# LIGHTBINDER

LIGHTBINDER SERIES

BOOK ONE

MICHAEL WEBB

WHATUP PUBLISHING LLC

# ALSO BY MICHAEL WEBB

---

**The Shadow Knights Series:**

Prequel Novella - Shadow Knights: Origine

**The Shadow Knights Trilogy**

#1 - The Last Shadow Knight

#2 - Rise of the Shadow

#3 - Shadow of Destiny

**Shadow Knights Generations**

#4 - Shadow of Betrayal

#5 - Shadow of Sacrifice

#6 - Shadow of Hope

---

**Treasure Hunters Alliance:**

#1 - Fortress of the Lost Amulet

#2 - Legend of the Golden City

---

**Lightbinder Series:**

#1 - Lightbinder

#2 - Soulbinder

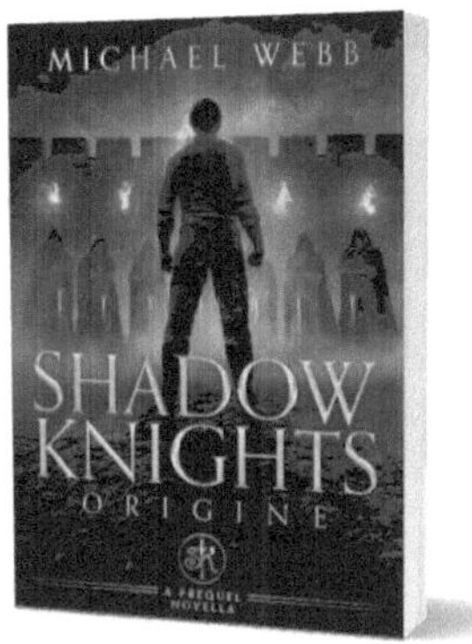

Get a FREE prequel novella to the Shadow Knights series - Shadow Knights: Origine - by signing up for my mailing list at www. subscribepage.com/michaelwebbnovels or scan this QR code

———

# CONTENTS

GREENSHIRE
FAYPORT
VALISTI
BELLHAND
DAIRLING
KALSHIA
MORVASK KEEP
GRASSMOOR
KALISTOR
LYNHARBOR
FAIRDRE
VERDANTH BAY
TWAINFORD
LAGRASH RIVER
DEADLANDS
THRAVIA
REVALLE
DUSTMERE
THRAVEN HILLS
KALSHIAN MOUNTAINS
HIGHBURN
GRAYGULF
VERRPORT

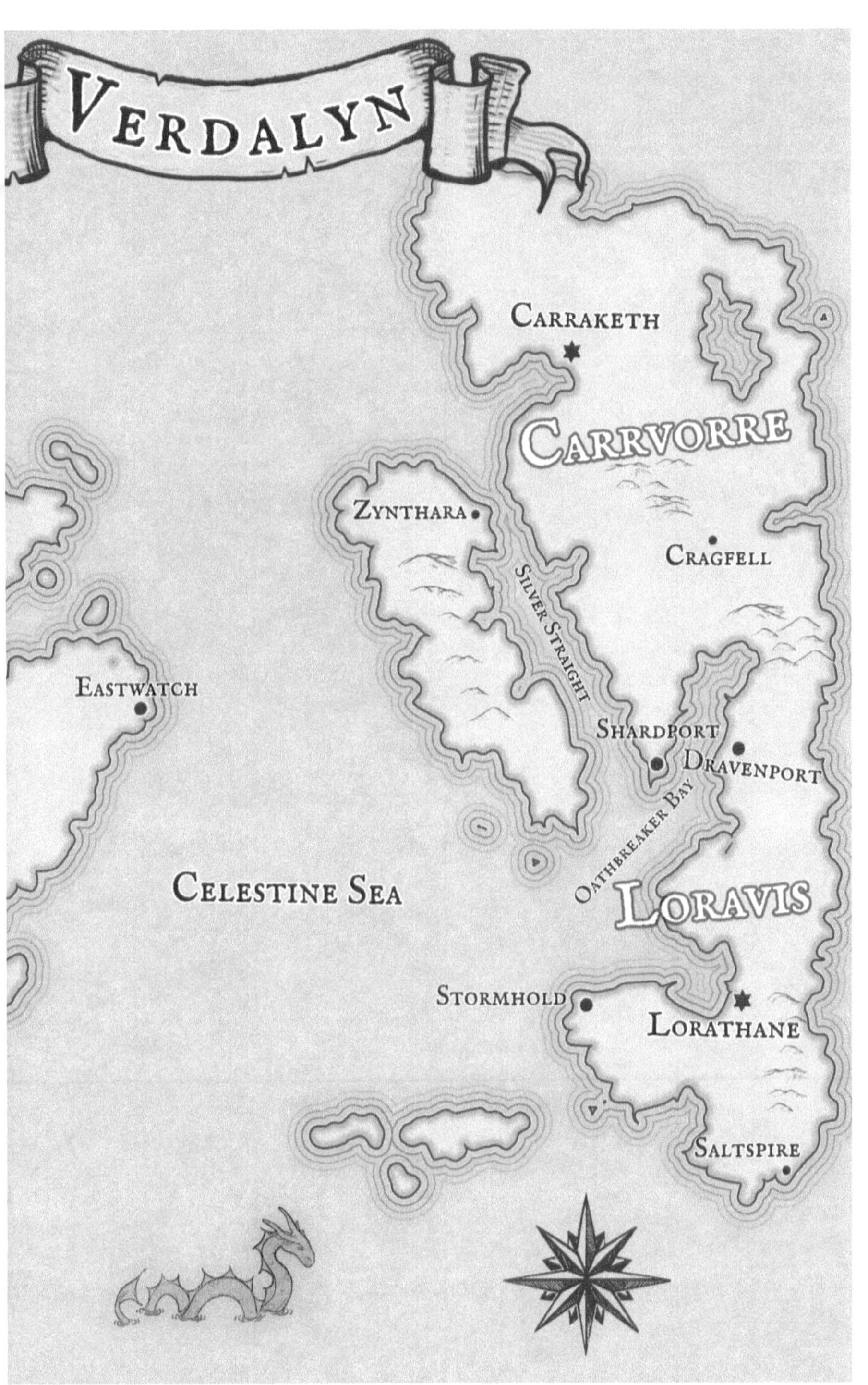

VERDALYN
CARRAKETH
CARRVORRE
ZYNTHARA
CRAGFELL
SILVER STRAIGHT
EASTWATCH
SHARDPORT
DRAVENPORT
OATHBREAKER BAY
CELESTINE SEA
LORAVIS
STORMHOLD
LORATHANE
SALTSPIRE

# PART ONE

## CHAPTER ONE

# DISTURBANCE IN THE ALLEY

Jarren woke with a start, knowing something was wrong. *Theft?* He had nothing worth stealing. *A beating?* He was used to them. The typical scent of mildew and rotting waste hung in the alley. Wooden boards under piles of burlap dug into his back in their usual fashion. The binder lamp at the end of the lane spilled the dregs of its light through the vertical slats in the pallets that hid his domain, overlooked in the forgotten corner of Kalistor.

What was unfamiliar were the two figures in deep hoods who stood a scant few feet away, oblivious to his presence. Jarren leaned closer.

"It must be soon," a man said in a deep voice.

"Be patient," the other replied. He sounded older and spoke with confidence. "It takes time to do it right."

"We are losing patience, and so is the king."

"Tell him I have it under control."

A foot twisted, grinding loose rocks into the alley floor.

"Every day you wait, our kingdom suffers," the younger man said. "The people suffer."

"And if it's rushed and fails, that suffering will continue. Let me do my job."

"We need that stone!" The man's shout echoed.

"We'll get it."

Jarren's breath grew rapid. His body felt squeezed by the tension filling the alley.

"Are you sure you haven't gone soft?"

Peeking out from his hood, the chin of the older man lifted as he took in a long breath.

"Are you capable of doing what needs to be done?"

The older man whipped a dagger from his cloak. It glinted like steel for a split second until it burst with light, piercing the air with a metallic thrum. A warm glow surrounded the blade, the hilt, and the man's hand, exposing the dark corners of the alley. "You want to find out how capable I am?" He held the blade forward, pointing the tip at the other man's hooded opening.

Jarren's heart pounded. Every muscle in his body tensed, trying to ensure he didn't move.

The younger man didn't flinch. His frame grew more erect as a rattling sound filled the alley. When he motioned upward, dozens of small rocks lifted from the ground, stopping to hover at chest height. He adjusted his hands as if prepared to push them forward. "You want to find out if *I* am?"

Jarren's breath came in short spurts. He glanced past the pallets, trying to judge if he could make it down the alley to get away. His legs felt like blocks of stone, fixed in place.

Both men stared at each other, threatening with weapons Jarren couldn't comprehend. Wanting to glimpse inside their hoods, he leaned closer. A traitorous board creaked beneath him, stopping his heart.

Both hoods jerked in his direction.

He held his breath. There was nowhere to run. No place to hide.

The older man stepped toward him and grasped one of the pallet's slats. With a rapid flick, he flung the wooden object through the air. It crashed to the ground, clattering as it rolled away.

Jarren held his hands up, staring at the tip of the glowing dagger. "I—I'm sorry. I was sleeping. I didn't hear anything."

The hooded men didn't even look at each other. They didn't

need to talk. The floating stones pivoted toward Jarren and then bunched closer together.

"Please," he begged. "I—"

The hands of the younger man jerked forward.

The last thing Jarren saw was dozens of stones hurtling toward his face.

# CHAPTER TWO
# SHILVAN PEAK

*Ten more feet.*

Kaleth gulped at the vertical rock face.

*An impossible ten feet. I'm going to let him down.*

An anxious ball tightened in his chest as his forearms and legs burned. His lungs strained for breath. Standing on a small ledge, the pre-dawn sun had grown bright enough to see by—much better than scrambling up the trail by the light of the full moon.

His father's head poked out from the lip of the climb. "You've got this, Son." The words were neither dismissive nor impatient. The proud smile covering Valorr's face exuded confidence. With a voice like warm butter and a casual affability, his father could calm an angry hornet with a simple greeting.

Kaleth's ball of nerves unraveled. His hands steadied as he blew out a breath. He stepped onto a jutting rock, then reached higher and wrapped his fingers around a crimp of granite. He scanned the face for where to go next, but nothing revealed itself. Perspiration dripped from his nose, disappearing into the sweat stain on his shirt. His tired arms threatened to give out. A groan accompanied his attempt to move a foot higher, but his fingers wouldn't hold. His boot slipped on a loose chunk of rock. "Gah!" Stone scraped his fingers as they ripped off the hold. He dropped back onto the ledge.

His father lowered into a crouch. Still smiling, he extended a hand.

Kaleth cringed and shook his head. "I can do it."

"I know you can."

The smooth words coated Kaleth with a wave of relief despite his building frustration. He pushed his glasses back up his nose.

"If you want to work it out, I'll wait. I know you'll get it. But we're not here to prove anything to anyone. We're here to enjoy the sunrise."

Kaleth stared at the rock, the sting of his hurt pride intensifying. The weakness in his arms felt more pronounced with each second.

His father's fingers wiggled. "Come on, Kaleth; see what's up here."

Kaleth nodded. Locks of shaggy brown hair fell in front of his eyes until he tucked them away. Putting one hand on the rock, he reached with the other. His father clamped on with a firm grip, then pulled. He pushed his feet against the wall, and his opposite hand pulled against the stone. Moments later, he rolled over the lip of the route onto the rounded summit of Shilvan Peak.

Kaleth brushed off his pants and stood. He kept his head down and pressed his glasses up again. *I should have been able to do that.*

"Hey." His father rested hands on his shoulders.

Kaleth lifted his chin.

Valorr's soft brown eyes sparkled. His short brown hair stuck up, glistening with a damp sheen of sweat. Lines crinkled at the corners of his eyes. His closed lips curled up. "You made it, and that's no simple task. I'm proud of you."

Kaleth's heart skipped at the soothing words. His pulse steadied. He breathed out, releasing the tension in his shoulders. His father pulled him close, wrapping his arms around Kaleth's back. The sweat on his shirt pressed against his skin, chilling him. His fatigued arms complained as they compressed.

Valorr pulled away, continuing to grin. He gestured toward the horizon.

Turning east, Kaleth's jaw dropped as he took in the view.

The first rays of the sun dappled the Celestine Sea, announcing the day with a fresh promise of life. Fiery wisps of clouds lit up the sky. Tucked at the end of Verdanth Bay, the eastern port of Lynharbor bustled in the early light. To the north, the rolling hills between Kalistor and Greenshire tossed long shadows over the lowlands. In the heart of Kalshia, rich farmland spread in every direction. Green pastures nestled amongst dark-blue rivers, lush forests, and vibrant cities.

"Storm's coming," Valorr said.

Kaleth followed his father's gaze to the west, where the massive Kalshian Mountains formed a snowcapped wall. Jagged black-and-gray crags reached to the sky like a row of teeth ready to tear into prey. The sun's early rays lit up dark clouds curling over the mountain range. "Do we need to hurry back?"

"No rush. It won't get here until late today."

Kaleth turned back to the fertile land of Kalshia. "I wish Mother could see this."

His father hummed in agreement. "I do, too. But in the shape she's in . . ."

"I know," Kaleth added. "I just mean . . . she would love it."

"Yes, she would. She'll be strong enough soon."

Kaleth's stomach tightened. His mother's six months of steady decline didn't leave him optimistic. He dropped the subject, hoping to not upset his father, then gasped when he turned toward the south.

The neighboring kingdom of Thravia stood in stark contrast to the lush landscape of Kalshia. Arid plains stretched between faded cities. Colored in grays and browns, the ground looked incapable of supporting life.

"I've never seen it from so high," he breathed. "I knew Thravia was bad, but it's—it's—"

"Barren," his father finished, frowning.

"How do they live? Can they grow anything? How would animals survive?"

His father paused for a long moment. "They get by," he finally said.

"Was it always like this?"

The tight shake of his father's head was out of character. Usually open about any subject, his reticence caught Kaleth off guard. He let the subject lie.

Valorr took a water flask off from over his shoulder. He handed it to Kaleth, then looked down the slope, where the capital city sprawled below them.

Back where they'd begun their early-morning journey, Kalistor shone in the morning light, perched at the brink of the Verdal Plateau. Water from the North Lagrash River plummeted over the edge, too far away for him to hear its thundering cascades. Where most of the land dropped off, a narrow path pushed precipitously forward. It navigated rocky outcroppings, first dropping through a saddle, then rising again to connect to Sky Fortress.

King Rhinean's castle perched atop the impenetrable promontory. The fortress contained towering spires and turrets nestled inside a thick wall that circled the top of the island in the sky. Within the hilltop stronghold, another building caught his eye. Opposite the castle's keep, but still protected in the fortress walls, the Lightbinder Academy tower rose from the nearby buildings. Kaleth adjusted his glasses and squinted.

Despite being short of the keep's height, the Lightbinder spire was no less impressive. Made of gray stone, its balconies and windows stretched up its length, ending with a chaotic roof of gables and sloped shingles. Having never seen past the fortress walls, the distant glimpse into the covert academy piqued Kaleth's curiosity.

He downed a large mouthful of water that coated his parched throat. He wiped his mouth and passed the container back.

With his father content to soak it in, Kaleth took several minutes to enjoy the view. The whisper of the wind soothed his fatigue. The beauty of the land refreshed his soul, and his heart rate slowed. His breathing settled to a normal rhythm.

Valorr broke the silence. "Do you know why I brought you up here today?"

"To see the sunrise?"

"To remind you to appreciate life." His father smiled. "You turn seventeen tomorrow, and you'll come of age in the eyes of the Kalshian government. You served me as an apprentice for three years, and I will be able to license you as a sage of Kalistor."

Kaleth smiled. "Just like that, huh?"

"You earned it. I sign the form tomorrow, turn it in to the city, and you can begin earning your own money. Assuming you still want to become a sage."

Kaleth's forehead pinched. "Of course. It's what I've been training for. All your classes. Do you not think I—"

His father stopped him with a raised hand. "You're ready. You know much more than I did when I started. It's just . . . the profession isn't always respected by others."

"Which is ridiculous," Kaleth said. "We've learned more than—"

"I know, Son. But some people measure worth by *doing* things rather than *knowing* things."

"You *do* things."

"Hammering a horseshoe or fashioning a leather saddle is easier to point to."

"We help people with their businesses. We advise city planners. We teach about sciences and math."

"Not everyone sees the value in that, and it's hard to find people to pay for these jobs." Valorr's mouth tightened. "The money isn't great, especially when you're first starting."

"There are plenty of rich people who need tutors for their kids."

"And we both know how that can end up."

The dark tone in his father's voice formed a knot in Kaleth's stomach. Valorr had learned the hard way how dangerous it could be.

"I don't need a lot of money."

His father nodded, then turned back to the city. "Very well. You have a clean record, so you can open a consulting shop, something I haven't been allowed in years. Things should be easier. You won't have to turn to—" His father's words cut off. His jaw formed a hard line as his eyes glistened.

Kaleth touched his father's arm. "You did what you had to. She needed it."

"Medicine that cost a fortune but did nothing."

"You made it work. You took care of us."

"Barely," he whispered.

"I'll open a shop and help with the money, and then we can afford what Mother needs. Tomorrow it all begins; just wait and see." The optimism felt forced, and an unsettled feeling in his gut remained. "It will be such a turnaround, people will wonder what our secret is."

"Secret?" His father puffed a grim laugh through his nose, then muttered, "If they only knew."

The curious words struck Kaleth, but his father didn't elaborate. Unsure of what to say, he turned to the west. "Where was it you came from, again? Near the mountains? Can we see it?"

Valorr dismissed the question with a wave of his hand. He wiped his eyes and then forced a smile. "Not from here. Come on. It will take a few hours to get back home, but we'll follow the northern trail this time."

Kaleth gulped. "You mean there's a *trail* we could have used to get up here?"

His father chuckled as he stepped toward a cleared path that exited the peak. Kaleth followed, shaking his head.

The gradual downhill was easier on his body. The dirt trail wound down the side of the peak. It descended through groves of fir trees and curved through meadows where butterflies flitted between wildflowers. A family of deelings raised their heads as Kaleth and his father passed within twenty yards.

Kaleth kept his eyes on the animals, confirming the faint lines on the adult females' flanks and the two pointed horns that protruded from the head of the singular male. "Classification test?"

His father shook his head. "Deelings? Too easy." He scanned the area until his feet came to a sudden stop.

Kaleth followed his eyes into a copse of trees where a rabbit nibbled at the base of a pine.

Valorr stepped closer. The rabbit's head popped up, freezing in position, ears alert. After a beat, it scampered deeper into the woods. "Interesting."

"What? The rabbit?"

"No." His father stepped into the shady area and crouched next to where the animal had been eating.

A cluster of half-eaten, red-and-gray mushrooms poked out of the ground. The long and thin stems ended at rounded tops that bulged as if they wanted to pop.

"Try this for classification."

Kaleth frowned. "Um . . . Realm: Plantia. Category: Stemmed. Group: Mushroom. Strain: . . . I have no idea."

Furrows dug into his father's forehead. "It's a reaper morel."

Kaleth sucked in a gulp of air.

Valorr ran a finger across one of their tops, then touched it to his tongue.

Kaleth grabbed his father's arm. "What are you doing?"

His father chuckled. "It's all right. Try it."

"Are you serious? Taste it?"

"Just a bit from the top."

Kaleth touched his finger to the mushroom. It was soft and spongy. When he wiped his finger across the surface, it slid on a coating of red powder that marked his skin.

"What's in this mushroom could kill a grown bear, but the dust is harmless."

Kaleth moved his finger to his mouth and tasted it with the tip of his tongue. The powder was smooth and tasted like an earthy honey. As the sweetness faded, a tinge of copper remained.

"They're rare to find in the wild," his father said. "Take a full year to mature."

Kaleth frowned, then turned in the direction the rabbit had run. "Wait . . . but what about—"

"The rabbit? Sure, they eat it."

"Wouldn't it kill them?"

His father shook his head. "Morel poison is unique. It takes longer to digest and for the poison to be absorbed. Same for humans. If you ate it, it would pass through your body, causing nothing more than a stomachache."

"Then why are reaper morels called the deadliest mushroom in Kalshia?"

"Well . . . it would *probably* pass through you. But if you hadn't drunk enough water or had some sort of external catalyst, it would speed up the process, and *that* would be deadly. Best to avoid it."

Deeper in the woods, galloping hooves tore through the underbrush, fading as the noise traveled downhill. Kaleth frowned. "What's wrong with the deelings?"

His father stood and scanned the woods. "Something has them spooked."

"Should we keep walking?"

A foxlike bark from back on the trail drifted into the woods, carried on the wind like the edge of a knife.

His father tensed. He held a finger to his lips, then motioned with a flat hand toward the ground. "Wait here," he whispered. Leaving Kaleth in the grove, he returned to the trail.

Kaleth's pulse raced. He had never felt unsafe in the woods, but the concern etched on his father's forehead was not typical. He peered through the drooping limbs, watching as his father slunk up the path.

*What was that? Fox? Wolf? Surely it wasn't a—*

A low growl punched through the trees, spinning Kaleth around. A dog-like animal with wrinkly, hairless skin stepped between the trees. Most of its black body looked burned, but it contained splotches of scabs. It had a protruding spine and spindly legs with claws at the end of its six toes. Eyes the color of blood stared at Kaleth while drool dripped from its protruding fangs.

Kaleth's breath caught.

*Realm: Animalae. Category: Mammal. Group: Panzer. Strain:—*

He could barely think it.

*Blood panzil.*

One panzil was dangerous enough on its own, but the real threat was that they never traveled alone. Guttural growls surrounded him as the rest of the pack arrived, bringing their total to six.

He considered casting a protection glyph in the dirt, but there wasn't time. Plus, it wouldn't help against so many. "F-F-Father." He tried to shout but barely made a sound. He looked desperately through the limbs and caught his father's eye—thirty yards away.

The lead panzil snarled as it crept closer.

Kaleth leaned back but had nowhere to go. Outrunning them was impractical. Fighting was impossible.

It leaped.

Kaleth raised his arms to block his face, but a yelp ripped through the air. The animal never arrived. Past his tensed arms, his father stood before him.

*How did he—*

Valorr pulled a knife out of the panzil's neck before tossing its limp body to the side. Following their leader, the rest of the pack converged.

"Kaleth, run!" his father shouted.

Frozen with indecision, Kaleth continued to stare with his jaw dropped.

His father's lightning-fast elbow to a snout knocked one aside. A kick and a jab with the knife took out another two.

"Behind you!" Kaleth shouted.

A panzil leaped toward his father's back, but it never arrived. With impossible speed, his father spun and tore the knife through the animal's hairless flank.

One more blood panzil remained. It lowered its head toward the ground and snarled, leaping sideways to get around Valorr's extended knife.

Breathing heavily, his father relaxed, stood up straight, and lowered his weapon.

Part of Kaleth wanted to step in and help. Part of him wanted to encourage his father to keep going. Instead, he stood dumbly while his father appeared to give up.

The last panzil bared its teeth and crouched, ready to rush. The animal's sudden burst of speed made Kaleth's heart sink to his stomach, but a second later, the intensity changed. The animal that had been full of energy and power seemed drained. It continued toward his father, but the fire was gone, like its strength had been sucked away, leaving a lethargic shell. Its red eyes flicked back and forth as if it couldn't understand what had happened.

Valorr stepped to the side and casually thrust his knife into the back of its neck. The torpid animal uttered a faint yelp as it collapsed. Three of the panzils lay dead or dying, and the others limped as they scurried off, whimpering, to disappear into the woods.

His father stood tall. He looked fresh, as if he'd just woken from a nap.

Kaleth's mouth felt as dry as sand. His legs shook. His pulse raced as he stared at the ground beneath his father. In the area where he had fought the panzils, the grass looked painted brown, as if it had suddenly died. "What just happened?"

Valorr's grim expression morphed into a smile. He stepped in Kaleth's direction until his leg gave out. He winced and moved a hand to his hip. "I'm getting too old to move like that."

Working his hand into the waist of his pants, his father massaged his hip, cringing as if the motion caused more pain. Pine needles on the nearest branch curled. The limb bounced up and down as if fanned by a light breeze. The verdant needles faded, turning from a healthy green to a sickly yellow. Snaps and pops filled the air like a wet log drying beside a fire. A louder crack ripped through the air as the suddenly dead branch fell from the healthy tree. His father straightened and sighed. He shook out his leg. Vigor of life gave his skin color.

"That's better." He chuckled and sighed. A sheepish grin covered his face. "I wasn't planning to show you all that today."

"What was that?" Kaleth's voice shook.

"That"—he punctuated the word clearly—"is my secret."

## CHAPTER THREE
# RETURN TO KALISTOR

When Kaleth followed his father onto Mercavor Street, the dazzling assortment of goods in the city market assaulted his senses. From sunup to sundown, the serpentine shopping thoroughfare slithered through Kalistor, boasting every product imaginable.

Attention-grabbing shouts from merchants blended with the haggling protests of buyers. Shoppers congregated under vibrant canopies, filling the air with the stale odor of sweaty bodies. Kaleth pushed through, jostling against the crowd. He ignored the rows of scarves, hats, and silver necklaces, all of which felt like a frivolous waste of money. He would have stopped to admire the colorful row of fruits and vegetables from the abundance of nearby farms, but he had to keep up with his father.

Past the vegetables, meat sizzled on grills. The savory aroma of spiced chicken and beef teased his nose and made his stomach growl. He didn't even bother to ask his father for money. They hadn't taken a midday meal since money had grown tight.

Once they left the market behind, they entered Grunwind, the neighborhood the rest of Kalistor ignored. The alleyways were darker. Windows contained a coating of grime. The tantalizing scent of meat had been replaced with that of rotten cabbage from refuse lining the gutters.

While they walked, Kaleth's mind reeled with his father's secret. Questions sprang up, one after another. What exactly had he done back in the forest? How had the panzil slowed down? What happened to the grass? Tired of being eaten up by the concerns, he glanced at his father. "Why won't you tell me about it?"

Valorr had barely spoken a word since the incident with the panzils. Keeping his eyes forward, he took several more steps before coming to a stop. "No one knows."

"What about Mother?"

"Not even her. As much as it pains me, it's for her own safety. I had been planning to share it with you when you came of age."

Kaleth swallowed a lump in his throat. "Sh-Share it with . . . me?"

"To teach you."

"You mean I'll be able to do what you did?" The thought of fighting panzils made his skin crawl.

"Not yet. But soon."

"When you mentioned a secret, I assumed you were talking about glyphs."

"I can't stress this enough, Kaleth." The usual smooth tone of his father's words formed an edge. His voice was deeper. "You must promise to tell no one."

Kaleth nodded.

"Say it."

"I promise."

"There's a reason you don't hear about it, and it's because no one else can do it."

The words sent chills down Kaleth's spine, but a curiosity ate at him. "What about Mother's illness?"

A crease formed in his father's forehead.

"If you can do . . . whatever that was, surely there's a way to get what she needs?"

The crease dug deeper, as if Kaleth had stumbled onto a topic that had plagued his father for a while.

"I considered it." Valorr's voice was softer. "Many times. Even without this ability there are ways to get what she needs."

"Then why don't you do it?" Kaleth didn't mean for his words to be so loud. He forced his volume to drop. "If there's a way to help, why wouldn't you take it?"

His father sighed and paused a long moment. "I would, but . . . she made me promise. I assured her I would not break the law. That's what I'm trying to do with the book I'm working on. It's taken longer than expected, but we're nearly there. If this doesn't work—" His father didn't elaborate. He set his arm around Kaleth's shoulders and gave a quick squeeze. "It's going to be all right, I promise. As for this ability . . . I'll teach you soon."

Kaleth reluctantly nodded, sensing it was all he would get from his father for the moment. Before he resumed his walk, a shaking snout caught his eye from where it poked out of an overturned crate. He crouched. A rust-colored dog with a white face and tail huddled in the container.

"Hey there, Charlie." The stray animal was a frequent visitor to their neighborhood. Kaleth wasn't sure if the dog had a name, but he had taken to calling him Charlie.

When he drew close, Charlie shrank back, shaking.

"Whoa, it's okay. I'm not gonna—"

He spied a bramble vine wrapped around the dog's leg. Thorns dug into the fur, staining it with dried blood. Kaleth's heart hurt.

"Oh, no. Here, let me." He moved slowly, making sure the animal didn't snap at him. "I can get that off you. It will just take a second."

Charlie flinched but didn't run or try to bite. When Kaleth rested a hand against his body, the shaking stopped. The dog huffed out a long breath of air as it calmed.

"Hold still a moment." He grasped the end of the vine and lifted Charlie's leg. Slowly, he unwound the briar. It moved in jerks as the thorns pulled free.

The dog winced. Faint whimpers reached his ears, but the animal didn't bolt. After disentangling the third loop of the vine, the last thorn pulled away, and Charlie was free. He sighed a note of relief, then began licking, wiping the patches of blood away.

"There. Isn't that better?"

Charlie turned to Kaleth and directed its enthusiastic tongue at his face. Kaleth leaned back and sputtered. "No, thank you. Not the face." The dog settled for his palms and fingers. Kaleth laughed at the tickling sensation.

"I think you made a friend," his father said.

Charlie limped out of the crate with a smile on his face. He nuzzled against Kaleth's legs. After a rub along its back, he trotted down the road with his tail wagging.

"Yeah, I think so." Kaleth's smile waned as he looked toward his father. Just beyond him, a path wound between two buildings toward the forest on the city's edge. The leaves created a dark shade over a dirt trail. The steady sound of the river came into focus—the river that ran past the old mill. In the distance, a wall of moss-covered stones blended into the woods. His stomach turned at the memory—the incident that had changed their lives.

His father followed his gaze. He stared for a moment, frowning at the path. "Come on," he said after a beat. "Let's get home."

THEIR HOUSE WAS the last in the row. Drooping tiles and rain-streaked walls identified a humble structure that had been there long before Kaleth was born. Many of the stones that formed the walls had crumbled years before. The propped-open red door brought a spot of color to the otherwise dismal scene.

"They're back," his sister's voice carried through the window.

The scent of something baking hit Kaleth as he stepped past the threshold.

Sora-el-Valorr took oversized mitts off her hands and set them on the kitchen counter. She crossed the room, heading toward their father until she paused to punch Kaleth on the upper arm. "Welcome back, Dinglebutt."

His sister, Sora, was younger by only a year. With blonde hair and eyes that were always observing, she brought character to any room she entered. Despite their frequent teasing, they were close, bonded by a childhood without privilege and the hardships that came with it. She left Kaleth to rub his arm while she went to hug their father.

The single room of their house strained to hold the few possessions Kaleth's family owned. His parents' bed took up much of the floor space. Two smaller beds—Sora's and his—peeked out from underneath it, running flush against the floor in the opposite direction. On more than one occasion, he'd hit his head on the bed above by waking too suddenly.

They only had space for two chairs in the center of the room despite having four people in the family. The wooden seats were hard with straight backs. Kaleth preferred the floor. His father's small desk pressed against a wall. The light wood grain was barely visible under the piles of odds and ends stacked on it.

On the opposite side of the room, a small counter and basin served as their meager kitchen. Shelves contained a collection of cooking supplies and ingredients, but they were never more than half full. An oven took up the corner. Its bricks rose to the ceiling and continued to a chimney that puffed smoke into the city air.

"Welcome home," his mother said from the bed.

Fenya-el-Garren propped herself up with an elbow. Wearing her usual faded blue nightgown, her matted blonde hair pressed against the sides of her smiling face.

"You must be thirsty." She winced as she pulled a blanket back and swung her legs over the side. "Sora just filled up a skin. I'll get it for you."

"No," Kaleth said, bounding to her bedside. He pressed a hand against her shin and cringed at the black discoloration on her ankle. "Thank you, but I can get it. You take it easy."

"Psh! I've been taking it easy for six months. I'm able to hobble across the house. It's good to stretch."

"The doctor said it's good to rest," his father interjected. "Movement like that is a strain on your lungs."

Fenya frowned but pulled her legs back under the blanket. A dry and crackling cough sputtered past her lips.

Kaleth grabbed the waterskin from the kitchen and drank several large gulps. The flask they had carried with them had been drained long before. After smacking his lips, he passed the skin to his father.

"What's that amazing smell?" Kaleth asked.

Sora shrugged conspicuously.

"Your sister wanted to make you a surprise for your birthday," his mother said.

"It's banana bread," Sora blurted. "I figured this way you'd owe me for *my* seventeenth."

"Bananas?" Kaleth said, his pulse quickening. "From Fayport? We can't spend money on those. We—"

His father's hand on his shoulder stopped him. "It's all right. I gave her the money."

"Our son only turns seventeen once in his life," his mother said. "It's a big deal and we want to celebrate."

Kaleth inhaled, letting the sweet scent fill his lungs. His eyes took in each member of his family, settling on his sister. "Well, it smells great. Thank you."

"How was the climb?" his mother asked.

The thought of the blood panzil attack and what his father did came to mind. Standing in their house, fresh questions surfaced. *Did Father use that ability at home? Did Mother truly not know anything?*

"We made it," his father said, interrupting his thoughts. "Just after the sunrise. What'd you think, Kaleth?"

He raised his eyebrows, then thought back to the scene from the top. "It was amazing," he admitted, forcing a smile. "We could see all the way to the coast. The clouds were incredible. They still are, in fact. Have you seen them?"

His mother shook her head.

"You've got to see." He stepped to her bedside and patted against the mattress. "Come on."

Fenya pulled the blanket back and angled her legs. In the manner they'd perfected through innumerable efforts, she scooted to the edge and leaned forward. Kaleth ran an arm under her knees and the other around her back. He inhaled and prepared to lift.

"Something smells good," a dark voice called from behind.

Kaleth abandoned his attempt to lift his mother and turned. His stomach dropped. Jairus, the "Night Saber," stood silhouetted in the doorway. The room grew silent. The temperature seemed to fall by ten degrees.

The beast of a man could not be mistaken—the "bringer of death and benefactor of pain." His bald head was always razor smooth. His trimmed black beard rounded out his face, and a scar was all that remained of his right ear. Kaleth wondered what had happened to it, but knew better than to ask. He'd heard of people being killed over the innocuous question. The man's neck was as wide as his head, sloping to a set of broad shoulders. Behind him, two similarly built men stood in the street.

"My men saw you passing through the square a bit ago, Valorr. Am I interrupting family time?"

No one answered. Kaleth's eyes drifted up to the protection glyph carved in the lintel. It remained clear and intact. He exhaled a silent breath.

"What do you want, Jairus?" Valorr asked after a long pause.

The man's face turned into a scowl. "You know what I want."

Valorr's eyes flicked to his desk. "You gave me until the end of this week. I still have five days, and it will be ready this time, I promise."

"I'm tired of your promises!" His voice boomed in the tight space as he took a step inside the room.

Sora shrank toward the kitchen, but Kaleth's father held his ground.

"The compendium is nearly finished. My payment from the Scholars' Council will be more than enough to—"

"You were supposed to have it a month ago, but you didn't. Then it was to be two weeks ago, but your wife was ill."

"She *was*," Valorr said. "Her cough, it was—"

"I don't care," Jairus said. "You needed help, and you came to me. Not the bank. Not a wealthy friend. Me. I took pity on you. I gave you what you needed, and you understood the stakes. Now, people are talking. They're saying I've grown soft—that my debtors can do what they want. Your negligence makes me look like a fool, and I can't have that. From the loans, supplies, and interest, you owe me one hundred gold, and I'm tired of waiting."

"You'll have it. I promise."

"Tonight."

The air stilled.

"You will have my money by midnight. If not . . . you've forced my hand."

"Forced your . . ." Valorr's lips trembled. "Meaning?"

"Leniency only weakens me. I must live up to my reputation."

Kaleth stifled a gasp. His mother grabbed his hand and squeezed, her arm shaking.

Jairus reiterated, "Midnight," then left the room. His goons in the street fell in step, and all three men left.

The silence in the room was so thick that Kaleth imagined he could touch it. His heart raced. "Can you do it?" he breathed.

His father looked at the thick book in the center of the desk. Its rich leather cover and golden clasps stood in stark contrast to the rest of the possessions in their house. Multiple inkwells and pens surrounded it. Scratch papers of notes and calculations piled high to the side.

Valorr nodded. "I can do it."

Kaleth caught the fear in his father's eyes. "How can I help?"

His father pulled out the chair by the desk and slumped into it. He forced a smile. "I'll be fine." He pushed a stack of papers aside, opened the leather cover of the book, and flipped pages until he stopped near the back. He glanced at a sheet of scratch paper as he dipped a pen into an inkwell. "Only one person can work on it at a time, and I only have one section to finish."

"The chapter on—" He glanced at the window, ensuring no one lurked in the street, then lowered his voice. "The part about the glyphs?"

Another nod.

"Can you skip it? Just leave it out?"

Valorr kept his head down, already writing. "The glyph chapter is what the scholars want most—the lost art known to a select few. It's why they're willing to pay so much for this."

"There must be something I can do."

Spry feet bounced into the doorway as a stocky young man appeared. "Good morning!" Jovi Strapper said, beaming and flashing his hands. After one look at the somber room, his tone changed. "Too hopeful? Perhaps . . . gloomy morning?"

"Jovi, not now," Kaleth sighed.

His friend lowered his hands and took a step inside. "Sorry. I saw Baldy leaving and thought you could maybe use something lighthearted." No one responded. "I, uh . . . came by to see if Kaleth wanted to go out for a pre-birthday celebration, but . . . is everything okay?"

"All is fine," Valorr said, stopping Kaleth from answering. "Kaleth, you wanted something to do? Go with your friend. Enjoy your last day free of responsibility."

"Father, I don't—"

"Actually"—he lifted a finger—"there is something."

Kaleth perked up.

"While you're out, find Erinth at the Hall of Sciences. Let her know the book will be ready shortly and I'll need payment today. And if it runs late, confirm I can bring it to her house tonight. Find out where that is."

"Sure. I'll find her."

"Kaleth." Valorr met his son's eyes and raised his eyebrows. "It will be fine. I mean it." He swept his hands, dismissing him. "Now get out of here. I've got work to do."

"If he needs anything, I'll help," Sora said before making a shooing motion with the back of her hand. "Now go, Binderbrains. Have fun."

Kaleth's shoulders released their tension. With his father hunched over the table, hard at work, he turned to his friend.

Jovi shrugged. "Can't say no to your father." He turned to the kitchen and worked his face into a goofy grin. "Hey, Sora. You look nice today."

Kaleth groaned and spun his friend around. "Okay, that's enough. Let's go."

# CHAPTER FOUR
# LAST DAY OF FREEDOM

Jovi shuffled his feet as Kaleth pushed him into the street. The arrival of his friend and his father's insistence that everything would be okay helped ease the sudden dread, although worry still lingered at the back of his mind.

Jovi gestured a thumb over his shoulder as they started down the street toward the square. "What was all that about?"

Kaleth shook his head. "My father's got a tight deadline on his book, that's all."

"Is this the 'Compendium of Knowledge' he's been working on for forever?"

"Yeah. It's pretty incredible. It covers mathematics, chemistry, economics, botany, physics . . . just about everything." He left out the part about glyphs. Although Jovi was his best friend, he was used to keeping his father's secrets.

"What's it for?"

"The Scholars' Council commissioned him for it. Since he can't tutor anymore—"

"Because of that Hightower kid?"

"Yeah."

"I still can't believe people listened to that bind-cursed idiot. He couldn't learn the material. It was clear."

Kaleth shrugged. "When a highborn kid accuses you of something, there's not much you can do."

"Anyone who knows your father knows better. He would never have attacked that boy's sister."

"People believe what they choose to believe, and no one wants to risk their reputations. We were just thankful they didn't haul him off to Morvask Keep. Anyway . . . this book was a way for the scholars to capture all the knowledge he has so it can be shared with others like advisors and educators. He's trying to finish it today." Kaleth laughed through his nose. "Despite the fact that no one in this city respects him, it sure seems they respect his knowledge a great deal."

*If only that would apply to Jairus*, he thought. His chest felt compressed like it was surrounded by a tightening band of rope.

"So, um . . ." Jovi looked his way with a mischievous smile. "Do you think your sister's changed her mind? I caught her eyeing me."

"What? No!" Kaleth pushed his friend hard on the shoulder. "If you don't stop it with my sister, I'm gonna mess you up."

Jovi paused, looking deep in thought. His head bobbed. "From the looks of your arms . . . yeah, I'll take that challenge."

Kaleth lunged with fists raised but Jovi danced away, cackling with lifted palms of surrender. "Come on, Kaleth. I'm only messing. Besides, your sister's a fine catch. Who would you rather her end up with? Some deadbeat you've never met or your best friend?"

"Deadbeat. Definitely."

Jovi pushed him back, then followed with laughter.

The sound of his friend chuckling loosened the tightness in his chest. Above him, a blanket of wispy clouds caught his eye. He frowned. They looked darker and more ominous than before. Kaleth wasn't sure if it was true or if he imagined it. He pushed the thought away.

After a short walk, the boys emerged into Ramble Square, the hub of the city that surrounded it on three sides. The fourth side of the square contained the best view in all of Kalistor. A short wall marked the brink of the Verdal Plateau, where Sky Fortress appeared to float in midair, just off the edge.

At the north end of the plaza, children covered a patch of grass, running and playing. Adults sat talking with each other on nearby benches. A dozen tables contained kamak boards where men and women faced off, moving pieces and focused in deep concentration. Kaleth smiled. The game always reminded him of his father and the late nights they stayed up playing.

"You wanna play kamak?" Kaleth asked.

"Ha!" Jovi scoffed. "And be utterly demoralized? No, thank you. I've got something else in mind."

An old man lying on a bench caught Kaleth's attention. His eyes were closed, and his chest looked still. His head rested on a bundle of fabric. The flowing brown robe covering him trailed to the ground. A city constable sat on a stool next to the bench. His slumped posture and casual attention indicated he'd had little to do but sit and watch.

"Old Man Telemus is unconscious again, huh?" Kaleth said.

Jovi followed his gaze, then chuckled. "Yeah. He's only been out for three days this time, though."

"What did he predict?"

"'A storm of sorrows,' whatever that means. It's supposed to hit tonight."

"Anyone could have predicted a storm." Kaleth pointed toward the mountains. "The clouds are obvious. That doesn't take mysterious powers."

Jovi raised an eyebrow. "But three days ago? I don't know. He does seem to be right more than he's wrong. What if he predicted something that was going to happen in twenty years? Would he be passed out the entire time?"

Kaleth shook his head. "I don't know." The old man's predictions were usually for a span of weeks or months, during which time he lay in a comatose state. Touching him sent him into a fit of seizures, so the city—who venerated his ability—posted a guard whenever he passed out. He stared at the old man, curious about how it might feel to be afflicted with such an ability.

Jovi's craning neck caught his eye. Kaleth looked behind them. "What is it? You see something?"

Jovi shook his head. "I thought someone was following us for a moment."

Kaleth groaned. "Not this again."

"It was just a mail porter. He's gone now."

"No one is ever following us. You've got to give that up!"

Unfazed, Jovi waved for him to follow. "Come on." He crossed the square to angle up Bridger Street.

Eyeing where his friend led, Kaleth frowned. "In Hightower? Are you sure?"

Northwest of the square, the city's gentry lived in the Hightower District. Kaleth generally avoided the area lest he find an opportunistic rich kid looking to show off fighting skills to his friends. Kaleth had been the recipient of such a display on more than one occasion.

"I know a guy who promised me free drinks," Jovi said. "Since neither of us can afford to buy anything, that limits our options."

Kaleth craned his neck as they walked up the affluent street. The road was wide and tidy. The air smelled fresh and clean. Painted homes contained decorated shutters and fancy porticoes. The people they passed wore spotless tunics, pressed and bright with sharp colors. He glanced down at his dingy gray shirt made of coarse linen. A tendril of heat crept up his neck.

Jovi's elbow nudged his ribs. "Check it out."

Kaleth looked up to see a man walking on the opposite side of the street. His jaw tightened.

The man in his thirties looked like a moving stone statue. His thick neck sloped to rounded shoulders. His chest and arms bulged with muscles so large his arms could barely reach his sides. Short brown hair matched the trimmed beard that framed a chiseled jaw. He wore a Lightbinder uniform, black leather with streaks of red. The man stopped by a dim binder lamp that hung along the street.

In a casual motion that seemed to have been repeated over a thousand times, the Lightbinder extended a hand toward the sun before redirecting it to the lamp. The glass object surged with a brief flash before falling dim again, ready to activate once the sun set. Having finished his work, the man continued down the street.

"That's so cool," Jovi muttered after they passed the man.

Kaleth didn't reply. He moved forward with his sight on the plaza ahead, trying to ignore the long-simmering anger he couldn't forget.

Plazas in Hightower differed from the ones in Grunwind. In Kaleth's neighborhood, trash filled the gutters, giving the air a rotten scent. Children played with reckless abandon, often loud, dirty, and barefoot. Adults were busy, moving with purpose.

In contrast, the open space ahead had a casual air. Adults lounged on benches, talking as if they had nothing better to do. The few children who could be seen played quietly together. The vibrant state of their clothes showed they knew little of tag, hide-and-seek, or binder wrestling.

Each step Kaleth took farther from his home pushed away the worry for his father.

"There it is." Jovi pointed to the center of the square where the Salty Boar Tavern waited.

Dark wooden beams lined the glass windows of the exterior, most of which were open, letting air in and noise out. Tables and chairs tucked against the building, butting into the street, and a stringed melody drifted through the open door. Two men in crisp suits stood talking at the entrance.

Kaleth frowned as he stared at the doors. "I'm not so sure this place is for us."

"Trust me." Jovi led the way past the outdoor tables to the last window where the pane was already slid open. He poked his head inside. "*Psst*, Fuzzy!"

Kaleth leaned closer. He spied a bearded man behind a bar who looked in his mid-twenties. The bartender glanced their way and nodded. He served a drink to a patron inside then grabbed two empty mugs with one hand and turned to a keg. The tied-up sleeve on his left side indicated he was missing an arm.

"Is he just giving us drinks?"

Jovi grinned. "Cool, huh?"

"How do you know this guy?"

"He spoke at a Blade interest meeting. He was in the army five years after graduating from the academy. After losing an arm, he withdrew to get a job in the city."

Fuzzy arrived at the window and set both mugs on the sill. "Good to see you, Jovi. Good luck tomorrow."

The mention of the academy and what was to happen the following day jostled Kaleth's memory. His stomach dropped.

Jovi picked up both mugs and thanked the bartender. He led the way to an empty street-side table.

Kaleth slid into a chair opposite him and touched the handle of a drink. "Tomorrow's Signing Day, isn't it?"

Already tipping the ale in his mouth, Jovi nodded.

"I'm so sorry. I forgot. That's why you want to celebrate today."

Jovi lowered his drink and wiped the foam from his lips. "Yup. It's your last day before you're seventeen, and it happens to be my last day of freedom, too."

"I'll be there to see you off. How do you feel?"

"Excited!"

The enthusiasm felt over the top. Kaleth raised an eyebrow. "Yeah?"

Jovi shrugged. "Mostly. A bit nervous, I guess. Ever since I first heard about Zanon's Rebellion and how it tore the kingdom apart, I wanted to be involved. If it ever happens again, I want to be able to help."

"Zanon's been dead over forty years. I don't think he's going to rebel again."

"Not him, but . . . you never know what could be next." He raised a finger. "Although, I have heard a rumor about him still being alive."

"Jovi. His head was cut off, and his body was burned in the square."

"Yes, but what about his ashes? No one knows where they are."

Kaleth groaned. "I can't do this. One good thing about you joining the academy is that I won't have to listen to your paranoid delusions anymore."

"You say that now, but you'll regret it the time you *don't* listen to me and I'm right."

Kaleth blew out a heavy breath. "So, you're set on Blades?" he asked, eager to change the subject. "At the academy?"

"For sure." Jovi grinned. "When you're born with this perfect physique, how could you not choose it? I thought about trying for Lightbinder, but I'd need your brains to go with my body to have a shot."

"There are other things you could do, you know. There are tons of jobs in the city." Kaleth raised his mug and took a drink.

"I *want* to do this. It's all I've been dreaming about for years."

"I know, but—"

Jovi's eyes brightened. "You should join me."

The thought turned Kaleth's stomach. He shook his head.

"You'll be seventeen tomorrow. You'll be old enough! Think how fun it would be—me and you training together in the academy—learning cool stuff. We could even be stationed together and spend all our time together. We could have each other's backs."

"I could never do it," Kaleth said. "Go into battle. Face off against someone trying to kill me."

"Blade's probably not for you, but you'd be a perfect Mender. Not as celebrated of a school, but still important. The army could use someone with your brain—the recruiters are always saying so."

A vivid image of the mill popped into Kaleth's mind, and a pool of anger flashed in his gut. "I want nothing to do with them."

Jovi leaned back as if making the connection. "You still hate the Lightbinders, don't you? Because of . . ."

Kaleth nodded. "I'm going to miss you, Jovi. I really am. But I could never join the academy."

Jovi blew out a breath. "I understand." He took a large drink.

An awkward silence lingered until Kaleth broke it. "How does your mother feel about you leaving?"

"Eh, she's fine. She keeps crying, but that's nothing new. She knows we need the stipend, otherwise things are gonna get bad soon." He nodded toward Kaleth. "What about you, then? A licensed sage, huh? You're set on it?"

Kaleth grinned. "I've been training for years. Father will certify me tomorrow, then I can open my own shop. He thinks having a storefront will attract a lot of business—much more than he's been able to generate." He looked up the street and appraised the buildings. "Maybe even in Hightower. I'm not sure. The people here are more likely to pay money for my services."

"And you would tutor rich kids and . . . teach people things?"

"Advise them."

Jovi frowned. "I still don't get it."

"Imagine someone has a business that's failing. They'd come to me. I'd help them with their budget and their business plan. We'd turn things around."

"And you're able to do that? Turn a business around?"

"Why do you think I've been working with all these stores over the years?"

"And they'd trust a seventeen-year-old to do this? To help them run a business they've been in for decades?"

Kaleth shrugged. "My job is to catch things they're missing. I'm sure it will start slow, but once I build experience and maybe get referrals, it should pick up. In the meantime, Father's taught me enough about hunting and foraging to get by."

Jovi's eyes drifted over Kaleth's shoulder. "Bind me," he whispered as his face twisted in disgust.

"What?" Kaleth turned, and the ale in his stomach soured.

Rayd-il-Stonne strolled up the street with perfectly brushed, thick black hair and a young lady by his side. Despite being Kaleth's and Jovi's age, he sported a full beard that made him look several years older. Tall, strong, and mean, he was the last person Kaleth wanted to run into. The pristine white suit he wore probably cost more than Kaleth's family spent in an entire year, but when your father is the exal general of the Kalshian army, cost isn't something to worry about. One hand wrapped around the leg of what looked like a roasted turkey, and the other held a glass of wine.

Not only was Rayd physically intimidating, he was smart and didn't even seem to have to try. Kaleth had watched from the crowd when Rayd won Kalistor's annual kamak tournament a month before. He had longed to enter himself, but the five gold entry was more than he could afford.

The girl walking with Rayd hung on every word he said, her eyes eager and mouth slightly parted. Coiffed hair tied up on her head. She wore a blue dress that covered her feet with a ruffled hem. She didn't even flinch when bits of turkey flecked on her face between his words.

Behind Rayd, a dog with rust-colored fur and a familiar white face trotted at his feet. Kaleth smiled to see that Charlie didn't even show a hint of a limp as he walked. The cuts from the thorns seemed to be doing well. When Rayd lowered his turkey leg, Charlie bounded closer, showing restraint to not snatch it out of his hand. Instead, he nudged the side of Rayd's leg, tongue lolling out the side of his mouth and a visible smile on his face. While continuing to walk, the young man kept his attention on the girl and pushed the dog away with his leg.

"You wanna hide?" Jovi asked.

Kaleth shook his head but kept his eyes on Rayd. "Last time was in a dark alley. He won't do anything here in the open." He swallowed a lump in his throat. *At least I hope he won't.*

Passing in front of the tavern, the rich young man's eyes wandered toward their table. Kaleth held his breath as their eyes met. Rayd paused mid-word from talking at the girl. His eyes narrowed, and a sneer curled his lip. After a short laugh, he turned back to the young lady and resumed his monologue.

Kaleth blew out a breath, releasing the tension from his shoulders.

Charlie nudged Rayd's leg again. "Get off," the young man muttered, pushing the animal away again.

Undeterred, Charlie trotted back with his mouth hanging open in a grin.

"I said . . ." Rayd rounded on the dog and put his weight behind a solid kick.

The hollow thud lasted only a moment until Charlie's high-pitched yelp drowned it out. The dog fell over. His legs scrabbled against the stone street to get back on his feet.

"Hey!" Kaleth's chair scraped as he jumped to his feet. "Leave him alone!" Seething anger ran through his veins. Without a thought, he took two aggressive steps until Rayd's glare stopped him in his tracks.

Charlie limped away, hanging his head. Faint yips sounded each time he bounced on his back leg.

"Kaleth," Rayd sneered. He strolled closer. "Are you looking for trouble, Grunny? Why don't you go back to Grunwind with the rest of your kind?"

Kaleth's heart leaped into his throat at the sight of the boy's full chest and strapping arms. He slunk backward. "No trouble, I just—I —" His gaze fell to the street. His voice quieted. "That dog didn't deserve to be kicked." He felt Jovi's presence at his back.

Rayd laughed. He passed his wine glass to the girl without looking at her. "Why don't you come over here and do something about it?" He tossed the remainder of the turkey leg to the street and began to roll up his sleeves.

Kaleth squirmed and kept his head down.

"Come on, Grunny. You think you're so tough? Why don't you prove it? It's easy to yell from a distance, but a real man can back it up." With his sleeves rolled back, Rayd stepped closer.

Kaleth kept his eyes down. The larger boy was only an arm's length away, rubbing his fists. Turkey breath wafted across Kaleth's nose. His palms grew clammy. Despite the anger inside, he didn't strike.

"Come on!"

Kaleth flinched.

Rayd roared with laughter. "You're worthless." He turned to head back toward the girl. "Almost as bad as your father."

The insult stung Kaleth's pride, and remembering Jairus' threat made it even worse. His temper flared. Jovi pulled back on Kaleth's shoulder, but he sloughed it off. Against his better judgment, he stepped forward, unsure of his own intentions.

*Stand up for Father. Stop and turn around. Ask him to apologize. Run away.* The options peppered his mind. With every step, the anger lessened, supplanted by his usual fear of the bully. When he was about to stop, his foot caught the leg of a chair. Gravity pulled at him, beckoning him to tumble to the ground. His arms flailed through the air. His legs struggled to keep him upright. The only thing that kept him vertical was both hands bracing against the back of Rayd-il-Stonne, who had just retaken his glass.

The muscular young man stumbled. His feet managed four lurching steps but ultimately failed to stay under him. He splayed flat across the stone pavers.

Kaleth's adrenaline surged through his body, battling with the terror that pricked his mind. *What did I just do?*

Jovi pulled harder. "Come on, man. Let's run!"

With his jaw hanging loose, Kaleth stared dumbstruck. He didn't move.

Amidst peals of laughter from onlookers in the plaza, Rayd flipped onto his back. The wine glass had shattered. Shards cut into his arms and neck, dribbling thin lines of blood down his skin. But the red that held Kaleth's attention was on his clothing. Crimson wine splattered the spotless white suit—the suit that would cost more than Kaleth could ever hope to afford.

The girl bent down to offer a hand, but Rayd pushed it away. His head lifted and his eyes stared, piercing with venom at Kaleth.

Kaleth and Jovi bolted. They left their mugs at the table and sprinted across the plaza. Kaleth's heart beat wildly. He could barely think. When they were about to disappear around a corner, he chanced a glance back. His legs slowed.

Rayd remained where he had fallen. He made no move to chase, but his vitriolic gaze left no room for misunderstanding. "You're dead, Grunny!" echoed over the cobblestones.

Kaleth gulped. *What did I just do?!*

## CHAPTER FIVE

# FIRST IMPRESSIONS

"Master Rayd, welcome home," the doorman said without warmth.

Rayd pushed past, not pausing when the man's eyebrows shot up. The bleeding in Rayd's arms and neck had stopped, and he'd managed to mostly clean himself. But there was little he could do about the stained suit. He crossed the marble entry room and beelined toward the stairs, stepping with light feet.

"Rayd, is that you?" his mother's voice echoed down the hall.

He froze but didn't answer.

"Thomas, who was at the door?"

The doorman froze as well. His eyes flicked between the direction of the question and where Rayd stood at the base of the stairs. His lips made a false start, cut off by Rayd's shaking of his head and the warning he tried to express through his eyes. Half of the doorman's mouth curled up. "Yes, Lady Delphine. Your son has just arrived."

Rayd gritted his teeth. He whispered, "One day I'll run this house, and you'll regret not having my back."

The doorman shrugged. "We'll see."

A second voice echoed through the house. "Come here, Son! I'd like to introduce you to someone."

The exal general demanded his presence. A watery feeling ran through his stomach. *I could pretend I didn't hear. I could leave again.* His shoulders fell. "Yes, Father," he managed in a tremulous voice.

His steps across the sitting room felt stilted. He spotted his parents through the windows, standing on the covered patio out back. He glanced down at his stained suit, then gulped as he exited through the open doorway.

Opposite his parents, a man Rayd didn't know wore an embroidered velvet doublet dyed a deep emerald color. The gold threadwork matched his rings and the lining of the wide leather belt. He stood with a woman dressed in a flowing silk gown with a tight bodice. Her long sleeves trailed over her hands.

"Let me introduce you to my son, Rayd-il-Stonne," his father said, beginning to turn.

The unfamiliar man's eyes widened. The woman's hand moved to cover her mouth, the long sleeve falling back to reveal her fingers.

Stonne-il-Malthus was dressed, as usual, in full military attire. His black uniform displayed numerous medals and ribbons that clinked together as he moved, but his perfect black hair remained motionless. The unctuous smile plastered on his face faded at the sight of his son.

His mother, Delphine-el-Draven stood next to him adorned in jewels and necklaces. Her gown sparkled with gems along the neckline. Its crimson color reminded him of the sections of his own suit that had been stained. Her silver hair had been tied up in a braid that rested atop her head. Rather than adopting a tender look of concern at the sight of Rayd, her eyes narrowed.

"What happened to you?" his father growled.

Rayd looked anywhere but at the exal general. "It's wine. It was an accident."

"My apologies, Warden Myrren," his mother said. "This isn't how we are. I wouldn't have called him had I known."

"It's fine, Delphine." The man touched the other woman on the arm. "It was time for us to be leaving, anyway."

"So soon?" Rayd's mother said. "You've only just arrived."

"Yes, but we have much to do. Thank you for the welcome to your city. I look forward to getting to know it better."

"Well, thank you for coming by," Stonne said quickly. "Good luck settling into your new role, and if you need anything from the army, please don't hesitate to reach out." He shook hands with the man and kissed the air next to the woman's cheek.

The warden headed toward the door. "Rayd, it's good to meet you," he said. There was little warmth in his words. The woman's nose lifted.

Rayd took a step out of the way, allowing the visitors to pass. He nodded but kept his eyes down as they walked by and proceeded through the doorway. He listened as their footsteps grew fainter. When he could hear them no more, he waited for the inevitable verbal assault that would follow.

"Do you know who that was?" Rayd's mother hissed.

He didn't.

"Myrren is the newly appointed Coinwarden of Kalshia."

Rayd's stomach dropped.

"He arrived only yesterday from Lynharbor. His wife is Seraphyne." She paused as if expecting a reaction. ". . . of Seraphyne Designs."

His insides churned. A political and economic power couple. His parents would have wanted to make a good first impression.

"And you show up like *this*?"

A surge of irritation ran through him. *It wasn't my fault.*

His parents waited.

"I'm sorry." The words grated as they came out.

"What really happened?" His father's question was quiet, but the veins on his thick neck bulged.

Rayd looked to his mother then back to his father. "I was with Athira in the square. We were talking when this *idiot* from Grunwind knocked into me and spilled wine all over my clothes."

"He . . . *knocked* into you?" His father gestured up and down Rayd's body. "And did all of this?"

Rayd clenched his teeth and nodded.

"And those cuts on your neck and arms." The exal general's eyebrow lifted. "That was from *knocking* into you?"

"Well, I—I fell. The wine spilled and my glass broke. That's what the cuts are from."

"What did you do?" his mother asked.

"What did I—" Rayd's protest halted at the appraising look on his mother's face.

"What did you do *to cause this*?"

He blew out a long breath. "This kid was mad when I wouldn't give his dog some turkey. He was trying to show off for his friend and pushed me down when my back was turned. He was a coward —nothing but a waste of breath."

"Who was it?"

Rayd shrugged. "It doesn't matter. Some kid."

"What was his name?"

Rayd swallowed hard. "Kaleth."

"Kaleth *who*?"

His pulse beat faster. "Kaleth-il-Valorr."

The exal general's body turned rigid. "We've talked about Valorr's son, haven't we?"

The reminder heated Rayd's blood. "He started it! I was minding my own business when he pushed me!"

"You know he's training to be a sage, don't you? His father—"

"His father is a disgrace," Rayd interrupted. "What he did to Morwyn's kid . . ."

"*Tsk!* He didn't do anything to her. Morwyn was saving face, and Valorr's family got a raw deal. What they don't need is people like *you* picking on them."

"It wasn't my fault!"

"Of course it was your fault."

Unable to stop it, his anger boiled over. "He! Pushed! Me!"

*Smack!*

The familiar backhand of Stonne-il-Malthus felt like an iron bar against his cheek. Rayd's hand jumped to his face, trying unsuccessfully to stop the sharp pain. The water that sprang to his eyes made his sight blurry.

"Don't you *ever* raise your voice to me!" The calm demeanor his father had managed eroded to a tightly controlled fury.

Rayd knew better than to fight back. He looked down until he sensed his father calming.

"Kaleth's family is poor. They have nothing, but he's working to make something of himself, and that's not easy to do. You wouldn't know."

Rayd's ears grew warmer.

"I grew up down the street from their house, poor and unknown. I trained day and night to be better—to advance—to get to where I am today. To have what we have. Valorr did the same thing, only with books and science. He chose to stay in Grunwind, though, and then he lost it all." His brows narrowed. "One wrong move—one bad impression, and their fate could be ours. It could be you."

"*Psh.* I will never be like that," he muttered.

"Valorr's son is trying. He's going to make something of himself. Hard work leads to perseverance, and perseverance leads to strength. That kind of strength is something you'll never understand, and I respect it. You should respect him, too."

*Respect.* The word echoed in Rayd's head like a taunt. His father was quick to use the word about titles, abilities, clothing, even food. The one person Rayd had never heard it reserved for was the only one he cared about: himself. He tried to fill the hole inside with anything that distracted or made him feel good, but nothing took away the ache.

"You prance around town with your girl-of-the-week, not caring what happens to the clothes *we* bought you, much less the reputation you endanger our family with."

"And tomorrow you go off to represent us at the academy," his mother added. "Please tell me you're contenting yourself with Blades."

Rayd lifted his chin, rankled by the comment. "I thought you valued ambition."

"Ambition, yes. Recklessness, no. You know what happens if you reach too high—if you try and fail. *Your* demotion out of the Light-binders is a disgrace your father doesn't need."

Rayd pictured himself part of the elite group. He imagined wearing the same uniform as his father. *He would have to respect me then.*

His mother inclined her head forward. "We've discussed it for years. Everyone knows you're perfect for the Blades."

"I'm very aware."

"So . . . ?"

Surprising everyone by surpassing their limited expectations of him was too tempting to pass up. He lied, "I haven't decided yet." Rayd knew exactly what he would choose.

"You embarrassed us enough tonight. We don't need a very public failure."

"Maybe if you had Kaleth's work ethic, things would be differ-ent," his father said. "He's the type of person who will outperform you at every step. You may swing a weapon better, but you will never be able to rise above what he's going to make of himself. Now leave. I need to write an apology to our new coinwarden."

Rayd slunk to the door, his blood heating with each step. His fists formed balls, flexing the muscles along his sizable arms.

*It wasn't my fault. I didn't start it.*

His teeth clenched.

*Kaleth-il-Valorr, I should never have let you get away.*

## CHAPTER SIX

# DEADLINE

Kaleth stared at the miniature kamak board, bouncing his leg and trying to ignore the stress permeating the room. He selected a black sword and moved the piece diagonally. A few seconds later, he played the other side, sliding a white warrior to take a black knife and put its tower under threat.

A hum pulled his attention to his father, whose head bent over the desk, nodding as he worked by candlelight. He scribbled furiously. Mother lay in bed, stifling the occasional cough. Steady rain pattered in the street and rolled in rivulets off the edge of the roof. A flash of light threw shadows into the room. A loud clap of thunder followed, and Kaleth jumped. He moved a white knife.

Jogging feet splashed through puddles outside the window. A moment later, the door opened and Sora entered the house, dripping water on the floor. She lowered her hood. "10:45." Her shoulders bounced from heavy breaths. "But that was at the square, so probably"—another breath—"10:50 now."

Kaleth's chest tightened. His mother coughed again.

"It's fine," Valorr said, not stopping his scribbling. "This is the last page."

"I hate this," Kaleth said, moving another piece but barely even paying attention to the strategy behind the move. "We're cutting it way too close."

"This section took longer than I anticipated." His father half-glanced over his shoulder at Kaleth. "How far did you say Erinth's house was?"

"It took me a bit to find it the first time," Kaleth said. "But knowing where to go . . . fifteen minutes' walk—faster at a run. Streets should be empty with this rain."

His father didn't reply.

Out of her wet cloak, Sora paced the room. She wrung her hands and glanced at Kaleth. It unnerved him to find her normally confident eyes swimming with fear.

Kaleth's stomach tightened. "But, Father, Erinth's house . . . it's just down the street from Lord Morwyn's."

Valorr's stylus paused. The tension in the room thickened. Kaleth hadn't wanted to distract his father, but he could hold the information back no longer.

His father resumed writing. "Get your cloak on," he said over his shoulder.

The order turned the dread in Kaleth's gut to anxious energy. Abandoning the kamak board, he grabbed his cloak off the hook and pulled it on. One arm stuck in its sleeve. His limb shook as he wriggled to work it through. Sora grabbed a coat for their father and held it ready.

A deep slap echoed from the desk. Kaleth jerked his eyes up. His father lifted his head and leaned back in his chair. His shoulders rose with a slow breath.

*Is he all right?*

When his father blew the air out, his body relaxed. "Finished."

The weight on Kaleth's shoulders eased. He smiled and stepped forward to look at the desk. The cover of the book looked as it had for months, but knowing it was complete made the gold seem brighter and the leather richer.

A long sigh from his mother ended with a weak cough.

Sora shook the coat that she held. "You ready?" she prompted. "You need to go, Father."

Valorr closed the golden clasps and snapped them in place. He grabbed a sheet of felted wool from next to the desk and wrapped the book up. "You prepared to run, Son?"

Kaleth closed the front of his cloak and tied it tight. "Yes, sir." He lifted his hood.

Valorr extended the bundled compendium. "Take it. I'm not going."

Kaleth's stomach turned. Fear gripped him from the pressure of what his father asked. "It's dark and raining. Lord Morwyn won't be out. He's not going to kill all of us just because you travel his street."

"That's exactly what he swore he would do."

"Yeah, but—"

"It doesn't matter. Kaleth . . ." He stepped closer and pushed the bundle into his son's chest. "I don't need to go. Just keep it dry. You can do this."

Kaleth swallowed a heavy lump. "Yes, I can." His words sounded more confident than he felt. He took the offered bundle and tucked it under his cloak. He kept one arm underneath it while his sister retied the sash, pulling it tight. The load felt secure, safe from the rain. Adrenaline raced through him. He flashed a nervous smile at his father.

Rain pelted his head when he stepped outside. His feet grew wet from the standing puddles, but he ignored the sensation. Adjusting his grip under the hidden bundle, he faced the center of Kalistor and ran.

The roads were empty, as he expected. Despite the rain, the binder lamps shone, illuminating the path along the street. He passed the occasional late-night traveler, bundled and hunched with their head down. His lungs soon hurt. They begged him to stop and walk, but he pressed forward without slowing.

Ramble Square was nearly deserted. A pair of constables patrolled, seemingly oblivious to the rain. A pool formed in a depressed area at the square's center, and abandoned kamak boards plinked with relentless drops of water.

His gait slowed when he spied the bench where Old Man Telemus had lain earlier that day. Both the man and the guard who had watched over him were gone. *His "storm of sorrows" must have arrived.* The thought did not sit well. Kaleth barreled into the narrow passage of Mercavor Street.

The daily market had been abandoned for hours. Carts were put away. Goods stayed dry, tucked inside the buildings. Most canopies were folded up, and the ones that weren't formed waterfalls that dropped to the stone path. At the closed-up clock shop, he angled up a street toward the center of the Hightower District. A clock in the window displayed 11:02.

*Plenty of time.*

His jogging slowed, partly from his aching legs and lungs but mostly because the area was less familiar. Another turn took him past a row of homes and a statue of some long-dead figure. Kaleth continued up the street. His boots splashed. His cloak felt heavy. The arm holding the bundled book against his chest ached from trying to keep it dry. He passed a smith's shop lit by the fading coals of its furnace.

*Almost there.*

He turned up the last street and his feet skidded to a halt. The road ended at an oversized door advertising a carriage shop. His breath caught in his throat.

*This isn't it. Where did I—?*

He spun, looking for the arched portico of Erinth's home that he had visited earlier in the day. It was nowhere to be seen. He jogged back along his path.

*Maybe it was the previous street.*

He increased his speed, acutely aware of the seconds passing. An ache grew in his side as his feet pounded the wet stones. He pressed his cramp with his free hand, but the pain didn't lessen. He turned up the next street, then stopped again. The gaudy entrance to the Hightower Bathhouse was something he would have remembered.

*I'm rushing,* he chided himself. *I should have been more careful of my turns.* He spun, calculating which direction he should try next. The overhang at the edge of the smith's shop caught his eye. He stepped under the cover and lowered his hood as if the fresh air might help him think.

Rain drummed on the roof above him. His breath fogged the air, making rapid panting sounds. He looked in one direction. The statue he spied in the distance didn't look familiar. He had seen a lot of similar roads earlier that day. He spun the other way. Past the turns he had tried, the road curved out of sight along a row of expensive houses.

*I didn't think it was that far.*

Amidst the drops of rain, he heard something—a faint splashing sound that contrasted with the repetitive cadence of the natural precipitation. He looked over his shoulder. Nothing was there except the rain-filled path lit by binder lamps. He checked in the opposite direction—nothing but dreary streets.

Two distinctive plinks of water hit the floor, perking his ears. The hairs on his neck stood on end. The drops came from behind him.

"You lost, Grunny?"

Kaleth spun. His jaw locked and his body tensed. Terror rushed through him, muddling his ability to think. Rayd stood before him with water dripping from the tips of his mussed hair.

"You're easy to follow, running around the city in circles."

Kaleth couldn't think of anything to say. "I—I—" He snapped into motion, running for the street. Before he'd even left the smith's covering, Rayd's iron grip on his arm held him in place. He strained against the hold, but the larger boy pulled him back toward the heart of the shop.

"You cut up my arm, and you ruined that suit." Both hands grabbed the front of Kaleth's cloak, shaking him. "Those clothes cost fifty gold. Are you gonna pay me back?"

*This can't be happening! Not now!* Kaleth didn't answer.

"I didn't think so."

*Crack!*

A fist slammed into Kaleth's jaw, ringing his ears and blinding him with pain. His glasses flew from his face and fell to the ground.

"That's for the pants." Rayd hit him again. "That's for the coat."

Kaleth couldn't see. His mouth was in agony. He teetered on his feet with his head drooping. He only remained standing because the other boy held him up.

His sneer turned as if the offense grew personal. "And this is for thinking you can rise out of Grunwind to be better than me." Rayd slammed his fist into Kaleth's stomach. "Gah!" The young man yelled, reeling and shaking his hand.

Kaleth had only felt a dull thud in his stomach. His sheltered book absorbed the fist.

"What's in there?"

Kaleth's fear of being caught by the bully intensified to a terror he had never known. *No! He can't find it!* He turned to run again.

"Not so fast." Rayd grabbed Kaleth around his neck and flung him backward. Kaleth slammed onto a table. The glow from the waning furnace lit the side of his face.

With blurred vision, he tried to push the boy away, but Rayd was too strong.

"Stay down!"

A fist in Kaleth's face cracked his nose. He nearly blacked out. The pain was so intense, he couldn't do anything but flail his arms. A warm, coppery taste filled his mouth. The world spun. Spots darkened his sight. A vague awareness of his cloak rustling brought him back.

"What's this?" Rayd said.

Kaleth blinked several times and lifted his head. Rayd stood a step back from the table. He unfurled the wool wrap that held his father's book. "Rayd, please. Give it back." His words bubbled with the blood in his mouth. His voice trembled. A gut-wrenching alarm rang in his mind.

Rayd laughed. "Please? You think if you grovel, I'm gonna let you off the hook? What is this? 'Compendium of Knowledge'?" He scoffed, then moved as if to toss it into the rain.

"No!" Kaleth yelled, jerking to a sitting position.

Rayd stopped, his mouth frozen in a smirk.

The pain of sitting up brought a blinding pain back. "I need it for my father. He's going to die without that book. Please! The rain will ruin it!"

Rayd's eyebrow raised as he cocked his head. "You think I care about your father?"

"Please," he whispered.

"Fight me for it," Rayd said.

"What?"

"You want the book back? Here it is." Rayd thumped it on a shelf next to him, then raised his fists. "Fight me for it!" The young man's knuckles were already stained with Kaleth's blood. His shoulders bounced, primed and ready to fight. Veins bulged on the sides of his neck.

Another wave of dizziness washed over Kaleth. The pain in his jaw and nose redoubled. He pictured himself walking into another round of pounding.

*I have to get the book!*

He slid off the table. His vision spun again. He raised an arm for balance and watched the lifted fists dancing circles. He longed to turn and run, but all he could picture was his father at home, waiting for him to return with the money. He imagined his sister watching out the window and his mother trying to keep their spirits up. A gut-wrenching thought planted in his mind.

*I can't beat him.*

"It's now or never," Rayd taunted.

Kaleth shook his head, a tear pooling at the corner of his eye. "I can't beat you. You know that." His shaking words hurt to enunciate. "But I *need* it. Don't throw it in the rain."

Rayd lifted his chin and stared down his nose. His eyes narrowed. "I won't."

A wave of relief washed over Kaleth. The tension in his body eased, but the pain remained.

"I won't . . . throw it in the rain."

The way he punctuated each word sent a chill down Kaleth's spine, like a trickle of cold water dripping from a roof spout. He held his breath, staring. His pulse thudded in his ears.

Rayd's mouth developed a wicked curl at the edge. "You will never rise above me." His eyes flicked to the side.

An empty feeling surged through Kaleth's gut as if it tried to warn him. His paralyzed muscles ached to spring into action, but they did nothing. By the time he realized the boy's intent, it was too late. His mind slowed, thoughts moving like syrup. His world shifted.

Rayd stepped toward the furnace, his move strong and sure. He raised his arm and flicked his wrist. The cover of the compendium opened as it twirled. Pages flapped. It landed with a fit of sparks, face down on the glowing coals. The dry paper ignited, bursting into a ball of fire.

"No!" Kaleth's scream filled the air. He stumbled toward the glowing red flames until an unseen fist slammed into his exposed gut. He squeezed his eyes shut, doubling over and gasping for breath. Air came in spurts. He sucked it in, wheezing. It took several long, agonizing moments until he could push the pain aside and lift his head. Past Rayd's menacing form, hungry flames devoured his father's book in the heart of the furnace. The book his father spent months on. The book that would pay off his debt.

The book that would have saved his life.

Gone.

He pushed past the other boy and grabbed a pair of tongs that hung next to the furnace. *It's not too late. It's not too late.* He leaned as close to the furnace as he could tolerate. Agonizing seconds passed while he fumbled with the tool, trying to fish out the burning object. With the end of the awkward tongs, he grasped one side and lifted. The compendium flopped open, burning on every surface. Flaming pages flapped. Blackened chunks fell. He lifted it slowly to him. When it had almost reached the opening, the spine tore and half the book fell back to the coals.

What he finally extricated from the fire couldn't possibly be worth anything, but he had to try. An amused Rayd, sporting a half-smirk, gave him a wide berth as he carried the tongs and the still-burning remnants toward the street. Kaleth tossed all of it to the ground once he'd stepped out from the protective roof.

A plume of smoke hissed into the air as the object contacted the water on the ground and the falling precipitation. Kaleth waved his hand, flapping the smoke away. The fire only took a moment to be quenched. Aware of the damaging water assaulting it, he tapped the cover to ensure it was no longer hot. Desperate, he picked up the remnant and brought it back to the dry table.

When it hit the wood, the remains of the compendium fell apart. Blackened pages shattered across the table. Wisps of destroyed paper blew away with the wind. He lifted the cover, and it fell from the rest of the pile of ash.

Kaleth was in shock. His mouth hung open, emitting sputtering moans. His stomach, jaw, and nose screamed in pain, but his heart ached worst of all.

Rayd chuckled. "Maybe next time, you'll know better than to mess with someone outside of your station."

The rain had eased but not stopped. Two pairs of footsteps approached in the street. With his body feeling numb, Kaleth turned to see what other misfortune had arrived. A flicker of hope built as he took in the sight of two constables passing.

"Sirs!" Kaleth raised a hand and stumbled out from the cover of the roof.

Rayd stared at him, piercing with his malicious eyes as if daring him to say something.

The constables stopped, the light rain dripping off their hats. They looked at Kaleth, then at Rayd, then back at Kaleth. One with a bushy beard raised his eyebrows. "Is everything all right here?"

The hope grew. "No," Kaleth said, aware of how beat up his face must look. He pointed a shaking hand at Rayd. "He burned my father's book. We're in debt to Jairus and we needed the money from that book to pay it. Jairus is gonna kill him! My father's going to die, tonight! Rayd just stole the book and threw it in that furnace. Now we have nothing and—"

A raised hand made him stop. "He took your book and burned it?"

Kaleth nodded. "That's right. Just now."

"Did he give you those wounds?"

Another nod.

"And your father's in debt to Jairus, you say?"

"Yes, sir." His heart pounded in his chest.

The two constables exchanged a glance. The bearded one turned to Rayd. "Rayd-il-Stonne, right?"

Rayd lifted his chin. "Yes."

The constable looked for a long time as if deciding what punishment was appropriate. "Tell your father, Valto says congratulations on his promotion."

"Yes, sir. I will."

Without another glance at Kaleth, the constables continued along the street.

Kaleth's stomach dropped. "No! Wait! He took it from me. He—" He stopped. He stared at the backs of the constables with his jaw drooping. They had no intention of interfering. *Rayd's father is too important.*

The other boy's deep and mirthless laugh shook Kaleth to his core. Rain drummed on his face. The blood from his nose ran down his chin and trickled to the street. He felt dead inside.

"See you around, Grunny."

Rayd strolled away, leaving Kaleth alone, hurting, and hopeless.

## CHAPTER SEVEN
# PAYING THE DEBT

K aleth slowed his pace when he approached their house, dreading having to enter. During the jog home, he racked his brain for ideas of what they could do. How to get money. How to stand up to Jairus. Nothing good came to mind. The only answer he found was that he needed to let his father know as soon as possible so he could figure out what to do.

*Father trusted me with it, and I let him down. He's going to kill me.*

His face still ached. His stomach felt like it was in knots. His chest constricted. He hadn't even thought to raise his hood against the rain, despite the water dripping down his scratched glasses.

The red door swung open. Sora's face fell the moment he drew close. "What happened?" she gasped.

He entered their house.

"Kaleth!" his mother cried, rustling the bed. "Your face!"

His father stepped closer and rested a hand on his shoulder. "Are you all right?"

The question broke his heart. *He's worried about me. He doesn't even know.* He shook his head, keeping his eyes on the floor. "No," he whispered. "None of us are."

His father glanced at Sora. "Grab some dried feldsthorn from the cupboard. We need to make a tea."

"No," Kaleth objected. His sister stopped mid-turn. "There's no time."

"What do you mean? Did you—" His father swallowed a lump, his face growing pale. "Did you get the money?"

Kaleth clamped his jaw tight to keep his chin from shaking. Tears welled in his eyes, blurring the sight of his father. "I'm sorry." The words were barely a whisper. He wiped at his eyes. "I was jumped. A kid in Hightower. He beat me up and—" It pained him to speak it. "And he burned the book."

His mother cried out. Sora gasped.

His father took in a slow breath. His face showed neither anger nor fear. "Burned?" he repeated.

Kaleth nodded. He pulled out the charred remnant of the cover and handed it to his father. His words trembled. "I couldn't stop him, Father. I'm so sorry. The book is destroyed. It's gone."

Valorr turned the cover over, inspecting it only a moment before he set it on his table. He turned back to Kaleth. In a calm voice, he asked, "Where are you injured?"

"Who cares!" Kaleth yelled, his fear and guilt fueling him with energy. "Jairus is coming. He's going to be here in a few minutes, and he will *kill* you!"

Valorr stepped closer and rested a hand against Kaleth's face. "Your nose may be broken. Your jaw looks bruised, but that's it."

"Father, stop! I'm fine. We need to do something for you, and it's all my fault!" The tears returned. He shook his head. "It's my fault. I'm so sorry, Father."

His father set both hands on his shoulders. "Kaleth, look at me."

He sniffed his runny nose and stopped shaking.

The tenderness in his father's eyes was the last thing he expected to see. "Thank you for trying," Valorr said in soothing tones. "It's not your fault, and I don't blame you."

The knot in Kaleth's chest loosened. He wiped his eyes and nose, then sniffed again.

"Now—" His father opened his stance to see the others. "We need to decide what to do."

"What if we explain it to Jairus?" Sora suggested. "We can show him the burned cover and tell him what happened."

"He won't care," Valorr said. "He wants money, not excuses."

"Is there anywhere else you can get one hundred gold from?" Kaleth's mother asked. "Would the Scholars' Council give you an advance? Surely you could replicate it with more time?"

"I tried that two weeks ago. They wouldn't budge."

The air in the room was tense. Kaleth paled at the only option he could think of. "We run," he breathed.

"Run?" Sora repeated.

His father nodded, his mouth a grim line. "Agreed. It's our only option. We leave now—make for Greenshire or Fayport. Jairus won't care enough to track us there."

All three heads turned to the bed. His mother's face was pale.

"We can carry you," Kaleth said. He glanced at Valorr. "Father and I can trade off. Maybe we can find a horse or a cart.

"We can do it," his father said. "Fenya? Sora? Are you in?"

Sora's eyes formed wide circles, but her jaw was set. She nodded. Kaleth's mother pushed her blankets back and angled her legs toward the edge. "I'm ready," she said.

A flash of lightning illuminated the window. A crash of thunder followed, shaking the house.

"It's going to be wet," Valorr said.

Kaleth nodded. "We'll dry."

After a beat, his father snapped into action. "All right, let's go. Sora, collect dried food from the kitchen—everything you can find. Include flasks for water. Pack the large pot, the medium skillet, and one ladle. Kaleth, grab your pack and fill it with the blankets from the beds and your and Sora's clothes. I'll take care of the rest. We leave in five minutes."

Kaleth, his sister, and his father rushed around the room in a flurry of motion. They grabbed packs, blankets, food, clothes, and anything important that could fit. Kaleth's body trembled as he worked. In a few minutes, Sora held an oversized sack, stuffed to the brim, Kaleth's and his father's threadbare packs stretched so far they barely closed.

"What's that?" Valorr asked, nodding at a bundle wrapped in a cloth in Sora's hands.

"Kaleth's gift." She folded a corner back revealing a loaf of banana bread. Her grim smile felt ominous. "I can carry it."

His father nodded, then slung his pack over his shoulders. "I'll carry Fenya to the edge of the city. We'll enter the woods, then we can trade off. Is everyone ready?"

Kaleth's cloak was on. His pack rested on his shoulders, weighing him down. His heart thudded in his chest as he opened the door. The protection glyph carved into the lintel made him pause. *We're protected in here.*

Valorr squeezed his shoulder. "It won't keep us safe forever. We need to go."

Kaleth swallowed hard, then nodded. He stepped through the doorway. The rain had not abated. It drummed on his head and filled the air with a steady rush of noise. He held the door for his sister. His father came last, carrying Fenya in his arms. She wrapped hers around his neck and leaned her head against his shoulder. He trudged through the door, weighed down by both the pack and his wife.

Kaleth glanced toward the center of the city. Dimmed by the driving rain, the binder lamps illuminated enough of the street to tell it was empty. "Good. I think we beat them." He turned east and froze as if ice shot through his veins.

His father and sister stood still, pelted by the rain. Over their shoulders, Jairus' two goons blocked the road. "Where do you think you're going?" one muttered.

Valorr turned and looked at Kaleth. "Take your mother and run," he whispered. "I'll hold them off. Find a place to hide."

One man held a crossbow, and the other pulled a knife. "I take it you don't have Jairus' money?"

Kaleth gulped. His mind told him to flee, but his legs wouldn't move. *What if he shoots me in the back?*

"Kaleth, listen!" his father yelled. "You need to—Aargh!" His face twisted in agony. He fell to the ground, knees hitting the street hard. Fenya rolled out of his arms onto the ground, grabbing her ankle and crying in pain.

"Father!" Kaleth yelled.

His face drained of feeling at the sight of Jairus. The man had arrived from behind, and his cloaked form stood over Valorr. Rain glistened on the man's bald head. He scowled, holding a bloody knife at his side.

Kaleth's father rolled onto the ground, his pack falling off. He pressed a hand against his side and groaned.

"I warned you the money was due today," Jairus said. "And now you've insulted me by trying to run."

Kaleth crouched next to his father. Blood seeped through Valorr's fingers, running as the rain washed it away.

Sora helped her mother up and aided her in limping back to their house.

"Father, what do I do?" Kaleth asked.

Valorr grimaced while panting. "Get ready," he managed through gritted teeth.

"Get ready? What do you mean?"

Jairus' smug grin faltered. His chest lurched forward as if taken by sudden fatigue. He pressed his hands on his knees.

"Are you okay, Boss?" a thug asked.

Jairus swayed, extending an arm for balance. "I'm fine." His words were curiously listless. He blinked multiple times.

"Get your mother," his father whispered. "We sprint for the woods."

Kaleth looked at Valorr and gasped. The pain-filled expression that was just there had been replaced by confidence. His intense eyes were ready to act. The weakness in his body was gone. "How did—?" He stopped when he looked at his father's side. A rip in his coat and the blood staining it remained. "You healed?" He glanced at Jairus, and it all made sense. *Father used his power like he did against the blood panzils.*

Valorr jumped to his feet and faced Kaleth. "As I said, I'll hold them off. You need to go!"

Kaleth nodded. Before he ran for the house, the sight over his father's shoulder stopped him. Jairus' man raised a crossbow, and a trigger flicked. *No!* He pointed and tried to make words. Nothing came out.

His father spun unnaturally fast, but it was too late. A bolt pierced Valorr's back. The look of agony returned. His back arched. He turned and flailed a hand behind him, groaning in pain.

"Do it again," Kaleth urged. "Do . . . whatever you did to—"

Jairus stepped in and plunged his knife into Valorr's chest, directly over his heart.

"No!" Kaleth yelled. He wanted to lunge at Jairus, but his feet remained planted. His mouth hung open.

His father fell again, collapsing onto his back. Rain pelted his face. He blinked, swatting weakly with a hand. The gaping wound in his chest gushed blood that covered his clothes.

"Father," Kaleth whimpered, crouching with him.

Valorr's eyes focused on him. His lips trembled. "It's okay, Son. Don't worry about me."

The weakness in his father's voice tore a cavernous hole in his heart. He choked on his words. "Can you . . . heal?"

His father coughed, blood spitting on his chest. He looked at the wound, then glanced around.

Kaleth also scoured the area, looking for any plants or signs of life. Dead stone, dirt, and thatched roofs surrounded them.

Valorr coughed again, then shook his head. "It's no use. Not from this."

Tears sprang to Kaleth's eyes, blending with the rain trickling down his face. A desperate idea came with a clearing of his sinuses. He dropped to the ground and pressed his finger into the muddy residue that covered the cobblestones. "I can cast a healing glyph." He sucked in a quick breath to steady his nerves. He muttered, "Focus. Intention. Action," as if speaking the words would help him achieve the precise purpose required to make a successful glyph.

*For my father. Heal his wounds.*

"Kaleth, it won't help."

He traced a circle, ignoring his father.

*Knit together his flesh. Repair his heart.*

The sparse mud only allowed an intermittent line. He clenched his abs to focus. Squinting helped him push out the chaos of the torrential rain, the looming enemies, and the mournful cries of his sister and mother.

*Let this mark focus on him—Valorr Gooding.*

Halfway through tracing the backward S of the glyph, his father's weak hand rested on his arm. "It's too much to heal."

"No!" Tears blurred his vision. He couldn't even make out what he'd tried to scratch out. The attempt was useless. He abandoned his failed glyph and looked around for a better place to cast it.

Waterlogged stones. Rivulets of silt.

Nothing.

"Let it go, Kaleth." Valorr gasped for breath. "Take care of your mother and sister."

Kaleth's jaw quivered. He couldn't give up, but what else was there to do? His father's peaceful gaze looked on him, giving him permission to stop. Kaleth wiped his eyes and nodded.

"Remember what you saw in the woods? That is your future."

A wave of terror washed through him like ice in his veins. He gulped, trying to swallow the fear that clawed its way up his throat. His voice trembled as he whispered, "How do I learn?"

Another round of coughing sprayed red. His father winced. "There's something you'll need to do first."

Kaleth leaned closer, his sight blurry.

His father's breath rattled. Blood thinned by drops of water covered his chin. He struggled to take in a breath, gasping and straining.

"Under the bed, on your side . . . loose floorboard."

Kaleth nodded. "What's in there?"

His father opened his mouth, but only a splatter of blood came out. He sucked in heaving spurts of air until he grew quiet.

Kaleth turned his ear. He waited, but no answer came. "What's there?" he repeated. A sinking feeling grew in his gut. When he turned back, the unseeing look on his father's face confirmed his fear.

The man who had raised him and taught him everything he knew was gone.

A torrent of tears flooded down his cheeks, but Kaleth wouldn't look away. He half-expected a sudden gasp and his father to be suddenly brimming with life—energy pulled from some nearby source. No breath moved his chest. No life lit his eyes. He would never again fill their house with his rich laugh or smile when Kaleth learned something new.

Footsteps approached. With tears streaming down, Kaleth lifted his face to see a blurry Jairus standing over him.

"Your father shouldn't have taken a loan if he couldn't pay his debt. He failed. Now . . . it's on you."

The words should have held more of a shock, but Kaleth was too numb to think clearly. He wiped his face, then dropped his head to look at his father again.

"Did you hear me?" Jairus asked. "One hundred gold."

"I don't have it," Kaleth whispered, lips shaking. "Does that mean you'll kill me, too?"

"Get it."

Kaleth laughed.

"You find this funny?"

He shook his head, the laugh fading. "It would take me a year to raise that much money."

Jairus stared for a long moment. The pattering rain was the only marker of the passing time. "Fine," he said. "One year. And if you don't have it—"

"I know," Kaleth said, devoid of feeling, "you'll kill me."

"No."

The answer was not what he expected. He lifted his eyes, but the hope he wanted to feel had turned to dread. A wicked grin grew on Jairus' face. "You pay me my hundred gold . . . or I kill your mother and sister."

The words confirmed his greatest fear and turned like a knife in his gut. Sora peeked from the door of their house. Her face twisted in terror, and she hadn't even heard the threat.

"I have connections everywhere: in the army, in the palace,

spread through Kalshia. If you run, I'll find them. And I'll make it hurt." Jairus waved to his men and headed back into the depths of the city.

Kaleth's gaze drifted to the rain-soaked street. Two packs of supplies and an overstuffed bag lay strewn in the rain. One of their cloths lay soaking on the stones. A fresh loaf of banana bread lay upside down in a puddle, having rolled out of its protection. Split down the center, water soaked into each half of his ruined present.

*One hundred gold in one year.* The amount sounded impossible. He nodded his head, thinking optimistically. *I can do it.* He'd need to scrimp and trade to open a meager consultant shop as a sage, but once it was running, he'd be able to bring in money. Some of the money would take care of the family and they'd set some aside to pay Jairus. A year is a long time. *But when I'm a licensed sage, I can—*

The horrifying truth hit him like a punch to his gut. His breath grew ragged.

*I'm not a sage.*

His eyes dropped to his father. A man who could teach him no more. A man who couldn't help him set up a shop.

*A man who can't certify my license.*

## CHAPTER EIGHT

# SIGNING DAY

Light came through the window, falling across Kaleth's eyes. Longing to fall back asleep, he draped an arm across his face, careful to not hit the underside of his parents' bed— his *mother's* bed. Footsteps shuffled through the kitchen, muffling a whimper. Something sizzled on the stove. Sora was up.

*Get up and help. There's so much to do.* His body didn't react to his mind's command.

The night before, he and Sora had spent hours digging a hole at the Freeman's Cemetery by the light of the binder lamps. You were supposed to pay four silvers for a plot, but if you dug it at night and left no marker, no one bothered tracking you down. Set in the heart of Grunwind, half the cemetery comprised unmarked graves. He and his sister had returned home only a few hours before the sunrise, filthy and exhausted.

He felt the impact of the traumatic night and tried to cling to any extra minutes of sleep he could get. When he rolled over, every muscle in his upper body complained. His chin ached, still in pain from the beating he'd received. He was about to close his eyes again when he spied the board his father referenced next to the wall, just past the edge of his mattress.

It was lighter than the others and chipped at the edge. Adrenaline attempted to flush the sorrow from his body, but it barely made a dent. Lying on his side, his hand drifted to the board. His fingers pressed against it. It argued with him but eventually slid. His fingers tucked around the edge.

His father's warning came to his mind. *No one knows. Not even Mother.* As much as he trusted his family, he had no interest in putting their lives in more danger than they already were.

*What if I ignore it?* he thought. *If I pretend I never heard about his secret, could all of this go away?* As tempting as it sounded, it wouldn't change things. His father wasn't coming back, and their debt wouldn't disappear.

He lifted the piece of wood, finding a hollow cavity below. Unable to see from where he lay, his hand fished inside. He cringed at the webs brushing his fingers. He tried to ignore the unbidden thoughts of massive spiders crawling on his skin. His fingers brushed something—paper. He lifted it gingerly, trying to avoid any noise. It was a note, folded over several times. His initial hope of the cavity being filled with money dissipated. Still, he knew whatever was on the paper was secret and—he imagined—valuable.

He lowered the board over the hole and slid it back into place. It squeaked as the wood grains pressed against each other.

"Hey."

His arm twitched. He slid the paper into his pocket.

Sora padded next to the bed, then crouched. Her tremulous smile looked forced, incongruent with her red and puffy eyes. "You awake, Kaleth?"

*Kaleth.* Not Brumblebum. Not Grubbynub. He nodded.

"How are you holding up?"

The question reminded him of the hopelessness of their predicament. He crawled out from his sleeping cave. "I'm not feeling great."

"Me neither," she said. "I slept maybe an hour until the nightmares came."

He didn't even consider doling out the teasing response he normally would have followed with.

"Come here, Son," his mother said, turning him toward the bed.

With swollen eyes of her own, Fenya looked as if she'd been crying most of the night.

In fact, each time Kaleth had woken, he heard faint sobs coming from above.

She extended her hand, taking his. "I know it's not what any of us planned, but . . ." Her chin trembled. A tight squeeze of her eyes sent a pooling batch of tears down her cheeks. She forced a smile and whispered, "Happy seventeenth birthday, Kaleth."

The words felt wrong as they mixed with the gloom that hung around them.

"The bread was ruined," his sister said. "So I'm making griddle cakes and eggs, instead."

He frowned. "Where'd you get—"

"Next door. I told Silvia it was your birthday."

His stomach growled at the aroma filling the room.

"Come and sit."

"Let Mother eat first. I'll run and draw some water." The monotone words spilled from him out of habit. He reached under the counter and found the bucket already full.

Sora's grim expression unsuccessfully tried to form a smile. "Already done. Mother's eaten, too. Maybe if you didn't lay in bed all day . . ."

He cringed, knowing he'd slept through it all. "I'm sorry."

She shook her head. "I'm sorry. I didn't mean it like that—just a habit. I'm glad you got some sleep." She sniffed. "Now, sit."

He exhaled through his nose as he dropped onto the stool at the counter. His sister flipped a griddle cake onto a plate, then spooned out a meager portion of scrambled eggs. Her trembling hand dropped a portion of the eggs on the table.

"Sorry," she said, picking them up with her fingers.

He found no joy in the special meal. The cakes—despite being perfectly cooked—felt dry. The eggs—a rare treat—tasted bland.

"We shouldn't be celebrating," he muttered. No one refuted the statement. "Father's gone, and now we're all doomed."

"We're not doomed," his mother said. "Valorr always said, 'All problems have two things in common: a pit to wallow in and a ladder to climb out.'"

Invoking his father's words made his blood run hot. He stuffed a bite of eggs in his mouth to keep from exploding at his mother.

"If your father were here, he'd remind you that the ladder may be hard to find, but it's there."

"Well, he's not here." Kaleth flinched at the bitterness in his own voice.

"Kaleth, please." Sora's words trembled like she was barely holding it together herself.

He pounded on the table, causing the plate to bounce. "He's not here because Jairus killed him!" His sister and mother jerked backward. "Jairus did it, he—" His words choked. "He's the one that—" Against his will, the events of the night scrolled through his mind. He tried to fight the memory, but the facts couldn't be changed. Moisture pooled in his eyes. "I had the book. I took it, and—" He swallowed hard. "It's my fault. I should have—"

"It's not your fault, Son."

Like a dam breaking, salty tears streamed down his face. He lowered his head and sobbed. Sora stepped to him and hugged around his shoulders, a rare, tender expression. He didn't fight it. Rather than run from the sorrow, he traveled toward it, hoping there would be relief on the other side. When the tears had run dry and the rest of his food was wet, he sat up. He wiped his eyes and nose. "What are we going to do?"

Neither his sister nor his mother answered.

"We barely have any food or any money. Jairus wants one hundred gold in a year's time, and I can't be certified as a sage."

"Can you speak with someone from the board and explain?" Sora asked, sniffing and wiping her own tears away.

He shook his head. "You have to start over with a new master."

"What about Farland or Howell? Surely they'd take you on."

"It's a two-year minimum. They're strict about that."

"I can sew," his mother said. "That can bring in something."

Sora nodded. "And I can wash laundry or maybe . . . get a job at the mill."

"No!" Kaleth shouted, louder than he intended. He looked at his mother. "None of us will be working at the mill. Besides, even that wouldn't be enough."

"If all three of us are doing what we can, that will bring in something," his mother said.

"We still need to eat, too. We need to live." He calculated the average rates of various jobs in his head. With what his mother, sister, and he could reasonably bring in . . . He swallowed as he multiplied the paltry sum by fifty-two weeks. *There's no way we can earn enough.*

"We'll figure it out," Sora said with forced confidence.

He nodded. "Thank you for making me breakfast. Even if I don't feel like celebrating, it feels nice to be thought of."

She smiled. "Jovi came by earlier."

He raised his eyebrows.

"You were asleep. He saw all the mess, and . . . I told him about Father. He felt awful but wanted me to tell you he stopped by."

"Shoot!" Kaleth's memory rushed back. "I forgot about today. Do you know what time it is?"

"Should be almost ten."

"It's Signing Day for the academy, and I promised him I'd be there."

"You should go," his mother said.

He shook his head. "We have too much to figure out. I can't leave you, now."

"Go, Fuzzlewort," his sister reiterated. "It's your birthday. We can climb Father's ladder out of the pit when you get back."

He did like the idea of doing something normal—something he'd planned to do before everything had gone wrong—as if the previous night had never happened. His sense of duty to his family kept him seated until his sister lifted her eyebrows and made a shooing motion with the backs of her fingers.

He chuckled. Despite feeling out of place, the bouncing air coming from his mouth boosted his spirits. "Fine. I'll be back soon."

· · ·

Thousands of people packed Ramble Square, causing Kaleth to have to push through the crowd to even enter. They came to see the dignitaries and pomp that came with each year's Signing Day—that and the free food. He cursed his luck for being late as he eyed the people he squeezed past eating bread and small chunks of cheese.

At the south end of the plaza, looming off the edge of the plateau, Sky Fortress dominated the scene. The path to get there ended at tall gates that hung over a precipitous drop. From there, the walls rose even higher, creating an oval-shaped protection around Kalistor Palace and the Lightbinder Academy. Crenellations ran the length of the fortress' rim, manned by guards who faced the square.

Where the path to the fortress met Ramble Square, a group sat in chairs on an elevated stage. A woman in a gray robe stood at the front of the platform, droning on about the storied history of Signing Day, the historical leaders who had joined the academy in the past, and the glorious futures they went on to have. The Kalshian flag flapped in the breeze over the platform. Its sky-blue top half was separated from fern green by a horizontal strip of white.

In front of the stage, dozens of tables sat on the ground. Young men Kaleth's age stood in front of the ones on the left while young women lined up in front of the ones on the right. Every line stretched well into the square. The hundreds of future initiates kept their eyes on the stage while they shifted their weight, waiting on the tables to register names. He spotted Jovi near the front of one of the guys' lines and pushed his way toward him as the woman in gray continued her monotonous speech.

"Heard you came by," Kaleth whispered when he pushed his way up to his friend.

Jovi sucked in a breath. He wrapped his arms around him and hugged him tight. Kaleth winced, still feeling the effect of his beating the night before.

Jovi pulled away. "I heard about your father and the book and everything. I'm so sorry."

Kaleth nodded as an image of his father's dead body came to his mind.

"Who burned the book?"

"I'll give you one guess."

Jovi's eyes grew wide. "Rayd? No way! That bind-cursed piece of . . . Did he give you those bruises?"

Kaleth nodded again.

"Hey," the guy behind in line said. "No cutting."

"I'm not cutting. I just needed to talk for a minute."

"I can't believe it," Jovi said. "He's here, by the way. Did you see him?"

"Where?"

Jovi pointed at the stage. At the end of the row, the young man sat erect. His chin lifted while his eyes stayed glued on the speaker. The man next to him was clearly his father. Aside from the clean-shaven face and advancement of twenty-five more years, he was the spitting image of his son. The man's black army uniform pressed into sharp lines with gleaming medals attached to his chest.

Kaleth's blood boiled. "Spoiled rich brat. He thinks he can do whatever he wants. Well, he's going to pay. I would rush the stage right now if I had a weapon."

"What do you need?" Jovi asked.

He looked at his friend, shocked by the earnest expression on his face.

"A knife?"

The offer felt tempting, but Kaleth shook his head. He couldn't imagine actually following through with the threat. "Not here."

"Yeah," Jovi looked around. "I guess not."

"Thanks for having my back, though."

The speaker's cadence changed. "And with that, I'd like to introduce you to one of the most powerful men in all of Kalshia, newly appointed to the highest position in the Kalshian army. Exal General Stonne-il-Malthus."

The crowd cheered as Stonne rose. With a chiseled jaw and leathery skin, Rayd's father looked as if he'd seen more than his share of fights. His muscular body suggested he had won them all.

Apparently, the man had grown up in Grunwind and even used to know Kaleth's father. Kaleth entertained a fleeting thought that perhaps the man could help with their situation, but then he remembered it was the man's son who had caused the problem. Stonne raised a hand to accept the cheers. The hard line of his mouth melted into a winning smile.

"Thank you, fellow Kalshians," he began, his words warm and inviting. He gestured toward the lines at the foot of the stage. "But the real honor here today is reserved for these courageous young men and women: Kalshian loyalists who will serve their kingdom, putting their lives on the line to protect the ideals that make this kingdom great. Your kingdom thanks you. I thank you."

The young men in line around Kaleth murmured with appreciation. It was no wonder the man had risen to his current rank. He knew how to work a crowd.

"While you enjoy security and freedom in the comfort of your homes, a war rages around you. Thravian warriors want nothing more than to rip our kingdom apart, to tear this city down to rubble and ravage our fertile land for their own gains. Kalshian soldiers hold the port at Lynharbor while the bulk of the army is stationed at North Twainford on the Lagrash River. Only last week, a battalion fought off an invasion of Thravians trying to cross the river. Thankfully"—a chiseled smile formed on his face—"we have the better army. Our Blades are stronger. Our Bows are more precise. Our Menders are wiser. And of course . . . nothing compares to our Lightbinders. The Thravians try, but they cannot compete. We must stay ahead of them as well as any future threats from Carrvorre or Loravis. We must be ready, not for what they bring today, but for the wiles of tomorrow. You initiates are what make us great. You are the future of protection for this great kingdom. Because you come here today, your families will be safe and our borders will be protected."

Kaleth rolled his eyes.

"To prepare you to enter this elite army, Lightbinder Academy was founded seventy years ago. Last year, we were devastated by the untimely loss of Headmaster Philbius. In his place, a new leader rises, ready to usher this academy and you initiates into the future. Please give a warm welcome to Headmaster Genoris-il-Justifore."

An older man approached the front of the stage and nodded as the general left. His thick, gray hair and wrinkled face placed him around sixty years old, but his poise and movement proved he was still physically capable. His brown eyes held a hint of blue that sparkled along with his teeth as he smiled.

"Thank you, Exal General Stonne. I am pleased to announce the taking of names is open!"

A rumble of excited conversation grew in the lines. The women who sat at the tables began taking names, and the lines moved forward.

"Are you sure you want to do this?" Kaleth asked.

Jovi nodded, grinning. "Can't wait."

Speaking over the rumble of conversation and the scratching of names, Headmaster Genoris added commentary. "In my first year as headmaster, I am thrilled to welcome you initiates. There is no greater honor for me than you placing your trust in us. The three years you'll commit to the academy will shape you into disciplined, capable warriors who are ready and able to defend this kingdom."

The line they stood in continued closer, drawing near the table and the lady who sat there.

"Three years," Kaleth shook his head. "I'm going to miss you. I hope you're able to leave for breaks."

"I'll come and visit when I can," Jovi said.

The headmaster continued, "Thanks to this year's bounty and his generosity, King Rhinean increased the academy stipend to one gold per week."

Kaleth jerked to attention, then leaned closer to his friend. "You get one gold per week for being here?"

Jovi grinned. "Yeah, nice, huh? They told us at the interest meeting. It used to only be seven silvers."

The boy in front of Jovi gave his name to the lady at the table.

"End-of-year bonuses have also increased," Genoris said from the stage.

"Wait, what?" Kaleth's heart pounded. "You get a weekly stipend *and* a bonus?"

"Yeah. The Lightbinders are up to seventy-five gold, now. Can you believe it?"

Kaleth held his breath. "At the end of the year?"

Jovi nodded, then turned to the lady at the table. "Jovi Strapper."

In a monotone, she repeated what she had said dozens of times. "Do you, Jovi, promise to serve the kingdom of Kalshia by committing three years of your life to the Lightbinder Academy?"

"I do."

"Wait." Kaleth grabbed his arm. "You get one gold per week, meaning fifty-two in a year. Then you get a bonus that can be up to seventy-five more at the end of the year?"

"That's right." He chuckled. "What? You having second thoughts about the academy, now?"

"Name?" the woman asked.

The boy behind in line pushed against Kaleth to get past him.

"No breaking in line," the woman said, glaring at the young man.

"But he's not—"

"No breaking!" she repeated. The stern look on her face showed she was not one to be messed with. She turned back to Kaleth. "What is your name?"

"My name?" Dull thumping echoed in his ears. He glanced at Jovi, whose eyebrows pinched together. He felt as if he stood in a fog and the world around him grew muted and distant. "Kaleth-il-Valorr," he whispered.

Jovi's jaw dropped. A broad smile washed over his face. "No way!"

"Do you, Kaleth, promise . . ."

The lady's words faded into the background, lost in his sea of thoughts. *Sora and Mother need me. I can't leave them to join the academy.* The thought of one hundred twenty-seven gold coins filled his head. *But I can't think of any other way to get it.* Jairus would be back at the end of the year. If Kaleth couldn't get the money, his sister and mother would be dead. *I must do this.*

The lady at the table looked at him with raised eyebrows. "Well?" she prompted.

Kaleth had missed everything she had said.

"Do you promise to serve?" she repeated, huffing.

His throat was dry. His fingers tingled. He swallowed a lump in his throat and whispered with as much confidence as he could pull together, "Yes."

CHAPTER NINE

# SELECTION CEREMONY

Kaleth stumbled away from the table in a stupor. *What did I just do?*

"What did you just do?" Jovi laughed as he hit him playfully on the shoulder. "That was amazing! We're going to the academy together. No more hating the army, huh? This is incredible!"

He didn't want to say anything about the debt to Jairus he was now responsible for. That was a burden his friend didn't need to hold.

*I'm joining the academy. I'm going to be in the army.* Kaleth's mind spun at the sudden change in his life's trajectory.

Headmaster Genoris had finished speaking, and the open area in front of the stage filled with mingling initiates from the various lines.

"What if you sign up for Blade, too?" Jovi shook his hands with excitement. "That would be so cool! We could train together—be stationed together." His face sobered. "You'd need to train hard, though. With your arms and legs . . ." He shook his head.

Name after name, young men and women registered at each of the tables. The mass of registered initiates grew larger. After what felt like an eternity, the lines in front of the tables finally dwindled to nothing. An excited buzz built in the crowd.

The woman in the gray robes raised a hand from the stage. "Do we have any more wishing to sign up? Do so now or wait another year."

Movement on the stage caught Kaleth's eye. Rayd left a seat from next to his father and hopped off the stage. He sauntered to one of the signup tables. While his movement oozed confidence, somehow, it seemed forced.

"Rayd's joining, too," Jovi said. "Man, that stinks. I'm sorry."

Kaleth's veins heated as he watched the young man give his name.

The woman in gray raised her hands. "Initiates, follow your instructors. You will choose your schools when you arrive inside the fortress."

Kaleth paled. "Wait? What? We're going now?"

"Yeah, what did you think we were gonna do?" Jovi said.

The swarm of bodies moved as one toward the break in the wall where the path dropped out of sight.

"I figured—" He spun toward the Grunwind District, where he pictured his sister and mother waiting for him to return. "I need to say goodbye. I need to explain."

Jovi's shoulders fell. "You can't miss the Selection Ceremony. That's what decides where you go."

"Kaleth!" A familiar voice cut through the din, and his sister pressed through the sea of initiates.

"Sora!"

Deep lines furrowed into her face. She latched on to his arm to fight the surge that moved them toward the path. "What's going on?"

Guilt clutched him. "I'm sorry. I had no choice."

"You're joining the academy?" Her eyebrows lifted as if she hoped it would be false.

Shame made him avert his gaze. He nodded, then whispered, "I had to. The money. It's the only way."

Her mouth hung open. She looked frozen as if a spell had turned her to stone.

"Hey, Sora." Jovi sported a crooked grin while he waved two fingers.

She didn't reply.

He hit himself on the forehead. "I'm sorry. Your father and everything . . . I forgot about . . . Never mind me."

"I'm sorry I won't be there to help with Mother," Kaleth said, ignoring his friend's mumbles. "I didn't think it through."

She finally blinked, then blew out a long breath. When she lifted her chin, a smile even crossed her face. "It's all right. We'll carry on."

"Move," a disgruntled initiate yelled, drawing attention to their lack of forward progress.

Kaleth held his ground. "Remember, she needs to soak the ankle twice per day, and when she's ready to walk, you need to—"

"Wrap it with the support," she finished. "I know. I can manage. Don't worry about us."

"I'll send money as soon as I'm paid. Use some of it for food. Her body needs greens and meat. And don't shop at that stand in the corner of the square. They charge too much. Go down Mercavor to the one with the dragon on the wall."

"Hey! Drogglebrains!" Her sudden energy caught him off guard. "I've been doing this just like you. I know what to do. You do your job and I'll do mine."

"Come on!" a voice called from the swarm of people. "Get out of the way!"

Sora released Kaleth's arm and stepped back. "Go. Do your best." The pressing crowd widened the distance between them.

Kaleth swallowed a lump in his throat. "Tell Mother I'm sorry and that I'll make things right."

Her mouth formed a reluctant smile.

"I love you both!" he called.

"I love you, too, Brother!"

The pushing crowd flowed around his sister until she disappeared amidst the throng.

Jovi's hand rested on his shoulder. "You all right?"

It took a moment, but Kaleth managed a nod.

*But will Sora and Mother be all right? Is this a mistake?* He didn't know, but he couldn't see any other way to do it. After he gave up resisting the surge of bodies, he fell in step with his friend and the rest of the initiates.

The path dropped only a bit before it leveled. While portions were too narrow for more than one person to walk at a time, most of the path accommodated two or three astride. An unfriendly shove could easily send him plummeting to an early death, so he appreciated having Jovi at his side. While his friend chattered on about how unsafe the path was, Kaleth imagined the logistical nightmare the fortress would have been to build.

Soon the trail climbed, circling along the side of the promontory. His legs ached and his lungs protested. One side of the road displayed a vertical wall while the other held a sheer drop. The wall intrigued him. Rather than bare rock, the cliff teemed with life, stretching up the fortress walls. Creeper vines snaked through cracks. Moss clung to the shadowy areas. Even small trees extended from the wall, their roots twisting through the rocky face. Birds flitted from hidden nests, and small mammals chittered to each other. A striped bird with a yellow head stared down at the procession of initiates, cocking its slender neck.

*Realm: Animalae. Category: Aeropist. Group: Bird. Strain: Striped Mountain Swallow.*

A head of styled black hair caught his eye in the crowd ahead. *Rayd.* The boy's shoulders strained his tight shirt from where they burst with muscles. Kaleth ground his teeth together.

"Have you decided what you want to do?" Jovi asked, breathing heavily.

Kaleth stared for several steps before finally shaking his head. "Sorry I'm a bit out of it. 'What I want to do?' What do you mean?"

"What do I mean?" Jovi chuckled. "Your school! It decides everything in the academy."

Kaleth shrugged. "I've tried to block out anything about the army or the academy for most of my life." He nodded ahead and lowered his voice. "I should probably avoid whatever Rayd chooses. But . . . if I end up in his school, I'll have a better chance to pay him back for what he did."

Jovi's nervous chuckle didn't give him an answer.

"I don't even know all the schools."

Jovi groaned. "For as smart as you are, you're pretty clueless. I'm signing up for the Blades."

"They're the ones who use swords, right?"

He nodded. "Swords, knives, spears . . . anything related to hand-to-hand combat. The best initiates even get horses to fight from. Training is supposed to be brutal, but I'm ready. By the time three years are done, we're supposed to be elite soldiers. The key traits they want are for you to be strong, brave, and a good fighter."

"While I'd love to train with you, I'm not sure that school is for me," Kaleth said.

Jovi laughed. "Yeah, I guess not. The Bows are also pretty great."

"I could maybe do that."

Jovi nodded. "They master all the ranged weapons—bows, crossbows, ballista, and even binder cannons."

Kaleth whistled. "Binder cannons. That would be cool."

"Initiates in the Bows are supposed to be quick and have good aim."

"What do they do in school? Shoot bows for three years? Seems like overkill."

"They head out to Twainford right away—both Bows and Blades, actually. I think most of the training is on-the-job. The three years is more of just a time commitment, and you're fighting as part of the army for most of that time."

"Tell me more about the Menders. What all do they do?"

"That's where I think you fit best," Jovi said. "They teach them medicine, science, anatomy . . . a lot of the stuff you've been learning for the last several years. They treat wounds, heal injuries, and perform surgeries. They also comprise the engineers. Those are the ones who plan fortifications and siege weapons. I think they stay here for a bit before they head to the battle lines. You need to be smart to make it with the Menders. I'm pretty sure you're bright enough. I doubt you'd be cut."

Kaleth frowned. "What do you mean?"

"You have to prove your ability to make it in those schools, and competition can be fierce. They have cuts at the end of the first and second years."

"If that happens, do you not get paid?"

Jovi chuckled. "Sure, you're still paid, but they put you in the Grunts."

"I've never heard of them. Is that another school?"

"Kind of. No one signs up for them, though. A few get to be smiths, armorers, and tailors, but mostly they do all the work no one wants: cook, clean, sharpen weapons, lug gear. Anything the rest of the schools need but don't want to do themselves falls to the Grunts. The schools want to keep the best, so any initiates that don't fit the bill get demoted. That's why it's important to choose based on where you'll fit. You *don't* want to get demoted."

"Yeah, I'm thinking Menders sounds like the right fit. But there's also the Lightbinders, right?"

A look of awe washed over Jovi's face. "They're incredible. They basically run the army. Rayd's father, the headmaster, and half the academy trainers came through the Lightbinders' school."

"Sounds impressive."

"Yeah, they're all impressive. Bodies sculpted of rock. Minds of geniuses. They only choose a select number at the end of the first academy year, so you'd have to be crazy to compete with them."

Kaleth nodded as a roiling sensation worked through his gut. *Menders. Blades. Lightbinders. Bows.* It all felt like more than he could handle.

"What is it?"

He snapped out of his trance and found his friend with lifted eyebrows. "What?"

"You have this . . . look. What's going on?"

His stomach lurched again. He kept walking, listening to the sounds of pebbles grinding into the path from hundreds of feet.

"I'm not—" It felt stupid to say. He had signed up for the army, but he didn't belong. "I'm not brave."

Jovi didn't laugh. He didn't dismiss the confession, and he didn't make a joke. His eyes grew soft, and he listened.

"When Jairus killed Father, I did nothing. When Rayd burned the book, I didn't even try to fight. In the woods, when—" He decided not to go into what happened with the panzils but shook his head instead. "I'm a coward. And what place is there in the army for someone like me?"

"Hey," Jovi shook his shoulder lightly. "There *is* a place for you. You have skills that leave everyone here *wishing* they were more like you. Not everyone has to be a fighter, but even if you are placed in a role where you need to, I believe in you. The thing about bravery is . . ."

Kaleth's ears perked.

Jovi's brow furrowed. He seemed to have run out of words. "The thing is . . . you can do it."

Kaleth chuckled. "Thanks."

"Sorry. I'm not great at giving motivational words of wisdom, I guess."

"No, it's fine. I appreciate it."

Snickers from over his shoulder caught Kaleth's attention. He peered behind to find two guys and a girl burst into laughter. "Hey. Everything all right?" Kaleth asked.

"What do you think, Roselle?" a guy said. "You all right?"

The girl narrowed her eyes. Fiery red hair dropped to her chin on one side of her head while the opposite side was shaved close to the skin. A small metal stud poked through her skin, sticking out on either side of her right eyebrow. "Yeah, I'm good," she said. "We were just wondering which school you were going to sign up for with those twig arms. I guessed Grunt, but Julas made a good point —you probably wouldn't make it."

The group laughed again.

Before Kaleth could respond, Jovi had stopped and pushed past him. "Kaleth is smarter than any of you. You're gonna *wish* he was part of whichever school you join."

Kaleth pulled his friend back. "It's all right, Jovi. I'm fine."

The group of three snickered again as the rest of the crowd carefully scooted around them, grumbling at the holdup.

Kaleth looked at the red-haired girl and turned his palms up. "I don't know what I'm doing yet. If Grunt is where I end up, then so be it. Good luck to you three. You all seem fit and could probably have your pick of any school."

Roselle smirked at the flattery, then ran her eyes down his body. "Ignore the scrawny limbs and you're not such a bad looker . . . for a future Grunt."

"You think everyone's a looker," one of the boys said.

She shrugged. "Have you been with a girl before, Kaleth?"

Heat crept up his neck. He swallowed hard and mumbled sounds that weren't even coherent in his own brain.

She stepped closer, but he didn't back up. Her tongue touched the top of her lip as she leaned in. Kaleth stared past her, focusing on the eager initiates trekking up the incline and trying to get around them.

"Don't be nervous," she whispered in his ear, her breath warming his neck. "If you're worried about making it . . ."

Her hand pressed against the inside of his thigh. She squeezed, causing him to flinch.

"I could teach you how to *grunt.*"

He jerked, stepping back and pushing her hand away.

Roselle and the two young men exploded with laughter. She winked as they walked around Kaleth and Jovi. "See you at the top, Kaleth."

His body felt warm, and his pulse raced. He leaned forward, pressing his hands against the tops of his legs and taking deep breaths.

"You all right?" Jovi asked.

"I think so."

"My advice . . ." Jovi pointed up the hill to where the redhead walked away. "Stay away from that one. She's trouble."

He swallowed to wet his dry throat and nodded.

"Plus, the red hair. That means she can get inside your mind and make you do things."

Kaleth rolled his eyes.

"But when those three are bleeding on the battlefield, we'll see how thankful they are to have you show up with your knowledge of how to save their lives."

Kaleth and Jovi fell in with the crowd, continuing up the path. The incline finally leveled out when the road reached the top of the cliff. Despite the elevation, Kaleth's neck craned even higher. He had never been so close to the fortress, and the towering sandstone walls made him dizzy. Guards looked down from the parapet, high above. Vines and growth were sparser than they were on the cliffs they'd passed, but still extended up much of the walls.

The crowd of initiates streamed through a set of opened gates, wide enough for four people to walk side-by-side. The giant metal barriers extended fifteen feet off the ground.

Kaleth's jaw dropped when he stepped through the gates. A wide, open-air corridor ran straight through to the center of Sky Fortress. Buildings lined each side, leading to a large, open section. Past the clearing, on the far side of the fortress, Kalistor Castle rose into the sky.

"This is huge!" Jovi said.

Kaleth nodded. The fortress looked large enough from Ramble Square, but its size seemed to double once they entered.

The passage they walked along was bare in the center, but where it met the buildings, plants clung to the edges. Sprigs of green poked out of cracks in the rock. Mossy tendrils crept up the walls, thinning the higher they traveled.

*Strange*, he thought. Plant life filled Kalistor on every street and square, but the amount of foliage that had taken over the fortress was on another level.

After walking a few minutes, the crowd arrived at the open area where their progress halted. A wall surrounded a large square courtyard with a grassy floor. A raised platform looked minuscule compared to the size of the space that could fit thousands of people. Adults in colored robes gathered on the platform while the crowd of initiates pressed toward the stage. The exal general and headmaster approached the steps to the platform. On the side of the courtyard opposite the castle, the recognizable tower of Lightbinder Academy rose into the air.

"I didn't expect to see you here," a chilling voice said.

Kaleth turned to see the imposing form of Rayd push through the crowd to stand next to him. His muscles clenched and his jaw ached anew. He took a step backward.

Rayd pointed at his face. "Looks like you fell down the stairs or something. Wait, you probably don't even have stairs at your house."

"Give me one reason why I shouldn't tell everyone here what you did," Kaleth said.

"Only one? Hmm." Rayd counted off on his fingers as he listed, "No one cares. It was your fault for snooping where you didn't belong. That book deserved to be burned. Telling on someone is a *great* way to earn respect in the army. Even if someone cared, who do you think would do something about it with my father standing up on that stage?" He wiggled his extended fingers. "Should I keep going, Grunny? What kind of impact do you think you're going to make, huh? With scrawny arms like those? Maybe I should kill you now and get it over with because you will *never* amount to anything in this army."

Kaleth's skin felt hotter with each word Rayd said. What bothered the most wasn't the injustice that had happened to his father, but rather that he had a difficult time refuting anything the bully said.

Jovi pulled his arm in the opposite direction. "Kaleth. Let's go."

He stumbled after his friend, thankful for the excuse to escape.

Rayd laughed. "That's right. Run away," he called out as Kaleth followed Jovi, meandering through the sea of people. "You know what? I'm glad you're here. Few people want to be Grunts, but we need them. And there's clearly nothing else you're qualified for."

They stopped moving when they could no longer see the other young man through the throng. "Thanks," Kaleth said, pushing his glasses up.

"You should avoid being near him," Jovi said. "Nothing good can come from it."

Kaleth said nothing but let his mind entertain the satisfaction that would come from slipping Rayd a knife while he slept. But even as he thought it, his body shuddered.

A trumpet blast jolted the crowd, drawing all eyes toward the stage. Guards lined the path where a man in a thick, purple robe approached. The train of his robe trailed behind him, dragging across the grass. Oversized gold stitches embellished the robe as well as the surcoat and doublet that peeked out from beneath it. A gold crown ringed with jewels and topped with pointed tips rested on his head.

"King Rhinean," Jovi whispered.

Kaleth felt the edge of his mouth curl up. He'd seen the king in the distance before but never from so close. The man walked in a shuffle with a bowed back and slumped shoulders, as if an invisible force pulled his chin down as he moved. Wisps of white hair peeked out from under the crown, but his snowy beard remained full and healthy.

The muttering voices hushed when the king took the stage. "Thank you, young men and women of Kalshia."

His weak voice barely carried to Kaleth's ears. It sounded scratchy and light, like it would fail at any moment.

"Your willingness to join this academy and prepare to enter the Kalshian army allows us to prosper. It's what keeps our kingdom free from oppressors. Your parents can hold their heads high, knowing you have brought the ultimate honor to your family."

The king continued, giving a rambling account of what made Kalshia great. Some of his words slurred, and others were too weak to be made out. Kaleth craned his neck forward but still missed much of it.

When he finished speaking, the king left the stage to a rousing applause—likely bolstered by his position rather than the content of his message. After a moment, the old man disappeared along the path he had come in by, escorted by his guards.

"That's something you don't see every day," Jovi said.

Kaleth's head swam. While he marveled at the prestige of hearing kings and generals, the uncertainty of his future terrified him.

Headmaster Genoris took center stage and raised his hand to settle the crowd. "Welcome, initiates, to Lightbinder Academy, your home for the next three years. The people standing around you, specifically the ones in your school, will live and train with you. They will sweat and bleed with you. Sometimes . . . they will die with you."

Genoris extended his arms and gestured to the square area. "This is the Grand Courtyard. We use it for ceremonies, academy meetings, and select portions of your training." He pointed to the tall, gray building at the side of the courtyard. "This is Central Tower, where the Lightbinders, Menders, and Grunts who remain here will gather for meals and classes. The rest of you will travel to Twainford where you'll drill onsite, within striking distance of the enemy."

A rumble of excitement rippled through the crowd.

"Before you are sent to your respective homes and receive your uniforms, you have to make the most important decision of your time in the academy—choosing a school. Welcome to the Selection Ceremony."

Kaleth's insides felt queasy.

"You may select any school you like, but that does not guarantee you will remain in that choice. Blades must be strong and brave. Bows must have clear sight and quickness. Menders must be fast learners and have strong stomachs. Lightbinders must be perfect at everything." His voice grew serious. "Do not choose Lightbinder unless you are confident of your abilities. The potential for glory is great, but, as you know, the stakes are higher. If anyone feels unsuited for any of the four primary schools, we encourage you to choose Grunts, today. While not glamorous, they do stay farther from the fighting, and the work is just as valuable."

Several of the surrounding initiates snickered.

"As mentioned in the square, pay has gone up this year. You

each will receive one gold per week, and at yearly anniversaries, select schools will receive a bonus, assuming you're not demoted."

Kaleth frowned. *Select schools?*

"Grunts still receive nothing. Menders are up to fifteen."

Kaleth's breath caught. *That's not enough! I thought—*

"Blades and Bows both receive twenty-five."

Panic raced through him.

"And our Lightbinders now receive seventy-five gold if they remain until their first year anniversary."

Kaleth's mind reeled. The plan to save his mother and sister unraveled before him. He felt trapped—locked in by a poorly thought-out plan. "It's not enough," he whispered.

Jovi kept his eyes on the headmaster but leaned closer. "What's not enough?"

"When the letter of your last name is called, come forward and line up. One at a time, you will announce your name and your choice of school, then join the principal of your color. During the choosing ceremony, tradition dictates all initiates remain silent out of respect for the choosers. There is to be no talking, laughing, or applause."

While the crowd grew silent, the five men and women in colored robes stepped down from the stage and spread out across the grassy floor of the Grand Courtyard. Despite hundreds of initiates filling the area, the whisper of grass under their feet reached all the way to Kaleth.

"Last names beginning with A, please come forward."

A couple dozen young men and women shuffled to the front, forming a line that stretched away from the stage. When they settled, the woman in a gray robe motioned toward the line of initiates.

The young woman who stood at the front had a ponytail of brown hair and the posture of an arrow. In a stilted voice, she pronounced, "Morgelle-el-Aaron."

The woman in gray inclined her head forward and raised her eyebrows.

"Bow?" The girl's declared school sounded more like a question than a choice.

The woman on the stage gestured her arm toward the principal in the yellow robe. With a measured smile and her chin up, the girl crossed the courtyard to join her new school.

"Olvas-il-Abbot," the well-built young man who was next in line bellowed. With his chest out, he announced, "Blade," without prompting.

The principal in green smirked as the young man headed in his direction.

The process continued, dragging on interminably. A clock on the wall gave Kaleth something to focus on to take his mind off his upcoming impossible choice. With his father being "Valorr," he would be near the end of the list. *Ten seconds per name. Roughly seven hundred people. That will be . . . one hour fifty-seven minutes.*

He measured the proportion of initiates collecting at each school to estimate what the eventual sizes would be. Blade was the most popular choice with ten so far. Bow was a close second at eight.

The three Menders so far looked of a similar build to him. Two wore glasses, one had a face filled with freckles, and all three were on the skinny side.

*Fifteen gold*, he thought. *Fifteen plus one per week. It's not enough.*

"Lightbinder."

A collective gasp filled the Grand Courtyard at the declaration. Kaleth jerked his head to the front of the platform where a young man stood with short blond hair and a chiseled jaw. Taller than Kaleth by a head, his neck looked like the trunk of a tree and sloped to bulging shoulders. He kept his chin up as he walked toward the principal in the red robe.

*Seventy-five gold* was all Kaleth could think.

The names continued, minute after minute, stretching into hours. The crowd in the center of the Grand Courtyard dwindled. Eighty percent of the initiates chose either Blades or Bows, but the numbers continued to grow in the others. Lightbinders were up to thirty initiates, and a handful had even selected Grunts.

The S's had lined up, and Jovi's turn would be soon. As much as Kaleth wanted to stay with his friend, the Blades were the last school he could see himself choosing.

"Rayd-il-Stonne."

Kaleth tensed. He spotted the unwelcome head of black hair standing at the front. He anticipated the school that would follow but did not predict the pause that preceded it. Rayd looked stiff. He stared at his father as if communicating through his mind.

"Lightbinder," the young man bellowed, abnormally loud.

*Of course*, Kaleth thought.

The exal general flinched when his son spoke. Rayd turned from his father and headed toward his new group.

Two heads later, Jovi announced his name. He lifted his chin and stared confidently back at the platform. "Blade."

Kaleth smiled as his friend crossed to the large group of initiates huddled around the green principal.

Standing alone, he felt conspicuous as the names continued. They finished the S's then the T's. He would be called soon. Despite having had several hours to think, his decision felt as impossible as ever. *If I choose Mender, the money won't be enough. It would only be sixty-seven gold. Maybe Sora and Mother could make up the rest?* He frowned at the thought of them saving an additional thirty-three gold on top of the expense of living. *Blades and Bows would be closer, but they're still not enough.*

He looked at the small but intimidating group around the man in red. Standing together, Rayd seemed to be the least of his worries amongst the other young men and women who looked more like pillars of muscle than humans.

"V's, please come forward."

The letter sounded foreign when it was called. Only a handful of people remained in the center of the Grand Courtyard, so no one blocked his route. As he walked, he noticed he was the only one moving. There were no other V's. His neck grew hot as he felt all eyes on him, judging him. It seemed to take forever to walk to the platform. His legs felt like lifeless stumps tromping forward. His pulse thudded in his head. Sweat dripped down his face. He pressed his glasses back on his nose.

When he stopped moving, he stared at the woman in gray. He opened his mouth. Through his parched throat, he barely croaked out, "Kaleth-il-Valorr." No further words followed.

The woman leaned forward and raised her eyebrows. "Well?"

He couldn't form words. He tried to clear his throat, but it only rattled. He glanced toward the Blades. Jovi watched him, smiling. Kaleth turned back to the woman and held his hands to keep them from shaking. A rough clearing finally loosened up his throat. He took a deep breath and forced his shoulders back.

"Lightbinder."

## CHAPTER TEN

# LIGHTBINDER INDUCTION

Muffled laughter peppered in with another echo of gasps. The woman in gray turned to the headmaster as if asking for his permission for the foolish choice to be allowed. The headmaster nodded.

Kaleth turned toward the group of Lightbinders. He watched the grass as he walked toward them, wishing he could be invisible. His hands tingled. The back of his neck felt like it was on fire.

When he passed the Blades, he lifted his eyes to find his friend. Jovi's jaw hung loose. His eyes were opened wide with a mixture of sorrow and terror. He shook his head and mouthed, *"What are you doing?"*

There wasn't time to explain. Kaleth lowered his head and trudged the rest of the way to the Lightbinders. When he arrived, the several dozen young men and women seemed to stand taller, crossing their muscular arms over their chests. Half the group stared at him with narrowed eyes while the others wore smirks of ridicule on their faces.

Rayd neither smiled nor looked down at him. The bully's face contained a complexity he did not expect to see and couldn't quite place. *Anger? Resentment? Fear?* None of his guesses made sense. Kaleth turned away from him and looked back at the courtyard.

The final names were a blur. His legs grew exhausted from hours of standing. He pictured his mother and sister, worrying about them taking care of themselves. He spent the time trying not to faint, waiting for the ceremony to be finished.

After the last girl joined the Menders, Headmaster Genoris declared the Selection Ceremony finished and instructed the school principals to take their new initiates away.

With the required silence ended, the new members of the Blades, Bows, and Menders turned to each other and celebrated with cheers and whoops. They clapped each other on their backs, shook hands, and even hugged.

The atmosphere in the small group of Lightbinders was thick with tension. Initiates stared the other candidates down as if appraising their abilities.

The man in red robes called out, "Lightbinders, this way." He led the way out of the Grand Courtyard around the side of Central Tower. Kaleth stared up at the building as they passed. He counted eight stories of balconies and windows stretching to a chaotic roof of gables and sloped shingles.

Kaleth looked over his shoulder, hoping a glimpse of his friend would settle his discomfort. The large group of several hundred Blade initiates followed a man in a green robe in the opposite direction. He couldn't spot Jovi.

As their group continued past the gigantic tower, the path led to the edge of the fortress, where it ended at a red doorway. When they drew close, the symbol of a flame became clear. Carved words across the top read, "Warriors are forged, not born."

"This is the Lightbinder quadrant," the principal said.

Kaleth had expected the man's tone to be harsh and demanding. Instead, his matter-of-fact demeanor was a pleasant surprise.

"Other than meals and classes, this is where you'll spend the next year of your life, at least those who remain that long." He passed through the doorway, and the pack of initiates followed.

*Those who remain*, Kaleth repeated to himself. The words formed a hollow cavity inside him.

An abundance of binder lamps lit the hall, spaced every few feet.

The warm glow illuminated a wide hallway with a high roof. Dozens of shoes clomped on the stone, echoing back to where Kaleth brought up the rear. The stone hall was bare at the center but clung to life at the edges, even inside where no sunlight reached. They passed several closed doors and multiple stairwells. After several turns, he worried about his ability to navigate.

Finally, the line of initiates spilled into a large room where five young men and one young woman lounged. "It's about time," one of the waiting boys muttered.

An oversized fireplace sat in the corner, cold and free from ash. The walls contained floor-to-ceiling bookshelves with two rolling ladders on each side. Stuffed couches and chairs formed multiple seating areas. At the end where the principal stopped, glass windows looked out to a grassy enclosure. Not as large as the Grand Courtyard, the space past the windows would hold everyone present with room to spare.

"Gather around," the principal said, standing on a short ledge in front of the window. Lifting the robe over his head, he folded the garment and tossed it in a corner. His brown hair was cropped short and stuck up in spikes at the front. Rusty-orange streaks mixed into his trimmed goatee. The leather Lightbinder uniform he wore held new significance for Kaleth. It felt more intimidating than when he'd seen it back in his regular life. Across the front, the diagonal handles of four knives stuck out of sheaths worked into the jacket. Leggings hugged his legs until they disappeared into high black boots. He wore a ring with a large green gem on his finger.

Kaleth cocked his head. The man looked familiar, but he couldn't place where he'd seen him before.

Two men and one woman in matching uniforms entered the room from the opposite side. One man walked to the chalkboard in the back of the room and began writing. The other two joined the principal at the front of the room.

"Welcome to the Lightbinder common room. The six young men and women behind you are second years," the principal said. "The lucky ones of you will be there next year."

Kaleth glanced over his shoulder along with most of the new

initiates. The older students in the back smirked as if they knew they were superior to the new arrivals. One young man tapped the end of a knife handle sticking out of its jacket sheath.

"I graduated as a Lightbinder eighteen years ago, and I've been the principal of the school for the last four. While Headmaster Genoris is in charge of the academy as a whole, I am in charge of the Lightbinders. You can call me Aurik."

Kaleth's blood ran cold. *Aurik.* He finally recognized him—the hair, the goatee. He remembered the way the man looked as he stared at the crumbling mill. He pictured with sharp clarity the cold reaction he gave when he saw Kaleth's mother's injury. *It was his fault.* He exemplified why Kaleth hated the army—no accountability and no thought for others. He clenched his teeth while he listened to the man he'd hated for months.

"You are the best of the best—at least those of you who are still with us next year. You will be well trained, respected, and feared by our enemies. This academy bears the name of our school for a reason. What we do goes far beyond what anyone else in this academy is capable of. Kalshia needs us, and for a lot more than lighting the binder lamps of the city. Who of you has seen what Lightbinders can do?" Aurik raised his own hand and scanned the room.

With a smug grin, Rayd's hand joined him in the air.

"Anyone who isn't the son of a general?" The principal continued to look, then lowered his hand. "There's a reason you haven't, and it's because we work hard to keep it that way. Even during your first year, you will only receive bits of information. We save most of it for your second year."

His mouth pulled up into a grin. "Would you like a glimpse?" He looked at the other two instructors. "Sorene? Falmouth?"

The man and woman who stood with him exited a door that lead to the courtyard. Aurik stepped to the side and gestured to the wall of windows. The second years in the back stood, craning their necks to see along with the rest of the group.

Sorene and Falmouth stopped in the center of the grassy space. Their bodies looked stiff as if they held their breaths, a thought disputed by their moving chests. They turned to each other and bowed. They lifted both hands, each bearing a sword and dagger.

Kaleth leaned forward. Elite warriors. Hidden abilities. It seemed too fantastical to be real. His heart rate increased. *What are they going to do?*

With a jerk of his hands, Falmouth's weapons hummed to life. A glowing yellow light wrapped around both the sword and the dagger, blade and handle included.

A collective gasp filled the common room. Kaleth's eyes grew wide.

Sorene replicated the move. The two instructors crouched and circled. The glowing swords seemed to give off their own source of light.

*What does the glow do?*

As if answering his unspoken question, Sorene stepped forward. She swung the sword in a diagonal arc. Falmouth brought his to a cross, but when the swords hit, light exploded from the weapons. Kaleth shielded his eyes from the sudden burst of luminescence. When he peeked around his hand, his jaw dropped. The instructors' legs moved at a regular speed, but their weapons and the arms that held them flew at an extraordinary pace. They traded a frenzy of blows. Their daggers and swords flashed in a barrage of motion, throwing bursts of light in every direction. The colliding steel boomed, even through the window.

With a slice as fast as lightning, Sorene's sword knocked a dagger out of Falmouth's hand. The knife twirled through the air until it stuck tip-first into the stone wall of the courtyard. Its glow quickly faded. The sparring match only lasted a few more moves until Sorene pinned Falmouth's sword against his body and held her dagger to his neck. The fighters panted as Sorene stepped back and released Falmouth from his vulnerable position. They both smiled and bowed once more. The crowd of initiates who had watched the frenzy in silent awe exploded into applause.

Kaleth forced himself to cheer through the abject terror that flooded his body. *Is this the same power Father had?* He inhaled sharply. The thought of his father reminded him of the secret from the floorboards, forgotten in the events of the morning. He slid a hand into his pocket and found the paper still there.

"That's as much information as you'll receive for now," Aurik said, bringing the crowd back to order. "That demonstration was a taste of what's waiting for those of you who make it."

A young man with dark skin and curly black hair raised a hand, his movement crisp and straight.

Aurik lifted his eyebrows. "You have a question . . . ?"

"Lainn, sir. Lainn Brawnfist." He brought his hand down to his side. "And yes, I do. You say we won't be learning much of that yet. What about our first year? If we're not training for lightbinding, what will we do?"

"Does anyone know the answer to that?"

The room was quiet except for a chuckle from the second years and the clacking of chalk on the board. Falmouth and Sorene reentered the room and joined Aurik back at the front.

In the center of the initiates, a girl with half a head of red hair spoke up. "We train our bodies."

*Great,* Kaleth thought. *Roselle, who thinks I should be a Grunt.*

As if hearing his thoughts, her eyes flicked in his direction. Initially, they narrowed as if anger simmered behind them and she weighed him as competition. Then her eyes widened with a playful twinkle. She mouthed, *"bodies"* at him as her brows danced.

Kaleth turned back toward the principal, feeling the back of his neck growing warm.

"Exactly," Aurik continued. "You drill. We will work your lungs, your legs, and your arms until they are falling off. You will haul loads until you vomit. You will run until your feet give way beneath you. And when you can't move another muscle—" He let a grin grow. "You'll do it all over again. Remember, warriors are forged, not born."

Kaleth's stomach turned just from listening.

"On top of that, we will drill your mind. Classes and books will pump you with knowledge. When you're not exercising, sleeping, or eating, you're studying and working on your skill log.

*Skill log? Great. Another hoop to jump through.*

The principal held up a small notepad. "Each of you will receive one of these to fill out over the next year. This is your skill log. Your squad leader will sign off, proving when you pass one of the listed skills. There are forty-five varieties listed in here to master: knife throwing, sword disarming, ironball carry, poison identification, history recitations, grappling competency . . . and much more. This measures not only your ability but also your motivation to get it done. If you wish to be here at the end of the year, ignore working on it at your own peril." He shook the notepad, letting a long moment of silence emphasize his point.

"Besides physical training, classes, studying, and skill work, you will face four exams."

*Exams?* What should have excited Kaleth carried a sense of foreboding.

"We test your strength and then your knowledge. At the end of the year, we will test your ability to handle fear. The first you'll have to pass will be a test of survival. And it will happen sooner than you may think."

A dropped pin could have been heard during the pause that followed.

"You chose the academy, and you selected this school. You opted to follow this path, and you know the risks. We don't coddle you like they do in the Blades. We don't give you a pass for your body if you have a strong mind like a Mender. And we don't accept anyone less than the best. Some of you will not make it through the first exam. Others will fail at the second. By the time we reach the end of the year, most of you will not be here for the second year." He held up his hand and showed off a ring that contained a large green gem. "One year from now, only six of you will receive one of these rings."

A pressure formed on Kaleth's chest. He felt like the air had been sucked from his lungs. *Only six!*

Aurik paused, sweeping his gaze across the room. "Six of you will progress to your second year in the Lightbinder school. A handful will be demoted at that year mark, but most of you, eighty percent of you standing here today . . . will be dead long before then."

Kaleth flinched, still struggling to get air. He moved his eyes around the room to gauge the reaction of the initiates. The other young men and women stared at the principal, held in rapt attention by his words. *Dead? He must have meant we become Grunts.*

"Outsiders criticize the harshness of our training. Politicians question the danger. We who have been through it understand its purpose. Lightbinders are the most powerful people in all of Verdalyn. It's critical our refining process is consistent with the excellence we expect. As a result, most of you will not survive the tests."

*He's serious.* Kaleth's pulse sped even faster, and his hands grew clammy. He looked at the gathering of perfect human specimens in a new light. They were his competition to stay alive.

"No killing other initiates," Aurik said. "Yes, the death of your fellow initiate means your chance of survival increases, so to prevent the dorms from becoming a bloodbath, we hold fast to this rule. Anyone in violation will be eliminated. Don't test us on this." His solemn gaze left no room for doubt. "First years are ranked. As you train and test, you will be compared to your fellow initiates, and twelve months from now, the top six names get rings. High ranks lead to advantages in some tests. This helps ensure only the best make it. If you find yourself near the bottom of the list, you better pull yourself together."

Kaleth gulped. The principal's gaze stopped on him as if he already knew what was going to happen with the weak, skinny initiate. *I shouldn't be here. This is a mistake.*

"Your dorm assignments are on the board in the back. Find your rooms and change into your uniforms. What's left of the day is yours, so get to know each other. Prepare your minds for what's coming, and make sure you get plenty of sleep tonight. Does anyone have questions before we dismiss?"

The initiates remained at attention as if the information presented had been expected.

Kaleth's hand trembled as he lifted it past his shoulder.

Aurik nodded at him. "Yes?"

Chiseled jaws and broad shoulders turned Kaleth's way. He cleared his throat to work out the catch in it. "If we die or get cut, is the year-end bonus paid to our families?"

Polite laughter filled the room. Aurik's shoulders bounced as he grinned. He swept his eyes across the initiates again, not even bothering to respond. "Anyone else?"

The lack of response gave Kaleth the answer he had feared.

"All right. I'll see you here first thing in the morning."

The crowd of initiates pressed toward the chalkboard, chattering. They scanned the board, then disappeared up the stairwell just outside the room. Unwilling to push through the intimidating group, Kaleth waited his turn.

"Can I have a moment?"

The question spun him around. Aurik stood next to him.

"Um . . . sure," Kaleth replied, trying to hold back the sudden anger that welled in him.

The man rubbed his goatee as if thinking of what to say. "Lightbinder isn't for everyone. That's why we give initiates a choice. The stakes are high and only the strongest live through the training. Generally, our initiates are of a certain . . . type." The man's eyes softened. "If you think you might have called out the wrong school by mistake . . . if this isn't the place you meant to be . . . I'm sure we can get you to the right one."

A shudder of relief rushed through Kaleth's body. *No more death. No more competing against perfect humans. I can choose any of the schools.* His heart sank when he remembered the reason he was there. *None of the other schools will pay what I need, which means Sora and Mother will be dead. But if I die in this school, they'll die all the same.*

The choice was death no matter what he did. A knot tightened in his gut.

Aurik's brow lifted, and a kindness filled his eyes. "Did you want to be in a different school?"

Kaleth's pulse pounded in his head. The question sounded thick as if blankets covered his ears. He swallowed the lump in his throat. *At least Sora and Mother have a glimmer of a chance with me here.* Lifting his chin, he shook his head. "No."

"You realize this means we'll expect the same results from you as we do everyone else?"

"I know."

Aurik nodded. When Kaleth didn't leave, the principal cocked his head. "Is there anything else?"

Kaleth ran through the words he wanted to say.

*"I remember you at the old mill, six months ago. You destroyed it. Three people died, and twice that were injured. My mother was hurt. Stones crushed her leg. Burning grain seared her lungs. The doctor said she may never walk or breathe normally again, and it was your fault."*

The confrontational words remained locked inside his head. "You're not just looking for the strongest," he said aloud. "You're looking for the strongest *and* smartest. I'm stronger than I look, and my mind is a razor. By the end of the year, my name is going to rank at the top of that list."

With his heart pounding, he spun and left the principal behind, walking to the board. His hands trembled. His gut clenched with stress. He had no way to back up the bravado he projected, and there was nowhere to hide.

*What have I gotten myself into?*

KALETH WAS PUFFING by the time he arrived on the fourth floor. The short hallway at the top of the stairs contained four wooden doors, and room 402 was the first one on the right. When he pushed the door open, the broad muscular back of dark-brown skin was the last thing he expected to see.

The other young man turned with a friendly smile already showing. The smile faltered when he got a look at who stood in the doorway. "You must be Kaleth."

"Not Kah-LETH. KAY-leth."

The boy nodded.

Kaleth stepped forward and extended a hand.

The other boy narrowed his eyes as if suspicious of the gesture. After a moment, he held out his own. "Lainn Brawnfist from Lynharbor."

Kaleth winced at the iron grip of the other boy. He shook his hand out after they let go. "Brawnfist sounds about right."

Lainn didn't respond. He wore the black-uniformed leggings but hadn't put on his shirt yet. His pecs and abs looked sculpted from obsidian and made Kaleth embarrassed to remove his own clothes.

"I'm from here in Kalistor."

Lainn pointed at Kaleth's nose. "What happened to you? You look banged up already."

"It's nothing." He shrugged, feigning indifference about his beating from the night before. "So, you, uh . . . always wanted to be a Lightbinder?"

Already turned away, Lainn worked a black shirt over his head. "Generally."

"It's been a dream of mine ever since . . . about an hour ago." Kaleth was the only one who chuckled at his joke.

Lainn pulled on his jacket but made no further comment. The rest of his belongings were already arranged in a tidy row on his bed.

The room was tight but larger than Kaleth was used to in his home. Each side contained a bed, a small desk with a stack of papers, a chair, and two empty shelves. A sheet and a blanket lay folded on his bed next to a pile of clothes—two pairs of leggings, two black shirts, one red-and-black leather jacket, and a pair of boots on the floor. He stepped toward the bed and tossed his skill log on the mattress. "Do you think we will—"

The click of the door stopped him. He turned to find Lainn exiting the room. His roommate pulled the door closed behind him with a slam.

Kaleth jumped at the noise. *It's all right. I'm not here to make friends.* He exhaled a long breath, forcing the tension out that he'd held all day. Alone at last, he pulled his father's scrap of folded paper out from his pocket.

A pang of guilt washed over him. *Father is dead because of me.* The reminder cut him deep, and the paper trembled as he held it by the corner. *I can fix my mistake. I can still save Mother and Sora.*

A tear threatened to trickle down his cheek, but he wiped it away before it had the chance to fall. Wallowing in grief wouldn't help his situation, so he focused on what he could do rather than what was in the past. Yellowed with time, the paper crinkled as he opened it up. His pulse raced. The answer to his father's secret lay inside.

He stared at the unfolded note, and his forehead tightened in a frown. There were no words. No instructions. His father hadn't written a message to him. It was an image. Four parabolic curved lines filled the interior of a circle, each being rotated ninety degrees. The center of the image, between the line intersections, displayed the letter F.

His eyes grew. *It's a glyph!* The glyph that held the secret to his father's abilities. As he stared at the paper, his brows knit together. His heart sank.

*But what am I supposed to do with it?*

CHAPTER ELEVEN
# FIRST TEST

A ringing bell jerked Kaleth awake, and he blinked in the darkness. After growing up in the same house all his life, it took a moment to remember where he was—in his dorm, lying in a bed of the Lightbinder Academy. Five chimes pealed through the window and reverberated in the hall.

*How early is it?*

Lainn rustled in bed on the other side of the room. Faint knocks and distant mutters sounded through the door. In a moment, the knocks arrived at their room, and the door opened.

"Get up, initiates," an unseen voice ordered. "Common room in five minutes. Come dressed but no jackets."

Kaleth mumbled a response, then sat up and rubbed his eyes. A flash of pain reverberated through his face at the familiar motion.

Lainn's feet hit the floor. A moment later, the binder lamp clicked on, filling the room with a glowing orange light.

*Those sure are handy*, Kaleth thought. *Too bad we could never afford them.* "You sleep all right?" he asked.

"Fine," Lainn mumbled.

"What do you think we'll do today?"

His roommate grunted something unintelligible as he shrugged.

*No early-morning conversation. Got it.* Kaleth threw on his glasses and a fresh set of clothes. *I'm not here to make friends. I'm here to become a Lightbinder.* The repeated thought left a pit in his stomach.

Half the initiates were already downstairs by the time he arrived in the common room. They stood huddled around the wall. He joined them in staring at the wall where a list of names had been put up overnight.

Fifty names matched with numbers in ascending order. Rather than read through the list of unfamiliar names, Kaleth skimmed to the end. As expected, "Kaleth-il-Valorr" took up the final slot with a "Fifty" next to it.

"Idiots," an angry voice muttered. The familiar timbre chilled Kaleth's blood. Next to the wall, Rayd stared at his name near the top and shook his head. "What are they even basing this on?"

"It's all from first impressions," another initiate said. "That's a great spot though. Don't worry about it. There will be plenty more for them to judge us on."

Kaleth scanned the list and found Rayd in spot five. The boy's gall felt ridiculous. Kaleth puffed a laugh through his nose that turned the general's son in his direction.

"You think that's something to laugh about, Grunny?"

Kaleth stepped back, wishing he could keep other initiates between them.

Rayd closed in. "What are you even doing here? You're no Lightbinder. It's a disgrace to us all for you to even be here. It's no wonder you're"—he glanced back at the rankings—"fiftieth." He uttered a laugh of his own.

Despite the advancing young man, Kaleth stopped stepping back. Rayd halted so close that Kaleth felt the heat of his breath. "We may not be allowed to kill each other, but who knows what might happen? After all . . . accidents happen here all the time."

Kaleth believed he meant the veiled threat. After a moment, he averted his gaze.

Rayd backed down and returned to the group he'd been speaking with. Kaleth scanned the list of names again. None of them meant anything to him until he spotted number nineteen. A shudder of fear combined with elation at the sight of Jovi Strapper's name.

"Surprised?" his friend's familiar voice asked.

Kaleth spun with his jaw dropped. Jovi stood behind him dressed like the rest of the Lightbinder initiates and sporting a crooked grin. "What are you doing here?"

Jovi shrugged. "I couldn't let you have all the fun, could I? We were an hour south of Kalistor when I asked if I could change. They let me transfer in last night."

Kaleth stepped closer, grabbing his friend by the arm and dropping his voice to a whisper. "Eighty percent of the people here are going to die over the next year. From those left, they demote all but six."

Jovi chuckled. "Uh . . . *yeah* . . . I know."

"How do—?"

"Everyone knows that, Kaleth."

"I didn't."

His friend puffed a short laugh through his nose. "Clearly."

"Why did you switch?"

"I thought you could use someone to watch your back." He nodded toward the ranking board. "Looks like you might need it."

Kaleth wanted to be angry with Jovi for his foolish action, but part of him celebrated at having someone on his side. He leaned in and wrapped his arms around his friend. Jovi hugged him back, squeezing with his muscular arms.

"Nineteen, huh?" Kaleth commented when he pulled away. "Not a bad first impression."

"I guess my size counts for something."

"Morning initiates!" Aurik entered the room.

The principal's voice was too cheery for such an early hour, a note added to Kaleth's list of grievances against the man.

"Today begins your first official test."

A burst of adrenaline rushed through Kaleth, flushing out any fatigue.

"As I mentioned yesterday, this is a test of survival. Lightbinders often find themselves at the front or even behind enemy lines. If you're not prepared to face the dangers of the wilderness as you are, we don't want to waste our time on you. The test is simple: spend four nights across the Lagrash River in the barrens of Thravia."

"That's it?" an initiate standing by Rayd asked. "Sleep outside for four nights?"

Kaleth cringed at the flippant question. He'd never been to the barrens himself, but he knew enough to have a healthy fear of them.

"Yes, Tyron, that's it." The head instructor fixed his gaze on the clean-shaven initiate who occupied slot number nine on the wall. "You *just* have to sleep outside. Of course, you'll need to avoid the dust serpents who like to curl up with warm bodies and barren lions who can track you from miles away. If you plan to use the rivers for water, I hope you know how to share with valsic dragons and blood panzils. And don't let a razech find you while you sleep."

Tyron's face turned pale.

Aurik panned his gaze across the rest of the group. "Shelter is scarce, food is practically nonexistent, and nights are cold. And if you plan to sustain yourself like the Thravians do, you better know the difference between edible and poisonous algae. To pass, you simply need to survive. Some of you will not."

He nodded toward the ranking board. "The top thirty initiates get to take a knife and flint. Top fifteen also receive a flask of water. The top ten will have two days of rations."

Rayd nudged Tyron and smirked.

"You will all be separated. No working together with other initiates."

Jovi sighed.

"And, as always, no killing each other. There is plenty to fear without worrying about each other. You *will* each get a choice in terrain though: river basin, plain, or mountain."

Kaleth's mind whirred into motion, thinking through all he knew of the Thravian wilds. Although he had not crossed the Lagrash to experience them firsthand, he'd had plenty of time in the Kalshian wilderness and knew enough theory from his father's lectures.

The river basin was the obvious choice because of its plentiful water source and the abundant algae that grew along the banks for food. But that also meant it contained the highest danger of predators. Any shelter he might find near the river was likely to be a den for valsic dragons.

The plains were the next most likely option. There was little shelter, food, or water, but the temperature would be agreeable, and there were few predators to worry about. If he kept his head down, he could pass the time with little effort.

The mountains would be a challenge. The terrain would be difficult to navigate, but the chief danger would be the cold. Blood panzils and barren lions would still frequent the area, but running into one would be unlikely. The varied terrain would provide a lot of shelter, and there would be wood for fires and water in the mountain streams.

*I'm not worried about food. I can live without it for a few days, but water is a must. And without a weapon, I need to consider the predators. Cold could be an issue unless I can make a fire.*

"State your preferred terrain in reverse order of ranking. Kaleth-il-Valorr, start us off."

The rest of the room turned in Kaleth's direction, waiting for him to choose. Jovi stared at him with raised eyebrows.

For an initiate with a supply of water, the plain would be the obvious choice. For anyone who had a weapon and knew how to use it, the river basin would be another safe bet. For someone going into the wilderness with nothing except their wits, the best choice was the most dangerous one.

"I choose mountain," Kaleth said.

Rayd snickered and muttered, "Fool," under his breath. While the other candidates took turns making their choices, Rayd whispered with Tyron and the redheaded initiate, Roselle.

As Kaleth expected, most of the initiates in the bottom half of the rankings chose the river basin, which is what Jovi selected. Once they arrived in the top fifteen, the preference for those supplied with water shifted to plain. It wasn't until Roselle's turn in spot eleven that another initiate chose mountain. She glanced his way with a mischievous look on her face. "Should be fun," she said as if to no one in particular.

*An odd choice for a highly ranked initiate*, Kaleth thought.

When Tyron made the same choice next, his gut twisted. When Rayd announced, "Mountain," he openly stared at Kaleth, turning his blood cold.

Jovi raised his hand when everyone had finished. "Can we change our decision?" A crease dug into his brow.

Again, Kaleth's friend was trying to protect him. A wisp of hope fluttered in his chest.

"Selection is finished," Aurik said. "You stick with what you chose."

The hope dissipated like smoke in the wind. Kaleth nodded in thanks toward Jovi even though nothing could be done.

Thirty-one initiates chose the river basin and fifteen selected the plain. It was only Kaleth, Rayd, and Rayd's apparent pals who had selected mountain, and their intentions seemed clear.

*So much for them not being allowed to kill.*

THE GROUPS DIVIDED into horse-drawn wagons and left Sky Fortress before the sun rose. Kaleth closed his eyes as they crossed the narrow path back to the city. He imagined a wheel catching the edge and plummeting off the cliff, killing him and dooming his family before he even had a chance to attempt becoming a Lightbinder.

After passing through Kalistor, the wagons worked their way down a serpentine path that dropped from the city to the lower ground. While those heading to the river and plain continued straight, Kaleth's group angled west. They quickly climbed, making up the altitude they'd lost in short order. In their new direction, the massive Kalshian Mountains loomed in the distance, while smaller peaks were much closer.

The ride itself was tense, uncomfortable, and long. A loquacious instructor named Falmouth sat up front and narrated about the path, the woods, and the dangers of the wilderness. Rayd, Roselle, and Tyron took the back row, whispering and laughing amongst themselves. Kaleth sat in the seat behind the instructor, listening to Falmouth spout familiar information he had known for years.

Roselle's teasing banter toward Kaleth from the day before seemed to have dried up overnight. A malice-filled glance in his direction prompted him to avoid eye contact. Her hands seemed to always be somewhere on Rayd's or Tyron's body, neither of whom seemed to mind.

The path the wagon followed could hardly be called a road. The ruts and bumps left much to be desired. Halfway through the trip, the plentiful grass and thick foliage grew sparser. Grass that had been green turned sickly, and trees that were abundant had spread out. The air even changed. Thick, humid air around Kalistor grew thin and dry. The longer they traveled, the higher they climbed. Riding on the wagon, the wind developed a chill that Kaleth's black shirt and leggings struggled to stop. In the mid-afternoon, patches of snow filled the shadows under scraggly trees and rocks.

The sun approached its final quadrant by the time they arrived at the Lagrash River. Falmouth continued to drive the wagon west. Few green items remained. Rocks lined the shoreline, covered with pink and orange algae. The river itself looked partially frozen. The center was fast enough to keep from solidifying, but white and blue encased the sides. On the far side of the water, the terrain rose, undulating in ridges and valleys filled with dead trees and scrub brush. After another half-hour of travel, the wagon rolled to a stop.

"I'll drop you off in staggered locations." Falmouth's breath fogged as he spoke over the river. After fumbling with a bundle at his feet, he sat up and tossed four cloaks back, one at a time. "You'll need these in the mountains so you don't freeze."

Kaleth took one and pulled his arms through the sleeves. It hugged his body, trapping his body heat against him.

"Who wants to go first?" Falmouth asked.

"I will." Wearing the new cloak, Tyron rose and then vaulted over the side of the wagon. Rayd handed the initiate his water flask, bag of rations, and knife in a belt sheath.

"The Lagrash is the boundary between Kalshia and Thravia,"

Falmouth said. "For the test, remain south of the river for the four nights. I'll be patrolling, so don't test me on this."

Tyron slung the supplies over his shoulders and tied the knife around his waist. "Good luck," he said to Rayd and Roselle. Before he turned toward the river, he directed an evil grin in Kaleth's direction.

Falmouth flicked the reins, kicking the wagon into motion again, heading north with the other three initiates. "The rest of you are this way."

Knowing where Tyron was dropped off proved reassuring to Kaleth. He hoped for plenty of distance, but while calculating the speed of the wagon and time to travel in his head, he paled at how soon again Falmouth stopped.

"Next?" the instructor asked.

Kaleth decided he would let the other two go first, then take the farthest drop-off. That way, he could travel west and avoid running into anyone. While he made his plan in his head, the silence in the back of the wagon grew unnerving.

"Which of you is next?" Falmouth repeated.

Kaleth turned around, but Rayd and Roselle only stared into the woods.

"Fine," the instructor said. "Kaleth, you're up."

The slight smiles that formed in the back row turned his stomach. He clenched his jaw, hoping the fire in his eyes would intimidate them. They still didn't look.

He rose from his seat. With nothing to carry, he threw a leg over the side and hopped off the wagon.

"Four nights," Falmouth said as he snapped the reins. "Cross the river, but be back here by noon on the fifth day."

While the wagon rode off, Rayd's head turned. Before they disappeared around a boulder, he lifted a shiny metal object—his knife—to ensure Kaleth could see it.

*I've got to make some distance*, Kaleth thought. *And quickly.*

He walked to the edge of the river, looking for a safe way to cross. The current didn't look intense, but falling in could lead to hypothermia without a way to get dry and warm. The edges of the water looked frozen solid. He tested it with one foot and backed off at the cracking and snapping issuing from the ice. Thankfully, rocks formed what looked like a trail to the far side.

He pushed his glasses up on his nose, then stepped on the first rock. A pink substance covered the surface. He bent down to look closer.

*Realm: Plantia. Category: Stemless. Group: Algae. Strain: Roseoalgorist or Pink Algae.*

Technically edible but tastes awful and provides little nutrition. Kaleth opted to ignore it as a food source. Keeping his arms out for balance, he stepped from rock to rock. The algae made it slicker than he would have liked, but he crossed without incident.

When he arrived at the barren, rocky soil covering the far bank, the import of the moment hit him.

*I'm in Thravia.*

The realization was equal parts thrilling and terrifying. The staunch enemy of Kalshia was not known for kindness or hospitality. Without a weapon or anything to defend himself with, he needed to ensure his presence remained unnoticed by any native Thravians.

He looked back across the river.

*But the more immediate danger is my fellow initiates.*

Not wasting any time, he faced the interior and began to trek.

The uphill trail he blazed taxed his lungs and legs. The chill that had cut through his clothes at the river dissipated as the effort from the uphill climb warmed him. When he noticed the sweat covering his forehead and soaking into his clothing, an alarm rang in his head. Sweat's purpose was to cool his body down. It felt good at the moment but could be deadly once he stopped. Not only would it dehydrate him, it would leach the heat from his body. He slowed his ascent, hoping to minimize the impact.

While he traveled, he kept his sights on a saddle that cut between the surrounding hills. From the vantage point, he hoped to survey the area and decide where to go. The ground was mostly barren, but a surprising number of trees decorated the slope. They all looked like they'd been dead for years, but it was encouraging to think that he could gather some dry wood for a fire.

*Water. Shelter. Distance from Rayd.* He repeated his priorities as he marched higher.

At the base of the mountain, snow dotted the ground in sporadic chunks, but as he climbed higher, the icy ground cover grew thicker. Before long, every step punched into the crunchy layer of frozen precipitation.

By the time he reached the saddle, the sun had fallen low behind him. The wind cut through his sweaty clothes and forced him to wrap his arms tight against his body. Despite the frigid gusts blasting him, he surveyed the scene.

The steep hill he had climbed descended only a bit on the opposite side before it climbed again and split into various snow-covered ravines and hills. He gave thanks at the sight he most wanted to see: a river. Judging from the topography, it must join up with the Lagrash just north of where he crossed. If he could find a sheltered place, far enough away from Rayd and the others but close enough to water, he could ride out the four nights until it was time to leave.

A burst of wind made him shiver. *For now, I need a safe place to pass the night.*

A rocky outcropping caught his eye on the backside of the saddle.

*Is that . . . ?*

He walked forward through the snow to inspect the conglomeration of rocks. The closer he grew, the more a recessed area revealed itself. A smile grew on his face, and he laughed aloud. A small cave cut into the rock. It was six feet tall and the size of his home in Kalistor. A pile of dead limbs had fallen and broken next to the entrance, ready to be made into a warm fire.

*It couldn't be more perfect,* he thought. *It's far from water, but I can travel down to get some during the day. I can't believe this was so easy to find.*

The thought sent a wave of disappointment through him.

*It was too easy.*

His shoulders slumped. He couldn't use that cave. If Rayd came to where he had crossed the river, the saddle he was at would be the obvious place to travel. Someone else could find it—someone who already had a knife to go with their superior muscles.

*I need to travel farther.*

After one more wistful look at the cave, Kaleth headed down the backside of the mountain.

WHEN THE SUN HAD DISAPPEARED, darkness covered the area like a thick blanket. Despite his shivering, Kaleth was about to stop and lay down when a half moon lifted above the mountains, reflecting enough light for him to make out the ground. The lack of vegetation allowed him to keep going. He walked for hours.

Eventually, his descent leveled out, then continued back uphill. His feet hurt, and his legs were exhausted. Moving kept him warm, and the distance kept him alive.

When he looked behind him to see if he could gauge the distance he'd traveled, a sight turned his insides to water. Up a long incline, centered in the saddle between two silhouetted hills, a glowing light flickered in the darkness. It reminded him of a binder lamp hanging from a castle balcony. He knew what it was. One of the other initiates was in the cave, confirming what he suspected but hadn't fully bought into.

*They're coming after me. And in the morning, they'll be down in this valley.*

He turned away from the light. His feet ached. His legs begged him to stop. Despite his waning strength, he moved one foot in front of the other and stumbled forward through the near darkness.

BY THE TIME DAYLIGHT RETURNED, Kaleth could barely walk. He felt as if he'd fallen asleep standing up. Blisters stung his feet with each step. His lackluster muscles had given up, and only sheer determination to stay alive kept him moving. His mouth was parched, aching for water to replenish his body. To add insult to his already dire situation, snow had begun to fall.

He felt much better about his location. He couldn't even see the saddle that he'd left the evening before. While walking overnight, he'd crossed two ridges and weaved around multiple ravines. As much as he wanted to keep moving, there was only so much he could do. If the others were lucky enough to find him in the maze of wilderness he'd crossed, it might just be his time to go. Thankfully, the falling snow would cover his tracks.

But before he could settle on a place to make a shelter to weather the next three nights, he needed water. And gushing somewhere nearby, his ears led him toward what he hoped would be a good source.

When he arrived at the river, he blinked multiple times. The effort of walking through the night had left him disoriented, but what he saw proved to be more than he could process.

He heard the river, but there was no water. He stepped closer to the noise. The ravine had settled into a natural dip. He was where the river should be. It sounded all around him. He looked down, realizing the truth.

*It's under ice.*

He kicked at the ground and his foot slid. The glassy ground covered a deep blue. He stepped back and appraised the river in a new light. The flat, smooth tributary meandered between boulders, stretching ten feet across and remaining inaccessible under the frozen top layer.

His chest grew tight until he forced himself to calm.

*It's okay. I can get to this.*

His first thought was fear of the ice cracking. His feet felt solid, though. A halfhearted stomp didn't break it. He walked up the river, looking for opportunity. His feet slipped in several places, but other than that, travel was easy on the cleared, flat trail.

In the center of the river, one area of ice looked thinner than the rest. The blue water appeared vibrant and deep. He scanned the shore until he spotted a rock the size of his head. He struggled to pick it up. He could barely feel his hands which had turned red long before. With the object in his arms, he shuffled to the spot. Heaving with both his legs and arms, he tossed the object as high as he could toward the river.

When it hit the surface, the stone crashed through the ice. It cracked up a round section just wider than the boulder. Shards of inch-thick ice jutted into the air. Water splashed over the rest of the frozen top layer.

Kaleth's mouth ached at the sight. Stepping back on the frozen surface, he crept closer to the hole, sliding a step at a time. Life-giving liquid teased him from where it flowed through the opened access. He dropped, touching the surface with his feet, knees, and hands, spreading his weight across as wide an area as possible.

He slid closer. The hole was just out of reach. He stared through the glassy covering that separated him from the water. One unexpected break and he would fall through. Without a fire or shelter, he would be dead.

A creak filled the air as a tremble ran through his arms. He stopped, his heart pounding. The water was available just ahead of him. One more move forward. He slid one knee closer. Then the other. He moved a hand and shifted his weight to it, but the creaking returned, louder. He held his breath. Having adjusted his weight, he made sure it would hold. Nothing more settled. Nothing threatened to break.

Slowly, he dipped a cupped hand into the water. Icy fire seemed to run through his veins as he brought the liquid to his wind-chapped lips. His throat rejoiced. It was bone-chillingly cold, but he sipped, handful after handful until his hand was fully numb and the complaint of his knees on the hard surface won out. Moving as carefully as before, he slid away from the hole until it was safe to stand.

His body shook. He tucked his hands under his armpits and tried to control the shivering. Being filled with water, one of his concerns was satisfied. Next, he needed to find shelter. The limestone cliffs that formed the walls of the ravine caught his eye.

Thankfully, he didn't have to look long. A few minutes' walk upstream brought him to a depression in the rock where a small cave jutted into the wall. It wasn't as wide as the one he had found the day before, but it was dry, protected from the wind, and empty of other animals. He grinned.

*It's perfect.*

## CHAPTER TWELVE

# TROUBLE IN THE WILDERNESS

Kaleth threw another log on his fire. The coals sparked and crackled, releasing plumes of smoke from the dank wood. Tucked in the partially enclosed space, the fire's heat kept him comfortable enough to sleep. And after walking through the night a few nights before, he needed it.

*Three nights down. One more to go.* He planned to get up at first light the next day and head back to the border.

He had spent most of his time huddled in the cave, wrapping his cloak as tight as possible, ignoring pangs of hunger, and letting his mind race through everything that had happened in the previous few days.

He worried about his mother and sister. His leaving had been sudden. His sister would have to handle a lot of responsibility. At least he had gotten to see her before he left, so she would understand.

*Do I even understand?* he thought. *I'm competing with the most elite prospects in Kalshia in a life-or-death competition for which I am outmatched and unprepared. What would Father have done?*

A pain grew in his chest at the thought of his father. He had been so full of life and wisdom. Despite living with nothing, he had been filled with joy every day. He had an uncommon amount of patience for every question Kaleth peppered him with.

Kaleth wiped his eyes to clear away the pooling tears.

*I can't believe he held a secret like he did all his life.*

He thought back to the glyph left on the piece of paper, wondering how it worked. His father had somehow drained energy from living things around him and used it to heal and power himself. *How did he do it? What was he able to take it from? And how did that glyph help?*

He glanced around the cave. Eight glyph attempts he had scratched into the rock wall taunted him. The F's with their curved lines inside a circle looked right, but he didn't feel anything different.

*Father took energy from other objects to use for himself. Was it powered by the glyph or by something inside him?*

There were no signs of life around—no plants or animals. The flickering fire caught his eye. *Fire has life.*

Some glyphs worked better when cast on different places. His father always said, "Potency requires efficiency," meaning using an efficient location led to a more potent glyph. Protection, healing, and containment worked best on walls. Summoning and warmth worked better on the ground. Cursing supposedly worked best on a ceiling, but Kaleth had never tried that one. Curious about trying other options, he touched a stick to the dirt in front of him.

"Focus."

Speaking aloud sounded strange, having been alone for so long. He tuned out the whistling wind and snow-packed landscape outside. He ignored the fire.

"Intention."

*Give me the ability to draw energy. Bind it to me.*

"Action."

With a steady hand, he drew. First was the circle, then the curved lines. Finally, he sketched the F in the center. He exhaled as he set down the stick. Nothing felt different yet, but that was okay.

His heart sped as he crossed his legs under him. He stared at the fire's flames, imagining the energy simmering inside and feeling the heat on his face. His hand lifted, fingers stretching forward. He reached out with every sense he could find. Shaking began with his hand, then extended up his arm.

While he tried to keep his body from trembling, the flame sputtered, surging his hope. But it came crashing down when he realized it was only the wind teasing the mouth of the cave. Kaleth lowered his arm and sighed. With a huff of frustration, he roughed his hand across the dirt glyph.

*One day, Father. I'll figure it out.*

An audible rumble sounded from his stomach. He placed his hand over the spot, wishing for food to settle the ache. He had cast a few summoning glyphs around the area to attract rabbits, but he hadn't seen any in the three days he'd been there. Summoning glyphs were one of the easiest to make and worked well, but only if an animal was in proximity. Pushing off the ground, he made his way to his feet. *If I can't eat, at least I can get more wood.*

Late in the day, the lowering sun and overcast sky left much to be desired in terms of visibility. He trudged up the slope, heading toward a gathering of dead trees that had supplied most of the fuel he'd already used.

Stick by stick, he piled broken limbs in his arms, skipping the small ones in favor of the larger branches. He grabbed a limb and was shaking off the snow when a flash of movement caught his eye. He stopped and scanned the ground. Nothing registered outside of the blanket of white and piles of rocks. He began to think he had imagined it when he spotted the animal's outline. Sitting motionless, a fat, white rabbit perched atop the snow directly over where he'd cast a glyph that was now buried. The hare blended in so perfectly, Kaleth could barely tell it was there, even when looking at it.

His stomach came alive, groaning as he imagined the animal roasting over his fire. He considered his options to kill it since the glyph didn't trap the animal in place. All it did was create a longing that directed it to move there. But if the rabbit sensed danger, nothing would prevent it from hopping off. It would be too fast to chase. One of the sticks he carried might work if he could get close enough. While inspecting the load in his arms, a gray rock at his feet emerged as the top option.

He squatted slowly, dangling his free arm at his side. Keeping his eyes on the rabbit, he patted the ground until his fingers found the stone. The size of a fist, it was the perfect size to do the job. Kaleth stood. He didn't dare drop the bundle of wood and scare the animal off. He moved one foot forward and inhaled. His arm lifted, readying to throw the object. The rabbit's whiskers flickered, but it didn't hop away. Kaleth's arm tensed, ready to fling.

More movement caught his eye, and he froze. Trailing the large rabbit, three smaller white bunnies hopped into view. The babies seemed less concerned with being spotted. Their heads were in constant movement. One even collided with its sibling when it hopped without looking where it was going.

The mother rabbit remained motionless, but Kaleth's resolve to kill it dissolved. *I can go without food for one more day.* His arm wavered, then lowered. When he dropped the rock in the powder at his feet, the animal scampered off with its babies following behind.

Kaleth's stomach growled again, reminding him of his body's needs. He shook his head. *I'm too soft.* He turned his attention back to the search for wood as a gust of wind cut through his cloak, reminding him he needed to get back to his shelter.

After dropping another small log on top of his armload, something new prickled his awareness. The hairs on his neck stood on end, and he froze again. His eyes danced between the trees. He spun on the balls of his feet. Nothing was behind him but the frozen ravine and the gray sky.

*What's wrong with me?*

His breath echoed in his ears. He spun again, nerves on end and sinuses clear. He peered through the gloom, trying to catch sight of Rayd or one of the others.

*There's no one there.*

Facing the trees, he backpedaled toward his shelter. His eyes had found nothing to worry about, but his mind still told him something was wrong. As he turned around to walk faster, the wind changed direction, and a musky smell crossed his nose.

He jerked to his left and faced the wind. His feet stopped, stuck in place. His wood-laden arms shook. A deep growl reached his ears, rumbling like loose phlegm in his chest as an animal stepped from behind a boulder into the open.

*Realm: Animalae. Category: Mammal. Group: Carnivorae. Strain:—*

He swallowed hard.

*Barren Lion.*

The beast kept its head down as it slunk forward. Rippling with muscles, the short gray fur blended in well with the barren landscape. Its back undulated with each step, its paws as large as Kaleth's hands. What concerned him most were the incisors, sticking out past its snarled jaws. He'd only seen one in pictures before, but the animal was unmistakable.

Running was hopeless. Staying still was foolish. Kaleth dropped the armload of wood and held on to a single thick stick. His only hope was to fight. He bent his wobbling knees and raised the poor excuse for a weapon.

"Go away!" Kaleth shouted. His voice trembled.

The lion's growl intensified. It paused to bare its teeth, then continued forward.

Kaleth stepped backward. He glanced around, searching for anything that could help. His cave was fifty yards away. It might as well have been a thousand.

With a roar, the beast lunged, moving like lightning. Kaleth's heart dropped. He extended his stick as if it would hold the animal back. The lion snatched the club in its mouth and clamped down. Teeth as long as Kaleth's fingers wrapped around his pitiful weapon, crunching into the wood. A twist of its head yanked the stick from his grasp.

Unarmed, there was nothing left to do but run. He spun and sprinted as fast as his legs could move. A roar bellowed over his shoulder. He looked back. The lion bounded toward him.

*I'm sorry, Mother. I'm sorry, Sora. I wish I could have saved you.*

The cave was too far. There was no way he'd make it in time. He winced as he pictured the beast landing on his back, ripping into his body. He imagined the agony.

A piercing yelp tore through the air. Kaleth didn't look back but continued pumping his legs, expecting to die at any second. The cave grew closer. He couldn't hear the snarling anymore. When he flew past the edge of the cave, a glimmer of hope sparked in him. He grabbed a stick from the dwindling pile inside and turned.

Breaths came in heaving gasps. His pulse pounded in his head. He stood behind his fire and stared toward the cave opening. The barren, white landscape remained as he'd seen all day. He clenched his stick. The muscles in his arm flexed, ready for action.

Nothing arrived.

Kaleth loosened his grip and lowered his arm. *Where'd it go?* Against his better judgment, he rounded the fire and stepped toward the cave opening. The snow stuck on his boots sloshed with each step. He craned his neck to see farther. Nothing surged around the corner. Nothing jumped at him. When he arrived at the mouth, his jaw dropped. Ten feet from the opening, the barren lion lay on the snow, motionless.

*Is this a trick? Does it play dead and lure prey to it?*

He racked his brain to remember what he'd learned about the animal, but nothing about faking death came to mind. He stepped closer. Its fur was still. Closer. He expected it to jump up and lunge at any second, but still he continued. A red spot in the snow drew his attention. He kicked the snow, sending a spray of powder onto the unmoving body. It didn't flinch.

Kaleth was only a few feet away. He kept his stick forward, ready to strike while he bent over. Poking out of a patch of snow, an unexpected row of gray feathers caught his eye. *What is this?*

He checked the lion again. No muscles twitched. It didn't even breathe.

Kaleth touched the feathers. They were stiff. He brushed the snow around it and a slender shaft of wood came into view. He wrapped his hand around it and pulled. The lion's lifeless body jerked as he yanked the object.

The arrow looked to be made of ash with a broadhead iron tip. Three rows of gray feathers formed perfect lines by the nock. Kaleth let the arrow roll from his fingers as his eyes jerked to his surroundings. Fear of the lion's jaws had been replaced by one of equal terror: fear of other initiates.

He walked backward, his head swiveling. The barren trees could hardly conceal someone. But high up the sides of the ravine, boulders grew aplenty. One would be easy to hide behind. *Did they mean to shoot the lion or me?* Either way, they could take him out if he continued to stand there. With renewed urgency, he jogged back to his cave. Feeling less exposed with the roof above him and walls at his side, he peeked his head out. The lack of visibility unnerved him.

*Someone is out there.*

His breath fogged. His heart pounded. Before his pulse settled, an unnerving laugh filled the air. He snapped his eyes to the opposite side of the ravine and gasped.

Tyron casually walked toward the cave with a gleaming knife held by his side. A smirk covered his ruddy face. "Do you know how hard it is to find someone out here?" he asked.

Kaleth stepped back, as if the walls of the cave provided protection rather than a place to be trapped.

"I found a few boot prints that hadn't been snowed over next to the river, but that lion's roar gave me the best clue." He glanced at the fallen animal.

Kaleth moved deeper into the cave, keeping his stick up. "Why are you here?"

"Isn't it obvious? We're in a competition, and you don't belong."

"You're worried about me beating you? Is that it?"

Tyron narrowed his eyes.

"You think I'm a threat, so you have to take me out when the instructors aren't looking?"

"I'm not worried about anything. You least of all," he sneered. "Rayd-il-Stonne, on the other hand, has a beef with you. It seems that you embarrassed him and turned his parents against him."

"I've never even met his parents."

"I may not care about you, but I *do* care about Rayd. His family has the connections I need to do anything I like once I graduate here. That makes you my enemy, and there's only one way to deal with an enemy."

"Where'd you get a bow from?" Kaleth asked.

Tyron flinched but didn't respond.

"Why'd you kill the lion if you wanted me to die? Or are you that bad of a shot?"

The other initiate paused when he reached the mouth of the cave. Without taking his eyes away from the boy, Kaleth bent to the fire and grabbed one of the longer sticks that was untouched at one end.

Tyron chuckled. "You think a flaming stick is going to scare me?" He raised his knife and danced it between his hands as he continued closer. "It's too bad Rayd couldn't be here to see you die. He would have enjoyed that."

Kaleth's heart pounded. With a wall behind him, there was nowhere for him to go. The threatening knife drew nearer. In Kaleth's periphery, against the wall, the protection glyph he'd cast stared at him with its three rings of concentric circles with the X over the smallest two. He could only hope he had done it correctly.

Tyron's face clenched as he inhaled. With a final step forward, he lunged with the blade.

Kaleth closed his eyes, pressing them tight. It could be the worst idea ever, but he trusted in his glyph-casting ability. His stomach clenched, as if his soft muscles could turn the hard steel of the weapon.

"Argh! Bind me!"

His eyes shot open as Tyron's knife hit the ground. The other boy recoiled, shaking his hand as if he'd punched it into a stone. A glance at his own body told Kaleth the glyph had done its job. Tyron hadn't been able to touch him. The marking on the cave wall shimmered before beginning to fade.

Swinging the larger club as hard as he could, he smacked it into the side of the initiate's head. The boy collapsed. He fell to the ground, groaning and clutching the side of his face.

Kaleth held the burning stick to an imperceptible line running up the cave wall. The flames tickled the vine until it caught, eating through the brittle strand. Not waiting to confirm if it had worked, he dropped the chunk of wood and sprinted for the cave exit. A snap of tension behind him told him he had only a moment to escape.

Tyron scrambled to his feet as Kaleth passed him in the narrow space. His hands flailed to grasp a leg, but Kaleth jerked free. Something rattled in the dark recesses above him. *Gotta get out!* The logs hidden in the cave ceiling barely missed Kaleth, but they thundered on top of the other initiate with a crash.

Kaleth burst from the mouth of the cave. He sprinted downhill, trying to put distance between him and his attacker. Nearing a corner, he glanced back in time to see a disoriented Tyron emerge from the cave, holding his head and stumbling with a face full of vitriol.

Kaleth's boots kicked up snow. His mind raced to think of where to go and how to escape. Frigid air seared his nostrils, and his lungs ached. He dashed over a pile of rocks and lost his feet on the surface of the river.

*Smack!* He hit the ice hard. His forearms screamed from the impact. With his attacker in pursuit, he scrambled to stand, only to find his legs slipping from under him again. By the time he resumed moving, an angry Tyron turned the corner and leaped past the rocks in pursuit.

Moving as fast as he could on the slick surface, Kaleth felt the other initiate gaining. Puffing and grumbling grew closer.

*I've got to get off this river*, he thought. He sighted a clear path on the shore. Before he could adjust his trajectory, a hard shove propelled him forward. His feet struggled to maintain purchase and keep him upright. A jolt of terror seized him. He fell, and the place he headed was the vibrant blue section of thin ice he had used to collect water. His hands hit first. One struck the ice and slid, but the other punched through. When his chest collided, the entire section of ice around him broke.

Water surrounded him with a bone-shattering cold. It pressed the air from his lungs and felt like knives stabbing him on every surface of his body. He tried to lift his submerged head out of the water, but it smacked into a hard surface. The current of the river pulled him downstream with an unseen grip, sliding his back against a barrier above him and ripping his glasses from his face. He flipped over and opened his eyes. A veneer of ice distorted his view of the sky. Upstream, he spotted the hole he'd punched through. He turned his body and flung his arm, grabbing the lip of broken ice. On top of the frozen layer, Tyron's cloudy form stepped into view.

Kaleth tried to pull himself toward the hole, but his arm shook. His muscles didn't work. His fingers slid down the edge until the current ripped him away.

Panic gripped him. His lungs begged for air. He slammed his elbows into the ice, but it wouldn't break. Tyron walked with him, keeping pace above.

*There must be a way out!* He hit the ice again, and a crack formed between Tyron's legs.

The other initiate stepped away from the danger. Standing on solid ice, he bent over, waving the knife through the air.

With his mind racing, Kaleth despaired. *Even if I break out, he's waiting for me.* He needed to breathe. He needed to get out of the water. *There's no hope.*

He pressed against the ice again, but it only pushed his body down. Another frantic smack from his elbow accomplished nothing. His lungs burned, but the rest of him was numb. The cloudy images through the ice darkened as if his eyes were giving up. His body twitched as if trying to conjure oxygen from some unknown source.

As if responding to his thoughts, Tyron's body jerked. Kaleth thought he imagined it until a long shaft through the boy's neck came into focus through a clear patch of ice. The boy fell, grasping at his neck.

*What happened?*

A moment later, someone new arrived. Someone shorter with curly black hair. The blurred form lifted something above their head.

*What is that?* He figured it out as the object hurtled toward him.

The boulder crashed into the ice just downstream of where he drifted, breaking through the frozen barrier and missing his body by an inch. When Kaleth's head broke the surface, he gasped for air. The sensation was odd, like his lungs wouldn't work. He sucked oxygen in spurts. His arms flailed at the edge of the broken ice until they contacted another limb.

The new arrival lay across the ice, stretching their body across the surface. They yelled something, but his muddled mind couldn't understand it. He barely felt it when they grabbed his arm. His sight grew hazy and the world around him spun. He was only vaguely aware of being pulled from the water. He tried to use his limbs to help, but they were like rag dolls. His head drooped. He felt nothing in his body. Free of the river and pulled off the ice, his body flopped onto the ground, shivering uncontrollably.

"Who are . . . ? What . . . ?" Kaleth tried to talk, but neither his mind nor body operated as expected.

He felt a faint pressure on his arm before his body rolled and lifted into the air. The ravine, the boulders, and the snow spun until he found himself staring down at a pair of legs and a blurry torso that held him in the air. Tyron's unmoving body lay atop the frozen river. Blood stained the ice, spreading from the arrow wound in his neck.

They moved in staggering steps toward his cave. Water poured off Kaleth's body and clothes, soaking the person who carried him. He tried again to talk but only managed muttering sounds. Shivering muscles convulsed his body, but his rescuer held him tight.

His eyes closed. Thoughts of Tyron, the river, and his family flashed through his mind, but the agony of cold prevented focus. Only one coherent thought stuck with him.

*Who is carrying me?*

## CHAPTER THIRTEEN

# WARMING UP

Disoriented and confused, Kaleth tried to push the haze away. His limbs dangled, numb and unresponsive. The ground passed by for several minutes as he was carried.

*Get to the cave*, he thought. *Just get to the cave.*

He tried to lift his head or speak, but the chattering of his teeth was all he managed. The path they took led up the ravine, but it didn't remind him of the path to the cave. They climbed higher. The person carrying him huffed with exertion, limping as they moved. After several minutes, the path ended at a protected overhang. A stone wall raised at an incline, leaving the area below it dry. A pile of blankets and supplies rested on the ground next to the burning coals of a fire.

Kaleth's feet lowered to the ground. Still shaking, he stared at the source of warmth, teetering to remain on his feet.

"Take off your clothes," the person said.

Kaleth turned and startled. The person who had carried him was a young woman around his age and shorter by a few inches. She had vivid green eyes and curly black hair that fell to her shoulders. A dark scar marked the line of her chin. Over dark olive skin, she wore bulky gray clothes that dripped water after carrying his soaking body.

*A Thravian!* he thought.

"Now," she repeated, the tremble in her voice matching the shake of her body. "Take them off!"

Barely processing what she said or the implications of her order, Kaleth fumbled with his soaking cloak. He tried to slide it off, but the wetness stuck to his shirt and skin. He attempted to grab the sleeve with his opposite hand, but his fingers wouldn't pinch the end.

While he struggled, the girl tossed several logs onto the fire. Once the wood was arranged, she removed her bulky outer layer, leaving a tight, wet tunic that clung to her body. The toned definition of her shoulders and arms proved how she could lug his body from the river. She draped her own soaking cloak on a nearby rock.

When she saw that he had yet to accomplish anything, she walked to him. "Here." She grabbed his cloak and worked it off. His limbs convulsed as he pulled them through the sleeves. Without pausing, she pulled up the hem of his soaking undershirt, exposing his chest to the frigid air. He expected to grow colder, but removing the wet shirt warmed him. She draped both items over a rock.

Kaleth's breathing was shallow and desperate. He felt like he could fall asleep standing up, but the shaking of his limbs kept him present. "Whoo'rr—whoo'rr y-y-y—"

She cut him off by yanking his wet leggings down.

Kaleth gasped. Fully exposed and barely coherent, he was cognizant enough to be embarrassed but not coordinated enough to do anything about it.

Her teeth chattered as she pulled his boots off one by one, then slid the rest of his clothes off over his feet. "Lay down," she ordered, pulling back a blanket that lay on the ground. "Get under here. On your side."

Kaleth obeyed, falling to the ground in an uncoordinated display of naked awkwardness. She pulled a blanket over his body and pushed a pillow under his head. His body continued to shake. His teeth chattered. He craned his neck toward the fire and saw the mystery girl set up his boots and leggings to dry.

*I would be dead if it weren't for her. I wonder what—*

His thoughts turned blank as she stripped her wet shirt off, pulling it over her head. Kaleth jerked his head back in the direction his body faced, looking out toward the ravine. A warming sensation crept up his neck, bringing a tingle of life to his frozen body. His ears burned as he heard more sounds of her undressing. A violent shiver shook his body.

*Warmth glyph!*

The idea came suddenly but took a long time to permeate his mind. He leaned forward and stretched a hand to the dirt. His arm shook and teeth chattered. He tried to focus his mind, but all he could think of was his unbearable cold and the girl undressing behind him. *To keep me w-w-w*—he couldn't even think straight. The outline he tried to etch in the ground contained jagged lines, useless in a proper glyph. He started again on a new attempt, but it was worse than the first.

He held his breath as the blanket rustled. His bare backside was exposed to the air for only a second until the girl lay down behind him, dropping the blanket over them both. Her skin pressed against his. He tried to stay still, but his body continued to shake. Her arms slid around him, pulling tight against his frozen skin. Unable to feel much, all he could sense was the pressure. He grasped his arms over hers, against his own chest.

"You need body heat," she explained, "and wet clothes would mean both of our deaths."

His teeth chattered as he nodded. His father had lectured him about cold-weather survival. In any other situation, an unfamiliar young woman lying naked with him would have been equal parts thrilling and mortifying. Under the circumstances, it terrified him.

After minutes with her body pressed against his, the blanket covering them, and the growing fire, tingling soon returned to his limbs. His uncontrollable shaking diminished, and his breath evened out. The shelter where they lay was higher up than the cave he'd been staying in. Through the barren limbs of several dead trees, he spotted it across the ravine. After losing his glasses in the river, it was blurry but still recognizable.

"Thank you," he whispered. His words rattled but no longer trembled. "Who are you?"

"Rest." Her breath tickled his neck. "We can talk when we have clothes on."

The flush returned to his neck, a welcome sensation of needed warmth. He closed his eyes to focus on managing his breath and keeping his limbs from shaking. The near-death experience brought one encouraging thought to his mind.

*I'm ranked forty-ninth now.*

A POPPING SOUND brought his mind into focus, and his eyes opened. A fire crackled behind him, throwing light on the nearby ground and trees, but the rest of the surrounding world was dark. It took a moment to remember where he was. He lay under a blanket, alone.

Nothing in his body shook. Nothing felt frozen. He wriggled his toes and balled his fingers. They worked and he could feel them.

"You stopped shaking an hour ago."

Kaleth turned toward the fire. The young woman sat around it, fully dressed, poking the logs with a stick. A bow leaned against the wall past her, and a quiver of arrows with gray fletchings caught his eye.

"Your clothes are dry—except your cloak. That will need longer." She set her stick down and collected his clothes from where they draped over rocks. Crossing to his side of the fire, she set the bundle next to his blanket, then turned around. "You can dress. I won't watch."

He chuckled. While he appreciated the respect for privacy, it seemed silly after the previous night. A chill washed over his bare skin as he pulled the blanket back. With the girl turned around, he dressed. Not only were the clothes dry, but they were warm from the heat of the fire, as if they'd been lying in the sun for hours.

Part of him wanted to return to sleep, but a myriad of questions tugged at his mind. He stood and moved to a seat on a rock beside the fire. The flames radiated an inviting heat. He extended his hands, relishing the warmth. A deep breath tested his lungs. As he clenched and unclenched his hands, he marveled at how well they worked.

The young woman turned around. "You're a Kalshian, aren't you?" Her piercing green eyes bore into him.

The blunt question brought a tightness to his chest. *Will she change her mind about saving me if she knows?* The curiosity in her eyes held no malice. He decided to risk it. "Yes."

Her face remained unreadable. She didn't lunge for a weapon. She stared back, her olive skin glowing in the firelight. A white scar following the line of her jaw caught his eye. Her steely exterior gave him the impression she'd dealt with some difficult things.

"I've never met one before," she said.

"At least not one with clothes on, huh?

She chuckled, a smirk pulling at her mouth.

"Thank you for saving my life," Kaleth said. "Twice."

"Twice?" She raised her eyebrows, then counted on her fingers. "The lion. That guy. Drowning. Freezing."

He laughed. "Okay, four times."

"Who was that? A slaver?"

He frowned. "Slaver?"

"They're common along the border. Kalshians hunt Thravians and sell them as slaves."

"No, he wasn't that."

She waited as if wanting further explanation.

"He was . . ." *in an academy, training to kill Thravians, just like I am.* "We're from the same city. He was trying to kill me, so I fled across the border to get away. I guess he was more determined than I realized."

Her eyes narrowed as if trying to read his mind.

Kaleth shifted in his seat, curious about who this strange girl was. "My name's Kaleth. What's yours?"

Her intense focus eased. "Felyra."

He smiled. "A beautiful name."

She flinched at the compliment.

"Do you live out here?" he asked.

"Nearby."

He nodded, pursing his lips.

"What?"

Kaleth shrugged. "You seem young to be wandering the wilderness."

"Says the guy who almost died four times."

He chuckled. "Fair point."

"Do you not think I can handle myself?"

"Sorry. I didn't mean to imply that. Yes, I'd say you can."

"My parents aren't far," she said after a pause. "Mother worries constantly, but my father encourages me to test myself. He's always pushing me to try things. To keep training. To get faster and stronger. That one day I'll need to do things on my own." A smile flashed across her face. "That's why I'm out here. I'm testing myself to make Father proud."

Kaleth managed a wistful smile and had to fight to keep the tears for his own father back.

She fished a necklace out from under her shirt. "He gave me this." The metal square at the end of the necklace displayed an engraved image of a small mammal. "It's a—"

"Silver-tailed ermine," he interrupted. "Right?"

Her jaw dropped. "That's right. Most people have never heard of them."

He shrugged. "I've been training to be a sage."

"The silver tails are fierce, known to defend themselves from predators ten times their size."

"Also extremely loyal," Kaleth added. "They'll sacrifice their lives for their family."

"That's right. As I grew older, Father said I reminded him of them." She tucked the necklace away again. "Now that your attacker is gone, where are you heading?"

"I'll probably leave once the sun is up." He tried to keep it casual but knew he would have to make good time to make the Lagrash River by noon.

His gaze drifted into the ravine. A faint bit of light peeked over the mountains, making the snow glow and the tree limbs look like twisted monsters. His eyes tracked to his cave, and a thought crossed his mind. "Have you been watching me?"

She crossed her arms. "I was here first, you know."

He had assumed he was alone. The thought of someone watching him for days brought a flush to his cheeks, a welcome warming sensation.

"How long have you been here?"

"Long enough."

"And you just let me struggle: collecting wood and getting water?"

"You seemed to do all right to me."

"Thravians hate Kalshians though, right?"

She didn't reply. A long pause built up the tension.

"Why did you save me?"

"Maybe I needed the meat from the lion."

"The meat you left down there in the ravine?"

She shrugged. "Maybe I felt sorry for you."

"Did you?"

She stared at him, her face unreadable once more. Her mouth opened, but it closed before she said anything. Her kind eyes flicked toward the fire. "I don't know why." The words were strained.

*She's lying.*

"Maybe I should have let you die."

The thought turned his blood cold. He felt vulnerable—alone in the Thravian wilds at the mercy of a warrior girl who outclassed him. "Well, I'm glad you saved me." He laughed, trying to lighten the mood. "Rescued by a girl with a chin scar."

Felyra's face turned hard in a flash. She jumped up and pulled a knife from nowhere. Kaleth scrambled backward and fell off the back of his rock, hitting his back flat against the hard ground. She leaned over him with her face furrowed and a knife waving in his face. "Girl with a chin scar? Is that how you see me?"

"No!" He held up his hands. "I'm sorry. I was just . . . I meant nothing by it."

"You take my help, then run back to your country with tales of maimed women who do your dirty work for you."

"That's not it. I promise."

"Now I see why everyone wants to kill Kalshians."

Kaleth gulped.

Felyra stepped to the rock that held his splayed-out cloak. "Dry enough. Here." She tossed the piece of clothing at him. "You're warmed up, and you'll live. Now, get out of here before I change my mind about how I think of Kalshians."

"I think the scar is great. It enhances your beauty," he said in a rush of honesty as he pulled on his cloak.

The hardened anger on her face faltered. Her mouth opened but froze before speaking.

"I didn't mean to offend you," he said. He buttoned his cloak and flashed the most genuine smile he could manage. "Again . . . thank you for everything. I will never forget you, Felyra."

THE PATH back to the border was easier than the trek in. Most of the travel was downhill, helping him make good time. Knowing Tyron was gone and that it was too late for the others to be hunting him allowed him to enjoy the hike. The sun still climbed in the sky by the time he crossed the Lagrash, so he sat on a rock to wait.

After a couple of hours, the same horse-driven cart clopped back down the path. Rayd and Roselle craned their necks around the driver and narrowed their eyes at the sight of Kaleth.

"Nice work," Falmouth said, looking impressed that he was still alive.

Kaleth climbed into the wagon, ignoring the glares from the two initiates in the back row. The wagon continued south, backtracking the route they'd taken on the way in.

"What happened to Tyron?" Rayd whispered.

Kaleth turned to look behind him. He fought to not smirk. "What do you mean?"

Rayd's eyes narrowed, but he didn't answer.

"I don't know. Was I supposed to know where he is?" He glanced at Roselle, feigning ignorance. "I feel like I'm missing something."

When neither of the other initiates said anything, he turned back around. Only then did he allow a smile to creep on his face.

## CHAPTER FOURTEEN

# RETURNING TO REVALLE

Felyra winced as an awkward step pulled at her hip. The ever-present pain radiated up the side of her body. She pushed it away and continued walking, settling into the cadence of her limping stride. She'd walked all day. Her feet hurt. Her legs ached. The heavy pack chafed on her shoulders, but she didn't want to stop and adjust it.

She walked beside the bank of the mostly dried-up South Lagrash River. All that remained of moisture was the orange and brown algae lining the banks. The dirt under her boots was hard. Small rocks kicked up dust as her feet sent them scattering. The rolling hills she'd left behind hours before had given way to the flat, arid plains of Thravia, stretching in each direction with little to break up the featureless view except the occasional dead tree. Gusts of wind picked up her curly tendrils of hair, waving them in front of her face.

While her eyes tracked the ground, she pictured the young Kalshian from the mountains. All her life, she'd been told about the enemy—how they stole from and murdered Thravians. And the first chance she had to encounter one, she'd saved his life. He had seemed like her—just trying to survive in the wilderness. She felt a moment of pity until his words "girl with a chin scar" ran through her head.

"Gah!" she shouted, kicking a rock and sending it skittering. Her fists clenched together.

*I was soft, and he's just like all the others. I should have let him die.*

She had enough to overcome as it was. She didn't want to add compassion to her list of weaknesses.

Continuing ahead, the air turned musty as she entered the algae farms. Stretching in each direction, the bright hues formed rows, providing the only color other than brown to be seen. Red and green were the predominant crops, but sections of orange, blue, and a small amount of black also decorated the fields.

Past the fields, the city of Revalle rose from the land. Clay tiles formed slanted roofs, raked to fend off the dust storms that ravaged the land. Passages between buildings kicked up clouds of dirt from the carts that trundled through the city. The city looked older than it was. The harsh environment left crumbling stone, building edges rounded by gritty wind, and faces of citizens that seemed stuck in a permanent frown. Little new had been built in the last forty years.

When she entered the city, the wind buffeting her hair lessened but didn't die. She pulled her pack higher on her back and marched forward. She passed Phyco Market where dried algae piled high in colorful stacks. The farmers who sold the crop looked no more happy to be there than the shoppers purchasing it.

Relaxing her mind, she took it all in at once. A woman piling algae into a basket perspired. A casual observer might assume it was from the heat, but Felyra caught the shake in the woman's hand as she opened her coin purse.

*She's unsure if she has enough money.*

Across the aisle from her, a vendor inched sideways as a man passed by his stall. The move was slight, just enough to open the line of sight to his product and block that of his next-door competitor. The customer stopped at the vendor's table.

Crows cawed, perched on an awning that draped over the market. The scent of dung wafted in, blowing from an alley where a donkey headed away. Behind her, the rustle of fabric flapped in the breeze. It could have been any clothes hanging on a line to dry, but Felyra picked it out without even looking. She turned her head and grinned. A fluttering apron, identifiable by sound from how the shape of its cut caught the wind.

She relished her ability to notice the world—to see things others missed. When she was younger, it hurt her head to try too hard. She berated herself for missing things, which caused her to try harder. Over time, the habit grew natural, honing her senses.

In the center of the city, the dried-up Fountain of Life couldn't appear more dissimilar than its name implied. A statue of sword-wielding King Thanean topped a raised circular basin. Grooves cut into the side of the basin were meant to spill water out into the larger pool below, but no water had run for the seventeen years Felyra had been alive. The name, Fountain of Life, was meant to inspire hope, but she usually heard it referred to by its informal title, Fountain of Dust.

The thought of dust left her mouth feeling dry. She opened her water flask and took a long drink, coating her throat.

"You need to mail anything?" a man lurking at the edge of the market asked.

She turned to him, still drinking.

"I can get a letter anywhere: Carrvorre, Loravis, even across enemy lines into Kalshia. Only two coppers per letter. Unless it's a rush, then it's six."

After swallowing her mouthful, she shook her head. "I don't have anything. Sorry."

"Find me when you do. I'm the best letter porter in West Verda-lyn." The man turned away, already looking for the next potential customer.

Past the fountain, she turned north, heading up the incline to the fortress that rose above the surrounding buildings at the top of the hill. Parapets jutted into the air. The weathered stone looked like a storm of dust had tossed a blanket of dirt against it. Through an arched opening, a passage led beyond the walls. A young man named Palric shuffled through with shoulders slumped. Felyra followed, exchanging a nod with the exhausted young man.

The far side of the passage opened up into a large courtyard. Older men and women stood waiting, ushering any arrivals toward tables holding platters of algae in various colors. Exhausted young men and women sat around the tables, eating and drinking as if it had been days without either.

Palric staggered forward until he collapsed in a seat. Two attendants swooped on either side. One held a vessel to his lips while the other collected green algae leaves onto a plate. The young man gulped the water.

"Name," a voice barked from the side.

Felyra glanced at the wall, where a scowling man with a square jaw glared at the newly arrived young man. Her stomach turned. *Captain Janduan Forcebane.* The forty-year-old sat casually, wearing his gray Soulbinder uniform with the hood pulled back.

"What's your name?" Janduan repeated with impatience.

"Palric," the young man breathed after swallowing a mouthful of water.

"Palric. That's right. Any injuries or medical concerns?"

The young man paused. It looked as if it pained him to think. "I've been dizzy and weak."

"From the lack of food. That's fine. Anything else?"

He held out his arm, showing off a dirty cloth that wrapped around his upper arm. "A razech tried to drain my blood while I slept. I ran it off, but it left a nasty wound."

Janduan wrote on his paper without looking up. The conspicuous blue ring on his middle finger caught the light of the sun. "See the medic when you're finished."

"Come and sit," a woman said, getting Felyra's attention by motioning her to take a seat at the table. "I'll get you some water."

"Name?" Janduan asked while still writing.

"I'm fine," Felyra assured the woman. "I'm not hungry."

"Not hungry?" Janduan looked up. "What are you—" The curiosity on his face turned hard. His eyes narrowed. "Ah . . . the cripple."

Felyra's muscles clenched. She stood taller and lifted her chin.

"So you survived, after all."

"I did, and I had plenty to drink." She lifted her waterskin, making sure the sloshing could be heard. "Are you thirsty? I have plenty left."

He didn't reply.

"Here," the woman tried again. "Come sit and get some algae. You must need some food."

Felyra didn't take her eyes off Janduan. "No to the water?" She lowered the container. "What was it you said to me before I left? Do you recall?"

His eyes narrowed even more. He used his thumb to spin his ring as if trying to remind her that he was superior.

"It was something like . . . 'You'll never make it and will be dead in a day.' Does that ring a bell?"

"Please," the woman tried again. "You need your strength. Why don't you take a seat and get something to eat?"

Felyra turned to the lady and pulled a wrapped object from her bag. She slapped the bundle on the table, echoing a thump through the courtyard.

"What is this?" The woman pulled the fabric back, revealing two preserved whole fish. She gasped.

"You had fish?" A wide-eyed Palric muttered with a frond of algae drooping from his lower lip. "Where'd you get those?"

The other men and women stood to get a better view.

"These were extra," Felyra said. "They're easy to catch in the mountains."

"The mountains?" He continued to gawk. "You traveled that far?"

"You can have them; I had plenty. Like I said, I'm not hungry."

Palric drooled, staring at the fish.

Felyra turned back to Janduan and stepped closer to his table. "'Dead in a day.' Do you remember?"

His jaw clenched even tighter as the sides of his mouth quirked down.

"Well, you were wrong, Captain."

She spun on her heels, leaving Janduan, slack-jawed-Palric, and the fish behind as she left the courtyard to enter the fortress.

·  ·  ·

THE BUNK ROOM held twenty-four beds stacked in pairs. About half the beds had packs laid on the mattresses. The rest had their wrinkle-free sheets pulled taut. Along the wall, a row of windows let in light, allowing a view of the clouds and the peaks of the Kalshian Mountains.

"Felyra!" Ruane Nimble left the group of young men and women she'd been talking with and bounced across the room. She stood out from the drab surroundings with her pale skin, blonde hair, and blue eyes.

The shout of her name and the sight of her friend brought a smile to Felyra's face. "Ruane, you made it. Everything went all right?"

Ruane wrapped her arms around her, squeezing. The human touch allowed Felyra's muscles to relax, a welcome sensation after a week of being on constant alert.

"I found a patch of wild red on an eastern tributary. There was enough moisture for me to siphon off a bit to drink, but I was still massively dehydrated. Algae was enough to keep me going, though. I saw valsic dragon tracks once, but, luckily, I never ran into one. How about you? You made it to the mountains?"

Felyra nodded.

"Was it cold?"

The thought of shivering next to Kaleth popped into her mind. "It was, uh . . . fine most of the time. I had a fire, and there was food and water."

"I should have gone with you, I guess. Did you have any trouble?"

She pictured shooting the other Kalshian boy through the neck, then fishing Kaleth out of the river.

"What?" Ruane's face screwed up in question. "There was something."

Felyra gave a short laugh. "It was nothing. There was . . . this boy."

Ruane's eyes widened, and a grin pulled at her lips. "Yeah?"

"No! It's not like that. He just—" She wasn't sure what she wanted to share. "He was all alone and in trouble—from a barren lion. I scared it off."

Ruane's grin turned mischievous. "A boy in trouble, huh? All alone, and you rescued him? Did he . . . *show you gratitude?*"

"What?" Felyra sputtered, pushing her friend in the shoulder. "He didn't do anything. He ran off into the wilderness, that's all."

Ruane's grin eased. "Pity. Could have been a good story."

A taunting voice cut through the room. "Looks like Cripp survived."

Felyra turned to find Graxon Thunderfoot crossing the room with his crew of sycophants in tow.

He paused and sneered as he passed. "You had enough yet? Decided you want to quit? Or maybe you decided you need a leader who's going to challenge you more. There's always room on my squad for a malformed limp monster like yourself. I'll show you what real training is like if you ask for a transfer."

A rush of heat crept up Felyra's neck. She puffed out her chest and stepped forward, close enough to smell the algae on his breath. "Do you have a problem, Grax? Did your mother drop you on your head as a baby?"

He scowled. "My problem is *you*, thinking you deserve to be one of us."

"You want to take this outside the fortress walls?" She touched the handle of a dagger on her hip. "Maybe you can show me how high and mighty you think you are?"

"I'm ready, now or anytime."

"Stop this, both of you!" Ruane stepped between them, pushing them back. "And Grax, don't be such a bind-cursed jerk! We're all on the same side."

The other boys chuckled. A smirk grew across Grax's face.

Easing back from her friend's push, Felyra spoke through clenched teeth. "To answer your question, no, I'm not quitting."

Grax shrugged. "It's gonna be either now or later, but suit yourself."

As the crew of young men passed, the last in the row, Thaylor, lingered. "Sorry about Grax," he said when the other boys were out of earshot. "I think you're right about that dropping on the head theory. There's no other explanation for how he is." Tufts of thick, black hair fell across eyes that held a surprising softness.

The tension in Felyra's shoulders eased. She chuckled. "Yeah, probably so."

"I'm glad you made it back." He smiled.

The anger that had just raged in her dissipated at his disarming words.

"He laughs about you joining our squad, but I keep hoping it will happen. It would be nice to have some beauty in the group."

*Beauty.*

There was the word again. Kaleth's words around the fire played through her mind. She pictured the hurt on his face when she'd kicked him out of her camp in a fury. A smile tugged at her lips.

*Maybe there is something to it. If both of them think—*

Thaylor's face changed. His kind affect morphed into a look of someone waiting at the punchline of a joke. A single laugh burst out.

*What is he—?*

He covered his mouth with a hand and exploded into laughter, turning to Grax and the others.

Felyra's back stiffened. Her jaw set.

Thaylor staggered to his friends and high-fived Grax, who joined him doubled over in cackles.

"Beauty! Woo hoo! Ha!" Grax spoke in spurts, fighting to take in air around the laughs. "You should have seen her face—she believed you. What a bind-cursed idiot! No one will ever find her beautiful."

She felt as if the air had been sucked from the room. The scar on her chin burned as if it glowed conspicuously.

Ruane pulled her sleeve in the opposite direction. "Come on. Let's get out of here."

Felyra stumbled after her friend. She didn't even bother to hide her limp. The familiar cadence of off-beat steps thumped on the wooden floorboards as they left the room.

The laughter behind intensified. "Look at her walk!" one of them shouted. The rest of the boys' words were lost in the cacophony of guffaws.

A fire of anger and shame burned through Felyra's veins. After years of ridicule, she told herself she was used to it—that it didn't bother her anymore. There was nothing anyone could say or do that would make her feel bad about who she was. She told it to herself over and over. And over.

And over.

She choked back a tear.

She hoped that one day, the words would finally be true.

## CHAPTER FIFTEEN
# WELCOME HOME

Initiates packed the Grand Hall by the time Felyra and Ruane arrived. A buzz filled the room, accented by slaps on the back and boisterous conversation amidst the must of dried sweat. The oversized chamber was square-shaped with a tall ceiling and windows on opposite sides. A chandelier of flickering lanterns dangled in the center, tossing light in each direction. Two more lamps sat on a raised stage at the far end of the room. The two young women kept to the back, settling against the wall.

"Hiding their boots at night. Taking their clothes while they bathe. Soaking their pillows with water." Ruane counted on her fingers as she rattled off the ideas. "Which do you like?"

Felyra shook her head.

"Maybe all three?" Her friend's eyebrows were lifted. "C'mon, Grax and his friends deserve it."

A smile washed over Felyra's face as she allowed herself to imagine the suggested retaliation. Finally, she sighed. "Thanks for wanting to stand up for me. It would just make things worse though."

At the front of the room, Headmaster Baloran Soulburn stepped on the stage in a crisp Soulbinder uniform. Using both hands, he lowered his gray hood.

"Welcome back to Revalle," he called above the din, raising a hand. The two flickering lights lifted off the stage, floating into the air, encased in their metal containers.

The murmur in the crowd dissipated. The lanterns floated back to the ground, settling with a clink as they touched down. No matter how many times Felyra had seen the power displayed, it invoked the same feeling of awe every time.

The headmaster's thick gray hair and deep lines on his face showed a weariness brought on by years of hard living. But the twinkle in his eyes reflected a vitality and exuberance that defied the challenges of his job.

"I'm glad to learn so many of you fared well over the last week. Thravians are strong, brave, and resourceful, and I had no doubt of your abilities."

A smattering of cheers filled the room.

"Unfortunately, we have five who have not returned."

The cheers faded.

"We may see them straggle in late. They may have run off. Or they may be dead. In any case, we mourn their removal from our ranks. Please take a moment of silence to appreciate the loss of your fellow Thravians."

Felyra's eyes drifted to the floor as he listed the names.

"Leifal Ironhand. Traavi Skymere. Chross Fendwhistle."

"Chross," someone from the crowd echoed in a solemn tribute.

"Evelyr Windmere. Julel Ironspine."

The quiet that followed felt heavy, like a wet blanket tossed over the crowd. Felyra hadn't been close with any of the missing initiates, but hearing their names out loud turned her stomach.

The headmaster continued, "You eighty-seven who remain are one step closer to finding your role. In moments like this, when we lose some of you, I encourage you to remember why we're here. Kalshia took everything from us. They used to be our brothers and sisters, living in harmony. We trained with them, side-by-side. We shared resources and lived in peace, united in defense against whatever may come from over the mountains or across the sea. Then they kicked us aside, leaving us to flounder in the barren wasteland."

He paused, looking around the room and locking eyes with those listening. "You are the hope for the future. You are the ones who will save this kingdom, restoring it to life and prosperity. We train all of you the same. You have the opportunity to prove yourselves with the strength of your body, the skill of your blade, and the sharpness of your mind. Every one of you will have a place in the Thravian army. Each of you will have value. Although only six of you will receive a ring."

He held up his hand, showing off a large blue ring that reflected in the light of the lanterns, something only he, Captain Janduan, and Instructor Peveral had the honor of wearing amongst the teachers. "You will be the best of the best. You will be the leaders this army looks to and relies on—our greatest hope against the enemy. The next stage of training will be difficult. It will test you like never before. Only the strongest of you will keep up. Only the cleverest will rise to the challenge. Only the most skilled will master the control you need. Very few of you will have what it takes." He let his gaze sweep over the crowd. "What it takes to be Soulbinders."

A surge of adrenaline rushed through Felyra's body. It was the goal she'd made years before.

"Here at Soulbinder Academy, we take our job seriously, and that is to prepare warriors for Thravia. Whether you make Soulbinder or not, every one of you has a place here. Every one of you has a purpose . . . and that is to defeat Kalshia and their Lightbinders."

*Lightbinders.* The word fixed in Felyra's mind—the cause of so much pain and hardship. Her blood burned at their mention—a deep-seated anger that had simmered for years.

*I can do it*, she told herself. *I will become a Soulbinder, and I will kill any Lightbinder who gets in my way.*

After the assembly dismissed, Felyra walked with Ruane. When her friend headed toward the stairs, Felyra grazed a hand across her shoulder. "I'm going to let my parents know I'm home," Felyra said. "I'll be back by dinner."

Ruane flashed a knowing smile. "See you soon."

The guards nodded when Felyra exited the gate of Soulbinder Academy's fortress. Initiates were free to come and go as they pleased as long as they showed up for training, classes, and exams. She turned west, heading into the Shanticlear District.

The west end of Revalle held the dregs of the city. Although the entire city showed signs of wear on the buildings, nowhere was it more apparent than in Shanticlear. The winds from the mountains hit the walls hard, eroding the stone and wood and leaving dusty remains. The people who lived there focused on surviving each day. Making their homes look presentable was the last thing on their minds.

Surviving in Revalle generally meant one of two professions. Most were algae farmers, tending the land on the east side of Revalle between the city proper and the South Lagrash River. The thankless job kept everyone alive, although years of breaking up hard dirt and reaping off the ground left bowed backs and arthritic hands. Farmers fed their families with the output and sold any extra for what meager pay they could glean. The hardy crop replicated quickly, keeping the supply high and the price low, although both the taste and nutritional value of the algae left much to be desired.

Anyone in Shanticlear who wasn't a farmer was usually a stone collector. The job was simple to learn but even more demanding on the body. Soulbinders needed a constant supply of rocks, their most common weapon. The challenge was to find the right size. Pebbles that were too small had no bulk behind them, but rocks that were too large required too much space to carry and effort to move. An adept Soulbinder could make do with whatever they found in their surroundings, but all carried a supply of stones to be safe. True harvesters scoured the barrens of Thravia, searching for the perfect stones. They spent the entire day roaming the sunbaked land around the city, filling carts and wheeling them around until they returned, exhausted and aching before the sun set. Masons, on the other hand, looked for larger rocks, then broke them into the size and shape they needed.

Felyra's family's home emerged after she turned a street corner. The building had chunks falling out where the mortar between stones had eroded. The faded shutters that bordered the single upstairs window looked more gray than their original blue. They hung askew, barely affixed to the wall. A planter box displayed outside the window, but nothing grew out of it.

The elderly couple who lived on the ground floor sat on benches in front of the building. They lifted their heads at Felyra's arrival and flashed grim smiles.

"Felyra," Sephany said. "Still making it, I see. Nice work."

"Thank you." Her limp felt extra conspicuous as she passed by the building.

"Tell your parents 'hello' for me."

She nodded and rounded the corner, making her way to the western edge of Revalle.

The stone markers would have felt less ominous had grass grown between them. As it was, the field of graves was no more than a large patch of dirt with slabs separating one from another. Felyra turned at the third row and counted seven markers from the left. She slowed as she approached. The chiseled names of Evelone-el-Geralln and Nemorr-il-Perrez decorated side-by-side stones.

On her previous visit, Felyra had brought a chisel. Despite the stones being only two and three years old, the writing was barely legible, worn down by the caustic winds. Her finger traced the letters of her mother's name, brushing the accumulated dirt to the ground.

"I'm back," she said.

She pulled a bundle out of her pocket and unwrapped the faded roll of cloth. A small dead fish stared back at her with its lifeless eye. She stepped to the flat rock next to her father's grave and placed the offering flat on the surface. She glanced around with raised eyebrows but caught no signs of movement. After a sigh, she turned back to her parents' graves.

"I passed the wilderness test." Saying the words aloud sent a sense of pride rolling through her. "You'd be proud of me. I was up in the mountains." She raised a palm as if to stop their concern. "I know it's dangerous. It wasn't too bad, though. I had a fire to keep warm and caught fish like you taught. It was a nice break from all the algae.

"I can feel the difference after all my training. My limp isn't gone, but I'm able to work through it. I feel stronger." A smile flashed over her face. "You should see me run now. I'm not the fastest, but . . . I can keep up. It drives the others crazy, especially the guys. They're starting to respect me more." Her pulse quickened after the lie. She swallowed hard and thought of the boys in the bunk room.

"They don't, uh, pick on me like they used to, and I'm making a lot of friends." Her mind drifted to Ruane, but there was no one else she could put in the friend category. "No boys of note. The others in the academy are pretty focused on training, and I'm too busy to pay them any mind. I *did*, uh, meet one in the mountains—a Kalshian." She lifted her palm again. "I know. Don't worry, I was careful. His name was Kaleth. He was running from a slaver or someone. He was . . ." She was about to say "kind" when his comment about her scar came to her mind. Her involuntary grin turned down. "He was like all the others—cared only about himself. He didn't kill me, though, so that was nice."

A meow turned her head toward the rock with the fish. "Pawleen, there you are."

The cat had first shown up around the time she and her mother contracted the wasting disease. The animal had perched in her window when she lay sick in bed. Felyra laid out scraps of food, but the cat came even when she had none to give. After her mother passed, Pawleen nestled with Felyra in bed, purring with sympathy while she cried.

Felyra's healing had been long and painful. When her jaw locked, it took a friend of her father and a nasty-looking knife to get it working again. She wept when she saw herself in the mirror for the first time after. But Pawleen treated her the same, even after she received her scar.

The cat pawed at the fish head as if debating whether to drag it off or stay a moment. With another meow, it sat on its haunches and waited.

Felyra smiled and turned back to the graves. "So now I'm a step closer to making Soulbinder. I'm not sure what's next, but I'm ready. As ready as I can be, at least. Few are chosen, but I think I can do it. All my life, you taught me to be observant—to see people and notice things, to process many things at once. From what I hear, the instructors look for that." She shifted her hips, sending a twinge of pain down her leg and causing her to wince. "I hope you'll be proud of me. Once I'm a Soulbinder, I'll join the front ranks. I'll be at the tip of the spear when we attack. I'll be able to kill the Lightbinders." A tear pooled at the corner of her eye. "I'll make them pay for what they did to you, Father."

With a final *meow*, Pawleen slunk off with the fish in its jaws.

Felyra felt heavy walking back to the academy. Living after her parents had both died felt like a responsibility—like she owed it to them to do something great. All she could do at the moment was give her best during training. She hoped that would be enough.

# PART TWO

## CHAPTER SIXTEEN

# CLEANING UP

"Kaleth!" Jovi called as Kaleth entered the common room. A dozen freshly cleaned initiates lounged around, huddled into groups. "You made it."

Weary limbs made the walk difficult. Kaleth nodded and joined Jovi where he sat with three guys and two girls. "Yeah. It was no trouble. We camped last night on the road back. Just got in now."

"Was it cold?"

He shrugged. "I managed. How was the river basin?"

His friend's eyes grew wider. "I tried to set up a shelter in what turned out to be a valsic dragon's burrow." He laughed. "You should see those things move. Thankfully, I had a knife or I would have been a goner. I can't be sure, but I think one of the instructors actually placed it there on purpose—to test me."

Kaleth ignored the conspiratorial comment. "Your group lose anyone?"

Jovi's face fell. "Four. Garolin ate something bad. He was non-verbal and convulsing when the wagon picked him up. Died on the ride back. A valsic dragon got Anenya. Two others never showed. Don't know what happened to them. I heard the plains group lost four, too. What about you?"

"We lost Tyron." Kaleth's stomach formed a knot as he spotted

Rayd glancing his way from across the room. "We don't know what happened to him, either."

"You should hit the showers. The group from the plains is there now."

"Showers?"

Jovi grinned. "You ever used one before?"

He shook his head.

"Neither had I. Have fun."

Kaleth had heard of showers, but he thought they were only stories people made up of the wealthy. Binder heaters warmed water in pipes and binder pumps pushed water through them. It made no sense, but who was he to say what was possible?

After retrieving clean clothes from his room, he found the showers on the second floor. A wall of steam hit him when he entered. It felt like walking into a bathhouse, only hotter and steamier. Tile covered the floor of the rectangular room. Benches lined the exterior with hooks on the walls. Divided by tiled walls, eight curtains blocked the sound of washing initiates and splashing water.

The candidates from the plains were already there. Both guys and girls used towels to dry themselves. Most were modest, covering themselves as best they could while dressing, but some conspicuously were not.

A young man with sculpted abs and a towel around his waist spotted him, then nudged the young woman next to him. She had a towel around her body and worked another through her hair. When she looked up, she scowled at Kaleth.

He grabbed a towel from a stack and moved to a bench on the far side, where he set his clean clothes and tossed his dirty ones in a pile. His neck reddened as he hurried to an open stall at the end of the line, closing the curtain behind him. A lever stuck out of the wall. Above it, a thin pipe curved up and over to end at a silver disk.

*Curious.*

He lifted the lever, then jumped to the side as water spouted from the disk above. It was cold at first but warmed after a moment. When Kaleth ducked his head under the stream, it was as if his body melted into bliss. The steaming water drummed on his head and poured down his skin. He groaned aloud, uncaring that others could hear. With the hot water soaking him in its glorious bath, he realized how cold he still was inside. He used a bar of soap to scrub his body.

Dirt and grit sloughed off his skin and mixed with the slurry of water until it disappeared down a drain set into the tile. He could have stayed there for hours. He massaged his scalp and scrubbed his whole body twice. Mostly he just stood under the falling water, basking in the magnificent sensation.

With his eyes closed and back to the shower head, he imagined he heard the curtain moving. Two hands slammed into his chest, jerking open his eyes. Kaleth backpedaled into the tiled wall, barely keeping his feet under him. A towel-covered Rayd came at him with a similarly attired Roselle just behind.

"What happened to Tyron?" Rayd asked.

Kaleth ran a hand over his face to push away the water. With his back to the wall, he had nowhere to go. "I told you. I don't know." A fist slammed into his gut, bowling him over.

"Liar!" Rayd shouted. "What did you do?"

Kaleth gasped for breath. Each shuddering gulp of air did little to ease the searing pain. His eyes watered.

"You want me to hit you again?" Rayd asked. "Tell me the truth."

Kaleth lifted his chin, terrified it would receive a punch of its own. One hand blocked his stomach while the other tried to provide a modicum of privacy. Over Rayd's shoulder, he spotted other initiates past the pushed-aside curtain scurrying out of the room. "He's dead."

Roselle breathed in sharply. "You killed him?"

Kaleth shook his head, wincing. "I didn't kill him, but he tried to kill me."

"You're a bind-cursed liar," Roselle said.

Rayd's eyes twitched. "How did he die?"

The image of Felyra and her bow and arrow came into his mind. It would have been easy to tell them about the warrior villager from

Thravia, but he felt oddly protective. Kaleth winced as he stood up straight. "It doesn't matter. He's dead. You want to punch me again? It won't bring him back."

Rayd and Roselle didn't seem to know what to do with his uncooperative spirit. Roselle's eyes unabashedly scanned down his dripping body, prompting a smirk to grow on her face.

Rather than wait for another punch, Kaleth pushed past his assailants, bumping shoulders with each before going to dry off.

THE LIGHTBINDER common room was lively, filled with the remaining initiates who had survived the wilderness survival test. They swapped stories of their time in the wild, laughed, and poked fun at each other for their brushes with danger. Kaleth lingered by Jovi, who was telling his dragon story to a group of five other initiates.

After Rayd and Roselle arrived, Aurik called for the group's attention. "Congratulations on passing the first test. In total, we lost nine initiates, which brings the number of Lightbinder hopefuls down to forty-one."

A rumble of approval rolled through the room.

"Today, we split you into six squads. You will train, study, sweat, and bleed with your group. It's true that only a portion of you will make it to year two in this school, whether in Lightbinder or elsewhere. Your goal should be for everyone in your squad to be on that list."

*Like anyone will care about helping me through*, Kaleth thought.

"To keep the squads fair, the top six on the board will be squad leaders, and we'll let you choose your groups."

Kaleth groaned. *Great. Another chance for me to be last.*

Aurik called the first six names, pointing out different areas of the room for them to move to. Each of the squads received a name: Raven, Iron, Claw, Tiger, Dragon, and Wolf. Rayd bumped Kaleth's shoulder hard as he crossed through the room to take his spot as captain for the Dragon Squad.

Picks followed along the ranking list, with captains calling out names one at a time. The first time a name was skipped was when the Tiger captain skipped Roselle, the highest ranked female. Rayd smirked when he called her for his squad next.

The next time it made it around to Rayd's pick, he paused.

Kaleth glanced at the board and froze. Jovi was the next name in the ranking list. *No! Not him!*

The general's son scanned the room until he found Jovi. His eyes narrowed. Next to him, Roselle leaned in and whispered. He turned to her and frowned, mouthing something in response. She shrugged. After a long pause, Rayd sighed. He waved a hand toward Jovi. "Jovi Strapper."

Kaleth's heart sank. *Great. My only friend has to partner with those two.* Jovi groaned as he left Kaleth's side to join his new squad.

The names continued to be called, and initiates moved to their groups. Previous relationships prompted lower ranks to be called sooner than expected, but most choices went in order.

When "Chyla-el-Banere" was called to Dragon Squad, Kaleth's gut twisted. Only six names remained, and if no one took him sooner, that would leave him for—

Rayd's head jerked in his direction. The captain seemed to have realized it at the same time. He shook his head, then turned to Roselle, gesturing and talking quickly.

When the names dwindled to Kaleth as the last choice, Rayd stood tall and lifted his chin. "Pass," he said.

Kaleth wanted to shrink into the floor. As much as he didn't want Rayd to choose him for his squad, he never considered how much more embarrassing it would be to *not* be chosen. A rumble of mutters ran through the room.

"You can't pass," Aurik said. "Kaleth is the only choice left."

"Other squads may want him. I'm willing to take the disadvantage of being a person down."

Aurik considered it for a moment. "Other squads? Would any of you like the final initiate?"

Kaleth's neck grew hot as the room of perfect physical specimens stared at him. He tried to look casual, like he wasn't flexing his arms and inflating his chest, but the effort was futile. Even with the attempt to puff up his body, he was sorely lacking compared to the others.

No one spoke up. The captains didn't even look his way, as if eye contact might volunteer them to take the unwanted baggage that would drag their squad down. Jovi's eyes were the only sympathetic ones. Had he been a captain, he would have taken Kaleth on the first pick, despite being the weakest out there.

"Sorry, Rayd," the principal said. "Kaleth-il-Valorr is on Dragon Squad."

Kaleth hung his head as he walked to their corner of the room. Rayd and Roselle sneered as he joined them. Jovi held up a hand to clap with him in welcome. His roommate, Lainn, was also on Dragon Squad. He stood with the rest of the group, frowning. The four other boys were all several inches taller than Kaleth, and the two girls had toned arms that put his to shame.

Rayd leaned down and whispered in his ear. "Don't worry, Grunny. You won't be here for long."

"Each squad's leader will be the initiate with the highest rank."

Rayd's chest puffed even larger than it already had.

"As rankings change, your leader could change. They will decide your training routines, split you into roles during exercises, and assign work if an initiate isn't cutting it. They should be strong, decisive, and have a high motivation for their squad to succeed. Leaders sign off on their team's skill logs while they need to get an instructor to sign off on their own. Leaders, you want your squads to succeed, which will reflect positively on you. Be fair on skill log sign-offs but not too easy. Be tough on drills but not harsh. If you fail in your responsibilities, you may find yourselves slipping down the ranks and replaced by another in your squad. And if the rest of you feel you're not being treated fairly, come to me."

The tension in Kaleth's body eased at the final statement.

"Leaders, come here for your squad's schedule."

Rayd sauntered to the front and took a sheet of paper from the head instructor. Leaders from the other squads followed soon after.

"All of you will have conditioning, strength, and weapons training each day, which will take up your entire morning," Aurik said. "After lunch, squads will have a rotating schedule of classes in strategy, chemical sciences, wilderness survival, and leadership. Afternoons have a block of time for mandatory study. And at the squad leader's discretion, there's time for an extra training session of their choice either before or after supper. Questions?"

Kaleth had plenty but was too intimidated to ask.

## CHAPTER SEVENTEEN

# CHEMICAL SCIENCES

Lunch took place in the dining hall on the ground floor of Central Tower. When it was finished, Kaleth joined the members of Dragon, Claw, and Wolf in ascending a wide set of stairs to the second level. Their first class was chemical sciences, a subject he imagined would be more to his liking than whatever strength training would look like when it kicked off the next day.

The classroom was set up in stations. Two chairs sat at each of twelve rectangular tables covered with beakers, basins, droppers, and burners. One side of the room contained an enormous network of cubbyholes in varying sizes. Kaleth recognized chunks of minerals in some, but most held various organic matter in cases or suspended in liquid. The back of the room looked like a raised-bed garden with sprouting greenery and rows of vines crawling up a trellis.

"Whoa, cool," Garod said, one of the other lower-ranked Dragons. He ran a hand across a row of green fronds.

"I wouldn't do that," Lainn warned. Lainn ranked twenty-third and had warmed little toward Kaleth despite being on the same squad.

"Why not?" Garod asked.

"This is a chemical sciences class, right?"

Garod shrugged. "So, what?"

"I imagine we may deal with some dangerous substances."

"I doubt the instructor would leave dangerous plants sitting out for anyone to touch." Despite the confident words, Garod looked at his fingers and rubbed them.

"Or he might trust his Lightbinder initiates to be wise enough to leave them alone."

Kaleth leaned closer to the plant in question.

*Realm: Plantia. Category: Fern. Group: Broadleaf. Strain:—*

He chuckled to himself.

*Fire fern.* Garod would feel a tingle in his fingers soon, but it would be harmless. A good lesson either way.

A door at the front of the room opened and Headmaster Genoris entered wearing gray instructor robes. He walked to the front of the room and stood behind a long desk. "Welcome Lightbinder initiates! Welcome! Please, choose a station, sitting in pairs."

Kaleth joined Jovi at the closest desk.

"This class is chemical sciences. I've taught it for the last twenty years, and even though I'm the headmaster now, I wasn't about to give it up. Menders spend a bit of time with me before they head off to Twainford, but you Lightbinders are where my passion lies." He held a fist in the air, showing off his green Lightbinder ring.

Looking around sixty years old, the headmaster moved and spoke in a sprightly manner. His thick gray hair formed a wave that bushed on top of his head. His brown eyes would look dull if it weren't for the twinkle in them as he spoke.

"You are the strongest, the bravest, and the brightest. Not only will you be our frontline fighters, but you will infiltrate the enemy's bases. Some will go undercover. You will kill without being noticed. You will escape when captured. You must be ready to do whatever needs to be done. More than your skill with a blade, this starts with knowledge.

"In this class, you will learn the secrets of our natural world and how they interact. You will become masters of poisons. You will study minerals and chemical reactions. You'll work with acids and elixirs. When you're not in my class, you will read. One of the Lightbinder tests centers on what you learn in this class." The headmaster paused as a murmur ran through the class. "That's right. It will be halfway through the year. If you don't pay attention in class, you likely won't live through the test."

The statement didn't bother Kaleth, who'd been studying similar material for years. It was the other tests that gave him pause. His eyes drifted to Garod. The initiate sat at the station diagonally from his with drops of sweat covering his forehead. He clenched, unclenched, and shook his hand in a loop. Kaleth chuckled to himself.

Genoris waved his arm in a flourish. "You may be wondering how chemical sciences will help you as a Lightbinder. I'll give you an example." He bent over on the opposite side of his desk, then stood with two objects. He lifted a glass vial. "Who can tell me what this is?"

Kaleth squinted, trying to make up for his missing glasses. Blue powder filled half the vial. He glanced around to see if anyone was going to respond.

Genoris held on to the cork stopper and shook the vial. "It's an absorbency powder. It's blue."

Kaleth lifted his hand next to his ear.

Genoris lifted his eyebrows and looked his way. "Yes?"

"Potannium?"

The headmaster's face brightened. "Correct. Well done. While not common in Kalshia, it's more prevalent in Thravia because of their algae fields." He lifted another object—a vial of orange and brown shavings. "And this is oxidized iron. If I needed a distraction, does anyone know what I could do with these materials?"

Kaleth smiled, seeing where he was going.

"What about you?" Genoris pointed at Rayd, who sat at the desk in front of Kaleth.

The Dragon Squad leader slunk into his chair and shook his head.

Kaleth raised his hand again, more confidently this time.

"Yes?"

He sat up straight. "Mix them together, then add water."

"And how would that help?"

"You could run or attack or whatever during the cloud of smoke."

A smile grew on the instructor's face. "What was your name?"

"Kaleth, sir."

He brought a glass of water out from behind the desk. "Let's see if Kaleth knows what he's talking about." The oxidized iron clattered as it poured on the desk. Next, he took the stopper off the potannium and shook it over the scattering of metal. A hissing sound grew. It spit flecks of sediment into the air, curling a faint amount of smoke.

A desk up, Rayd leaned to Roselle and muttered, "Can't hide behind that."

After letting the objects simmer a moment, Genoris raised the glass, then tipped it. The liquid poured in a stream. When it hit the blue-and-orange pile, the faint hiss turned into a gushing roar. A wall of smoke billowed into the air, hiding the headmaster and the entire front of the classroom.

The initiates exclaimed in awe. Several chairs jumped back.

Jovi leaned toward Kaleth. "Nice call," he said over the roar of the reaction.

It took a moment for the smoke to settle, and when it did, a rumble grew amongst the initiates. The headmaster was nowhere to be found.

Rayd scoffed. "Anyone can duck behind a desk. That doesn't help much."

"True," a voice called from the back of the room.

Kaleth spun to find the headmaster leaning against the door they had entered at the back of the room.

"Ducking wouldn't help much, but a Lightbinder with knowledge of chemical science could use it to escape altogether." He proceeded down the center aisle of the room, nodding at Kaleth as he passed his station. "Nice work, initiate."

Kaleth tried to keep his smile reserved, but it threatened to take over his face.

The headmaster didn't break out any more demonstrations but dove into a lecture on chemical reactions. Kaleth found all of it to be review—topics his father had taught him years before. After an hour and a half, the rest of the initiates looked like their brains were about to melt. When class was dismissed, the initiates stood and headed toward the door.

"Kaleth," Genoris said, turning him around. The headmaster beckoned him to the front. "Spare a moment, please."

Jovi grinned. "Way to impress the headmaster," he said. "Good luck."

Unsure if he was in trouble or about to be congratulated, Kaleth walked against the crowd toward the front of the class.

"Come with me," Headmaster Genoris said when Kaleth reached the desk at the front. He walked to a door at the side of the room and held it open.

Outside the room, a stone hallway glowed with binder lamps. Genoris walked down the hall, then stepped into a small square room with no windows or other passages. Kaleth paused at the entrance.

Seeing his reluctance, the headmaster chuckled. "You've never been on a binder lift before, have you?"

Kaleth's eyes grew wider as he shook his head. He had only heard of the invention. Once he entered the room, Genoris pulled a lever on the wall. The room rumbled, and the floor shook. Kaleth's hands shot to the walls to keep from falling. The passage they had just walked through disappeared as their box moved upward. A strange sensation of pressure against his body made him feel heavy. Soon it lessened as the binder lift smoothed out its ascension. When it slowed, his weight moved in the opposite direction, as if he were being flung into the air by some unseen force. The lift stopped, and a new passage opened where the old one had been moments before.

The headmaster led the way down a short hallway that opened into a vast room. A massive desk stacked with papers and various objects sat facing two chairs and a cold stone fireplace. Bookshelves with innumerable leather-bound volumes lined the walls. The ceiling was conical with a circular lattice of wooden rafters, sloping up from all sides of the room to reach a peak at the center. Another hallway led off the opposite end of the chamber, and a door cut into the wall next to the fireplace.

"This is my office," Genoris said. "Last year I was in the staff quarters, but this summer I moved in here."

"It's nice."

The headmaster managed a mischievous grin. "You haven't even seen the view yet." Genoris opened the door and motioned for Kaleth to take the lead.

When Kaleth stepped forward, his jaw dropped. A circular stone balcony extended from the tower. He walked to the end and set his hands on the railing. Kalistor Palace filled his sight. The keep was the only structure other than the Lightbinder's tower that rose above the fortress walls. The bulk of the keep was impressive. It contained jutting towers, sloped roofs, precipitous walls, and countless windows. Looking down showed him the roofs of the academy buildings, the Grand Courtyard, and the rest of Sky Fortress. They all seemed cobbled together in a patchwork of tile.

To the north, over the gap that separated them from the plateau, Kalistor glowed in the afternoon sun. The capital city looked healthy and vibrant, emphasized by the greenery growing everywhere and the deep blue of the waterfall that tumbled from its edge. In the other direction, miles to the south, the greenery faded, giving way to the barren lands of Thravia. Behind the towering keep, the Kalshian Mountains dominated the view, maintaining their snow-capped wall to the west.

"Quite the view," Kaleth said.

"I come out here to think. It feels good to monitor our enemy." He pointed south. "You see it there?"

Kaleth followed the headmaster's finger. The air was clear. He imagined he'd be able to see the city of Revalle as a speck on the horizon, but without his glasses, it was a blur.

"Revalle. Where the enemy makes their plans to attack us. Their Soulbinder Academy is very similar to ours. Did you know they came from here? Before the war, we trained Lightbinders and Soulbinders together, here in Kalistor."

He shook his head. "No, sir, I didn't. What is a Soulbinder, exactly?"

"Your mortal enemy. A Soulbinder is the only thing that might threaten a Lightbinder. If you run into one, kill them before they can kill you. We'll talk about it more in school. All in good time, though."

"Why'd they leave?"

Genoris frowned. "They betrayed us." He stared to the south in silence. His jaw clenched as if remembering a past injustice.

Kaleth sensed he wasn't getting any more information about their rivals. "What about Lightbinders? I see these binder lifts, binder cannons, and, of course, binder lamps. How does that work? Do you . . . capture energy in an object or something?"

A grin formed across the headmaster's face. "Very good. It's a lot like that. Energy comes from light—the sun, fire, even reflections—and it's put into objects like a lamp or a cannon. Then those objects release the energy when we tell them to."

"Like shooting a cannon or raising a lift."

"Or lighting a lamp. We're even experimenting with lightning."

Kaleth cocked his head. "What do you mean?"

"It can be captured like anything else. What do you think happens when it's released?"

He sucked in a long breath. "I can only imagine."

Still grinning, Genoris waved Kaleth to follow him toward a set of steps that descended from the side of the balcony. "I'm curious about you, Kaleth. That's why I asked you up here. I always take an interest in the top candidates of the academy. I get to know them and help guide them if needed. You stand out but not in the ways I'm used to seeing."

Kaleth began down the steps. "Um . . . thank you?"

"Your knowledge in class impressed me. First years rarely have much grasp on the elements before they arrive. Where did you learn?"

"My father taught me."

"Is he a scientist?"

"A sage. Valorr Gooding."

The headmaster nodded as if the name was familiar. "Interesting. And here you are, training to be a Lightbinder." After descending the steps, they reached a flat area of the roof where they had to walk around a massive decorative stone. Kaleth considered what a monumental task it must have been to get something like that up there. A structure with short walls and an angled glass ceiling waited on the other side of the stone. Genoris pushed open the doors. "You may recognize some of what's in here."

Kaleth entered. When he stepped into the rooftop building, the temperature rose. Herbs, plants, and vines formed rows growing from raised dirt beds. "It's a greenhouse."

"It's one of the few places in the fortress that receives enough sun."

"Sporadicus fern. Tenthalite. Morbius sprout." Kaleth pointed to a squat green frond with yellow flowers at the end. "Is this yellow-hearted vetril?"

The headmaster nodded with a grin.

Kaleth stepped back, keeping his hands far from the fronds.

Genoris laughed. "It won't jump out and bite you. Do you know what vetril is used for?"

He shook his head.

"Most people don't. It's a subverter."

"Interesting," Kaleth breathed.

"You mix this with a common poison like berryflayer, and the usual cures won't work. You'd need something with a heavy concentration of redroot to neutralize it." He pointed to a leafy stalk sticking up in the back row. Where the stalk met the ground, its green changed to a sharp red before it disappeared under the dirt. "Thankfully, I have that as well. But yes, I grow many specimens. I create salves, poisons, and antidotes. We use them for the army's supplies as well as for Mender training and our chemical science class." He pointed at a row of vines hanging from a trellis. "I even make my own wine—a hobby of mine."

Kaleth scanned his eyes over the plants. "I've spent a lot of time in the wilderness. Many of these, I've never seen."

"I'm very proud of my collection. Most Lightbinder initiates couldn't identify all that you just did."

Kaleth felt smug but tried to avoid showing it.

"As you saw, none of your classmates knew what you did about potannium and its reaction. I assume time around your father was to thank for that."

The reference to his father felt like a knife in his gut. He managed a nod. "He taught me a lot."

"Why are you here, Kaleth?"

His lips parted, then remained frozen. He was not prepared for the question. *Do I tell the truth about the debt? Do I lie about always wanting to be a Lightbinder?* "Does it matter, sir?"

Genoris chuckled. "Not to me, but it will to you. Training to be a Lightbinder is one of the most difficult tasks in all of Verdalyn. You compete against the best. Every task is arduous, and the consequence of failure is often death. No one gets where you are lightly or without serious thought."

*Without serious thought?* Kaleth laughed to himself. *He's wrong about that.*

"I grew up poor on the outskirts of Lynharbor. I came here because I wanted to make a name for myself. I was tired of people ignoring me, so I vowed to stand out—to be someone who left a mark on the kingdom. When you're being pushed to your limits, only one thing will keep you going, and that's your answer to the simple question, 'Why are you here?'"

"I guess . . . I'm here to protect my family."

The headmaster raised an eyebrow. "Noble. Personal. But unusual."

Kaleth frowned.

"We typically get young muscle-bound men and women with dreams of glory. They want the prestige that comes with being part of an elite force. With that comes ego, pride, and selfishness. But you seem to have none of those. You look like you could barely carry a jug of water, and you don't seem interested in personal glory." A smile grew on his face. "I like you, Kaleth. Instructors aren't supposed to play favorites, but I hope you do well." A furrow dug into his forehead. "Watch out for the other initiates. I know what challenges are coming, and they're going to be difficult. You'll need to dig deep and train hard if you're going to survive."

"Yes, sir. Thank you, sir. I will."

"Tomorrow morning is your first conditioning and strength class?"

He nodded.

The headmaster's lips pressed together. "Good luck."

CHAPTER EIGHTEEN
# CONTAINMENT GLYPH

Bells followed by a rapping sound on the door jolted Kaleth awake. "Five minutes! Binder Court for conditioning. Don't be late!"

Kaleth wiped his bleary eyes as he propped himself on an elbow. The open window filled the room with a crisp breeze that helped rouse him. The night spent in his dorm bed had been a welcome change from the cold ground of the mountains. Despite having been warmer and more comfortable, he had hardly slept. His body was tight and stressed. His mind had spent most of the night anticipating the physical punishment that was to come.

Lainn was already awake. He sat on the edge of his bed and fiddled with the leather seams on his boots as if they were out of place.

"Not looking forward to this," Kaleth said, trying to achieve a lighthearted tone.

His roommate rose and grabbed his jacket. He paused at the door. "You coming?"

"Yeah." Kaleth pressed his hands against his face and groaned. "I'll be there."

Lainn left without another comment, pulling the door shut behind him.

With the room empty, Kaleth fell back on his bed and exhaled. *Five minutes. I can afford a moment.* He cycled through ideas of what awaited him downstairs. He couldn't imagine any scenario where strength and conditioning training would help distinguish him from the other initiates. It was bound to be embarrassing, and it was sure to be painful.

Voices drifted through the window where other initiates must be gathering in the courtyard below. He sat up and groaned. As much as he wanted to avoid what came next, the last thing he wanted was to make it worse by being late.

He stood, grabbed his clothes, and got dressed. When his boots were tied and his jacket was buttoned, he blew out a deep breath. "Can't delay it any longer." He grabbed the knob of his door and turned it, but when he pulled, the door didn't budge. The knob slipped through his fingers, and he frowned. He tried again, gripping tighter and pulling harder. Nothing budged.

He looked at the bottom of the door to ensure nothing blocked it. He twisted the knob again, but the door bolt spun freely. *What is going on?*

"Hello? Is someone out there?"

He imagined other initiates pulling the knob from the opposite side, trying not to laugh out loud.

"Lainn? What did you do?"

He leaned his ear against the door and froze. No sound echoed back.

No longer trying to be delicate, he banged his fist against the wood. "Hello! Can someone help me? The door is stuck!" He pulled again, jerking his body in pulsing attempts to yank it open. After several tries, he stopped, breathing heavily. *What is going on?*

A gasp filled the air as he sucked in an involuntary sharp breath. The door hadn't budged, and the startling truth hit him. It didn't even rattle in its casing. That wasn't the sign of a lock that wouldn't open. *It's the sign of a containment glyph.*

Kaleth had only cast one once. His father had him practice at their home, trapping Sora inside, but he had never had a valid chance to use it after that.

*But who here would know how to use it?*

He banged louder, shouting and kicking against the door. No one replied, and the door didn't budge. As time ticked by, he grew more desperate. Being ranked last in the academy was bad enough. Showing up late to conditioning would only make things worse.

He rushed to the open window and stuck his head outside. A couple dozen initiates gathered in Binder Court three stories below. He sucked in a breath to shout but then stopped with full lungs. *What am I doing?* How would it look for the last-placed initiate to get stuck in his own room, yelling down to be rescued? That would be worse than showing up late.

The open window of the room next to him caught his attention. Four feet of mortared stone filled the space between the sills. He didn't know their names, but a Wolf and Iron initiate stayed there. He leaned forward to judge the distance. *I can reach it.*

A gust of wind ruffled his hair, making his stomach jump. His eyes drifted down. With a racing pulse, he imagined what would happen if he fell. The risk was too great. It was ridiculous to consider, but the alternatives were few. He looked at the window again. The chances of him making it to the window were much higher than the chances of his rising to the top six ranking in Lightbinder Academy.

*I'm a goner no matter what I do. But I might as well not turn the principal against me out of the gate.*

Holding to the side of the window, he hopped both feet on the sill. A momentary balance check forced his hand to grip tighter.

*This is a bad idea.*

More initiates had arrived in the courtyard. They would be starting at any moment.

Kaleth pivoted both feet to where his toes pointed toward his room. He braced his hands against the opposite sides of his window, then craned his neck to check the distance. It was a stretch but doable. *I'll be able to reach it.*

He scooted his feet toward the right side, then worked both hands to the same edge of the window. Leaning his body to the right allowed him to grip with his left hand. One finger at a time, he released his right. A swooping feeling rushed through him as he stretched his arm over the open space.

*Not far enough.*

The stone wall was smooth, too smooth for his fingers to grip anything. He needed to lean more. His heart jumped in his chest. With only two points of contact on his window, his body swung.

*No! No! No!*

He gripped tighter and lowered his center of gravity. The swinging stopped. His right foot and hand dangled over the drop. His boot scraped the stone, finding nothing that amounted to any semblance of a foothold. His palm pressed flat against the wall. The skin on his fingers found the slightest purchase.

Kaleth swiveled his head, sighting the other window. A wave of dread rushed through him.

*Still too far!*

With his body drooping, his arm couldn't reach. He dug the toe of his boot into the wall, fighting for any grip that would allow him to push against it. While he strained his toe, he pulled against his left hand, trying to lift himself higher. His left foot felt useless until he pulled back against the edge of the window. The effort brought him closer to the wall and allowed him to rise higher. A surge of hope ran through him. With nothing to grab, he couldn't creep his fingers across the surface, but he could lean farther.

His left hand held tighter as he angled his body. His foot pulled back, straining to keep his body close to the wall. His right hand drew nearer. *Only a few inches more.* His palms filled with sweat. His pulse thundered in his ears. He tried not to think about the yawning drop below him, but the wind ruffling his hair made it impossible to forget. His right foot scraped the wall, losing the tentative grip it had. His left hand held on with all its might. The sweat building under his fingers made the effort increasingly impossible.

For a second, he considered giving up and returning to his room. But that would leave him back where he started. Plus, he wasn't sure he'd even be able to get back to his window.

A fresh placement for his boot gave him a boost of confidence.

He leaned with fresh vigor. His fingers stretched. They touched the edge of the opposite window's casing. *Almost there!*

He loosened the grip with his left hand, allowing his hold to slide to the tips of his fingers. Across the gap, his fingers inched around the window casing. His tips touched the window. He tried to grip it, but he couldn't yet. His left hand slipped farther, and he felt his body losing it. When his fingers gave out, he gasped. He held nothing but air. With no grip on the wall, he pushed with his left foot. Angling farther, the fingers of his right hand slid past the inner edge of the opposite window, unable to grasp it.

*This is it. All the planning to save my family—the risk of joining the academy. It was all for nothing.* He prepared for the drop—for the eventual crash of broken bones and pain.

His body fell to the side. He was about to yell when his fingers wrapped around the bottom ledge of the window and caught. Higher than his head, his left foot lost its perch and slid off the sill of his window. While his legs swung like a pendulum, he slapped his left hand to join the right. It held, too. Holding the window with both hands, the weight of his swinging legs tried to yank him off the wall. Somehow, his tenuous grip didn't break.

He allowed a quick smirk before putting all his focus on getting inside the building. He pushed his toes against the flat wall while he pulled up. He gritted his teeth, grunting as quietly as he could. He slung one bony elbow over the lip, then the other. His arms scraped as he wriggled himself through the opening.

He collapsed on the floor between the beds of the other dorm room and allowed himself a quick moment to lie on his back. His arms ached. His legs quivered. He gasped for breath from the quick but sudden effort. *I can't believe I did that! If only Father could have seen it.* Valorr would have been terrified that he attempted it but proud that he made it.

Aurik's commanding voice outside the window jolted him to action. Kaleth jumped to his feet and peeked out the window. No one looked up. His high-flying actions had gone unnoticed. Filled with the renewed fear of being late, he hurried out the door, relieved that it opened without trouble.

Having made it to the hall, he stopped outside of his room. He ran his eyes along the doorframe until he found it. The containment glyph had been carved on the left post near the floor. The circle with the three arced lines was clear to see, even though it had already begun to fade after having achieved its purpose. Anger burned through his veins. As if he didn't have enough stacked against him, confirmation that someone had tried to stop him made him even more upset.

"I'M HERE!"

All eyes turned to Kaleth as he jogged to join the other initiates in the center of Binder Court.

Aurik paused mid-sentence from his speech. "Tardiness doesn't help if you're trying to rise in the ranks, Kaleth."

"I'm sorry, sir. My door was stuck." He narrowed his eyes and looked at Lainn. "I won't let it happen again."

His roommate cocked his head with what looked like a curious expression.

Aurik cleared his throat. "As I was saying . . . conditioning and strength are vital for all Lightbinders. You will chase down enemies. You will carry heavy weapons and wear armor. You will battle a dozen fighters at once. Without conditioning, you will not survive. It will be an integral part of your training this year. If you cannot handle it, you won't be here long."

As much as the talk of conditioning dismayed Kaleth, he had other problems on his mind. He sidled next to his roommate while everyone listened to the principal.

When Lainn noticed his presence, he angled his head and whispered. "Stuck door? That's pretty weak, Kaleth. Especially when your roommate made it on time without trouble. Maybe next time, you just get up when I do, huh?"

He didn't hold the vitriol back. "Maybe if my roommate wasn't trying to sabotage me, I'd be more willing to stick with him."

Lainn frowned. "What do you mean?" He wasn't taunting. He

wasn't playing coy. His brows knitted together. "Why would I sabo-tage you?"

Kaleth was ready to shoot back a retort, but the point was valid. Getting rid of him accomplished nothing positive for his roommate. "You didn't . . . *jamb* the door after you left?"

"No!"

The heads of nearby initiates turned at the emphatic word.

"I closed the door, so you'd have privacy to change, but I didn't —" He shook his head. "No."

Kaleth swallowed hard. *Someone* had cast that glyph. He soft-ened his tone. "Was there anyone else in the hallway?"

Lainn paused as if thinking. "No one in the hallway, but I passed Rayd and Roselle lingering by the stairwell on the third floor."

*Of course.* He found Rayd in the crowd. The squad leader had been watching him but his gaze jerked toward Aurik when Kaleth looked in his direction. *That's just great.*

Aurik clapped his hands together, wrapping up his speech. "With that said . . . who's ready to get started?"

The crowd grunted in affirmation while the pit in Kaleth's stomach widened. Escaping from his room felt like a victory, but the real problem had yet to begin.

## CHAPTER NINETEEN

# IRONBALL INTRODUCTION

"To warm up, grab a small ironball." Aurik gestured toward a pile of rounded, gray spheres. "Your job is to carry the weight on your shoulder and jog through the main corridor inside the fortress. Jog past the Grand Courtyard, then head to the entrance gate. Once you reach it, come back to the Lightbinder doors. Complete that length four times, then return here to Binder Court. Do *not* turn around early. Shortcuts in training will affect your performance in the tests. Squad leaders, make sure your teams do the work. Remember, you live and die by your squad. Don't leave anyone behind."

Rayd turned toward Kaleth and glared.

"Okay, squads. Go!"

The other six members of Dragon Squad ran toward the pile of weights. Feeling less enthusiastic, Kaleth jogged behind. The ironballs turned out to be exactly what they sounded like: balls of solid metal. Each weight had a colored handle sticking out of the side. The initiates each selected one of the smaller balls with green handles.

Kaleth wrapped his hand around one and tried to lift it to his shoulder like the others. When the ironball passed his hip, his arm gave out. He dropped the ball back to the ground. Ignoring the frown from Rayd, he lifted the object again, using his left hand to balance it as he moved it to his shoulder. It was heavy, but when perched on his shoulder, the burden felt manageable.

Jovi bounded up, seeming as if his own burden was made of air. "Everything all right? What happened to your door?"

Kaleth's thoughts were on the balancing weight. "I'll fill you in later."

In the pile of weights, he spotted larger ironballs with yellow handles. *I hope we don't have to lift those to our shoulders.*

"Dragons, let's go!" Rayd called.

Rows of massive red-handled weights caught Kaleth's attention at the far side of the pile. Blood drained from his face. He might not even be able to lift those off the ground. *It's all right*, he told himself. *One thing at a time*. With the small ironball on his shoulder, he jogged after the other initiates.

Navigating through the passages of the Lightbinder building kept everyone's speed slow. When they exited the facility, initiates spread out in the wider corridor. Kaleth wanted to pick up speed, but as soon as his mind formed the thought, his legs felt heavier. His body slowed. While he struggled, the other initiates seemed to flourish with the increased room. Their strides increased, lengthening the distance between them and Kaleth.

His lungs no longer felt fresh. An ache grew in his legs. Every step put him farther behind the others. By the time he passed Central Tower, the rest had already exited the far side of the Grand Courtyard. When he entered the open space, he glanced at the stage on his right. The memory of committing himself to the elite school ran through his brain.

*I wish there had been another option.*

When he made it to the opposite end of the courtyard, other first years were already passing him on their return trip. Rayd ran with Roselle, keeping his head up, avoiding eye contact with him. Kaleth angled to get out of the way, but Rayd's trajectory adjusted with him. Kaleth stepped aside more purposefully, but the other boy followed. About to collide, Kaleth spun at the last second, taking the brunt of a hard shoulder against his chest and dropping his ironball.

"Watch it," he shouted.

Rayd and Roselle laughed, looking back over their shoulders and smirking.

Kaleth rubbed his chest and allowed himself a moment to take a few deep breaths. His legs thanked him for the reprieve, but he needed to keep moving. Lugging the weight back to his shoulder, he resumed his slow jog.

When he passed Jovi a moment later, his friend paused. His brows pinched together. "You making it?"

Kaleth struggled to answer the question. Jovi turned and backpedaled, waiting for a response while distance grew between them. "I'm fine," he finally managed. The other initiate frowned, but all Kaleth could do was turn around and continue moving.

Any other initiates were a speck in the distance by the time he turned at the fortress gates. The visual reminder of his lack of ability sprouted tendrils of despair in his mind. *How can I ever hope to beat any of these people?* His legs plodded forward but felt as if he ran on stumps. His lungs begged him to stop, but he continued. Even though the pace was barely faster than a walk, he kept going.

*Four laps*, he thought. *I can do this.*

As the multiple trips down the corridor progressed, the other initiates passed him sooner and sooner. While he rounded Central Tower on his second return trip, the lead runners lapped him, wrapping up their third lap before he'd finished his second.

"Move it, Grunny! You're a disgrace to your squad!"

Kaleth jumped at the words yelled at his back. Moments later, Rayd thundered past, looking as strong as he had when they had first started.

During his third trip, the rest of the initiates lapped him. Jovi gave him some encouraging words, but they did little to boost his spirits. When Kaleth lumbered back to the Lightbinders' door for the third time, the six other members of the Dragon Squad were the only ones remaining in the corridor. Several leaned against the wall as they waited on him.

"Finally," Roselle muttered as he approached. "We're gonna look like idiots to the other squads."

"They won't judge us all based on one person," Lainn said.

Rayd blew out an exaggerated sigh. "Enough rest, squad. Let's go."

The five initiates bent over to pick up their weights.

Slowing to a stop, Kaleth's gut twisted in a knot. "This is . . . only three," he uttered between gasps.

Rayd turned toward him. "What?"

He gulped. "This is my third lap." He sucked in more breaths. "I still have one more."

Everyone but Jovi erupted in groans.

"Forget it," Rayd grumbled, waving the group toward the door. "It won't matter. We look bad enough as it is. Let's go."

Approval to skip a lap gave him a surge of hope, but Aurik's words about taking shortcuts rang in his head. *If I'm going to make it through this, I need to do the work.*

Kaleth shook his head. "I need to do one more."

A fresh round of groans rang in the air.

Jovi picked up his weight again. "I'll run with you."

Kaleth would have smiled had he not been too exhausted.

"Come on, Jovi," Roselle said. "Your squad leader said we go."

"And our school principal said to not leave anyone behind," Jovi said.

Rayd pressed a heavy finger into Kaleth's chest. "He doesn't count. He shouldn't be in our squad. But if you two want to run another lap, have fun. The rest of us are going back."

With his weight on his shoulder, the squad leader entered the building. Roselle, Garod, and Chyla followed on his heels. Lainn stayed behind.

"You gonna run with us, too, Lainn?" Jovi asked.

The other initiate shook his head. He placed his weight on the ground, then adjusted it to where the handle ran parallel to the wall. "I've done my work. It doesn't make sense to go again, but you're right . . . Aurik said to not leave anyone behind. So, I'll wait."

Kaleth nodded. "I'm sorry, guys. I know I should just head back, but—"

"Don't apologize," Jovi said. "You're doing the work and not taking the easy way out. That's gutsy. I'd offer to carry that weight for you, but ..."

"I've got to do it."

Jovi nodded. "I figured."

Feeling less alone than he had during his entire time at the academy, Kaleth began his last lap with a friend by his side. Jovi didn't talk, just ran with him, matching stride at a much slower pace than his usual.

On the return trip, a line of six jogging initiates caused Kaleth to forget his fatigue for a moment. Five young men and one woman jogged in a row with yellow ironballs on their shoulders. They ran in perfect cadence at a faster rate than Kaleth could have even managed without added weight. It was the second-year Lightbinder initiates. They didn't even spare him a glance as they passed.

"You think we'll look like that next year?" Jovi asked when they had passed.

The question caught Kaleth off guard. He played into his labored breathing to explain his slow response, but the reality was he hadn't pictured himself being alive the next year. "Yeah, I think so," he answered.

When they rounded Central Tower, a surprising sight waited at the end of the corridor. Lainn was there as expected, bending to pick up his weight when he saw them. The shock was the other three members of their squad. Kaleth wanted to thank them for waiting on him, but the scowls on their faces showed a reluctance to be there.

"You all change your mind?" Jovi asked as they slowed.

Rayd huffed a mumbling response, then picked up his weight. "Let's go."

Lainn leaned toward Kaleth and Jovi when the others had left. "Aurik made them come back and wait."

Kaleth's stomach dropped. *Another reason for them to hate me.*

He continued down the corridor, following Rayd and the rest of their squad. When they arrived back in Binder Court, the other groups snickered. They were already working on a series of strengthening exercises, but all Kaleth could think about were his jelly legs, aching lungs, and sore shoulder.

"Dragon Squad, you need to do better," Aurik barked.

The hair on Kaleth's neck bristled at the reprimand.

"The rest of us were fine," Rayd said. "It was—"

"*You* are squad leader, Rayd-il-Stonne," Aurik said, getting in Rayd's face. "The results of your squad are your responsibility. Get it together. The other squads have already started, so each of you grab another green weight and follow what they do."

The enraged look Rayd leveled in Kaleth's direction could have melted iron. "You heard him," he grumbled to his squad. "Grab another weight."

The movements they had to do were past Kaleth's ability. The initiates pressed the weights over their heads. While keeping them up, they lunged the length of the courtyard. They performed squats, push-ups, sit-ups, and a move where they had to lift the weight from the grassy courtyard to above their heads in one move.

Most initiates struggled. They could manage a handful of moves, but then tired. They often took breaks while Aurik or their squad leaders yelled at them to keep going.

Kaleth could barely complete a single movement. Only being able to get one weight above his head, he dropped it every time he tried to lunge. He managed a few push-ups until Rayd forced him to set the weight on his back like the others. Then he just collapsed on the ground. Sit-ups were manageable until he reached the count of ten, when his abs decided not to work anymore. His body felt like a beat-up mess that dripped sweat and hurt everywhere. Every attempt he made felt weaker as his muscles wore out. When Aurik called for the initiates to stop, Kaleth collapsed to the ground and rolled onto his back, sucking in air.

"That was rough," Jovi said, leaning over with his hands on his knees. "I can barely feel my arms anymore."

"Yeah," Kaleth muttered between breaths, relaxing his head against the grass. "I couldn't—the weights—"

"What are you complaining about, Grunny?" Rayd said. He kicked Kaleth in the side, not hard enough to hurt, but enough to be annoying. "You didn't even do anything."

Roselle snickered beside the squad leader.

"Give him a break," Jovi said. "He's trying his best."

"That's his best? I'd hate to see what his worst looks like."

"And his name's Kaleth."

Rayd's eyebrows lifted and his mouth pulled into a scornful smile. "To me, he's a bind-cursed piece of trash from Grunwind who has no right to be in this school or in my squad. So, I'm gonna call him *whatever I want!*"

The other squads looked their way, and an awkward silence filled the courtyard.

The squad leader muttered, "How could anyone respect this?" as if speaking to himself. His voice caught. Something deep inside tugged at unseen emotions.

After a moment, Rayd looked at Kaleth and returned his voice to a regular volume. "You're holding our squad back and making us all look bad. It's an extra training session for you. Back here before supper. Jovi, since you seem so ready to defend him, you'll work him out."

Kaleth's heart sank. Not only would he have to do more work, but now his only friend was being dragged into it, too. He pushed himself to a sitting position, his abs groaning from the effort. "Why'd you trap me in my room?"

Rayd's jaw tightened. His eyes flicked to Roselle's before turning back. "Why would I care to trap you in your room?"

"You tell me. Do I intimidate you? Do you think I'm a threat to take your spot in the top six?"

Rayd's bellowing laugh bounced off the courtyard walls, so loud it felt forced. "Take my spot? Hardly." His voice was strained.

"Why do you desperately want me out?"

Rayd froze like he'd been caught cheating on a test. His neck undulated as he swallowed hard. "Any fool would know that." He cleared his throat to fix the breathy catch in his words. "You bring our squad down. You just proved that with this morning's embarrassing display. And worst of all, you make me look bad." He bent down closer to Kaleth's face. "Of course, I want you out."

"How did you—" Mentioning glyphs would invite questions. He lowered his voice. "On the door frame, that was you? You know how to . . . ?"

Rayd stared back, still as stone.

*Fine, don't admit it.*

Aurik clapped to get everyone's attention. "Some of you performed well in that session, but most of you were sloppy and weak. The next Lightbinder test is one of strength, and it will be here before you know it. If you want to have any chance of surviving, I suggest you figure out how to do better here. Now, bring your weights." He motioned for the spread-out initiates to gather around him.

A hand appeared in front of Kaleth's face. He took it and allowed Jovi to pull him to his feet. "Don't worry about Rayd. His father dropped him on his head when he was young."

Kaleth's legs wobbled, but he remained on his feet. "He's not wrong about my strength, though. I just don't have it."

"Yet," Jovi added while they walked. "You don't have it, *yet.* Some people are born with it, but most have to work for it. This is your time to work."

Kaleth nodded. "I just hope there's enough time until that test. And I hope for the sake of my body that we get to rest from now until our afternoon session."

"How are you all feeling?" Aurik asked when everyone had arrived around him. "Tired?"

Mumbles of affirmation answered back.

The principal smiled. "Good. Now it's time to run again."

Kaleth's head drooped. *So much for a rest.*

## CHAPTER TWENTY

# THE BLOCKADE

Felyra's stomach dropped when she rounded the corner. A tight ball constricted inside her, sending waves of nervous energy shuddering through her body. She had imagined running the Blockade dozens of times, but there was a difference between visualizing it and facing it herself.

A narrow path of wooden slats was elevated off the ground. The boardwalk stretched across a field, turning back on itself twice to make three lengths of obstacles. The first section tested balance. Much of the path was no larger than the width of a boot. Gaps in the course required jumping to narrow planks at varying heights and angles. Near the end, a straight section passed through a gauntlet where other initiates waited to hurl swinging sandbags. Felyra had seen many young men and women taken out by an unsuspecting bag when they kept their eyes too focused on the path. Only about half the initiates made it through the balance section. She was determined to be one of them.

The middle part of the Blockade required focus. The path was wider but filled with obstacles trying to knock the initiate off. Ropes ran from a box to the edge of large wheels that hovered over both sides of the path. From the spokes of the looming devices dangled wooden boards, heavy ironballs, and oversized sandbags. When the box was activated, the wheels turned, creating a dizzying array of objects dancing in and out of play along the entire section. Hesitating initiates were taken out by a swinging object they had overlooked. The success rate of the middle portion was worse than section one.

For the few initiates that made it to the final length of the Blockade, the obstacles grew even more dangerous. Instead of dodging sandbags, initiates had to keep their eyes on swords and axes. Propelled by more ropes, various weapons swung and jabbed along the length of the path. The section required those running the path to have a mastery of both balance and focus, but the true test was their bravery. It was rare for any initiates to make it through. Most fell off while dodging a weapon. Several froze in their tracks, refusing to move forward. The previous year, one initiate had even died, or so Felyra had heard. An axe ripped a gash in a young woman's leg, cutting an artery. The initiate bled out in seconds on the grass.

Standing in front of the starting platform, Captain Janduan rested his hands on his hips and scanned the crowd of initiates. "The Blockade will test your balance, focus, and bravery. If you want a shot at becoming a Soulbinder, you need to stand out. And they'll be watching." He nodded toward a row of instructors seated along the closest battlement—four men and one woman. Headmaster Baloran took the spot at the end of the line. "You get two tries, then you move on. Falling is a fail. Freezing in fear is a fail. Dying is definitely a fail."

He waved a hand toward the wooden box where the ropes emerged. As if responding to his will, the ropes moved, pulled back and forth by an invisible force, controlled by soulbinding.

"Line up and get going."

Felyra's heart beat steadily, thumping in her head. Her hands felt clammy as the clump of initiates jostled for position.

Four near the back of the line headed to the sandbag gauntlet. Grinning, they took positions on platforms, pulling the dangling bags next to them to be ready to hurl at the initiates who made it that far.

The first to climb the ladder to the starting platform was her squad leader, Fenris. The young man's blue eyes lit up with eager anticipation. He held back his broad shoulders, staring down the course he was about to attempt.

Going first showed courage and initiative, but it also was risky —not getting to learn from the failure of others. Felyra was content to meld into the line near the back.

"Fenris Wardragon. First year," he called out, looking up toward the battlement.

The instructors each turned to papers in front of them and scribbled the start of their notes.

Fenris paused only a moment at the edge of the platform before surging forward. His steps were light and purposeful. He navigated the straight, narrow beginning portion, holding his arms out on each of his sides. At the end of the path, he jumped without hesitation. His body looked light, touching down on angled blocks before leaping to the next. He whisked through the next sections, pushing at what Felyra thought was a reckless pace.

It was impressive on its own to make it through the sections of the Blockade, but to truly impress the instructors, initiates tried to be the fastest one to do so. Even if someone failed, a performance could still impress if the portions they completed were quick and confident. While Felyra wanted to be fast, her primary goal was to keep from falling off.

Fenris slowed for the first time when he arrived at the gauntlet. The closest sandbag swung on its rope just ahead of him, having been flung by a too-eager initiate. Fenris crept forward on a narrow beam, eyeing the remaining three bags. He scurried ahead of the next one but took the third on the shoulder. While his arms windmilled, the final bag tipped his balance past what he could recover. He dropped to the dirt and released a frustrated groan.

His second attempt looked similar to the first, but he timed the gauntlet better. One bag glanced off him, but he avoided the others. The watching crowd applauded when he arrived at the end. Fenris gave a quick wave, then turned his attention to section two. Rotating obstacles swung and danced along the precarious route.

The young man passed a half-dozen of the impediments until an unseen baton took out his legs and knocked him off the course, onto his back.

Before he even hit the ground, the next challenger was already mounting the ladder to get ready. The instructors' heads moved to their papers in unison as they all scribbled something about the fallen Fenris.

The candidates continued one after another. Most uttered cries of disgust when they fell, landing on both feet after losing their balance. A few took nasty hits to the head against the wooden slats of the course. When they collapsed to the ground on their back or side, the crowd gasped. They generally recovered after a moment, but one young woman was so dazed, she had to be carried off.

"Graxon Thunderfoot. First year."

Felyra cringed as she turned to the start of the course, where Grax faced the wooden path. As much as Felyra hated to admit it, he made the challenge look easy. The balancing during section one appeared to come naturally. His eyes darted between the swinging obstacles as he danced his way through section two. He wasn't the first to complete it, but he was the first who didn't break a sweat while doing so. She wasn't counting in her head, but his speed had to have been the fastest yet. His smirk faded when he approached section three. Steel scraped as swords jabbed in and out. He took a moment to glance down the path.

"You've got it, Grax!" Thaylor yelled from where he waited by the ladder.

Grax moved forward. He ducked and twirled, inching along the path. Felyra wished a blade would catch him by surprise—not to kill him, but to cut him enough to leave a nice scar across his face.

A yelp made her jump as Grax clutched his shoulder and fell off the path. She held her breath. Guilt crept into her mind for wishing him ill, but after a moment, he waved at the crowd to show he was all right.

After restarting section three, his second attempt made it only slightly farther. He passed the place where he had previously fallen but lost his balance after ducking under an axe. Felyra released the tension she had held, thankful to not have to hear him bragging about completing the course.

After a few more initiates, Felyra found herself at the ladder. Rather than put off the inevitable, she climbed it after the girl in front of her fell in section two. When Felyra stood, a rush of heat crept up the back of her neck. All eyes were on her. Ruane nodded in encouragement, but her legs still wobbled. She glanced up at the wall where the instructors waited.

"Felyra Nightwind," she croaked.

The garbled sound earned a few snickers from the crowd. She clamped her jaw shut, cringing as a familiar pop resonated through her skull. She imagined the scar on her chin but avoided touching it as she usually did to ease the pain when her bones clicked. When she turned to face the course, the only thought in her mind was that she had forgotten to tell her year.

*I can tell them, but I'll sound like an idiot adding it on now. Does it matter though? They know what year I am. But will not saying it show I can't follow instructions? Is it worse to do nothing or to look foolish by admitting I forgot?* She shook her head. *All they see is a girl with a chin scar. I don't need to give them one more thing to laugh at me about.*

"Hello?" Captain Janduan said in an agitated tone. "I said . . . year?"

Her ears grew even hotter. The crowd all looked at her, waiting. *I'm so stupid! I didn't even hear. Chin scar—that's all they see.*

"I'm first scar," she blurted.

She tried to swallow the words back. It was too late. The other initiates roared with laughter until a sharp rebuke from the watching instructors quieted them. She wanted to run. The platform she stood on looked like a nice place to hide underneath. Her entire body was tense, burning with embarrassment. She forced a mumbled, "I meant *year*. First year," from her mouth.

Felyra turned away from the lingering snickers that surrounded her and faced the narrow path ahead. It looked even narrower up close. She stood at the edge of the platform and took a deep breath. Her boot toed the line where the first section began.

*Forget about them*, she told herself. *Fast and confident. Balance . . . you can do this.* She lifted her arms by her sides and stepped forward.

The memory of laughter faded. Her confidence grew with each step. Feet tracked in front of each other. With her arms out, she felt solid and balanced. She moved quickly. When the gaps arrived, she didn't pause. She leaped over the first space, alighting with one foot on the narrow landing. The following jumps felt rhythmic. She danced across the gaps with solid feet and confident posture despite the dull pain throbbing from her hip down her bad leg.

The angled portion that followed required her to run, bounding to the opposing ramps before her feet lost their purchase. She stepped over logs and ducked under barriers, all while keeping her center of gravity under control. Her confidence wavered when she arrived at the final challenge of the first section.

Grax stood on the first platform, smirking as he held a sandbag waiting to be flung. "Come on, Cripp," he taunted. "Show us what you've got."

Felyra waited, hoping he would swing the bag prematurely. She feinted a lunge forward, but he didn't bite. Her feet inched forward on the narrow beam. She held up her hands, ready to deflect the projectile.

Grax's eyes narrowed as he pulled his bag farther back. The rope it dangled from was taut. The muscles in his arms bulged, ready to fling the object toward her.

Another step. Eyes locked. She held her breath.

He faked a throw, but she didn't fall for it.

Another step. She was nearly past him. *Can I make it without him throwing?* She pushed one hand against her hip, trying to press out the ever-present pain in her leg.

*Slam!*

A heavy object collided with the side of her head. Her view of the world shifted as her body fell. Grax and his un-thrown sandbag turned sideways. His mouth dropped open before a howling laugh pierced the air.

It took Felyra a moment to realize what had happened. She'd forgotten about the other three initiates waiting to knock her off the beam. Time seemed to slow as she tumbled off the course. Failure and humiliation were all she could think about until her head hit something new. An unyielding edge of wood—the side of a platform.

The light dimmed as her body crumpled to the ground. The last thing she remembered before passing out was the surrounding peals of laughter.

CHAPTER TWENTY-ONE

# TORCH TATTOO

Walking with Jovi, Kaleth stumbled into the dining hall, mentally and physically exhausted. His squad mate had taken it easy on him during their late-day training session, letting him move as slowly as he needed and pretending not to notice when he skipped reps. Kaleth's legs still felt like noodles. He expected each step to be his last before collapsing onto the ground, but somehow, he kept going.

The savory scent of meat made his mouth water. They joined the curving line that stretched from the entrance of the hall, around the side, and to the back of the room. Lainn brought up the rear and turned when they arrived.

"How was it?" the other initiate asked.

Kaleth barely had the energy to grunt, so he felt relieved when Jovi gave a generic response of, "Not bad." Despite the words being incorrect, he didn't have it in him to correct him.

Jovi leaned closer to both Kaleth and Lainn. "Be careful with your food. They may try to poison it."

Kaleth groaned and then pinched the bridge of his nose.

"That doesn't make sense." Lainn cocked his head. "We're academy initiates. It would be counterproductive to try and kill us."

Jovi shrugged. "Could be a clever way to test us—see who is

smart enough to detect it. All I'm saying is be careful if your food smells like berries."

"Berries?" Lainn said. "So what if there are berries in the food?"

"Not all poisons smell like berries, Jovi," Kaleth said.

Jovi shrugged again. "Ignore at your own peril."

The oversized room was square with curved lines twisting into designs across a vaulted ceiling of rich wooden beams. Chandeliers of binder lamps dangled over twelve long wooden tables with benches on either side. Menders already filled half the seats, identifiable by their black-and-blue jackets. On the opposite side of the room, Lightbinders filled in the other tables.

The line continued forward, and soon Kaleth took a bowl and a spoon from a stack of dishes. Grunts in brown waited behind a counter with disinterested frowns on their faces. One scooped a heaping serving of stew into his bowl and the next broke off bread to hand to him. A third filled cups with water from a pipe. He turned a knob on the top and water ran or stopped, depending on which direction it turned.

*Wow, that's handy.* Kaleth thought.

Jovi lifted his plate to his nose and inhaled.

Kaleth rolled his eyes. Still, he leaned his head slightly forward and sniffed. All he smelled was meaty stew. No berries. He laughed at himself, then shook his head. Loaded with a plate of food and a cup of water, he followed Jovi to the tables and sat across from him and next to Lainn.

"Even though eighty percent of us aren't supposed to live through this year, I prefer the all-or-nothing method of the Lightbinders," the well-built initiate next to Jovi said, talking around a mouthful of stew. "Can you imagine trying out for the Blades only to end up serving food to everyone else like those Grunts?"

Lainn shook his head while using his spoon to arrange similar ingredients together in his bowl. "That doesn't make sense. You can't know if you'd prefer something if you've never experienced it."

The initiate sighed. "I'm saying I'd rather be dead than be a Grunt."

"Yes, but you can't *know* whether—"

"We know what you're saying," Jovi interrupted. "Both of you."

"Have you two met Lorenzo?" Lainn asked. "He came with me from Lynharbor."

Kaleth nodded at the initiate with short brown hair and a thick beard.

"You're Raven Squad, right?" Jovi asked.

Lorenzo nodded, swallowing another mouthful. "I've been training for this since I was a kid. My father was a Blade—served for twenty years until he caught a dagger in the kidney from some Thravian who ambushed their camp at night. I'm here to get even. I want to make them pay, and what better way to do that than by being the best there is? So it's Lightbinder or nothing for me." He pulled the collar of his jacket back to reveal a tattoo of a torch under his collarbone. "Torch. Light. Lightbinder. I thought it was cool."

Despite Lorenzo's impressive form and driven attitude, Kaleth remembered him in spot thirty-six out of the forty-one left. He marveled at the young man's determination.

His rumbling stomach reminded him to not forget about the food sitting in front of him. He spooned a mouthful. The stew was hearty, filled with beef, potatoes, and carrots. If there was a bright side to him surviving a few days with the Lightbinders, it was the food he got to eat.

"What's your story?" Lorenzo asked. "Kaleth, right?"

"Yeah," he mumbled, covering his mouth.

"How does someone like you end up with us?" He held up a hand in apology. "Sorry, I don't mean it as an insult, it's just . . ."

"It's all right. I know what you mean." Kaleth swallowed. "To be honest . . . it was a series of unfortunate events, culminating in me acting out of ignorance." He chuckled. "I knew nothing about this place or what Lightbinders were."

Lorenzo whistled. "Rough luck."

"Now I'm just trying to make the best of it." In the quiet that followed his words, Kaleth's ears grew hot. He sensed someone close, as if a body hovered over him.

Jovi's lifted eyes looking past his head confirmed it. He turned to find Rayd's imposing form looming.

"How did he do?" The question was for Jovi, but Rayd stared at Kaleth.

Jovi cleared his throat. "He did . . . great. We repeated some of this morning's exercises. He kept up."

Rayd sneered and puffed a burst of air out of his nostrils. "Do it again tomorrow. I want him working every day until he's either dead or is no longer embarrassing me."

Kaleth's heart dropped. The day had been brutal. Hearing he had to repeat it indefinitely was a tough blow. When the squad leader left, the appraising look on Lainn's face piqued his interest. "What?"

Lainn cocked his head. "You may not be the typical Lightbinder candidate, but I have to say, I'm impressed."

Kaleth's sinuses cleared. *What?*

"You're clearly outmatched. There is little hope you'll survive the year, but . . . you're here. And you keep trying. Commendable."

Kaleth smiled. "Thanks."

"Although your judgment may be questionable, your brain is sharp, as we saw in class with the headmaster. If you can somehow get your body in shape and learn how to fight, you may have a shot."

*Learn how to fight*, Kaleth thought. Of all the things his father had taught him growing up, that one was skipped. But it wasn't the only thing he didn't teach him. The day in the woods with his father's secret ability came to mind. *Speed, strength, power. That's what I need. If only I'd been able to learn it before he died. That's what I need to make it through this school.*


"Kaleth."

The voice sounded distant.

"Kaleth, hello."

It felt closer. Through much effort, Kaleth blinked his eyes open and found Aurik standing at the entrance to the common room, propping his hand on the wall. The presence of the man who had ruined his mother's life jolted his body with adrenaline.

"Head up to your dorm," the principal said. "I imagine that would be more comfortable and restful. Training will begin before you know it."

Kaleth discovered a book with plant diagrams laying open on his lap. He wiped a cold wet spot on his cheek. "What time is it?"

"Just after midnight."

The common room was empty. He had fallen asleep reading, searching for anything that would help explain his father's ability. "I'll head up."

"Just so you know, I see your effort, Kaleth."

The words were not what he expected. They eased the simmering anger, but it was far from gone.

"We want everyone to work hard, but some coast because they have natural ability. What you've shown so far . . . that's what I want to see from everyone. Just thought you should know."

An unbidden smile worked across Kaleth's face, but he quickly forced it away. Unable to bring himself to thank the man, he managed a nod of acknowledgment.

Aurik left and Kaleth re-shelved *Forces of Nature, Energy Explained* and *Plants: A Discourse*. He didn't remember having fallen asleep, but he remembered not finding anything helpful. He sighed. *There's got to be something, somewhere that can help, and I'm pretty sure the powers these Lightbinders have are linked.*

The scrap of paper his father had left him wouldn't leave his mind. Curved lines and the letter F. *What do they mean?*

Leaving the common room, Kaleth paused at the steps to the dorms. The memory of the vaulted ceiling of the dining hall came to his mind, spiking his adrenaline. *There were curved lines there. Could they be related?* He set a foot on the steps but didn't continue up. After wavering a moment in indecision, he turned and headed down the hall.

No one was out that late. He navigated the empty Lightbinder halls and the deserted main passage of the fortress. Binder lamps illuminated the path, and a smattering of stars interrupted the dark cloud of blackness in the sky.

He felt exposed. He wasn't doing anything wrong, but sneaking around after midnight would raise questions if anyone found him. The creak of the Central Tower doors made him cringe when he pushed them open. He glanced over his shoulder. No one was there. Taking a deep breath, he entered the building, passed through the exterior hallway, then entered the dining hall.

The lamps were low, but they provided enough light. A shiver ran down Kaleth's spine. The hall was empty. It felt strange. The savory smell of meat from earlier was gone after the Grunts had packed up and cleaned. A pungent odor remained. It reminded him of vomit and rotten eggs but had a hint of sweetness to it.

His eyes lifted to the ceiling and squinted to help with his blurry sight. The curved lines intersected and crisscrossed in a similar pattern to his father's glyph. It didn't form a circle, though, and he couldn't find any F letters hidden in the design. *It's similar, for sure, but . . .* He sighed. The similarity didn't help him understand anything more. It explained nothing about his father's power or help with his current predicament.

A yawn forced its way out. His thoughts turned to morning conditioning, and he decided the best thing he could do at the moment was to get whatever sleep he could. He turned and trudged toward the door. As he spun, the rotten odor strengthened. *What is that?* Something on the back wall caught his eye. His feet stopped. His arms and legs trembled. He covered his mouth, forcing back a gag reflex.

A lifeless body of a young man stuck to the wall, attached as if hanging on a hook. His eyes were closed. His pale face was frozen, contorted in a scream of pain. With his jacket unbuttoned, a horizontal slash across his belly spilled guts down to the floor.

Kaleth's eyes locked on the young man in the red-and-black jacket. His short brown hair and thick beard could be a number of people, but the tattoo was unmistakable. With the jacket hanging loose, an inked torch stuck out from the young man's undershirt. *Lorenzo.*

After having handled his father's body, seeing death up close did not rattle him as he would have expected. All he felt was numb. Lorenzo had been like him, though, young and eager. He felt for whoever the young man left behind, but after living each day prepared to die at any moment, Kaleth found himself surprisingly callous.

Words written on the stone wall caught his eye. He stepped closer and squinted. Painted in blood, the now-dried letters had dripped at the corners.

———

*Death comes this year to the academy.*
*Leave while you can, or all will die.*

———

THE THREAT SEEMED NO LESS dangerous than daily life as a Lightbinder initiate, but he found the message curious. *Who did this?*

Footsteps worked their way past his ruminations. His gaze drifted above the hanging body to find Headmaster Genoris looking down at him from the staircase on the opposite side of the wall. "Kaleth, what are you doing here?"

He jumped. "Nothing!" An icy hand of fear gripped his throat.

The instructor's brow furrowed as he completed descending the flight of stairs. "Nothing? What are you looking at?"

Kaleth flicked his eyes between Lorenzo and the headmaster as he stepped away. He sputtered sounds but nothing that formed words.

Once down the stairs, Genoris rounded the banister and gasped. He stood still and remained silent for a long moment. "Did you do this?"

"No! I swear, I found him just now."

"What are you doing here?"

"I-I was hungry. I came to see if there was any leftover food."

The headmaster didn't reply but stepped closer to the body. He ran his eyes over the victim. His jaw looked tight as he read the scrawled words in blood. "Who else knows about this?"

Kaleth shook his head. "I don't know. I just—I just showed up, and it was here."

Genoris turned from the body to face Kaleth. The tension in his face softened. "Are you all right?"

Kaleth swallowed a lump in his throat. He forced a nod. "I think so."

The headmaster entered an alcove by the door and grabbed a thick rope from where it was tucked against the wall. He pulled down, and a bell rang out. Once. Twice. The resonance echoed through the hall.

"Return to your dorm," Genoris said. "The staff will be here soon. I will fill them in and we will handle this." His eyes turned hard. "Don't speak a word to the initiates. Someone wants to spread fear and disrupt what we're trying to do."

"But who?"

"We'll get to the bottom of it. Now, go."

Kaleth nodded, then walked toward the door, his eyes glued to the dead initiate. When he exited the hall, he took in a deep breath. Fresh air filled his lungs. It pushed most of the scent of death from his nostrils, but some lingered. His shoulders released their tension. His arms relaxed.

When he drew near the Lightbinder building, Aurik exited the doorway and startled. "Didn't make it to your room yet, huh?"

Kaleth put his head down. "I'm heading there now."

Before he passed through the doorway, more adults in gray robes caught his eye, down the corridor to the left. They made their way from the staff quarters—summoned by the bell, like Aurik.

As he navigated the Lightbinder hallways, he couldn't shake a question—something that nibbled at his mind with no logical answer.

*What would make someone inside the academy want to kill everyone?*

CHAPTER TWENTY-TWO

# STRATEGY CLASS

No word of the mysterious death spread the following day. As the headmaster requested, Kaleth kept quiet despite wanting to say something to Jovi and Lainn. Still, he listened in on conversations, expecting something to come up. Aurik gave him a suspicious look during conditioning but said nothing.

During lunch, the dead body and the smell of death were gone. Not even the bloody lettering remained. The explanation for Lorenzo's disappearance was that he quit and left overnight.

The class after lunch was called Strategy. Kaleth had been looking forward to it due to his love of beating his sister in strategy games. He, Jovi, and Lainn walked up the grand staircase and began down the second-floor hall toward the classroom.

"I still don't get Lorenzo quitting like that," Lainn said, taking long strides to step over the repetitive cracks in the floor.

Kaleth's stomach clenched.

"I've known him since we were little. This was his sole focus growing up. He wanted to be in the army, and he wanted to be a Lightbinder. It makes no sense."

"Yeah." Kaleth cleared a catch in his throat. "It is odd. He seemed like a good guy."

"He knew how tough this training would be, but even then, he would have told me if he was going to quit."

"I'll bet something else is going on," Jovi said. "A secret we're not supposed to know."

Kaleth's heart pounded. The phantom smell of death fixed in his mind.

"Maybe the school eliminated him," Lainn suggested. "Either way, he knew the difficulty when he signed up. We all did."

"Well . . ." Kaleth started.

Jovi chuckled. "Well, maybe not all of us."

The strategy classroom was down a hall from where they had chemical science. Individual desks were arranged in neat rows with the instructor at the front of the room. Kaleth took a seat next to Jovi.

"Welcome to your first class on strategy," the professor greeted.

He looked to be in his mid-thirties with straight brown hair. No Lightbinder ring adorned his finger, and judging by the shelves of bandages and salves around the room, Kaleth assumed he doubled as an instructor for the Menders.

"I am your instructor, Beram. Lightbinders are not only faced with challenging situations when in battle, but they often advance to become captains or generals. Strategy makes the difference between winning a battle and winning a war."

Kaleth straightened in his chair, focusing.

"Strategy is planning ahead. You must evaluate a situation and project both possible and likely outcomes. A plan that only focuses on what's *likely* is doomed to fail. You must have given thought to what is *possible* because that is where even the best strategies unravel. Know the goal. Know the obstacles. Consider ways to get around obstacles and achieve the goal while minimizing risk. No strategy is perfect, and no plans are foolproof. How could we recruit Loravis as an ally against Thravia? How could we position ships in the Silver Straight to neutralize Carrvorre's navy? If Thravia wanted to break prisoners out of Morvask Keep, how would they do it?"

He paused, letting his words sink in. "Let's practice. Imagine you're a Thravian and Sky Fortress holds something valuable that you want. Only accessible from inside the fortress walls, it's buried in a chamber deep underground, locked behind a door that is protected by two Lightbinders."

Kaleth's interest piqued again.

"When Thravia infiltrates our fortress, they don't storm the castle, and they don't raze the city. They scurry through our tunnels to try and steal this hidden object . . . theoretically. Imagine you're the enemy. You're outside the walls of this academy and have an army at your disposal. What strategy would you use to get in and steal this hidden object?"

The class was quiet for a long moment.

An initiate from Iron Squad raised his hand. "Attack with a large force at night?"

Beram raised his eyebrows as if waiting for more. "Is that it?"

"Um—" The initiate's eyes grew larger until he shrugged.

"That's not a strategy, it's a tactic. Strategies involve multiple tactics with contingencies for when they fail."

Lainn lifted a hand. "Night is a good time because most of the academy will be asleep, but a large force would be more likely to raise an alarm. I'd attack with a small force—eight people. Take out the guards on the walls or sneak past them. Once inside the walls, they can find their way down to the hidden chamber and kill the guards."

"Kill the guards?" Beram repeated as a question. "The Lightbinders? How?"

"Um—" Lainn's confidence faltered. "I-I don't know."

"How would you get past the fortress walls?"

Lainn shook his head.

"I'd attack during the day," Rayd blurted.

"Oh?" The instructor's eyebrows raised. "Why's that?"

"Sure, people will sleep at night, but guards will be on alert. They'd expect an attack. I'd wait until there was an event or ceremony—something distracting."

"What's your name?"

"Rayd-il-Stonne."

"That's right. The exal general's son. Inspired idea, Rayd."

"To get over the walls, I'd use grappling hooks," Rayd continued. "Scout from the nearby hills to find the area that's the least guarded. Have two people scale it at the same time so they can watch each other's backs. Once they're in, take out any nearby guards with bows. Then either let others up the walls or open the gates."

"And how would you get past the Lightbinder guards in the hidden chamber?"

Rayd paused. "Poison gas?"

"Is that a question?"

"No, sir." He sat up straighter. "Mix up some sort of gas and toss a container of it in the room. If the guards stay, they die. If they try to flee, we cut them down."

Beram nodded. "Not bad, initiate. There are plenty of holes in your strategy, though."

Rayd frowned.

"What if guards on the walls see your grappling hooks? They could cut the ropes before your scouts make it up, or at least sound an alarm. The battlements are open and visible. If one guard was taken out, it would be easy for others to notice. Infiltrating with a stealth group is harder once an alarm is raised. Whatever distracting ceremony you were counting on to help would be moot. And gas in the chamber is not a bad idea. You might have to wait longer than you like to let it clear out, but it's possible."

Beram turned to the rest of the class. "Strategy is about anticipating what could go wrong and minimizing the risk of failure. What could be done differently in this scenario?"

No one answered.

"What would you do to increase your odds?"

Kaleth lifted a hand. "Start a year ago."

Soft chuckles from other initiates filled the room.

Beram didn't laugh. "What's your name?"

"Kaleth-il-Valorr."

The instructor strolled down the aisle toward him. "Go on, Kaleth."

Rayd angled in his seat and glared at him.

The back of Kaleth's neck grew hot. He cleared his throat. "To have a better chance against Lightbinders, I'd have more people. From what little I know about their abilities, I imagine a handful of people would struggle, no matter what tactics they use. That many people would be difficult to sneak in, but what if the rest of the guards and the people inside Sky Fortress were dead?"

More laughs filled the room.

"Everyone dead?" Beram said.

"That's right. A while ago, I would have had a young-looking Thravian fighter pose as a Kalshian and join our academy."

The other initiates in the room grew quiet.

"Ideally a few of them—to try for Lightbinder. Have them train and learn the ways of the academy. After a while, whoever's still here will have skills, connections, and trust. Living and training inside the fortress gives unique access to a lot of things. They could share secrets with the enemy, take out guards, leave the fortress gate unlocked . . ."

A horrific thought came to Kaleth. *Lorenzo's dead body in the dining hall! Could insider spies from Thravia have killed him?*

"Excellent thought, Kaleth," Beram said.

"If everyone in the academy were dead, I could stroll through the gates with as many people as I wanted. There would be no help for the Lightbinder guards against my large force."

"And how would you kill everyone to begin with?"

His mind stopped working. All he could think of was Lorenzo's face frozen in agony. "I-I don't know."

"Initiates are vetted," Rayd said. "It wouldn't work. You list your family when you sign up, and they're checked out."

The instructor nodded. "It's true. They are. Still . . . is it impossible?" he shrugged. "Promising idea, Kaleth."

Kaleth beamed and Rayd scowled at him.

"In this class, we will go through many exercises like this. The purpose is for you to practice critical thinking, anticipating problems, and minimizing risk. A well-planned strategy is more likely to end in victory, but even the best plans go wrong at least once. Your job is to ensure errors are salvageable. For now . . . let's move on."

Beram headed back toward the front of the class. "Another exercise you will get used to in here is games of strategy, pitting you against each other. Can I have two volunteers?"

He reached the front of the class and turned. No one in the class responded. "Very well," he said. "Let's start with our two strategy titans. Kaleth and Rayd, come up please."

Kaleth's stomach jumped. He slid out of his chair.

"Good luck," Jovi whispered.

Beram squatted behind his desk, then lifted a wooden object. When Kaleth saw the pieces, he held his breath. It was a kamak board.

Roselle chuckled. "Put him in his place, Rayd."

The smirk on Rayd's face was so sharp it could have cut metal.

Beram set the board down and had the initiates face each other. "Do you both know how to play?"

Kaleth nodded.

"Yes," Rayd said, still smiling and already positioning the black pieces on his three rows of the ten-by-ten board.

"Rayd won the Kalistor Open this year," Roselle shouted.

The instructor raised his eyebrows and nodded before turning to the class. "Kamak is the ultimate test of strategy, foresight, and responding to your opponent. A plan is only good until your adversary pulls it from beneath you. Two towers you must protect, eighteen knives who move one space in any direction, eight swords who can move up to three spaces, and two warriors with unlimited range. To win, threaten one of your opponent's towers with two pieces."

Predictably, Rayd set up in the Tyrashian defense: two towers clustered in the corner, surrounded by a row of knives then a row of swords. It was how he had won the championship match in the tournament. Kaleth remembered his play—patient on defense and ruthless on attack, carving through his opponent's field with warriors.

Kaleth placed his first tower on the right side of his board, one space off both edges. Rather than group the other tower next to it for easy defense, Kaleth placed it on the opposite side.

Rayd snorted a laugh.

"What?" Kaleth asked, second-guessing his unconventional setup.

Rayd shook his head, smirking. "Nothing."

Kaleth completed his setup, spreading his white knives, swords, and warriors throughout his squares.

"Only ten seconds per move," Beram announced to the class. "After one warning, time violation calls from the judge result in a double-move by the opponent. You don't win by thinking through every outcome because of the pace of play. It's achieved by thinking quickly."

Rayd picked up a knife of each color, rustled them in his hands, then held out closed fists. Kaleth tapped the one on the right. Rayd's smug grin grew as he opened the hand to reveal a black piece.

"Black begins," the instructor announced. "Players, are you ready?"

Kaleth nodded. His heart pounded.

"The rest of you, pay attention. At the end, we'll discuss their tactics and what could be improved."

Rayd scanned the board without a care showing on his face. He touched one of his central knives and waited.

Kaleth lifted a clammy hand, ready to respond. The pause seemed to last forever. When Rayd finally moved his knife forward, Kaleth's clumsy fingers knocked a middle-row sword over by mistake. He scrambled to set it back up, then countered with a knife of his own.

The play was fast. As most openings went, they alternated piece exchanges. Twice, Kaleth tried to set up a double-single exchange, but Rayd wouldn't take the bait. As the board cleared, space to maneuver grew, signaling the true beginning of the match.

Rayd was the first to move a warrior. He moved it to the center of the board, just out of reach of Kaleth's pieces. On his next move, he slid his other warrior diagonally forward, stopping it in line with its pair.

Kaleth inhaled sharply. He had a sword positioned three diagonal spaces away that could take it. *Was that a mistake? Did he not see my piece?* He hovered his fingers over the sword. His mind played through the next moves in his head while he counted: *Four . . . five . . . six . . .*

He saw it. It was a masterful setup. A classic double-warrior gambit. He baited Kaleth to take the powerful piece, which would leave one of his own towers exposed to the other warrior. One threat was nothing to worry about, but a lurking sword waited within striking distance to get the lock on Rayd's next move.

"Time warning for Kaleth," Beram said.

Kaleth moved a knife a single space, ignoring the tempting capture of the warrior. Sweat beaded on his forehead.

Rayd shrugged. "Too bad. I was hoping for a quick finish. Either way, I'll just take this."

Kaleth's stomach dropped. He saw the move before his opponent touched his piece. The sword slid three spaces through the gap he had just created, capturing one of Kaleth's warriors.

Mumbled comments echoed through the class.

Kaleth took the sword with his adjacent knife, but the exchange did little to ease the sting.

With a two-to-one warrior advantage, Rayd went on a devastating offensive push. He took knives and swords left and right, clearing out Kaleth's side of the board. He arranged several single threats on a tower, but Kaleth thwarted the game-ending locks by blocking or scaring off the attacking piece.

With little time to think between moves, Kaleth turned his attention to the opposite side of the board. *I won't win by just moving around in defense.* After a positioning move of Rayd's that didn't threaten anything, Kaleth slid a knife toward his opponent's cluster of towers.

Rayd frowned. His fingers had hovered over his attacking warrior, but he paused to check out his tower arrangement. After a shake of his head, he moved the warrior as planned.

Kaleth ignored the predictable attack Rayd planned. Instead, he moved a sword two spaces across the gap.

Rayd followed through with his planned next move, taking a knife and threatening the sword that waited diagonally behind it.

Kaleth ignored it again, moving his piece a space farther, putting him in position to attack two different swords and double-covering himself from behind.

Rayd touched his warrior but froze. His eyes traced the path Kaleth's pieces made, and lines formed between his brows. Kaleth counted in his head. Rayd removed his finger from the warrior.

"Time warning for Rayd," the instructor said. "The next violation for either player results in a two-move penalty."

Rayd abandoned the warrior he wanted to move. He grabbed one of his vulnerable swords on the opposite side of the board and grumbled as he moved it out of the way. Allowing a hint of a smile, Kaleth picked up his piece and took the other one.

The minor loss rattled Rayd. No longer could he focus solely on attacking. His eyes shifted across the board between moves. The glisten of perspiration formed on his brow. His following moves were cautious. Both players pushed the limits of their time.

Rayd moved a sword within striking distance of one of Kaleth's towers. "Threat."

Kaleth scanned the board. One of Rayd's warriors could achieve a lock in two moves. He moved a knife to block the path.

"Threat," Rayd said again, moving his other warrior to the opposite side of the board.

Kaleth's pulse quickened. Both his towers were under threat, and he couldn't defend each of them. A handful of moves from one of a few different pieces could complete the lock. His own pieces dwindled. Only one warrior, two swords, and a half-dozen knives remained. He held his breath, counting the seconds. When he reached *six*, he turned his focus across the board and moved a sword three squares toward the corner.

Without even a single threat, Rayd had little to worry about. He moved a sword around a knight, staying one space out of reach.

*He has three moves until lock.*

Kaleth slid his lone warrior six spaces to pair it with his attacking sword.

Rayd answered by moving a warrior. He flashed a cocky grin. "Two moves until lock."

Kaleth returned a smirk of his own as he touched his sword. "Are you sure about that?" In a smooth motion, he slid his piece two squares to take one of Rayd's knives—a knife that bordered both of Rayd's towers. "Threat."

Rayd's smile vanished. He stared at his own towers, eyes flicking to each piece while his mind scrambled to calculate. "How would you—?" His hand hovered over the board. "You can't get to me."

Kaleth held his smile. He kept his arm close, ready to make his next move.

Rayd's hand moved back to his attacking warrior, but his confidence in his plan seemed shattered. His fingers hovered, but his eyes remained on Kaleth's attack. "You don't have it." His focus turned back to his original plan.

"Time violation," Beram called. "Two moves for Kaleth."

"Bind and break me!" Rayd yelled.

Kaleth sucked in a breath. Grinning from ear to ear, he moved his warrior past both towers. Using his second turn, he slid the piece around the back, taking an unsuspecting sword and placing not one but *both* towers in game-ending locks.

"Lock," Kaleth said.

"Double lock," Beram clarified. "Incredible. Kaleth wins!"

The class erupted into applause.

Rayd stood in a huff. "It's not fair! He didn't have the move and made me take too long."

"He didn't *make* you do anything," the instructor said over the uproar. "Strategy takes many forms. Sometimes playing your opponent is just as important as playing the pieces."

Kaleth's pulse pounded in his head. He glanced at the other initiates, smiling at their cheers. Jovi pumped his fist from his seat.

*Who knows?* Kaleth thought. *Maybe I'll actually have a shot at this.*

## CHAPTER TWENTY-THREE

# KNIFE INSTRUCTION

After a crushing morning of conditioning, Kaleth groaned at the sight awaiting them in the courtyard. Instructors carried armloads of swords, knives, and staffs, then set them in piles. They dragged out a half-dozen wooden logs that were attached to metal poles. The logs stood upright—*practice dummies*.

Aurik motioned for the initiates to gather around. "Today, we begin weapons training."

The crowd bubbled with excitement.

"Combined with conditioning, this is the foundation of your ability as a Lightbinder. An initiate who cannot find their way around how to use a weapon has no place with the Lightbinders. During this first year, your practice swords and knives are dulled, but they can still do damage, so be careful. We live by two rules with weapons training. One, don't be so careless as to kill a fellow initiate. If you do, you will join them in their fate. And second . . . don't be so careless as to get killed.

"We'll rotate squads through disciplines. Claw and Iron, you'll both work swords with me and instructor Falmouth. Raven and Wolf, you get staffs with instructor Norum. Dragon and Tiger, you'll join instructor Sorene to work with knives."

Despite his pulse thumping, Kaleth exhaled in relief at the

thought of working with knives. Compared to the heavy swords or clunky staffs, he figured knives would be the easiest weapon for him to manage.

Instructor Sorene looked like she could handle herself with a set of blades. Tight braids pulled her blonde hair back in rows, pinning it against her head. Her sizable neck and toned shoulders made Kaleth jealous. "Grab a pair and follow me," she ordered, not looking back to see who complied.

The two knives Kaleth chose weren't the pictures of elegance he'd expected. Marks riddled the scuffed metal blades. The wooden handles were smooth but lumpy in spots. They scraped when he rubbed the blades together.

Sorene pulled two daggers from the sheaths across her chest and waved them in the air. Her perfectly crafted metal blades gleamed in the light. "The six who make it to your second year will receive ones like these. Now, spread out so you don't kill each other."

Kaleth found space. He held his knives and kept his eyes on the instructor.

"For the first few weeks, you'll perform a variety of drills. Repetition will train your body to get used to the movements. Soon, you'll spar with each other."

Kaleth's stomach twisted. He glanced at the other initiates and imagined having to fight them for his life.

"First drill—hold your knives up and ready."

Kaleth faced the instructor again, gripped his weapons tighter, and lifted his hands to be ready.

"No, not like that."

It took him a moment to realize the instructor stared at him. She lifted her hands and waggled the daggers that were held in a reverse grip. A glance on either side confirmed the other initiates already held their weapons correctly. Kaleth gulped as he looked at his hands—wrapped around his daggers in a forward grip.

"Turn them around," Sorene said. "Wrap your thumb around the end so your hand doesn't slide down the blade when it strikes something."

Kaleth adjusted both knives, holding them in reverse and resting his thumb like a cap on the hilt.

"Combat with two knives is complex and only for advanced fighters."

*Great.* Kaleth's thoughts dripped with sarcasm. *Sounds just like me.*

"Once you become Lightbinders with enhanced strength and speed, it becomes much easier. Because of this, dual-knife wielding is one of our favorites. Fighting with knives is not like using swords. You're not trying to block your opponent's knife; you block their arms or hands. You don't clash your blades back and forth, it's all about measure—controlling the range between your bodies. Stay out of their reach and come inside when you're ready to strike."

Kaleth nodded, holding his knives up and watching intently.

"Your first drill is called the Circle of Thrusts. Follow me." Sorene turned around, facing in the same direction as the initiates. She stabbed at shoulder height. "Thrust, but imagine an opponent blocks your arm."

Kaleth stepped forward, stopping his arm after a half-lunge like the instructor demonstrated.

"Hook the knife in a circle to clear the imaginary arm. Once it's out of the way, slash back across it."

Kaleth spun his wrist, then pivoted at the elbow. In a quick flick, he brought the knife across his body, imagining it slicing across a man's arm.

"Circle thrust." Sorene moved her knife in a circle, then struck forward. "Finish with a quick jab." The final move was at head height. Her hand popped like an attacking snake.

Kaleth mimicked the move along with the rest of the initiates.

"Now, repeat with the other hand."

Repeating the moves with his left hand was more awkward, but he muddled through.

Sorene turned back around. "Take it slow, be deliberate with your movements, and thrust with power, like you're trying to break through chainmail. Cycle through the moves while I watch. Alternate arms and pause between rounds."

Kaleth thought through the moves in his mind. He acted them out, slowly. Each swipe of the knife felt purposeful. He imagined his opponent trying to avoid his strikes. The motions grew faster. Movements flowed together, one after another. He grinned, relishing the feeling of power that came with the increased confidence.

"Keep your arm higher," Sorene said, looking at him.

His motion faltered. He restarted the sequence, thrusting higher.

"Better. Watch your circle thrust. You're stabbing *into* the body, not just tearing their clothes."

The height. The angle. The power. The more he thought about it, the less natural it felt. His neck grew hot as he felt the instructor's eyes bearing down on him.

When he rested, he glanced at the other initiates. Their moves were sharp and precise. Their arms snapped with power as if they'd been practicing it all their lives.

Standing at the front of the group, Rayd stood out as if a binder lamp shone on him. His knives looked like extensions of his body. He flowed through the motions as naturally as breathing. His hands jerked, and his elbows snapped. Arms moved, strike after strike, with deadly precision and punishing force. He didn't sweat. He didn't even look like the moves took effort.

Kaleth's shoulders slumped. *Another area where I'm behind everyone.*

They learned two more drills that each strung various motions together. One focused on dropping an opponent to the ground, and the other simulated fighting multiple assailants. As they continued the repetitions, his arms grew fatigued. He paused longer between rounds. He struggled to keep his arms up. His lungs labored to fill his body with oxygen.

When they broke for the day, he slumped over, sweating and weak. His arms felt like noodles. A nauseous feeling clawed up his throat. He closed his eyes, extending an arm to prevent the wave of dizziness from taking over. After taking a moment, he stumbled to join the others.

"Lunch is in twenty minutes," Aurik called. "Squad leaders, find a spot to gather your teams. Check in to see how everyone is doing."

The Dragons looked to Rayd, who frowned. He glanced around, looked up, then pointed toward the sky. "Let's go on the roof."

Kaleth's legs, arms, and lungs all protested as he trudged with his squad two flights past his dorm room's floor. He wouldn't mind the effort except that the other initiates seemed to make the climb without a struggle.

At the top of the stairwell, a doorway opened to a flat terrace. Wooden benches faced each other, centered between low stone walls that bordered the rooftop. Past the barrier, other buildings of Sky Fortress jutted in various heights and shapes, all of which were dwarfed by both Central Tower and the castle.

Trying to catch his breath without his squad mates noticing, Kaleth stepped to the edge of the building. Their height matched that of the fortress' outer wall. Despite the sun beaming down on them, the air was crisp. A light breeze fluttered Kaleth's hair and buffeted his jacket.

"Grunny, get over here," Rayd called.

Kaleth spun, then hurried to join his squad. He sat on a free bench.

"First, I'm supposed to remind everyone to be working on your skill logs and not wait until the end of the year. Sign off on them with me to prove your ability."

Roselle smirked. "I already have seven done." Her hair was braided on one side, forming a "V" shape over her ear.

Chyla lowered her chin and muttered, "I didn't know there was a skill slot for 'weaving limbs with your squad leader.'"

Stifled laughs popped around the circle.

Roselle's eyebrows lifted. "Ooh, is there?" Not backing down from the gibe, she stared Chyla down. "That'll be next."

Kaleth thought of the blank skill log sitting in his room. He needed to start on them if he were to have any chance of standing out. But the idea of working with Rayd made him think of nothing but failure and insults.

Rayd cleared his throat and adjusted his seating position. "Also, I'm supposed to check in with you. So . . . anyone have a problem?"

No one answered.

Lorenzo's death in the dining hall filled Kaleth's mind. The instructors hadn't said a word, and it didn't seem anyone else knew what really happened. Genoris had told him to keep quiet, to not scare the others. It made sense, but they would all want to know.

"Kaleth?" Jovi looked at him with curiosity etched on his forehead. "What is it?"

Kaleth's eyes widened as the rest of the squad turned his way. "It's-it's nothing," he sputtered.

"He has plenty of problems," Roselle said. "We'll be here all day if we open that box."

"No," Kaleth protested. "It's not that."

"Maybe he just needs to release some tension. Loosen up." Her mouth raised on one side. "You need a *woman* to help you out?"

"I'm not supposed to say." The moment the words left his mouth, he regretted them. His squad mates leaned forward with raised eyebrows.

"Not supposed to say . . . what?" Roselle asked.

His mouth shut tight. He couldn't share the details, but he would look stupid if he backed down. He swallowed a lump in his throat.

"Come on, Kaleth," Lainn encouraged. "You can tell us."

After a moment of deliberation, he shook his head.

"You idiots," Rayd said. "Grunny doesn't know a bind-cursed thing. He's messing with you."

"No, that's not it," Kaleth protested, his mind whirling.

Roselle chuckled. "You just want to feel special, huh? Want to make us think you know something we don't?"

"He wants us to start asking around about secrets so we'll end up looking stupid," Rayd said.

"You don't care about anyone, do you?" Roselle asked. "You just want to feel important."

"Lorenzo didn't quit!" Kaleth blurted.

A moment of silence followed. The others frowned.

"What do you mean?" Lainn asked.

"He didn't quit. He was killed."

Rayd scoffed. "He was killed because he quit?"

"No, it's not that. He didn't quit at all. He was killed for no reason—disemboweled and hung on the wall of the dining hall."

A long pause followed the admission.

"I knew it," Jovi breathed.

Roselle snorted. "In the dining hall. Sure."

"He hung on the wall with a message written in blood. 'Death comes this year to the academy. Leave while you can, or all will die.'"

Most of the squad frowned, while Rayd and Roselle openly laughed. "All will die?" Rayd repeated. "Hung on the dining room wall, huh?"

"I swear," Kaleth said.

"Then how come we haven't heard anything of it?"

"Genoris said not to tell. He didn't want anyone to panic."

"You expect us to believe that a Lightbinder initiate was murdered, the instructors are covering it up, and you're the only one who saw it?"

"Well . . . the headmaster saw it."

"I believe it." Jovi raised his hand, emphasizing the words.

"You'd believe any conspiracy," Lainn said. "That doesn't make it true."

Rayd shifted his weight. After a moment, he barked a laugh. "Disemboweled. Ha! Nice try for attention, Grunny. I'm not falling for it, though. You all see? I told you he wants to make us look like idiots."

Everyone but Jovi frowned and turned away. The rejection stung. Kaleth had never counted on popularity or motivating others, but discarding his words as lies hurt in a way he had not expected.

"What else?" Rayd scanned the squad. "Any *real* problems?"

Kaleth bit his tongue. Continuing to argue wouldn't give him anything new to share.

"Chemical sciences is tough," Chyla said. Jovi nodded. "All those plants and compounds to memorize . . ."

"One of the elimination tests is supposed to be on knowledge," Roselle said, her words cutting, "so you may want to try harder."

Still reeling from the group's rejection, Kaleth lifted a tentative hand. "I wouldn't mind hosting some study sessions."

Lainn scoffed. "You can't be serious."

"Why not? My father's taught me that stuff since I was little. I don't mind helping."

Jovi nodded. Chyla looked interested but hesitant.

"There's nothing that says we can't help each other," Kaleth argued. "If we want our squad to be strong, we should—"

"Why would we want that?" Lainn interrupted. "Only six of us make it at the end of this year, right?" He pointed at the bodies one by one. "I count seven here already, and that's just our squad."

"Sure, not all seven of us will make it as Lightbinders, but we can at least live through the year. If we work together, we can help each of us overcome our weaknesses. That will at least help us against the initiates in the other squads. Everyone will have something they could use help with at some point."

"I don't have any notable weaknesses," Lainn said. "Why should I help you overcome yours if it means there's less chance for me to make it? I like you all fine enough, but . . ."

"He's right," Rayd said. "At least one of us can't make it—likely more."

Curious eyes turned to Kaleth. He took a deep breath. "Jovi's been helping me with extra conditioning sessions, and—"

"You can stop those," Rayd said. "If you had ten years to condition, you still wouldn't get where the rest of us are."

"He *is* getting better," Jovi said.

The insult from the squad leader rolled off Kaleth's back, but Jovi's words stuck with him. "You think so?" His eyebrows lifted, heart hopeful.

"I do. It's tough for you to see because you're still just as exhausted, but the rests are less frequent."

"It's pointless," Rayd said. Roselle sniggered.

Kaleth ignored the squad leader. "Yes, we compete against each other. Some of us are likely going to die and several will probably get cut. But Jovi's been helping me. I may be a lost cause, but I'm getting better. And I know a few things about chemical science. I'd be happy to teach anyone who wants to listen, so maybe *you* can get better." He pointed at Rayd. "And our squad leader looks to be one of the best fighters in our entire class. I'll bet we could all learn something from him. What I'm getting at is . . . what if we helped each other be the best we could? Why compete against forty other people on your own when you can compete against thirty-four people with others by your side? We're not all going to make it, sure, but if we build each other up, each of us will have a better chance against the other squads."

The group was quiet. Kaleth scanned their faces, which stared back with curious expressions.

"I've changed my mind." Lainn nodded. "That logic makes sense. If we work together, it would give each of us better odds of surviving."

Kaleth tried to keep a grin from showing.

"I'm in," Chyla said.

"Of course I am," Jovi added, beaming.

Garod nodded.

"Maybe we can meet in the common room after dinner," Kaleth said, "for anyone interested in studying chemical science."

Rayd threw up his hands. "If that's how you want to spend your last four weeks alive, so be it."

Kaleth frowned. *Four weeks?*

"Is that the next test?" Jovi asked.

"It's the strength one," Roselle confirmed.

Kaleth's stomach dropped. "I-I forgot that was so soon."

"You can't escape it, Grunny," Rayd said. "It doesn't matter how much strength conditioning you squeeze in. The test weeds out the best from the rest. It's like a game of kamak. They want the warriors, not the swords or knives. You don't even qualify to be on the board."

Kaleth's pulse grew quicker. *He's right. I'm out of place here.* No matter what he did, there was no way to get ready in time.

Jovi broke the thick silence. "Didn't he beat you at kamak?"

Garod and Chyla snickered.

Rayd glared at Jovi. "Are you disrespecting your squad leader, initiate?"

Kaleth's friend straightened, but he didn't apologize for the insult.

Lainn turned to Kaleth. "Four weeks or not, I'll join you."

Kaleth nodded, but a despairing thought wouldn't leave his mind. *How am I supposed to improve that much in four weeks? It's hopeless.*

## CHAPTER TWENTY-FOUR

# THE IMPORTANCE OF FOCUS

Two days after her injury on the Blockade, the medical team released Felyra. A lump still marked her head where she'd hit the platform, but the throbbing pain had finally eased. Being later in the afternoon, she hurried down the main corridor to the initiate classroom where her peers should be.

When she opened the wooden doors, silence echoed back. The chairs were empty. No instructor stood at the front. She frowned, standing in the doorway.

"The parapets."

Felyra turned to find a weathered man with a broom, pausing in his sweeping of the hallway. "I'm sorry?" she asked.

"The class." He gestured toward the south staircase. "If you're looking for them, they went up on the parapets."

Felyra thanked the man and headed toward the stairs. Her bad leg twinged as she began the ascent. She ignored it, wincing as she hurried and ignoring the stiffness in her limbs from days of inactivity.

A baking heat greeted her when she exited the stairs. The sun hovered high above, and the fortress' battlements provided little shade. Strung in a messy line, her fellow initiates stood along the wall, facing the heart of Revalle.

A piece of cloth covered Thaylor's eyes, his black hair drooping over it. "Um . . . three?" he said.

Captain Janduan frowned. "No, there are four. What about Thravian flags?"

"Six?"

The other initiates laughed.

"Not even close," the captain said. "Three. That's enough. Take it off."

Another initiate pulled off the covering.

"You all need to pay better attention. If you want to be the best, you need to operate at the highest level. You need to always be—" Captain Janduan paused mid-sentence as he noticed Felyra.

The rest of the crowd glanced her way. Ruane smiled.

"Nice of you to join us." The captain's words carried a sharp edge before they slipped into sarcasm. "If you can't be here every day, it's no problem. Just join us whenever you feel like it."

Felyra hurried forward, squeezing past a few shoulders to stand next to Ruane.

"Are you all right?" her friend asked.

She nodded, keeping her eyes on the captain.

"As I was saying . . ." Janduan drawled. "You must take it all in at once. You can't pay attention to only one thing. A Soulbinder's focus must be on many places at the same time. Let's all try it again."

Felyra allowed her gaze to drift east of the fortress, along with the rest of the crowd.

"Notice those walking along the street. What are they wearing? Where are they going? Why do you think they are going there?"

Felyra's eyes danced between the six people passing in front of the fortress gates.

"But don't forget about Phyco Market. What flavors can you spot from here? Who is shopping? Who is selling? What about the windows of the buildings? Do you see anyone inside?"

"How's your head?" Ruane whispered.

Felyra turned away from the market to observe her friend's furrowed brow. She touched the lump on the side of her head where it had hit the platform. "Still tender, but much better than before. Did I miss much?"

"I made it halfway through section two of the Blockade."

A combination of pride and jealousy ran through her. "That's great, Ruane."

"Yesterday, we did more conditioning, then some dagger sparring. Grax was a jerk again, so not much new."

The captain's voice boomed, "Trouble paying attention, Ruane?"

Felyra cringed as her friend turned toward Janduan.

"I'm sorry, Captain," Ruane said. "I was making sure Felyra was all right."

"Was your assignment to check in on her?"

Ruane shook her head.

"If you're fighting the Kalshians and their Lightbinders come at you, will you tell them to hold on because you were busy talking with a friend?"

She didn't reply.

"Ignoring orders leads to chaos, and distraction will get you killed. Do you want to be the one that lets the enemy slip past the line? Are you so incompetent that you can't stay focused for one minute?"

A glisten of moisture welled in the corner of her friend's eye.

"She was checking on me after my injury," Felyra blurted. "It was just a moment. Give her a break."

"A break?"

The tone in the captain's words sent a shiver down her spine.

"Will the Lightbinders give you a break because you're not paying attention?

"Just because she was talking to me doesn't mean she wasn't paying attention," Felyra said. "Did you ever consider that some people might process more than your brain can handle?"

She cringed even as the words left her mouth. The gasps along the battlements matched the intensity of the captain's glare. *Too much*, she thought.

"Bold words from a girl whose brain can't process the image of a sandbag swinging toward her head," Janduan taunted.

Several snickers dotted the crowd. Felyra wanted to jibe back, but there was nothing she could say to minimize her failure on the Blockade.

"Perhaps you wish to demonstrate the splendid state of your own mind? Maybe you can prove how observant one can be while distracted."

She stared back at the captain, then dropped her voice and enunciated, "Gladly."

Shifting hips and a chorus of mutters filled the crowd.

The captain puffed air out his nose. His eyes narrowed as they held hers for a long moment. "Blindfold."

A sweaty rag appeared from behind to cover her eyes. Faint light made it through, but not enough to see anything. Her pulse quickened at the salty must invading her nostrils. Her ears perked at each shuffle of feet that gave space around her.

"All right, observant one," the captain began, "how many people are shopping in the market?"

"Do you mean how many—"

"No questions," Janduan barked. "The Lightbinders won't let you stop and talk before they run you through with their lightning-fast, glowing blades."

"Four," she answered.

"An old man walked in front of the fortress. What did he carry in a basket?"

She pictured his shuffle in how the man moved up the street. "Flowers and a bottle of wine."

His tongue clicked. "Across the street, what is visible through a window on the second floor?"

"The window on the far left has an empty planter perched outside. The next one is open, showing the corner of a bed with ruffled sheets, and the last one contains a white-and-black cat licking its paws—at least it was a moment ago."

"What about your fellow initiates?"

"What about them?"

"They stand with you on the battlements, but one of them is absent. Tell me who it is."

Her forehead pinched. She couldn't see through the blindfold, but her mind played back through her arrival. Face after face whisked through her memory. Whenever she thought she'd figured out a missing name, the image of that person a moment ago flashed in her head. *So many names. How can I possibly think through them all?* Her palms sweat. None of the names she could think of had been missing.

"Who is it?" Janduan asked.

Her mouth hung open, begging to say the correct name, but nothing accurate came to her mind. She lowered her chin and shook her head.

"Not even a guess?"

"I-I don't know," she admitted.

He exhaled in disgust. "Your incredible skills of observation allowed you to guess one out of four questions. The Lightbinders have arrived, and congratulations, you are now dead."

Her jaw tightened. "What did I miss?"

"You got the cat, but that was it."

"Are you sure about that?"

Her question sent a murmur rippling through the crowd.

"Excuse me? Do you want me to send you to lockup for insolence?"

"I'm only asking for clarification about your questions. In the market, did you think it was five? Because the woman with the rags isn't shopping. She's begging for coins. You can tell by her cup and how she lingers at the entrance. The answer to how many are *shopping* is four."

She pulled the rag off from over her eyes and blinked at the sunlight. She found the captain frowning as he looked toward the market. Turning toward the city, she spotted the old man with the basket who stood before a door next to the market.

"And how can you say I was wrong about the flowers and wine in his basket?"

"The flowers were right," Janduan said, "but there was no bottle of wine."

"It's under the flowers."

The captain scoffed. "I didn't ask for guesses about what might be there."

"No, you asked what *is* in the basket. And I told you, there are flowers and there is a bottle of wine under them."

"You can't know that."

"Sure I can." She pointed down from the fortress wall at the man. "That is Pevingal. Four years ago, his wife died on his sixtieth birthday. Recently, he's taken to calling on Lady Ewell. He visits her daily with a bundle of flowers . . . and a bottle of wine."

"Humph," Janduan muttered, his frown covering his face while he continued to stare. "Either way . . . you didn't pay attention to your fellow initiates when you arrived."

"I did though," she said, standing straight. "I thought through everyone and they were all here. My guess is no one is missing."

Janduan's face twitched. A few chuckles peppered through the crowd. A smile on Ruane's face told her she had hit the mark.

A distant squeal drifted on the wind, turning the group toward where Pevingal stood outside a building. The door stood open, and a woman hugged around his neck, pressing a bouquet against him. When he extricated himself, he reached into his basket and lifted a bottle of wine.

A few initiates "oohed" in unison.

She stared the captain down. "Keeping your focus in multiple areas is about more than just seeing what's around you. It's about putting puzzles together. It's observing what you see, and even what you don't." Felyra smirked. "I know it's late in the day, but don't worry, Captain . . . there's still time for you to learn something today."

A deep laugh bounced from the shadowed stairwell, turning Felyra's head along with the others. Feet crunching on the crusty dirt that coated the stone wall, Headmaster Baloran stepped forward. His laugh redoubled in strength.

Felyra shrank at the man's presence, aghast at her bold words.

"Looks like you've met your match, Captain," the headmaster said. "Maybe you should give her some credit instead of trying to trick her."

Janduan bristled. "It's important we require a lot. If you expect me to—"

"I expect you to treat them all fairly."

The rebuke cut through the air, ushering a heavy moment of silence. Janduan nodded. "Of course, Headmaster."

"I think that should be about it for your class today, yes?"

"Yes, I—" He cleared his throat. "We're finished." The captain raised his voice. "Class dismissed."

The initiates moved in sync toward the stairs. Conversations picked up as they jostled for position. The headmaster stood by the stairwell, letting the young men and women pass him.

"Nice job," Ruane said at her side.

Felyra smiled. "Thanks. I need to bite my tongue, though. Janduan's going to make me pay for that comment."

"Maybe, but you've been out for two days. You needed to catch up on your insults."

"I need to catch up in a lot of ways. I haven't had any conditioning in days. My leg is liability enough as it is, and it feels like it puts me even further behind."

"It's probably good. It's helpful to have a few days off to rest."

Headmaster Baloran held up a hand as the two young women moved to pass him. "Stay, Felyra. I'd like a word."

Her stomach dropped. Ruane continued forward, her wide eyes staring straight ahead. Felyra stepped to the side to let the rest of the crowd pass. The initiates filed past, with Captain Janduan bringing up the rear. The scowl on his face made her cringe.

When everyone had passed, the headmaster gestured for her to follow as he stepped out onto the wall.

## CHAPTER TWENTY-FIVE

# HEADMASTER WISDOM

Felyra followed as Baloran circled the parapets. When they passed the courtyard, she spotted Ruane, who looked up from below. Felyra shrugged as if answering the unsaid question of what the headmaster wanted with her.

Steps led to a higher level. They continued farther. More steps. On the north side of the fortress, Baloran stopped at the tower. Felyra took the spiraled stairs behind him, ducking her head to keep it from hitting the cramped roof.

A stronger wind flapped her hair when they emerged on top of the tower. The snow-topped Kalshian Mountains rose to the west, jutting into the sky as if to assert their dominance over the rest of the land. The world to the north turned greener the farther her eyes tracked. Her teeth clenched when her gaze fell on Kalistor, minuscule against the horizon.

"How are you, Felyra?" His voice was gentle.

"I'm good."

"Your head—is it okay?"

She shrugged. "It's fine."

"I'm sorry about the Blockade. We try to make it as safe as possible, but it's impossible to escape all danger when you're preparing as we do."

The reminder of her failure stung. "Really, it's fine."

"I had meant to visit you in the infirmary, but, well . . . I've been busy. I'm sorry."

"You don't owe me anything."

"But I owe Nemorr."

The reminder of her father sent a twinge of sorrow through her heart.

Baloran pointed at the river. "Did you know we used to play there when we were little?"

The question perked her up. She knew very little about her father when he was young.

"Of course, the South Lagrash wasn't a trickle of muck and algae then. It still had *some* water and even a few fish in it. There used to be a tree on the east bank that leaned over the water. We'd climb up in it and pretend to be lookouts against invaders." He smiled. "We were as close as friends could be."

It was difficult for Felyra to imagine the land having been fertile at one point, but she relished the idea of her father playing in it. "What happened to you two?"

Baloran exhaled. "Both our fathers were farmers. Some families had already transitioned to algae, but ours were some of the last to hold on to the old crops. We both helped until we were of age, but our true desires were to join Soulbinder Academy."

Her eyebrows raised. "My father? Nemorr-il-Perrez? He wanted to fight?"

He chuckled. "That's right. He mellowed in his age, but you should have seen him when he was young. We had swords made from branches. He left welts all over my body when we sparred."

"Why didn't he come, too?"

"His father died—the season before we were both to join. His mother couldn't manage on her own—not with two younger boys to care for—so Nemorr took over their family's crops. I joined the academy, and he stayed in the fields."

"I never knew all that. He talked little about his past."

"We kept up some after we split, but it was difficult. Our lives went in different directions." The headmaster lowered his chin and fixed his stare ahead. "I saw him the day it happened."

A lump formed in Felyra's throat.

"Lightbinders snuck in from across the river, entering the city unnoticed. I was on guard, on the battlements where your class just stood. No one had seen anything when binder cannons blasted against the fortress walls. The noise was deafening. Stone chips flew in every direction. While the barrage rained on us, squadrons of their Blades mixed with Lightbinders stormed the gate.

"We returned fire as best as we could. Soulbinders sent projectiles into the attacking force and archers picked them off. When their resistance faltered, they melded into the city. Some citizens took up arms with whatever they had to help drive them off. Nemorr had been returning from the fields when the attack took place. I watched as he swung a hoe at a Lightbinder. The man's glowing sword moved like a force of nature, knocking the tool away and running him through before I could even blink."

Felyra's insides churned. Her fists formed into tight balls as her sight grew blurry.

"I'm sorry." Baloran shook his head. "I shouldn't have brought it up."

"It's okay." She wiped her eyes and sniffed. "I appreciate it. That's more than I ever heard about it. It's helpful, especially with me being here and all."

"Is that why you joined?"

"The academy?" She was about to shake her head but then stopped. "Maybe. I want revenge against the Lightbinders. He was all I had left, and they took him from me. Plus, I didn't have a lot of options. What else is a young cripple supposed to do once her parents die?"

"I wouldn't exactly call you a cripple."

A short laugh puffed from her chest. "You'd be one of the few here. Have you seen me walk?"

"I have. I hear you walked to the mountains during the trial. Seems like you get along all right."

"I may get somewhere, but I look stupid doing it with this limp.

It's all anyone else sees." She uttered a mirthless laugh and ran a hand along her chin. "Unless I stop moving, then all they see is this scar."

"Some people focus on things like that, but in the end . . . they're just idiots." He winked.

The frank comment brought a smile to her face. "The main reason I'm here . . ." She took in a deep breath, then blew it out. "I want to be special. I want people to be in awe of me for my abilities. I want them to see my blue ring and know that I have incredible skills they can only dream of. I want them to ignore my scar, forget my limp, and only see me as a powerful warrior."

"You're a highly capable young woman. You're here learning and contributing, just like the rest of them. And from what I observed in your class just now, you're doing a fine job."

A spark of encouragement welled inside. "Splitting my focus is something I've always felt natural at. My father drilled me on it since I was little."

"And that's an important criterion for being chosen as a Soulbinder. I see you during conditioning and weapons training. No one tries as hard as you."

"I'm not sure if that's a good thing or not. Some of them don't have to try."

"And that will only get them so far. Eventually, they'll get to something difficult. If they're not used to putting in effort, they'll find themselves unable to overcome it. I'm not the only one who chooses, but you should keep at it and don't give up hope."

"I shudder to think about not being selected. I can picture it now, getting cut and being put in an infantry squad led by someone as rude as Grax or as mean as Captain Janduan. Of course, I'm sure Grax will make Soulbinder, too."

"Most aren't selected," Baloran said.

"Why does Janduan hate me so much?"

Baloran paused with tight lips. "The captain can be . . . harsh. I know. He was trained by Celedar Wardragon."

Her eyes opened wider at the reference of the legendary Soulbinder.

"Old Silver Hair is great in many ways, but his training style was unrelenting. Teaching at the academy wasn't the best fit for a warrior such as him, but he made his mark. Janduan absorbed a bit of that style. The captain's intentions are good, though. He wants to promote the best candidates to be Soulbinders just like we all do."

"And he doesn't like me because I'm not perfect?"

"Nobody's perfect," the headmaster's eyes drifted out to the city, "including Janduan. He has his own challenges to overcome."

Felyra's eyebrows lifted. She waited, hoping deeper secrets would be revealed, but nothing else came.

"Still, everyone is needed. Unless Kalshia one day changes their tune, we cannot stop trying."

"Why do they attack us?"

The headmaster frowned. "What do you mean?"

"They all live in their land of plenty, yet they focus their efforts on us. Why?"

"They want our gems."

Her eyes flicked to the blue ring on his hand. "But they have their own. Are they just so hungry for power that they want everything?"

"Few people know this, but . . . the soul gems were originally held in Kalistor."

Her eyes opened wider. "Before the split?"

He nodded. "When our kingdoms were one, the academy in Kalistor was the only one, and they trained Lightbinders and Soulbinders together. Forty-four years ago, Thanean was merely King Rhinean's brother, living in Kalistor. After Zanon's Rebellion, he determined it was too dangerous to keep the soul gem and the light gem in the same place, controlled by the same people. So, he broke into the vault, took the blue gems, and fled to Revalle. Of course, Rhinean wanted them back, so he attacked. Thanean anticipated it, though. He already had fighters ready to defend. The conflict between them was what led to the Rift—splitting the land into Kalshia and Thravia. We created our own academy here and have been training Soulbinders ever since."

"And Thanean held his brother off?"

A grim look flashed across Baloran's face. "He protected the soul gems, but he didn't realize Rhinean's plan. Failing to regain the gems, Kalshia's focus shifted to something much more sinister—something that has left Thravia reeling for forty-four years."

Felyra frowned. The tone in the headmaster's voice had shifted as if contemplating a dark secret. Her throat felt dry. "What happened? What did they do?"

The headmaster started to speak, then stopped himself. After a pause, he shook his head. "I shouldn't have said so much. I'm sorry. If you're chosen for Soulbinder, you'll find out more."

Her shoulders lowered as she breathed out. Something he said prickled in her mind, though. "You said King Thanean thought it dangerous to keep the gems together. What does that mean? What happens when they're kept together?"

He didn't answer.

"Did something happen forty-four years ago? Something with the gems?"

"That's enough, Felyra." His words were gentle but direct. "I'm sorry. But it's not safe to talk about."

Her mind worked even faster to process the implications of his avoidance of the issue. Danger. Secrecy. Gems with powers. *What is he keeping from us?*

"I, uh, know you feel like an outsider with your . . . limp and everything. Did you know I have a son?"

She shook her head.

"He has a brilliant mind, but he has physical struggles."

His effective change of subject perked her interest.

"The doctors call it a palsy. His arms don't work the way they're supposed to. They shake whenever he puts them under strain. He can't even drink from a cup without tremors spilling it everywhere. When it first showed up, his friends turned on him. They ridiculed him for his inability to do simple things. It was devastating for him to endure and for me to watch."

"I can imagine that would be tough."

"He's fourteen now though, and his perspective has changed. At first, he grieved the fact that he wouldn't be able to join the academy and follow in my footsteps. But now, he's more content."

"What happened?"

"He accepted that his inability to do physical tasks wasn't a failure on his part. It wasn't because he was broken or that he had done something wrong to deserve it. It simply *was*. Rather than mourning things he couldn't do, he got excited by what he *could*."

"And what's that?"

"He's smart, and he's good with people. He realized that, palsy or not, he could be an excellent banker, so he's been apprenticing at the Bank of Thravia. He's no longer sad about his lost dream because he sees purpose and ability in what he's doing."

Felyra's lips pursed. Her gut twinged as if a knife pressed against it. "What are you saying? That I should forget about being a Soulbinder because of my physical limitations?"

The headmaster's brow wrinkled as he cocked his head.

"You think I can't keep up with the others and that I should find a job where my leg won't be a liability? So, I should see purpose in . . . what? Selling algae in the market? Maybe being a washerwoman?"

"No."

Her words grew faster as frustration built. "You can keep your advice. I don't need your limits placed on me. For years, people have been trying to tell me what I can and can't do."

"Felyra, please—"

"No! I'm *done* with listening to people who tell me I can't do it! I *can*! I'm stubborn. I'm a hard worker. I may not win every challenge, but I keep at it until I do. My bad legs will not hold me back, and no one will keep me from trying. You'll see. When you select the Soulbinders, I'm going to be the first choice, the one that everyone wants because they can't imagine winning the war without me."

The headmaster no longer tried to interrupt. He stared back with eyebrows cocked.

"I'm glad your son has found his place, but you won't bring me down with your confinements on what I *can* or *should* do. Other people may settle, but I won't. So, you can take your motivational story and shove it!"

Her chest heaved after the outburst. Fire raged through her veins. She was ready to fight—ready to run. She was capable of anything.

The headmaster didn't immediately speak, but only stared back at her. "Are you finished?" he asked after a pause.

She lifted her chin. "Never."

"Good."

His wry grin took her aback.

"If you had let me speak, you would have heard that you and my son are different people. While you are both very smart, he doesn't have your grit and ability to push through difficulty. As a result, it's helpful for *him* to find a place that allows him to shine in his strengths without forcing him to contend with his weaknesses. You, on the other hand, will work. You can push through pain to get your body to perform. The limp you often remind yourself of is not a limitation because you don't allow it to be one. Your strengths are many: focus—as you proved just now in class, intelligence, and a very strong work ethic. My son's story wasn't meant to convince you to wash clothes but to keep working at what you're doing because that's where your gifts lie. Despite some setbacks, you're doing what you're passionate about, you're highly capable, and you have a good chance of being selected, so don't give up."

Heat crept up her neck and flushed across her face. "Sorry," she mumbled.

He waved the apology away. "Don't worry about it. Your fire drives you, so don't let it go out. Still . . . listening to what others are saying could be something to work on."

She nodded. "I am—I mean . . . I will."

"Good." Baloran's gaze drifted north toward Kalistor. "Because Kalshia and their Lightbinders aren't content to leave us be. They continue to train recruits, and they will bring the fight to us again. To stop them, we will need all the help we can get." He turned to Felyra. "To put it plainly . . . we need you."

## CHAPTER TWENTY-SIX

# FAMILY INSIGHT

Kaleth stared across the table, watching Jovi's brow bunch up in deep concentration. Chyla, Garod, and Lainn joined him in waiting on his friend.

The window to Binder Court was already dark, being a bit after sunset. Across the common room, the six second-year initiates laughed around the fireplace. A handful of first years scattered around the room, poring over books.

In the weeks since Dragon Squad decided to work together, no other teams had latched on to the idea. While Rayd and Roselle never joined them, the rest of their squad grouped up every night after dinner to talk through what they'd been learning in classes.

"Eidelflower?" Jovi said.

"Is that a question or an answer?" Kaleth asked.

Jovi lowered his chin and spoke with more confidence. "The antidote to vascoth poison is eidelflower. Grind the petals and stem and brew it in a tea. Take it within four hours of exposure or the poison will be too far gone."

"Correct," Kaleth said.

Chyla grinned, but Lainn frowned. "I thought it was gunny root," he said.

"You'd use gunny paste if the poison got on your skin, but if you ingest it, eidelflower is the best antidote."

"That's right," Lainn said. "Man, there's so much to remember."

"You'll get it," Kaleth said. "It just takes time. You all want to go over acidic reactions again?"

Jovi rubbed his forehead. "I think I'm about done for today. I don't think my brain can handle much more."

"Maybe we should get to our rooms early," Garod said, his lip curling, "before someone cuts out our entrails and hangs us on the wall."

Chyla sniggered, but Jovi only pursed his lips. Kaleth ignored the barb. Heavy steps in the doorway drew his attention to their principal's arrival.

"First years, I recommend getting extra sleep if you can tonight," Aurik said. "The strength test will be here early tomorrow, and you'll want to be rested."

Kaleth's stomach twisted in a knot. The studying had helped him avoid thinking about it, but the reminder brought the fear rushing back.

Jovi looked at him. "You'll do fine." The waver in his friend's voice contradicted the confidence he tried to impart. "You've improved a lot."

"Yeah, you've made a ton of progress, Kaleth," Lainn said. "You should be proud."

Kaleth swallowed the lump in his throat. "Thanks."

Knowing most initiates died over the course of the tests, Kaleth expected the following day to be his last. If he'd been able to figure out his father's secret ability, he would have felt much better. He'd tried casting his father's secret glyph multiple times in different settings, but nothing ever worked.

"Thank you for helping us with all of this studying," Chyla said in a somber tone. "It *has* been helpful. You may not be the typical Lightbinder initiate, but you've proven your worth in my book."

"Knock it off," Jovi said. "You're talking as if he's a goner."

No one responded, but Kaleth knew what they were all thinking —he was about to die.

"Have you considered . . . going to see your mother and sister?" Jovi asked.

"What? Quitting?"

"No. Well . . . that's always an option, too—"

"I can't quit."

Jovi turned his hands up. "I just thought . . . they're close by and you haven't seen them in weeks."

"We can't leave the academy."

"Why not?" Lainn said. "I don't think they ever said that. You could ask Aurik."

Kaleth's eyebrows raised. The other Dragon initiates looked at him, waiting. Aurik lingered in the hall, talking with instructor Sorene. The thought of asking a favor from the man turned his stomach, but the idea had merit. "I guess it can't hurt to ask."

He rose from his chair and approached the principal, waiting until the man turned in his direction.

"Would it be possible for me to visit my mother and sister? They're in town and seeing them should only take a few hours."

Aurik stared back. His eyes seemed to pierce into his soul. "You signed up for the Kalshian army, committing to three years. Are you trying to run?"

"I would return tonight."

"If you are afraid of tomorrow's Lightbinder test, you can always drop. Usually, being cut would move you to the Grunts, but your aptitude in class is strong. I may be able to pull some strings and get you in the Menders."

The offer felt like a surge of air in his lungs. No more Lightbinders. No more strength test. No more Rayd and Roselle trying to kill him. Menders was where he belonged, and he could make it right.

His lips parted. Aurik and Sorene waited for his answer. He began to agree until he remembered the fifteen gold bonus paid to Menders. *It's not enough.* His mother and sister would die. His chin pushed forward as if trying to say the words.

He cringed when he spoke. "Thank you, but no."

Aurik's shoulders fell as he exhaled.

"My mother she—" A wave of anger raced through Kaleth as he remembered whom he spoke to. He choked back the bitterness that threatened to come out. "She's injured and sick, and I haven't seen her in six weeks. I'll be back tonight, I promise. You'll see me here tomorrow morning, ready to take the test."

The principal looked to Sorene and then back to Kaleth. After a long pause, he nodded.

WALKING through Grunwind felt strange and familiar at the same time. It was a street he'd walked thousands of times, but the buildings looked different. The air felt thicker, reminding him of the tragedy that had happened the last night he was there.

His life had changed so much over the previous six weeks. While he *was* getting stronger, better conditioned, and more skilled in combat, all he could think about was the fact that he was constantly exhausted, sore, and mentally drained.

His family's house looked worse than when he'd last seen it. The fading binder lamp across the street revealed the chipping red paint on the door flaking more than usual. A few of the drooping tiles on the roof had fallen off. More chunks of stone that used to make up the walls had crumbled. Although the house had always been difficult to keep up with, his father had been quick to handle any repairs without fail.

His heart pounded as he stepped to the door. A sudden fear of how they would react washed through him. After all, he had left them at the time they most needed help. Taking a deep breath, he delivered a quick double-tap with his knuckle before turning the knob and pushing it open.

Lit by a lone oil lantern that hung on the wall, Sora spun from where she hunched over a pot on the stove. A salty tang filled the air, mixed with a hint of sage. His sister's blonde hair fell across her face, looking darker than when he'd last seen it. The sleeves on her grimy dress pushed up past her elbows. A spot of soot marked her chin. Her eyebrows raised, then her nostrils widened as she inhaled sharply.

"Kaleth!" The breathy greeting came from his mother. She lay in her usual spot on the bed, but she appeared worse than when he'd last seen her. Her eyes looked tired. Sunken cheeks emphasized her lack of nourishment. Her unwashed hair was tousled and stringy. A weak cough followed the greeting.

Sora dropped her ladle and crossed the room. Kaleth prepared himself for an insulting nickname and a punch in the arm, but she wrapped him in a hug instead. "We were worried we might never see you again."

Kaleth held her in return. He nearly flinched at the feel of her bony collarbone and shoulders. His reasons for everything he'd done came flooding back in a rush. When he and his sister broke their embrace, he moved to the side of the bed. "Mother," he said tenderly.

She beamed with joy. Tears already fell down her cheeks. The bed creaked as she leaned forward, extending her arms.

His hug for her was gentler. A rasp in her breath increased his concern. "We're not normally allowed to leave," he said as he pulled back from the embrace. "They gave me permission because—" He stopped to contemplate.

*Why did he let me go? Is it because he expects I'm about to die and this would be my last chance to see them?*

"I guess I caught my principal in a generous mood."

Sora sat on the edge of the bed. "Thanks for sending the letters. So . . . Lightbinders, huh?"

Heat crept up the back of his neck. "Yeah, I'm working toward it."

"Kaleth, you shouldn't have done that," his mother said. "We could have found other ways to make up the money."

He shrugged. "Maybe. I had little time to think about it at the moment."

"But I hear Lightbinder initiates *die.*"

His mirthless laugh bounced his shoulders. "Tell me about it. I'm making it so far, though." He gulped at the thought of what was to come the next day.

"You look . . . bad," Sora said.

Kaleth cringed. "It's hard. We're always running, lifting, or fighting. I never knew a body could take so much. We have a lot of classes, too, but they're not so hard. Mostly stuff Father taught me already. My roommate, Lainn Brawnfist—yes, his handshake is like a rock—he was distant at first, but he's warmed up." He didn't mention anything about Lorenzo's mysterious death.

"What happened to your glasses?" his mother asked.

He touched his face where they used to rest. "Uh, yeah, I lost them. It's all right though. I'm getting by without them."

"How's Jovi doing?" Sora's eyes sparkled. "I can picture him as a Lightbinder."

"He's—" The dreamy look on her face gave him pause. *Great. Just what I need.* "He's still making it. Doing pretty well. Our group started at fifty and is down to forty-one now. Jovi is ranked seventeenth."

"What are you ranked?" Sora asked.

His throat tightened. "Me, um . . . enough about me. How are you two? Are you getting the food you need?"

The faces of the two women fell in unison. "We're getting what we need," his mother said, forcing a smile back. "Your sister is taking great care of me."

"I got some work at the laundry today," Sora said. "That's why we're eating so late tonight."

He glanced at the stove where a pot simmered. Inhaling, he tested the air. Traces of potatoes mixed with a sharp aroma. "Is that pinlock needles?"

The grimace on his sister's face confirmed it. "We got potatoes from the garden, but we use them sparingly. The, uh . . . pinlock is plentiful from the woods."

"To trick your stomach into thinking it's full." He sighed. "Are you getting any meat?"

Sora looked about to speak, but nothing came out. She looked at their mother as if searching for help.

"Silvia brought us some eggs," Fenya blurted. "At least she did once, a few weeks ago."

The silence that followed felt heavy. Kaleth gestured to the pot on the stove. "If you were about to eat, please don't let me hold you up."

"Can you stay and eat with us?" Sora asked with raised eyebrows.

The question warmed his heart. They were eager to share the little they had with him. "I already ate, but I'd love to stay a bit. You both go ahead."

Sora ladled out two bowls of the thin stew. Kaleth delivered one to his mother before taking a seat at the table.

"And how about you, Mother? How are your lungs and your ankle?"

"I'm actually doing well," Fenya replied after swallowing a spoonful. "Much better than before."

Sora's dark expression drew Kaleth's eyes before she forced a smile.

"My breathing is improved, and I'm able to get around more. I —" One hand flew to her mouth as a cough erupted. She leaned away, hacking, too weak for the effort to clear much inside of her. The other hand held the bowl to keep it from spilling. "The coughs are—" She coughed more. "—not as bad as they—" A final rasping wheeze ushered in a moment of quiet while she sat still. "Not as bad as they sound. They have been getting better."

Sora's eyes told him otherwise.

"And my legs are stronger. The right leg is good, and I can put a bit of weight on the left." She touched a wooden crutch leaning against the side of the bed. "This helps me hobble around the house, at least."

Sora nodded and swallowed a mouthful. "She *has* been able to get up. Can't walk anywhere else, but the crutch is good for the house."

"I don't suppose you've been able to see a doctor at all, have you?" Kaleth asked.

His mother slurped on a spoon, then shook her head. "It costs money."

He nodded, expecting the answer. *Money.* The word covered the room with a heavy weight. The debt filled his mind. One hundred gold. It was what prompted him to join the army—what forced him to choose the Lightbinders.

Thunder rumbled somewhere in the distance, adding to the heaviness in the room.

"Has Jairus been by?" he asked.

Sora nodded. "He checked in last week. We had scrimped together a few coins, but he took them for the debt."

"How much debt is left?"

Sora's shoulders drooped. "Ninety-nine and a half."

While it didn't surprise him, the figure hurt to hear. He reached into his pocket and pulled out a small stack of gold coins. "This should help."

Both his mother's and sister's eyes grew. "How much is that?" Sora asked, setting her spoon against the rim of the bowl with a clank.

"Six." A twinge of pride ran through him as he spoke the number aloud. "I get one each week."

His mother covered her mouth with her hand as tears welled in her eyes. "Kaleth, we can't—"

"Of course you can. That's why I did this. It's *my* debt now."

A tentative smile formed on Sora's face. She took the coins with soft hands.

"Use a bit to get some food. I'll be bringing more back as the year goes on. You need something with more substance than pinlock soup. Get some eggs from the market, some more vegetables, and maybe some chicken."

His sister's eyes grew wider as he listed off the ingredients.

"At the end of the year, I'll get a bonus of seventy-five coins. That should cover the debt and then some."

Thinking about the debt warred with the comforting feeling of being with his family again. His father's absence was a conspicuous hole, but it felt good to be back in his home. The protection glyph carved over the doorway caught his eye. Having failed to help with his father, who died only steps outside of its protection, it remained clear and unused.

He pointed to the glyph. "Let me know if this gets used and fades. I'll come and cast a new one."

His mother smiled and nodded. "Thank you." Her smile grew as her eyes drifted wistfully to the glyph. "Valorr and his glyphs. He sure loved them."

"I've used a couple already at the academy. It's been helpful." He purposely avoided details about how they had been used.

"He spent so much time trying to create new ones. He'd try them on the floor and on the walls, attempting with wood, then stone. 'Potency requires efficiency.'"

Kaleth chuckled. "Yep, that was Father."

His mother's grin grew wider. "He even tattooed one on his body, if you can believe it."

"Really?" Kaleth and Sora both said together.

"It was from before we met. Below his hip, here." She pointed to the side of her leg. "I think he was embarrassed because he made sure no one ever saw it."

"He tattooed a glyph on his body?" Kaleth felt his brow pinching together. "Did it work?"

She shook her head. "I don't think so. He never tried another one."

*Strange that he would never have told me. Like he wanted to keep it a* —he sucked in a breath. *A secret.*

Sora looked at him. "Are you okay?"

His breath came quicker. His racing mind spun for a long moment until he forced a smile. "Yeah, of course." He turned to his mother, trying to act casual despite his pounding heart echoing through his body. "What, um . . . glyph was it that he tried?"

She shrugged. "I don't know. He didn't talk about it. It had some curving lines in a circle, then a letter at the center. G or J or . . . H . . ."

The words sounded muddled. He held his breath. "F?"

"That's it. Did he show you?"

It was as if a lamp made of hope lit inside him. Kaleth struggled to respond because of the cascading thoughts streaking through his mind. "No." His voice was breathy and distant. "But he mentioned something about it."

"Are you sure you're okay, Kaleth?" Sora said. "You have beading sweat on your forehead."

"Do I?" He wiped his brow and chuckled. "It is warm in here, I guess. Plus, my, uh, principal didn't give me long to visit. I should actually probably be heading back so I don't get in trouble. I'm really sorry. I wish I could stay longer."

His mother managed a tender smile. "I'm just glad you came. It's so good to see you, Kaleth. Will you be able to come back soon?"

His chair scraped as he pushed it back and stood. "I'm not sure, but I will if I can."

He gave long hugs to both his sister and mother. His pounding heart urged him to rush, but he forced himself to give them a proper goodbye. He waved as he left the house, hoping it wouldn't be the last time he saw them.

He took the path back to the fortress at a jogging pace. Time was short. If he was going to figure out his father's secret, it had to be that night. The strength test would be the end of his journey unless he could solve the riddle. Lightning rippled through the sky, illuminating the western hills with an ethereal glow. Rolling thunder followed before long.

Sweat covered his skin after hurrying across the narrow path and the long incline back to the fortress. After waving past the guards at the gate, he rushed inside. Kaleth found a bottle of ink in the Lightbinder's common room and a needle from the supply room. He stopped on the fourth floor to get the folded piece of paper from his desk. Lainn was already asleep, breathing deeply under his blanket. With a pounding heart and clammy hands, he made his way to the rooftop terrace.

The clouds blocked the moon, so the rooftops were dark. Kaleth could make out the walls of the fortress and the silhouette of both the castle and Central Tower, but little beyond. After tapping on a binder lamp, he hurried to a bench.

He unscrewed the lid to the bottle of ink, flattened the scrap of paper, and pulled the waist of his pants down on one side. He adjusted his weight to the opposite hip. The bare skin of the exposed side seemed to glow in the lamplight. He dipped the needle into the inkwell, then paused with it next to his skin.

He pushed the next day's test out of his mind. He tried to ignore the storm that drew closer. *May this glyph allow me to draw energy from other forms of life, like my father.*

He pressed the needle against his skin. The ink touched the exterior and transferred to the epidermis. It wasn't enough. If he wanted to mimic what his father had, he needed to get it under the surface. He pressed harder, wanting to avoid going too deep. The needle pushed the skin in. A sudden break delivered the ink underneath the surface and registered a sting in his brain—like the prick of a bee. He winced.

The needle slid out easier than it went in. A speck of ink remained under the skin, and a small bead of red dotted the surface. He released his breath then looked back at the drawing. His mouth turned down in a frown.

*This is going to take a lot of work.*

A flash filled the sky, closer than before. The following thunder took only a few seconds to arrive. Kaleth considered if it would be better to move somewhere else, but the rooftop's seclusion appealed to him, so he stayed. He turned his father's drawing upside down, so it would match his perspective. Then he dipped the needle in the ink again.

Finding the right pressure for the needle grew easier as he progressed. The inked design grew, marked by pricks of blood. Drops of sweat beaded on his forehead, a side effect of the constant, low-level pain.

When he had finished the F and part of his first curved line, the rain began. The drizzle was light, so he didn't scurry to leave. He pulled the bottle of ink close and leaned his body to keep the rain from hitting it or the canvas of his skin. Lightning and thunder repeated, still seconds apart.

The process took longer than he'd anticipated. The spots of ink gradually formed a design, but each painstaking prick of the needle felt insignificant compared to the overall task. While he managed the sting of each jab, the constant piercing of skin had a cumulative effect. His vision wavered, and an unsettled feeling grew in his gut.

The rain intensified. It thrummed against the back of his head, soaking his hair and dripping underneath his clothes. Splattered drops found their way to his hip, causing spots of blood to run down his leg. A crack of thunder boomed, concurrent with a burst of lightning that tore through the sky. Kaleth flinched, nearly knocking over the bottle of ink. He was on the last portion of the tattoo. The intensifying storm caused him to hurry.

He pricked his skin with less caution. The flares of pain were more acute as the needle dug deeper. He gripped the tool, flying between the bottle and his skin. The beads of blood grew larger in his final, careless pricks. The dizzy feeling that had left his brain fuzzy grew more pronounced. He steadied himself between jabs to ensure he didn't mess up the design.

As if backing into a spider's web, his hair felt as if something pulled it. His skin prickled. The static charge built until a bolt of lightning ripped through the air, crashing into the heart of the fortress. Kaleth flinched. But rather than explode the buildings with damage, it seemed to melt into the top of nearby Central Tower. The bolt flowed along its jagged line and disappeared into the tower as if something sucked it up. A muted "pop" filled the air rather than the expected peal of thunder. He turned back to his hip and blinked water off his eyelashes.

*Only a couple more pricks.*

The end was in sight. The driving rain splattered around him. His hip was wet, running with a fluid mix of red and black. Despite the mess on the surface of his skin, his father's design took shape underneath.

Kaleth jabbed his skin and winced at the depth of the puncture.

*One more.*

He dipped the needle into the ink. Drops of water fell from his hair to plunk the back of his hand. Bracing his wrist against his leg, he pressed the needle into the final spot. The needle pierced his skin and delivered the last blot of ink to complete the design.

A wave of relief flooded him. He closed his eyes and craned his neck back, stretching the muscles that had been hunched and tight. Rain fell on his face. While it didn't wash away the fear that had permeated his thoughts, it allowed a modicum of hope.

*Maybe this will do it. Maybe this design is all I need.*

A burst of thunder shook him from his reverie. He wiped the rain from his face and rushed to return the lid to the bottle. Holding the waist of his pants away from the tattoo site with one hand, he grabbed the bottle and stood.

The lingering pain from countless jabs splashed a wave of heat across his face. The dizziness he had felt while sitting reached a new level of intensity. He stepped toward the stairs, eager to get out of the rain. The terrace spun. He extended his arm for balance, but his legs wouldn't travel in a straight line. Each step lumbered closer until the doorway leading to the stairs fell on its side. As the doorway moved, Kaleth struggled to process what was happening. He felt light, as if sleep beckoned him.

He was only vaguely aware of a hard thud against the side of his head. The stairs no longer drew closer. The weight of his eyelids overshadowed his desire to get out of the rain, and he gave in to the pull of unconsciousness.

CHAPTER TWENTY-SEVEN

# THE STRENGTH TEST

A distant shouting echoed in Kaleth's dream. Urgent but hopeless. Familiar but strange.

"Kaleth!"

It called again. Kaleth's awareness of the voice grew clearer. Something hard lay against his side. His muddled brain pushed away the cobwebs, providing clarity to a throbbing ache that beat against him. He blinked his eyes open. His face lay in a puddle.

*Wha—What happened?*

He lay on the floor of the rooftop terrace. His stiff limbs ached as he sat up. The throbbing in his head intensified. He held a hand against it. The pressure did little to ease the pain.

The events of the previous evening came flooding back to him. The rain. The tattoo. He stretched to get a look at his hip. The waist of his askew pants covered part of it. He lifted the stained fabric from his skin. A near-replica of his father's tattoo displayed on his hip. The skin was still red and swollen, but most of the blood had washed off in the storm. What was left looked good.

Kaleth laughed to himself. *Let's hope it works.*

"Kaleth!"

He gasped. The voice called from over the edge of the terrace. Ignoring the beating pain in his head and the ache in his side, he made his way to his feet. The sun had just risen to the east, peeking over the horizon. He struggled to the edge and glanced down at the blurry group of initiates who gathered in the grass of Binder Court. Fear rushed through him.

*The test! It's starting!*

"I'm here!" he croaked. He cleared his throat as a few heads looked up. He waved an arm. "I'm coming!"

Bouncing off the walls of the staircase, he ran down the multiple flights. He adjusted his pants, cringing at how they rubbed the sensitive skin on his hips. He tightened the strap on his jacket.

*I can't believe I passed out. I need time to practice. I haven't figured out how to use this power yet!*

He grasped at fleeting thoughts as he descended. Grass. Animals. People. Energy. Strength. He had nothing around him to try it with. When he reached the ground floor, a stream of Lightbinder initiates jogged away from Binder Court toward the building's exit.

"Kaleth," Aurik barked.

Kaleth jerked to attention as the jogging principal slowed to a halt, letting others pass.

"I gave you leave, trusting you'd return on time."

"I did, sir," he panted. "I came back last night. I just—I slept in."

"Initiates are on time, always! Especially on testing days."

"I'm sorry, sir. It was an accident."

"If you miss a test, you don't get a pass—you're out."

"I'm here now, sir. I can still test, right?"

The principal blew out a frustrated breath. His tone softened. "Kaleth, you of all people need to be on your game today. I hope you find the strength you need." He resumed jogging and waved a hand for him to join the group.

Relief washed through Kaleth until two hands grabbed him by the jacket and shook him.

"What are you doing, Grunny!" Rayd yelled. "You made me look like a bind-cursed idiot this morning."

"I'm-I'm sorry."

"Not knowing where my squad is," he muttered. "If you weren't about to fail anyway, I'd kill you myself."

Kaleth kicked up into a slow jog, merging with the other initiates. Jovi pushed through the crowd to join him.

"Are you all right?" he asked. "What happened?"

His father's warning about not telling anyone stuck in Kaleth's mind. He couldn't think of a good explanation without giving away too much. He shrugged. "I couldn't sleep, then I finally fell asleep on the roof."

"We all thought you ran, trying to get away from the test."

Kaleth chuckled. "It crossed my mind."

"Then I thought, maybe the disemboweler got you, but obviously he didn't. Did you see your family?"

"Yeah, for a bit. They're doing—okay. I'm glad I went. Any word on what the test is?"

Jovi shook his head.

Kaleth thought through his body as he jogged. He had grown in strength during his weeks in the academy, but the poor night of sleep left his legs and arms weak and sore. The tattoo on his hip remained in his thoughts. He looked at the mossy greenery lining the halls, wondering how to pull energy from it as each step jostled him. He clenched his stomach, trying to grasp at any tendrils of strength he could find. The color of the plants didn't change; neither did the sensations in his body.

The line of jogging initiates exited the Lightbinder building and turned right. The corridor led to a staircase that climbed the fortress wall. Each step up left him more winded. When they arrived at the top, Kaleth hunched over, sucking air into his lungs.

"Welcome to your second test," Aurik called.

Kaleth forced himself upright to see what the principal referred to. Along the south battlements, dozens of stone merlons had somehow been pulled away from the edge, and small glowing boxes had been attached to the ends.

"When activated, these binder boxes will push the merlons back to their original positions, flush against the outer wall. The only thing that will stop them is weight—a lot of it. And you'll only have two minutes from when the merlon begins moving."

Kaleth gulped when he noticed the weight the principal referred to. On the close side of the wall, six red-handled ironballs sat in rows next to each station. Much larger than the green ones they'd been practicing with in Binder Court, Kaleth wasn't sure he'd be able to lift even one of them.

"You'll need all six of your weights resting against the moving object plus your own body pressing against it to stop the wall from pushing you off. Rolling the weights is not allowed, but you may drag them if you wish. If you can arrest the merlon's progress, the binder box will shut off. If you can't . . ."

Everyone's eyes drifted to the edge of the wall.

". . . it will be a long drop. If you fall, I recommend hitting head-first. The ones who land on their back or legs end up wailing in pain until we can get down there to put them out of their misery. And anyone who steps out from behind the obstacle to avoid it is cut."

Kaleth tried to swallow the lump in his throat, but it felt caught, like a rock he couldn't crush or breathe around. *This is it*, he thought. *If I can't do it, Mother and Sora are going to die.*

"Kaleth?"

His name snapped him from a trancelike state. Aurik stared at him, pointing a hand along the battlements. *How long have I been standing here?*

"Find a station."

The other initiates either already stood by one of the near merlons or were walking along the wall to reach the farther ones. Kaleth moved slowly, his boots dragging along the stone. He stared at the piles of weights as he passed. The meager progress he'd made in strength since he'd arrived was nothing compared to what was being asked of him. He had expected a spike of adrenaline—a rush of energy from a fight-or-flight reaction. Instead, he felt hollow and weak.

Jovi had taken the second-to-last station to be next to him. "Good luck," his friend said. Deep furrows dug between his brows. He pressed his lips together in a sorrowful, knowing expression.

The final merlon looked bulkier than the rest. The glowing binder box appeared brighter, and the balls of iron looked heavier. The only way he could survive was to figure out his father's power. With the tender tattoo still stinging his hip, Kaleth scanned the ground for any sign of life: moss, weeds, or even a small animal. The battlements were clean, nothing but stone. He had no source of power to pull from and no idea of how to do so even if he did.

He glanced at Jovi, who rested a hand on the merlon and stared at his own weights, ten feet away. The sorrow was gone. His face pinched in focused determination.

"When your box activates, you begin!" Aurik projected from the far end of the initiates.

A surge of nerves ran through him, sparking him to life. His heart beat faster. His sinuses felt clearer. He looked at his stack of ironballs. They taunted him, sitting in a pile. He touched his fingers against the stone side of the merlon. The surface was smooth, worn down by years of wind.

Aurik, Falmouth, Sorene, and Norum had spread out along the wall, spacing themselves between the long row of initiates. Ten stations down, Norum touched the binder box of a young woman from Claw Squad with her hair pulled back tight. She jumped toward her weights and squatted as the stone barrier began a deep hum that combined with a rough grinding sound. Kaleth watched long enough to see her stand back up, holding one of the ironballs in front of her body. She tottered side-to-side as she struggled under the weight.

Norum progressed down the line, starting each merlon and sending the waiting initiate surging to action. Kaleth's mouth grew dryer with each activation. The tips of his fingers trembled against the stone. He pressed his boot into the grit of the battlements.

Norum touched the box connected to his station. The light glow intensified, and a rumble began. "Go," he called.

Kaleth pushed off the stone and hurried to the pile of iron. Each weight looked the same size, so he started with the closest one. The object was round but had a handle worked into the top. He squatted, keeping his back straight and chest up. Both hands wrapped around the grip. He paused for two beats of his heart and a quick breath. With a surge of power, he pulled with his arms and pushed with his legs. The weight strained his hands. It felt heavier than he'd anticipated. His grip held, but he couldn't lift the weight off the ground.

After a moment of straining, he stopped his effort. He kicked out his legs and shook his hands. After another deep breath, he squatted over the weight again, spreading his legs wider. They trembled as the ironball inched off the ground.

*I'm doing it! I'm doing it!*

Standing with the weight in hand, Kaleth shuffled his feet toward the edge of the wall. The jostling movement swung the object, straining his hands even more. After a few lumbering steps, his body couldn't take it anymore. He gasped as he dropped the weight with a thud.

He panted and stepped back from the object. A sinking feeling rose in his gut. He had only moved a quarter of the distance. The sliding merlon reminded him he had no time to rest. Despite his protesting legs and arms, he returned to the weight and gripped it. His efforts to stand with it again were unsuccessful.

*No! This can't be happening!*

He strained his muscles but still couldn't lift the object. Desperate to move it, he turned his feet. Rather than lift it, he attempted to slide it forward. The change in tactic worked. The ironball moved. It was only a few inches, but it was better than nothing. Encouraged, Kaleth adjusted his feet and slid it again. The weight crept across the parapet, moving toward the shrinking gap at the edge of the wall. After several short bursts of movement, the ironball made it to the opposite side of the sliding barrier.

Kaleth nurtured a foolish hope that when the merlon touched the single weight, it would somehow be enough to stop its momentum. That hope was dashed the second they touched. The sliding wall continued forward, pushing the weight with it as if it were a pebble. It had already traveled half the distance to the edge.

Kaleth's heart sank. Gasping for air, he glanced down the battlements. Jovi worked on his fourth weight, and the other initiates looked to be in a similar place.

A shriek tore through the air from somewhere along the wall. The yell faded quickly as if a victim had plunged to their death. The sound sent a chill through him, but he had no time to dwell on it.

*I can't do it. There's not enough time.*

He touched his hip where his tattoo hid beneath his pants.

*What do I need to do, Father? How do I make this work?*

No answers returned. No ideas came. He scoured the wall again but found no traces of plant or animal life. Jovi caught his eye. He entertained trying to steal his energy for a second, but quickly dismissed it. *I couldn't do that to him even if I knew how.*

Kaleth closed his eyes. The scent of sweat and fear filled his nose. The wall scraped closer to the edge. He reached out with his senses, searching for anything that could help, unsure of what it would even feel like.

A prickle flitted through his body, and his breath hitched. *What was that?*

Life.

He felt it—a thread of a growing object filled with energy and vitality. He spun to find the source but saw nothing. His heart pounded harder. He took a step toward the edge of the wall. The long drop loomed, sending a wave of dizziness through his body. Keeping a foot away from the edge, he leaned forward. From Ramble Square, the precipitous path wound up toward the fortress, one hundred feet below. Kaleth gasped when he saw it.

Vines.

They clung to the wall, growing in thick clumps with broad leaves. A desperate hope filled his chest. He closed his eyes and clenched his muscles.

*Father, please help me.*

He touched the spot on his hip. A slow breath steadied his pulse. He blocked out the grinding of the stone wall and focused on the vines. Life. Energy. Power. His fists clenched. He inhaled a slow breath, willing the energy from the plant to come into him.

A tingle rippled at his hip, then shuddered down his leg. Kaleth gasped. He pulled harder at the invisible threads. With each passing second, his body transformed. The fatigue in his legs evaporated. His arms felt fresh. The aching in his lungs eased, and the weight on his chest lifted. He pulled again. The energy continued to flood him, past anything he'd ever experienced. His muscles felt like rocks. Power filled his body.

His eyes shot open. Quickened breath came from the thrill of power instead of fatigue. He sighted the pile of weights and strode toward them. A quick bend of his knees allowed him to wrap both hands around the handle of the next weight. He stood as easily as if he rose from a chair. He felt the bulk of the object, but carrying it posed no trouble. It was as if he were out for an afternoon stroll. Back at the moving wall, he chuckled to himself as he set the weight down beside the other.

The next object felt just as easy. While returning with the fourth, heat washed over his face while he was halfway back. His brows pinched together. The casual stride he'd adopted devolved into staggering lurches of his feet. The strain on his arm flared. When the burden became unbearable, he dropped the iron weight, having barely made it back to the sliding merlon.

Sweat had burst across his brow. His lungs struggled to get the oxygen they needed. He bent over and rested his hands on his knees, heaving for air. The stone wall continued to slide, but it moved slower than before. He blanched when he realized how little space he had left to stand.

*Only a moment left!*

He closed his eyes again and pushed the tendrils of his mind over the wall to seek any energy he could grasp. The vines were there again but fainter than before. He breathed in their life, letting it fuel him. He pulled as hard as he could, desperate for the energy to bolster his muscles. The power filled him, but not as readily as it did the first time.

With only a few seconds to spare, Kaleth rushed around the corner of the merlon. The final two weights taunted him from where they sat. He crouched and grasped a handle with each arm. The weight was significant, but he stood. Each arm rested at his side, hands clutched in a sweaty grip. He staggered back under the unimaginable weight, watching the remaining ledge grow narrower. His mind told him to forget about it—that it was too late. But his body forced him onward.

The other four weights were close to being pushed off the lip. Carrying both weights made him too bulky to walk forward, so he turned sideways and shuffled into the path of danger. His back faced the open air and the long fall it contained. Wind brushed his hair, threatening to pull him off the wall. He stared at the merlon that moved inexorably toward the edge. As soon as he found spare ground space, he dropped the last two balls of iron against the moving barrier.

A scream sounded from somewhere down the line.

His wall groaned. Despite the six iron weights, the binder box continued pushing, inching the stone object toward the brink. *It's not enough!* The backs of Kaleth's feet hung over the drop. A gust of wind ran up the wall, tossing his hair. Standing on his toes, he leaned forward and pressed his hands against the merlon. Push too hard and he'd send himself over the lip. He pressed as hard as he could. His toes strained to maintain their grip. His balance threatened to tip while sweat poured down his face.

Another yell reached his ears. Closer this time.

He turned a boot sideways, pressing it against the base of the wall. With no room, the other leg waved in the open air. The six ironballs had reached the end of the ledge and dangled their weight over the lip.

A growl rumbled in Kaleth's throat. It grew louder as he pressed harder. A swoop in his stomach flared when he felt his center of gravity shift. He no longer balanced over the ledge, but fell away. With his last second, he dug the side of his foot in and pushed harder with his hands in a surge of effort.

A click sounded from the other side of the barrier, and the merlon stopped moving. A gasp escaped Kaleth's mouth. His push turned into a desperate grasp at the top edge of the stone object. His arms stretched, and his fingers held, preventing him from dropping off the side.

The wind continued to tease his hair, but everything else was silent. One foot remained on the narrow ledge, but the rest of his body hung over the drop. He managed a nervous laugh while a smile tugged at his lips.

*I did it!*

A gust of wind reminded him he wasn't out of danger yet. Working hand over hand and using the narrow ledge for his feet, he made his way around the stone object. When both feet regained solid footing and his body no longer dangled over a precipice, his limbs shook.

"Kaleth!" The breathy exclamation of his name turned him to the closest station, where Jovi hunched over his knees. His friend's chest heaved, but he had lifted his head toward him with a hanging jaw. "You made it!"

Kaleth managed a weak smile. "Barely."

"That's incredible. How did you—" The creased lines on Jovi's forehead grew thicker. "Last I saw, you had hardly moved anything. You carried them all?"

Kaleth felt his ears redden. He nodded.

Jovi beamed. "All that training. It must have paid off."

A glance down the row showed the rest of the initiates in various stages of exhaustion. At the far end, Rayd stood tall, barely looking winded. His merlon appeared to have stopped close to the start of its path. The squad leader's shoulders faced Kaleth while a deep scowl covered his face.

The magnitude of what had just happened hit him like a smack in the face.

*I can't believe I did it!* His father's power worked. He had drawn energy from a vine to give him the strength he needed. *A vine!* An incredulous chortle escaped his mouth. He survived the trial—the one he had felt the least capable of passing.

Pulling back the hem of his pants, he gasped to find the tattoo remained. Not that he expected a tattoo to disappear, but normal glyphs faded after they'd served their purpose. *I guess tattoo glyphs are different.* He covered it up again. Even though it was hidden, the mark on his hip felt conspicuous, like anyone who saw it would know he was a fraud.

*I'm not, though.* He smiled. *I lived.* He looked out from the wall while he let his breath settle. Past the square, the narrow alleys of Grunwind twisted and turned, leading to the edge of the city. It was small from his height, but he recognized the roof of his parents' house. He swallowed hard. *Mother's house.* He was one step closer to saving her and Sora. One *big* step.

While staring over Kalistor, his eyes widened. Even across the city, the buildings weren't blurry. He blinked several times and waved a hand across his face. *I can see.* The poor sight that had plagued him for years seemed to have healed.

The mysterious power pricked his mind. Even though he'd made it work, he still understood next to nothing. A step closer to the edge of the wall made his vision spin. He touched the stone merlon for balance. While he wanted nothing more to do with the steep drop, he had to know. He leaned over the edge and gasped. The vines remained where they climbed up the fortress wall, but the greenery was gone. The lush leaves and vibrant tendrils had shriveled to yellow-brown scraps of the life they once held. Halfway down the wall, the color returned, morphing from the death pallor to the lively green it had all been minutes before.

What terrified Kaleth the most wasn't the fact that the vines had died but rather the shape they made. Extending in a parabola to his right and left, the dead foliage formed a perfect arc that conspicuously centered on his station. He held his breath.

"Grunny!"

Rayd's call made Kaleth jump. Had he not been holding on, he might have tumbled over the edge. He spun to find his squad leader standing with crossed arms, two stations away. The rest of the initiates already headed back toward the steps they'd taken to get there. Dozens of Grunts dressed in brown worked in teams to clear the iron weights, set the merlons to their original positions, and remove the binder squares.

Rayd beckoned for him to join the others. "Get a move on. We've got morning conditioning. By some dumb luck, you didn't die here today, so that means you have more work to do."

Kaleth grinned. He had lived through the toughest test he could imagine. "Can I get you to sign my skill log?" He fished the log out of the inside of his jacket and extended it toward the squad leader. "Ironball carry for weight? I'd say this counts, right?"

With pursed lips, Rayd looked to where Kaleth's merlon had stopped. "I can't sign you off. I didn't see anything."

"But . . . I moved them. You can see they're over there, now."

"If I don't see it happen, I can't sign off on it." A smirk grew on his face. "It wouldn't be fair." Dropping the subject, Rayd turned and walked off.

Kaleth tucked the log back in his jacket. Despite the frustration with Rayd, he couldn't be brought down. He walked taller as he joined the progression of initiates. For the first time since his father had died, he had reason to hope.

## CHAPTER TWENTY-EIGHT

# INCREASED SUSPICION

After pushing his body to its limit during the strength test, conditioning was brutal. Kaleth lagged even farther behind the other initiates than normal. Every patch of moss and clump of weeds he passed begged him to suck its energy into his body. He could ease his pain and improve his performance, but the terrifying thought of losing control and someone noticing what he could do kept him from trying.

During weapons training, Dragon Squad worked on the broadsword. Kaleth followed through the movements, but he felt slow. The blade seemed bulkier than usual. After having tasted the ability to draw in extra energy, everything paled in comparison.

When they returned to the common room after morning practice, the ranking board held everyone's attention. Nine initiates had failed the strength trial. Two had been pushed off the wall when they ran out of time. Several gave up, stepping away from the edge just before the end. Garod, from Dragon Squad, tripped on an iron-ball and fell over the side halfway through the test. Dropping to six squad members was a sobering reminder for the group. The remaining candidates had their rankings updated by how they fared on the test and their performance in daily training and classes.

As he expected, Kaleth remained at the end of the list, ranked thirty-first. His abilities in the classroom couldn't overcome his physical liability. Rayd must have impressed the instructors to move up to slot three. Roselle congratulated their squad leader by slapping his butt. Despite the high ranking and the playful smack, his face never changed from a frown.

Kaleth dipped his spoon into his soup, but his eyes were fixed across the dining hall. Headmaster Genoris and Instructor Beram engaged in conversation. Kaleth wished the headmaster would notice he was there, that he'd survived the strength test, but the man had yet to look.

"How'd you do it?" Lainn asked before he even sat, joining Jovi, Chyla, and Kaleth at the long table of the dining hall.

Kaleth froze with a spoonful of soup in his mouth. He raised his eyebrows.

"Garod couldn't make it in time. Even Tuomo and Marc from Raven. They weren't the *strongest*, but . . ."

"But, what?" Kaleth mumbled around his mouthful of soup. "What are you saying about me?"

Lainn blushed and squirmed in his seat.

Kaleth allowed a smile. "I'm teasing you. I know . . . I was the worst."

Lainn chuckled and his shoulders relaxed. "I wasn't saying *that*. I meant . . ." His words faded, leading to an awkward silence.

Jovi leaned forward and looked at Kaleth. "You were the worst."

The group burst into laughter, Kaleth included. He nodded. "I think I just needed that extra push—you know? My life was on the line. I think it helped me find an extra bucket of strength I hadn't been able to tap into yet."

His squad nodded as he spoke.

Kaleth shrugged. "Maybe I'm stronger than I realized."

"That's two trials down," Jovi said, "and we're still here. Two more to go this year. What is next? Fear?"

"Knowledge," Lainn replied. "Whatever that means."

Kaleth relaxed. He welcomed something that didn't focus on

physical abilities. "We'll keep studying in the evenings—reviewing everything they teach us."

A commotion across the dining hall turned their heads. The Mender initiates at the far table had stood, looking toward the door and blocking Kaleth's view of whatever they stared at. A feminine scream ripped through the room. He jumped to his feet.

A Lightbinder initiate stumbled through the door, Atheas on Tiger Squad. Blood poured out of his mouth and dripped down his chin. His jaw moved as if he tried to speak, but only moaning sounds came out. His black-and-red jacket had been ripped open, and a bloody mess streaked across his bare chest.

Bow and Lightbinder initiates swarmed toward the door, surrounding the stumbling arrival. The clamor of the room blocked whatever the young man tried to say.

Kaleth pressed forward, rounding the end of the table to get closer. He peered over shoulders and around heads.

"Quiet!" someone near the victim yelled. "Let him speak!" The crowd hushed. "What happened, Atheas?"

The young man's jaw moved again, but no words formed—only more moaning.

The horrifying truth hit Kaleth as another initiate spoke it.

"Someone cut his tongue out."

Gasps filled the room. Atheas' eyes rolled back in his sockets, and he swayed. Initiates reached to steady him but couldn't prevent him from collapsing to the ground. The silence evaporated as voices clamored to be heard. The crowd pressed closer in various states of concern and curiosity.

A twisting feeling pulled at Kaleth's gut. The memory of Lorenzo hanging on the wall rushed to his mind.

The noise faded. Those closest to the initiate took steps backward.

"What's going on?" a voice called from the top of the stairs. Professor Beram led several instructors who descended.

"He's-He's dead," someone muttered from the crowd. "And there's a message on his chest. In blood." Silence filled the room.

At the end of the instructor line, Headmaster Genoris looked like the wind in his sails had disappeared. His shoulders slumped, and his eyes found Kaleth's.

"What is it?" Beram asked, quieter as he pushed through the crowd to arrive near the dead initiate. The room seemed to hold its breath as those near the body stared down with focused attention.

"What does it say?" Genoris asked, his voice projecting through the room.

Beram stepped back. His chest deflated. "It's a warning. It-it—" He stopped speaking.

"Read it." The headmaster's command left no room for discussion.

"*You ignored my last warning,*" Beram read in a shaking voice. "*Initiates will continue to die until you listen.*"

The heavy silence weighed on Kaleth's shoulders.

A Raven Lightbinder cut through the quiet. "What warning?"

The crowd turned toward the stairs where the headmaster had paused halfway down. Pinned by their stares, he appeared more uncomfortable with each second of silence. An exaggerated swallow preceded clearing his throat. "This academy exists to train the next generation of warriors to defend Kalshia, but someone is attempting to thwart what we're doing here. Yes, there was another attack. An initiate was killed weeks ago."

A rumble of mutters rolled through the room.

Genoris raised a hand. "The instructors are handling it. The irrelevant warning was of no consequence."

"Death comes to the academy? Leave while you can?" Lainn's voice carried through the room. "All will die?"

Kaleth turned to his squad mate and found the young man looking his way. *He believes me.* A grim smile pulled at his mouth.

"Yes," Genoris admitted, catching Kaleth's eye with a glare leveled in his direction, "that was the message."

"And you kept it from us?" a faceless voice called from the Bows. Other voices added to the building chaos.

"We had a right to know!"

"What are you doing about it?"

"We should leave before we're next!"

"I expected this would happen," Jovi said to Kaleth.

Genoris raised both arms and projected over the tumult. "Fear and intimidation are weapons of an overmatched adversary. This threat is a desperate attempt to put us on edge and cause dissension in our ranks. We must not give in. The academy staff will find who is doing this, and we will stop them."

The disquiet in the room settled some, but many initiates continued muttering.

Kaleth stepped closer to Atheas' body. Blood surrounded his mouth and dripped down the side of his face. The writing on his chest streaked and ran, still wet. The macabre sight was hard to stomach. A dark line across the initiate's leather jacket caught his eye. Kaleth frowned.

"I'm gone," a voice said. A young man in a yellow jacket walked to the door of the dining hall. Five other Bows joined him, then two Lightbinders followed, members of Claw Squad. The remaining initiates looked far from settled.


"Hey."

Kaleth looked up toward the whisper. Lainn and Chyla had turned around at their desk.

"Sorry for not believing you," Lainn said. "About Lorenzo. I didn't want it to be true, so I think it was easier to ignore."

Kaleth shrugged. "It's no problem."

"Who do you think's doing it?" Chyla asked.

"It's gotta be a Lightbinder student, right?" Jovi suggested.

Chyla nodded. "That's what I was thinking."

"It doesn't *have* to be," Lainn said. "Why do you think that?"

"They're hitting Lightbinder initiates and threatening to kill more," Jovi said. "Who gains by Lightbinders dying or leaving?"

"Initiates trying to make the top six," Lainn said.

"Exactly. If they kill the competition or scare them off, it makes it easier for someone to make it at the end of the year."

Kaleth's eyes darted around the room. The other initiates hunched over their desks, discussing with their partners. Headmaster Genoris paced between the tables near the front of the class. "It could be a Thravian spy," Kaleth said.

"Now you sound like Jovi," Lainn said.

Chyla's eyes widened. "Like you mentioned during strategy class?"

Kaleth nodded. "That could explain their motivation."

Lainn frowned. "Yeah, but . . . we're just initiates. What does someone gain by killing us off one by one? I'm sure we'll still have at least six at the end of the year to make Lightbinder."

"Which is why I think it's an initiate," Jovi said.

Lainn thought for a moment before adding, "Maybe it's more than one."

The thought hadn't occurred to Kaleth. It was chilling to consider but made sense—coordinating multiple killings in secret would take help.

"Eyes on your own desks," Genoris boomed.

Lainn and Chyla spun back around.

Kaleth's attention returned to the seven colored vials sitting on the desk before him. The aromas coming from the liquids mixed in the air, creating a sharp, peppery scent. Before him, notes on color, viscosity, and scent filled a sheet of paper. He'd even added comments about taste—based on what his father had taught him.

"More than one," Jovi breathed at his side. "It makes sense."

"Yeah, it does," Kaleth admitted. "I'm guessing it wouldn't be anyone from our squad. There's no time to get away to do something like that, unless it was Rayd and Roselle. They're on their own more. But they're ranked so high that I bet they'll make it on their own without having to kill everyone."

Genoris clapped his hands, bringing the class' attention to the front. "All right, that's long enough. Who wants to go first? Would someone please describe and identify the first vial?" His head rotated on a swivel, taking in the room. A young woman from Claw raised her hand. Genoris gestured toward her. "Go ahead."

She lifted the first glass tube, holding it toward the light coming through the window. "Color is reddish-orange. Smells of blood-thorn and citrus. It's thick, clinging to the sides of the vial. This makes it sangrell, or . . . the Mediciner's Poison.

The headmaster smiled. "Very good. What does it taste like?" The Claw initiate blanched, causing him to chuckle. "No, you don't need to drink it. Do you have any idea?"

The lines on her forehead deepened before she shook her head.

"Orange and lilac with earthy accents," Genoris said.

*And it sticks to your throat*, Kaleth thought, remembering testing it under his father's supervision.

"Do you remember what it's used for?"

The furrows in the girl's forehead lessened. "Um . . . doctors use it."

"Yes."

"They . . ." She glanced at her table mate, but the young man sitting with her only shrugged. "They give it to people who are sick?"

"Sick with what?"

She thought for a moment, then shrugged.

"Cenrrheic worms," Genoris said, causing the class to squirm. "The parasites in your gut cause your body to expel its contents. You become unable to hold down food or water, then you die of dehydration. The sangrell poison acts within hours, burning the lining of your stomach. It gives you uncomfortable bowel movements for a week, but it also kills and flushes the worms."

Kaleth's father only had him try a small sip so he could remember the flavor and sensation. Even that small amount had caused him discomfort for a couple of days.

"What about the second one?" Genoris asked.

Jovi's hand shot up.

"Yes?"

Jovi lifted the container with a green liquid. The potion was a common sight, displayed in the windows of all apothecary shops. "Heartsoothe," he began. "An antidote that cures half the poisons found in nature."

"Good," Genoris said. "Where does it come from?"

Jovi shrugged. "A heartsoothe bush?"

The class laughed.

"Heartsoothe is brewed from the leaves of the sporadicus fern," Genoris answered. "Yes, it is found through Kalshia and cures a variety of poisons: black tiger, lincerric acid, berryflayer, death-bloom"—he pointed back to the previous vial—"sangrell . . . and lots more."

Jovi sat down, looking content with himself.

"Next?" the headmaster prompted.

Rayd lifted his chin along with a hand.

"Yes, squad leader. Please describe and identify the next one."

Rayd touched the third vial. "Deep blue color. It smells of berries with a hint of juniper. The liquid is thin. It's supposed to have a sharp, tart taste."

"And its name?"

"Bellick—although it's often mistaken for its benign counter-part, barrill, which is used to reduce inflammation after injuries. Bellick's berry flavor makes it an excellent choice to mix with an enemy's food."

Jovi whispered to Kaleth, "Berries. See, I told you."

Kaleth rolled his eyes.

"And how long does it take to kill a man?" Genoris asked.

"Symptoms show in an hour, and they'll be dead in three."

Genoris smiled broadly. "Excellent. Is there an antidote?"

The smirk on Rayd's face faltered, giving way to deepened lines. "I'm not sure."

The headmaster spread his arms in a grand gesture. "Nature exists in balance. For example . . . the fire fern growing at the back of my class."

Kaleth glanced back and looked at the green fronds Garod had touched on their first day.

"It causes irritation and tingling when you touch it because the oil in its leaves reacts with our skin. Ground squirrels prefer to burrow in their midst, though. Why?"

Jovi lifted a tentative hand. "Because they're not affected by the oils."

"Yes, so why would they burrow there?"

"Because everything else reacts to it?"

"Correct," Genoris said. "Potential predators steer clear of the plant, leaving the squirrels hiding in their midst. Plants and animals rely on each other to survive. This is balance. Like a symbiotic relationship, there's always an antidote to a poison. Droppings of the squirrels can make a salve that neutralizes the pain of the plant." The headmaster paused, but no one seemed to have anything to add. "So an antidote to bellick?"

Kaleth racked his brain, but couldn't remember anything.

"What makes it deadly?" Genoris asked.

"The bark of the bellberry bush," Rayd answered.

"Fresh bark. Yes. When brewed in juniper tree sap, the oils from the wood strips become concentrated and potent. What exists to counterbalance the bark's poison in nature?"

The instructor scanned the room, looking at each desk. The class was quiet.

Kaleth brought up an inkling of an idea from the recesses of his brain. He lifted his hand. "Constructor ants?"

Genoris beamed again. "What about them?"

Kaleth's pulse quickened. "They live on the bushes, don't they?"

"You tell me."

He swallowed a lump. "If I'm remembering correctly, constructor ants ingest the outer layer of the bellberry bush, then regurgitate it to build their colonies. I wonder if something about the ants' digestive process counteracts the poison."

"An excellent supposition, Kaleth," Genoris said. He winked, then opened up to the entire class. "The initiate is correct. Constructor ants live in harmony with the otherwise-deadly bellberry bush. A dozen of these ants ground in a mortar then brewed into a tea create a reliable antidote to the bellick poison."

Jovi chuckled then muttered, "Ant-idote."

Kaleth rolled his eyes.

"But there is a problem. The tea is unique. It takes around five hours to work through your system and counteract the poison."

Kaleth frowned. "But you'll be dead in three."

"That is where shock nettle comes in."

Kaleth was familiar with the rare plant and its unique properties, but he wasn't sure how it would heal someone from a poison.

Genoris lifted a glass jar from behind his desk and set it on the table. Green leaves filled the jar to the brim. He placed a glass of water next to it. After sliding on a glove, he selected a leaf from the jar.

"Shock nettle leaves—difficult to find. They grow on the slopes of the Kalshian Mountains . . ." He allowed a grin. "Or upstairs in my greenhouse."

*Realm: Plantia. Category: Shrubae. Group: Nettle. Strain: Shock Nettle.*

Keeping his hand clear of the water's surface, Genoris dropped the leaf into the cup. A hum filled the air. The leaf danced on the surface, moving in jerks. The water trembled as if a gigantic beast walked next to it.

"Do you hear that?" The headmaster asked. "A current runs through this water. If you drink it . . ." He paused, allowing a grin to grow on his face while he watched Kaleth.

His father's lesson about reaper morels and how a catalyzer could speed their absorption came to mind.

"It would shock the antidote, making it work faster," Kaleth finished.

"Exactly! Incredible, isn't it?"

Kaleth found it all fascinating, but he struggled to stay focused. As the class continued discussing the line of poisons, his mind wandered back to the dying initiates and the threat to the academy. The memory of the sounds Atheas and his missing tongue made caused him to shiver.

*Two people dead and more will come.*

He had enough to worry about just trying to stay alive through Lightbinder training. Another threat felt like too much to wrap his mind around. Even so, the fear in the eyes of the other initiates during lunch stuck with him.

They finished talking through the rest of the samples—a mixture of poisons derived from plants and animals. All were familiar to Kaleth.

"That's all we have for today," Genoris announced. "Does anyone have questions?"

The room was quiet for a long moment. A blonde girl from Claw lifted a hand. "Do you have any idea who is killing initiates?"

The headmaster's face soured. "Any questions about what we discussed in class?" he clarified.

The girl persisted. "I heard Seppo from Iron Squad is missing, too."

"He's the guy with the tattoo around his neck and the triangle beard, right?" one of her squad mates added. "He's gone?"

"That's what someone told me," the girl said. "Do you think the same person who's killing the initiates took him, Headmaster?"

Genoris' jaw was shut tight. The room waited for an answer that he didn't look interested in giving. "I haven't heard about Seppo being missing, but I can assure you the trainers and instructors are doing everything they can to put a stop to it. You all have nothing to worry about."

The hollow words did little to ease the tension in the room.

"Time is up." He shooed a hand toward the door. "Next class will get into reactive minerals. Review what we went over today. You never know when your life may depend on it."

CHAPTER TWENTY-NINE
# TOWER CONNECTION

Kaleth joined his squad, exiting the door. His feet followed one after the other, but his mind was elsewhere as he traversed the hall.

"I spent time with Seppo," Lainn said ahead of him to Chyla and Jovi, pulling Kaleth from his stupor. "We talked on the ride to the plains for the first test. He was from Grassmoor."

"I sat by him yesterday at supper," Chyla said.

"Really?" Jovi leaned in. "Was he all right?"

"He was, then. Seemed like it."

"Do you remember his rank?" Jovi asked.

"Mid-twenties, I think," Chyla said. "At least before today. Why?"

"Twenty-four," Lainn said.

"Just curious if I would move up, if he's really gone," Jovi said.

"Jovi!" Kaleth chided.

His friend shrugged. "What? I'm not *wishing* him dead. Just curious."

*Twenty-four*, Kaleth thought. He stopped when his squad mates began down the stairs that led to the dining hall. "You all go on. I'll catch up," he called as he turned around.

Kaleth pushed past the crowd of departing initiates until the hall was clear. He passed the classroom they'd just left and continued along the passage until he entered the square compartment of the binder lift. The lever on the wall worked just like he remembered. When he pulled it, a lurching motion indicated the room was rising. A short period later, it stopped and opened up. He followed the hall to find Genoris' office.

The headmaster faced the back wall and dusted his hand over the ridge of an exposed stone brick. He appeared transfixed, lost in deep thought. On his desk sat a cluster of four spherical objects, each about the size of a fist.

"Headmaster," Kaleth greeted. "Is everything all right?"

Genoris turned and forced a smile. "Kaleth. Welcome. Yes, everything is fine." He stepped toward the chair behind his desk, but his feet hesitated. "To be honest . . . no. My mind has been troubled lately."

Kaleth frowned. He hadn't expected such a candid response. "Because of the killings?"

The headmaster inhaled a deep breath, then nodded. "Leading the academy is a challenging task."

"Being *in* the academy is more challenging than I imagined, too." Kaleth picked up one of the round objects from the desk and readied to toss it.

"No!" Genoris lunged forward, extending his hands. Kaleth froze. "Don't toss that."

"Sorry. What is it?"

The headmaster plucked the sphere from his hand and gingerly placed it back on the desk. "Have you heard of binder orbs?"

Kaleth shook his head.

Genoris nodded. "All in due time. We'll talk about them next year. Congratulations on passing the strength trial—no easy feat, especially considering . . ." His words faded as if he had second thoughts about the end of his sentence.

"Thank you, sir."

"What changed?"

Kaleth thought of the tattoo hiding beneath the waistband of his pants. "What do you mean?"

"From what I hear, you struggled in training. I can tell you've grown stronger since you arrived." The headmaster pointed to his body. "The improvement in muscular definition is clear, but even so . . . not quite what we're used to."

"I think the stakes helped me dig deeper—do it or fail. It's motivating. I found strength I didn't know I had."

His squad mates had accepted the explanation, but the headmaster only stared for a long and quiet moment. "I don't think that's it."

Kaleth's throat ran dry. He shifted his hips. "What do you mean?"

Genoris gave him a moment to squirm before he headed toward the balcony doors and waved for him to follow. The view outside was as epic as Kaleth remembered: the castle, the city on the cliff, and the distant, barren lands of Thravia.

Genoris leaned against the railing of the circular balcony and crossed his arms. "There's something else in there, more than digging deep. When we first met, you said you were here to protect your family. You weren't speaking in the general sense of keeping the kingdom safe, were you?"

Kaleth swallowed to wet his throat. "No, sir."

"Would you like to talk about it?"

The invitation to share was a welcome offer. The softness in the headmaster's eyes eased the swirling in his gut. "We're in debt." The words cracked as he spoke them. "We fell on hard times, and my father was—" He choked back the emotion that threatened to bubble to the surface. "He was killed."

"I'm so sorry."

"Now, the debt is on me, and my mother and sister are the collateral. If I can't raise the money by the end of the year, they're dead, too."

"How much do you owe?"

"One hundred gold."

The headmaster's eyes widened. After a moment, a sparkle of recognition filled them and a soft chuckle escaped his lips. "One hundred . . . the wages of a Lightbinder. That's why you signed up."

Kaleth nodded.

"It explains so much. Why someone like you would—" Genoris didn't finish his sentence.

Kaleth averted his gaze. It was foolish for him to have signed up. His desperation had purpose despite being against impossible odds. His eyes landed on the Thravian buildings of Revalle that sprang from the barrens, far in the distance but newly sharp to his sight.

"My parents died when I was fifteen. My brothers were two and four years younger than me, and they needed money. That was a major factor in why I joined, too. For you . . . there's something else, isn't there?"

He turned back to the headmaster, who squinted at him.

"Saving your family is enough to drive a man to the edge of the world, but something else motivates you."

Kaleth looked down and frowned. His thoughts turned to Rayd: the smug grin, the privileged upbringing, the look on his face when he threw his father's book into the fire. The exal general's son. Number three in the Lightbinder rankings. Naming the up-and-coming initiate and admitting Kaleth wanted to kill him wouldn't do him any favors.

"*Someone* caused my father's death," he said. "And that person deserves to pay."

The headmaster's eyebrows raised. "Revenge. A dangerous motivator."

"I understand how foolish it—"

"Dangerous . . . but powerful."

Kaleth stared at the headmaster, noticing the heavy lines that had appeared on his forehead.

"I understand the feeling. When I was an initiate, another boy wronged me. He was highborn; I was lowborn. I embarrassed him by besting him in a sparring match. He had grown up training with a master-at-arms. What he didn't know was that my father—the finest cutpurse in all of Lynharbor—had trained me with daggers since I was old enough to walk. In the showers, I gained a vague sense that something was wrong when everyone left at once. I turned too late and was hit with a sack of iron pellets across the face. They wouldn't stop beating me no matter how loud I yelled. He and his friends left me a mess, bleeding and bruised on the floor of the showers. I lost two months of training while I recovered."

Kaleth cringed.

"I wanted him to pay—him and his friends. My thoughts took me to some bad places—so dark they terrified me. I wrestled with it every day while focusing on taking care of myself. In the end . . . I graduated as a Lightbinder, and he did not."

Kaleth leaned in, waiting for more. "Did you . . . ?"

"Did I kill him? No . . . I didn't. I tried to forget about him. I received help from others to get better, and I focused on my work. It's been over forty years, but I still remember the terrible things I dreamed about doing to him. Those thoughts never leave me."

"That's awful."

"Revenge. It's powerful, motivating, and easy to follow. But when you tread that path, you often find yourself in a place you never wanted to be."

"It's Rayd," Kaleth blurted.

Genoris' eyebrows lifted.

"Rayd-il-Stonne killed my father, and the constables wouldn't do anything."

"I see. A difficult person to take revenge against, for sure. Like him or not, we need Rayd. And don't forget that killing fellow initiates is strictly dealt with. I trust you're not planning to do anything about it."

Kaleth swallowed a lump. He wanted to shake his head, but his muscles wouldn't move. His voice turned breathy. "I'm not sure I'm brave enough to do anything even if I wanted to."

"Bravery." The headmaster lifted his chin. "Don't sell yourself short, Kaleth. Just like the antidotes to poisons, bravery can be learned."

His heart beat quicker. "How do I learn it?"

"I'll tell you my secret."

He leaned closer, ears perked.

"What holds you back from doing something brave?"

"Um . . . fear?"

"Exactly. Fear keeps people from trying something new. It prevents attempts at greatness if there's a hint something could go wrong. But what if nothing could go wrong? What if there was no path that could lead to failure or pain?"

"No risk of getting hurt? I guess I wouldn't hesitate."

"Fear comes from inside you. It's your mind telling you all the ways something *could* go wrong." The headmaster's eyebrows lifted. "But what if you told yourself something different?"

"What do you mean?"

"Focus on the outcome you *want* to happen. Picture yourself winning the fight. Imagine the girl saying yes. Don't let your mind entertain the thought of failure. Fear does nothing but hold you back from trying. If you want to be brave, push fear back and replace it with thoughts of what you want to happen."

"Push the fear back," Kaleth nodded. "It sounds easy when you put it like that. I'll work on it. Thanks."

"Now, when it comes to Rayd, take my advice, Kaleth—put your effort into your own training and block out anything that distracts you from it. Instead, find something you enjoy and put effort into that. I focus on my gardening in the greenhouse and my science experiments. Both bring me great pleasure."

The mention of experiments tugged on his curiosity. "Last night, during the storm . . . I saw a bolt of lightning hit this tower. But nothing seems to be damaged. And it was strange, like the tower absorbed it or something. Do you know what happened?"

The edge of Genoris' mouth pulled up. "Yes, I know what happened. It was late, but I was up here." He motioned Kaleth to follow him to the flat area of the roof.

After descending the steps, Kaleth put the pieces together on his own. A faint hum came from the decorative stone that sat in front of the greenhouse. The closer he got, the more his hair stood on end. "You used your Lightbinder ability to harness lightning."

The headmaster's broad grin took over his face. "And I infused this stone with it. Incredible, isn't it? To my knowledge, I'm the first one to do so."

Kaleth hovered his hand near the surface. "Is it . . . safe?"

"You can touch it, sure."

He rested his hand on the stone. A faint tremor ran through his body, but it didn't hurt. "What do you do with this?"

"The power of a Lightbinder comes from the ability to both store light energy and to use it. Imagine a stone holding the power of a lightning bolt at the front lines of battle."

"It could kill the enemy?"

"If concentrated . . . sure. It could take out a handful of people. More importantly, it could burst through a fortress gate. Or if spread out over a large area, it could send a shockwave through their entire force. Imagine all of Thravia's army dropping their weapons and shaking for a solid minute while our soldiers lay waste to them."

He patted the stone. "This one was just an experiment. The lightning will stay trapped for months—possibly years unless released safely back into the sky. Incredible, huh?"

"Yeah."

"I'm guessing lightning is not what brings you up to my office today, though."

Kaleth cleared his throat. "No, sir, it's not. I had a thought about Seppo."

The headmaster's eyebrows raised.

"I've been thinking about the deaths since we found Lorenzo in the dining hall. I had assumed it was another initiate, possibly a spy from Thravia taking out other candidates so they could insert themselves in an elite army position. But the more I think about it, the more it makes sense."

"What makes sense?"

"I think it might be an instructor."

"An instructor? Behind the killings?" Genoris shook his head. "Impossible. I know every one of them personally. They all came through the academy. They're loyal fighters of Kalshia and have been for years. The newest we have is Wentworth, the Mender principal, but she spent three years in the academy, then four more years fighting and killing Thravians. Most have been here longer than that. Why do you think that?"

"Seppo is ranked twenty-fourth. Lorenzo was thirty-three when he was killed. And Atheas was only one spot ahead of me. If an initiate is behind all of this, what's the point? They aren't a threat to anyone. They're not going to take one of the top six slots. If someone wanted to take out competition, they would focus on the higher-ranked initiates."

"And you're thinking that leaves instructors as the only options?"

"Lightbinder instructors."

Genoris' head jerked.

"The bloody messages all point to a student being behind it. The knife wounds on Lorenzo and Atheas could have been made by anyone with access to a blade. But Atheas had something else. Scorched leather."

The headmaster frowned. "What do you mean?"

"A dark line ran across his jacket. A knife couldn't have caused that. Getting too close to a fire wouldn't either. But what about a long, burning object?"

"Like an infused sword of a Lightbinder?"

"Exactly."

Genoris rubbed his chin as if deep in thought.

"I know it's not you. You were in the dining hall when someone would have been mutilating Atheas. And the second-year initiates have been out on patrol for the last week. But other professors with Lightbinder skills or any of the four Lightbinder trainers could be the culprit."

"But what motivation would they have?"

Kaleth frowned. "I'm not sure. It's possible, though."

The headmaster's furrowed brow smoothed out as he forced a smile. "Sure, it's *possible*. But what's likely is that Seppo's still around somewhere and the stories about him missing are only rumors. Or even *more* probable is that he chose to leave and didn't tell anyone."

"I guess so. But what if he turns out to be the next victim? That could confirm—"

"It wouldn't *confirm* anything," Genoris said. "But . . . it's worth looking into. I'll check with Aurik to see if someone is missing."

"What if he's the one behind it?"

"I said I'll look into it."

A reluctant smile pulled at Kaleth's face.

Genoris led Kaleth up the steps, then back inside the office. "We *are* working on it, I assure you. Ever since Lorenzo died. I meet with the staff every day, and this is our top priority. We're tripling night patrols. Blade guards are being paired with Lightbinders. In the rare possibility that an instructor is involved, we have enough of us working on it. We'll stop them. We'll make sure no one else is hurt."

"Thank you, sir." He tossed a thumb toward the hallway. "I should probably get back. Thanks for listening and for the advice on bravery. I'll work on it."

"Thank *you*, Kaleth, for coming to me."


GENORIS WATCHED the initiate's back as Kaleth exited the room. The smile on his face relaxed. *An instructor working as a Thravian spy . . .* he hummed in thought. A *whoosh* indicated the binder lift left the floor. He spun on his heels and rounded the desk. His hand touched the wall, fingers touching the edge of a stone block. His pulse thumped in his head. The surface of the rock was hard and gritty. A crack ran down the side where the stone met a line of masonry. He tensed his muscles and pulled. The wall pivoted, opening to reveal a cavity.

Crouched on the floor, a young man cringed at the flood of light in his dark space. He turned his face away, pushing his triangle beard away from his neck. The gag in his mouth permitted nothing more than a dull moan. Dried blood covered the side of his face, originating from a black gash on his forehead. His torn, cream tunic was dingy from grime. Blinking, he turned to face Genoris. The moaning grew louder, bulging his neck tattoo as he shook his bound hands.

"Now what are we going to do with you?" the headmaster asked.

The captive stilled.

"It seems people are getting suspicious, speculating it could be an instructor involved." He pulled a dagger from a sheath at his waist, and the captive's eyes widened. "'What if Seppo turns out to be the next victim?'" He scoffed, then frowned. "Sorry, Seppo. I had big plans for you. I was going to string you up at the entrance to the Grand Courtyard for everyone to see, but I can't do that now. Kaleth has put a wrinkle in my plans. I guess I can't kill you in public."

Seppo's forehead eased, and his eyes softened in hope.

"That means I'll have to kill you in private." Genoris flicked his wrist and ripped the blade across the initiate's neck.

Seppo's eyes bulged. Bright-red blood streamed over the black ink of his tattoo. The young man thrashed in his alcove, straining against the binds that held him. The jerks of his arms and legs softened until he grew still. His head lolled back and his eyes remained open, frozen in a death stare.

Genoris wiped the knife against Seppo's tunic, cleaning the blood from the blade. "I may need to take a fresh approach with my plan," he muttered aloud. "Looks like Kaleth-il-Valorr might need to be one of my next victims."

# PART THREE

## CHAPTER THIRTY

# THE EXPEDITION

When Felyra's eyes opened, dread seeped through her being. No longer protected by the blissful ignorance her patchy sleep provided, she focused on what was to come. Her pulse spiked, fueled by adrenaline. She'd been dreading the day for weeks, but there was no getting around the Expedition.

Combining physical conditioning with weapons training and patrolling skills, they had heard rumors of the grueling test from the moment they began at the academy. It had terrified her then, and the feeling had only intensified since.

Half of the initiates yawned, stretched, or wrestled with their packs while the other half had not roused yet. Felyra swung her legs over the side of her bed, determined to not put it off.

Ruane hopped down from the bed above. "How'd you sleep?" she asked.

Felyra's eyes ached as if something pressed against them. "Awfully. I couldn't take my mind off what's coming."

"You're going to do fine."

She scoffed. "Easy for the girl with two good legs to say."

"Two legs isn't everything, Felyra. You have heart and drive—"

"You mean stubbornness."

"—far past most of the people here. It's something they look for. Didn't the headmaster tell you that?"

"We'll see. It still doesn't mean I'm looking forward to this."

Breakfast was a somber ordeal, the mood tainted by what came next. Felyra gulped down as much food as she could, knowing the energy she was about to expend. Their stuffed packs lined the courtyard, leaning against the walls. She had filled hers with clothes, food, water, and a blanket the day before.

"Grab your gear and line up with your squad," Captain Janduan barked.

Felyra hurried with the others to comply. Each initiate had a shoulder sling for their swords that went on first. She fitted hers and slid the steel weapon in place. It was more challenging to draw than when sitting on her hip, but the position would allow the mobility they would need. Her pack went on second. It wasn't heavy yet, but she dreaded what it would feel like after carrying it for hours. Geared up and ready, she gathered with Ruane and the other eight initiates in Fenris' squad.

"Do you think Grax's pack looks a bit heavier than the others?" Ruane whispered.

Felyra looked at the initiate who adjusted his pack as if he couldn't get it comfortable. "I don't know. It looks like—" Her friend's mischievous grin stopped her words. "What did you do?"

Ruane's grin grew wider. "I may have tossed a few Soulbinder stones in there."

"Ruane!"

The outburst drew attention from others in their squad, but they lost interest as Fenris called for their attention.

"This is going to be tough," the squad leader said. "All I ask is that you give everything you have and that you don't make me look bad out there. Once we make it through this, we prove to ourselves we can do anything."

Butterflies flitted in Felyra's stomach. A twinge of pain flared in her hip, though they hadn't even begun yet. She couldn't tell if it was real or only the anticipation of discomfort.

Janduan stood by the exit of the courtyard and held up a hand.

The squads grew silent. "One week—that's how long this will last. We'll cover forty miles a day, and it's going to be brutal. If you want to succeed, let me give you some advice."

The initiates perked up, standing straighter.

"One of the most common mistakes initiates make during the Expedition is not eating and drinking enough. Your body needs fuel, and even though you won't want to consume anything, you'll break down if you don't. Fuel up whenever you can. The second issue I often see is relaxing once we stop each day. When we break for camp, your work isn't finished. We spar in the evenings, honing your skills when you're tired. I expect the same effort and intensity with anything I ask of you in camp as we do when on the trail. The final issue we see is not keeping up."

Janduan's eyes found Felyra's, causing her stomach to twist.

"We won't slow our pace to accommodate any of you. You must be able to keep up. If you can't, find your way back because you don't have a place with us." He let the words sink in. "Any questions?"

A puff of wind dropped a sprinkling of dust over the courtyard. It tickled the loose hairs on the back of Felyra's neck. She would not be the one who couldn't keep up. She would prove Janduan wrong.

"Remember, it's just me and you out there, and I'm the authority. If anyone can't handle that, feel free to head home now."

Receiving no comments, the captain flicked his head, then jogged through the courtyard exit.

Felyra's legs felt like wooden blocks. She kept up with the others, but each step felt like she was watching from outside of her own body. Her pack jostled on her back, rubbing against the sword's sheath.

The familiar path through the streets of Revalle only took a few minutes to run. The men and women they passed stopped to stare. While the large majority had never experienced what they were about to undertake, they all knew enough to respect—and pity—the initiates.

A musty smell filled her nose as they exited the city streets and jogged into the midst of the algae fields—green on their right and a large patch of red on their left. The thought of running for a week while fueling her body with nothing but algae made her stomach turn. If they were lucky, they'd range closer to the border and find some actual meat.

The dry South Lagrash River posed little obstacle. Initiates jogged down the bank, stepping over patches of orange algae before they climbed the opposite side and set off in a northeasterly direction.

The jogging pace they established wasn't too aggressive, but the thought of maintaining it for most of the day felt daunting. An ever-present ache simmered in her hip as she focused on each step. Her cadence didn't match the others. The rest of the initiates settled into a rhythm of equal strides, but Felyra's legs made an offbeat tempo as the right leg compensated for the pain it generated with each step.

Dust filled the air as the group tracked across the dirty, flat plain. She regretted her decision to hang near the back but didn't have the energy to sprint to move up near the front. Before long, her mind turned into mush, unable to focus on anything but taking in a dusty breath. She fought the pain in her legs and followed the rest of the group.

An hour into the run, Janduan stopped jogging and motioned for everyone to drop their packs and take their first break. Sighs filled the air as packs sloughed off shoulders and dropped to the ground. Felyra pulled out a canteen of water and slaked her thirst. Despite having no appetite, she forced down some dried green algae, knowing her body needed it.

"How are you holding up?" Ruane asked after swallowing a mouthful from her canteen.

Felyra thought through the state of her body. Her legs kept her upright, but they were so numb she could barely tell they were there. A throb of pain pulsed on the right side of her hip. As much as she tried to ignore it, her body wouldn't let her.

She put on her best face while trying to avoid cringing. "I'm keeping up."

"How's your leg?"

"It's fine!" Felyra regretted the sharp outburst when her friend flinched. "Sorry, I'm not upset with you. It hurts, of course, but I'm trying to move past it."

"It's all right. You're doing amazing. I'm barely hanging in there."

Felyra rubbed both hands on her own shoulders, massaging their dull ache. "I'm wondering if those rocks of yours were put in my pack by mistake though." She managed a weak smile. Her breath settled the longer they paused. The throbbing in her leg diminished but wouldn't disappear. She counted seconds in her head, dreading the moment the break would end.

When the captain called for everyone to put their packs back on, groans echoed from each initiate. Felyra took one last drink of water, then followed suit, cringing when her pack settled on her back. Janduan waved them forward and took off at what felt like a faster clip than before they'd stopped.

While the rest had given her a moment to feel somewhat normal again, the reprieve vanished within seconds of resuming the run. The agony in her hip returned. Her shoulders ached. And her throat felt dry and cracked, even though she had just drunk her fill.

While they ran, Felyra fought to keep pace with the bodies in front of her. The few initiates that were behind passed her, leaving her the last in line. She struggled to keep up, and the gap between her and the others continued to widen.

The sight of Captain Janduan falling back in the line after letting others pass caused her stomach to turn. Her steps picked up. She closed the gap to the next runner before the captain made it back to her.

"What are you doing back here, Cripple? You can't keep up with the others?"

Her lungs worked hard to breathe. She didn't have it in her to respond to the jibe. The captain fell in line behind her, talking over her shoulder as she kept her eyes on the pack of the runner ahead. She tried hard to regulate her stride, but the limping cadence would not be quelled.

"You think you deserve to be a Soulbinder, but you're the worst at every physical challenge we have. Good luck being selected. You might as well give up now. You know you don't deserve to be here. You know all the others are better than you."

His words cut through her in a way even the pain in her hip couldn't. *He's right*, she thought. *The others are faster and better. What am I doing here?* She entertained the thought of stopping. The possibility filled her with a surge of excitement. The pain would end. She could breathe again. The hit of each footstep echoed in her mind, joining forces with the captain to convince her to give up. The rhythm of her steps slowed, increasing the distance to the next runner.

The captain's laugh filled the air. "That's what I thought. Time to quit. We only take the best of the best, and you should know that cripples could never be Soulbinders."

Felyra sucked in air as she continued. Labored breaths filled her muddled ears. Each step jostled her body with pressure and pain while she replayed his words over. *Cripples could never be Soulbinders?* Her jaw tightened until her teeth ached from the pressure. She thought about what obstacle he had to overcome that the headmaster had alluded to. Through a concerted effort, her stride lengthened. The gap to the next runner shrank as she pushed her body to move faster.

*He will not talk me out of this.*

*I will not give up.*

*I will not—*

Something hit her foot, causing it to catch the back of her other leg. Her stomach leaped into her chest. Options scrambled through her mind, but there was nothing to do except tumble forward, falling to the dirt. Her hands scraped the trail. The forward motion slid her across the arid, rocky ground. Small stones tore across her face and arms. She yelled after sliding to a stop, more from frustration than from the actual pain. She scrambled to remove the pack off her head and rise to her feet. The jogging initiates closest to her looked back at the commotion as they slowed.

"What are you doing?" Janduan barked at them. "Keep moving!"

The initiates jumped back into action, resuming their jog that took them farther away.

Felyra brushed her forearms and cheeks. Dirt and pebbles peeled off, dropping to the ground. Most of the cuts were surface-level red scrapes, but a few shone with blood. She cringed. The pain would come when the adrenaline wore off.

"Are you giving up?" Janduan had stopped next to her. His hands rested on his hips. "If you can't keep your feet under you, maybe you should turn around."

She looked at the ground, scanning for whatever she had hit. Her embarrassment turned to anger. Nothing was there. "You tripped me," she panted.

A malicious smile covered his face. "No proof of that. All I see is you covered in scrapes, letting your training class get away. Now, are you going to end this charade and head home, or are you going to hurry and catch up?"

She gritted her teeth and shot daggers with her eyes. Although she tried to minimize the motion, her heaving chest gave away her exhaustion. She turned toward the other joggers, noting the growing distance between them. Her leg throbbed. Her feet ached. Her lungs begged her to give up. Groaning, she slung her pack over her shoulder and tucked her arms through the straps. Each step felt like moving through thick mud as she resumed a slow jog toward the others.

*I will not give up.*

*I will not let him win.*

A scraping sound caused her to look over her shoulder. She gasped. Having been pulled from its sheath, her sword floated in midair, held in place as if by magic. *Or held by a Soulbinder.* She danced to the side, worried Janduan was going to use his ability to drive the blade into her side. When the sword turned around and the hilt dropped near her legs, the captain's intentions grew clear. Continuing to jog, Felyra reached down and grasped the hilt before it could be thrust between her legs to trip her again. When the weapon was firmly in her grip, she felt the invisible control fighting against her cease.

*Ha! He won't get the best of me.* Saying nothing, she worked the blade over her shoulder and slid it back into its sheath.

A harder kick knocked against her foot, knocking it against her other leg again. She splayed her arms, readying herself for another tumble onto the gritty surface. Her footsteps clomped onto the ground, her arms windmilling to help keep her upright. She stayed up and forced herself to keep jogging.

Janduan belted a laugh, seeming unconcerned that his second effort had failed.

Felyra angled her body as she continued forward. She looked at her feet, keeping part of her vision where she ran and the other part making sure the captain didn't trip her again. He jogged closer and feigned another attempt, causing her to stutter-step. He laughed again, then seemed to back off.

"They're getting farther away," he said.

She gulped. He was right. She allowed a more upright posture as she increased her speed. Her hip ached from the angled way she ran, trying to go faster. She continually looked down, ensuring the captain didn't trip her again. She stepped lively, lifting each foot in an exaggerated motion.

*This is ridiculous. Why should I have to put up with this when no one else does?*

She entertained the idea of trying to trip him back but dismissed it. There was no telling the suffering he would put her through if she tried that.

"You're never going to catch them with this ridiculous effort. I won't trip you again. You can run regularly."

He was right. She couldn't run as fast while trying to watch him. Sighing, she faced forward and picked up her pace. Her ears burned, straining for sounds of the captain closing in. The crunching dirt filled the air, combined with her panting. The backs of the other runners drew close.

When she had almost caught up, Janduan's footsteps pulled her attention back. She looked down. His feet were right next to hers, positioned to strike. She stepped lightly, warding off the expected attack. She tried to maintain her faster pace while keeping her eyes on both of their sets of feet.

*He said he wouldn't trip me. Was that just mind games? Is he going to leave me alone?*

A shove in her back gave the answer she had feared. Her feet stumbled forward, pounding the ground. She tried to keep upright, but gravity won. Trying to save her tender hands and arms, she turned her shoulder in, hoping it would absorb the impact better. The collision shook her body. While her arms avoided repeating the same injuries as before, her face did not. The side of it scraped across the gritty surface, sending dust into her mouth and eyes. When her body stopped moving, she lay still. Opening her eyes would confirm the reality of what had happened, so she kept them shut.

The captain didn't wait for her. His low chuckle filled the air as he jogged on. "No one told you to stop," he shouted ahead. "Keep moving!" Footsteps grew distant.

Felyra lifted her face off the ground. Dirt worked past her lips and tainted her tongue. She wiped her eyes, knocking dust from them. She blinked to clear them. After wiping grit from her cheek, bloody streaks covered her hand. She used her arms to prop herself up. Her breath labored as she watched the dusty cloud of initiates jog away, driven by Captain Janduan.

Her sight grew blurry. Tears pooled in the corners of her eyes, followed by a trembling jaw. The sting across her arms, shoulder, and face intensified. She'd spent half the year training to be a Soulbinder only to be pushed to the dirt and left behind by a captain who hated her.

Tears fell freely. She alternated between sniffing and sucking in breaths to satiate her exhausted lungs. When her pulse settled and tears dried, the group of initiates was only a dusty speck in the distance. She wiped her face, wincing at the grit in her eyes. Sharp pain radiated through her body as she worked her way to her feet. She brushed her arm again, knocking more rubble from where pebbles stuck to her skin.

She looked back toward Revalle. The tallest buildings looked like nothing more than bushes in the distance. It would take all day and into the night to walk back. *And then what would I do?* she wondered. She hadn't considered any other job since her father died, putting all her focus on becoming a Soulbinder. There was no one left in the city for her. Ruane, her only friend, had run off with the other initiates.

Tears welled in her eyes, threatening to burst anew. "No!" she belted. She wiped her face and set her jaw. After adjusting her sword in its sheath, she hiked her pack up on her shoulders. The first few tentative steps were nothing more than a walk. Her leg and hip ached. Her hands, arms, and face stung. She forced her feet to move faster. The speed wasn't nearly as fast as the pace the captain had set, but it was the best she could do. She kept her eyes up, pushed her legs to keep moving, and followed the cloud of dust as quickly as her aching body allowed her to move.

# CHAPTER THIRTY-ONE
# CAMPING BY THE LAGRASH

Felyra's pace settled to a fast walk as the sun moved across the sky. She lost sight of the jogging group, but the beaten path was easy enough to follow. She continued forward, hoping they would stop soon and she could catch up.

Her body had long run out of energy. Fueled by anger toward the captain and stubborn pride, she continued placing one foot in front of the other. No one could say she gave up. No one would say the captain got the best of her.

The terrain morphed from a flat, barren plain into rolling hills. While not green with foliage, a smattering of brown bushes and leafless trees decorated the landscape. Eventually, the sun drifted to the horizon. When the trail was nearly too dark to see anymore, voices carried on the wind. After traversing a hill, she sighed and relaxed her shoulders.

A rudimentary camp sprawled before her with a modest fire burning in the center. Packs and bedrolls littered the ground. Marking the border between them and Kalshia, the Lagrash River flowed on the far side. Filled with actual water, the sight made her dry throat ache. The group of initiates stood in a circle, each one slumped with a long face and drooping limbs. They remained upright, but a few appeared to lean on each other to maintain it. In the center of a sparring ring, two initiates faced each other, holding wooden staffs.

Felyra stumbled forward. She dropped her pack and sword at the outer edge of camp, then made for the ring of initiates. Her feet shuffled against the ground. Her body had gone numb long before, but dropping her pack and the presence of other people caused it to prickle with feeling again.

Young men and women startled as she pushed through the ring of bodies. They didn't even mask the horror when they looked at her face. She heard words of "blood" and "scrapes," but a muttering of the word "cripple" was the only one that bothered her. She scanned the observers for Ruane but couldn't find her anywhere. When she turned her attention to the action in the ring, her stomach turned.

Ruane backpedaled as her staff blocked Grax's attack. The clack of wood split the air multiple times until it changed to a dull thud and an "oof." Ruane bent over, clutching her side while Grax gave her space to recover and return to the center.

Grax looked exhausted. His shoulders slumped. His breaths seemed to take the effort of his entire body. Ruane looked as bad as Felyra felt. A fresh red welt in the shape of a staff marked the side of her face. She struggled forward, trying to keep her staff raised.

"Don't give your enemy time to recover," Janduan called from the side. "That's one of the biggest mistakes you can make in battle. Finish them while you can."

Grax's eyes flicked toward the instructor. "Of course, Captain." He paused to take a breath. "But today we're only sparring, right? I thought I should give her time—"

"Sparring is practicing. If you practice weakness, you will exhibit weakness when it counts."

Grax turned back to Ruane and readied his weapon. The light in his eyes didn't have the fire Felyra was used to seeing. Ruane remained hunched, favoring her left side. When Grax lunged with the staff, his half-hearted strike seemed weak. Ruane deflected it and the two after, but she failed to stop the swing that struck her across the cheek.

Felyra flinched as her friend spun and fell. Ruane dropped her staff and landed on her hands and knees.

"Good!" Janduan shouted. "Now show her what it means to be beaten."

With heaving breaths, Ruane looked up with pleading eyes.

Grax frowned. "But, sir, she's—"

"Your opponent will lure you in and, when you least expect it, they will stab you in the back. If they're not collapsed on the ground, then they have fight left in them. Do it!"

Felyra's fists clenched into tight balls. Her veins were on fire, stoking the rage she felt toward the captain.

Grax lifted his staff and stepped closer. The hesitation on his face only lasted a moment.

Stepping from the ring of onlookers, Felyra rushed forward. She grabbed Ruane's discarded staff and lifted it in time to stop the blow. Ruane gasped.

Grax's eyes opened wide. The shock seemed to start from her sudden presence, but then his face screwed up as he focused on her physical state. "What happened to you?"

Felyra pushed against his staff with what force she could muster. "She's had enough!"

Grax backpedaled after being flung away. The whites of his eyes grew larger as Felyra surged forward. "I didn't want to hurt her," he explained. "I was just . . ." He trailed off as her path became clear.

Felyra stormed across the circle, passing Grax and heading toward the captain. The pain and fatigue in her body were a distant memory. Fueled by rage, her muscles felt like stone.

Janduan cocked his head as she approached. "How dare you interrupt my training? You should have headed back to Revalle when you had the chance."

The growl in her chest started low, then crescendoed. She gripped the staff with both hands, wringing the smooth wood against her skin. Initiates near the captain backed up. The oblivious man realized her intent too late. His eyes opened wide. He ducked too slowly. The butt of the staff collided with the side of his head, making a loud *smack*. Janduan spun in a half-circle before he fell to the ground, clutching his face and moaning in pain.

The other initiates gawked in silence. All Felyra heard was her own labored breathing and the throbbing pulse beating in her ears.

The captain flopped to his knees. He spat a wad of bloody saliva with specks of white onto the ground. He continued groaning and touched his mouth. Where a row of teeth should have been, a bloody gap revealed a missing section.

The intensity with which she had attacked him sobered her. The adrenaline pumping through her system faded, leaving her cold, tired, and aching. Janduan's face morphed from creased lines of confusion to a fury she hadn't considered.

Muttering filled the circle of initiates. While no one condemned Felyra, they didn't rush to back her either.

"You *dare* assault me?" Janduan roared. "You want to be considered as a Soulbinder, but you strike your captain. Ha!" Drops of blood flew to the ground from his laugh.

Felyra lowered the staff and took a hesitant step backward.

"You stumble in here long after the others, having been unable to keep up, hoping what? That your tardiness will impress me?" The captain stood upright. Vitriol filled his face with blood dribbling down his chin. With a flick of his fingers, three stones lifted off the ground, then hovered, threatening to hurl at anyone who would threaten him. "You can't run. You can barely fight. You've only made it this far because the headmaster has a soft spot for cripples. You would have been better off if you had died from whatever caused that scar. It would have saved us from having to deal with you all this time, and *we* wouldn't have had to look at that hideous face of yours."

Snickers burbled through the crowd.

Felyra clenched her jaw so hard her teeth ached. Her limbs shook as she tried to think about anything but his words, hoping to avoid crying in front of everyone. The scar on her chin was all she could think of.

"As nice as that would have been, we don't have to live with it much longer." A wicked, gap-toothed grin washed over his face.

"Striking an officer is a capital offense. You'll be executed for this. Tonight."

It felt like a horse had kicked her in the stomach. She gasped for air. Her eyes flicked between each of the floating rocks. Turning in each direction revealed nothing but initiates who wouldn't lift a finger to help.

Ruane had found her feet. Her only friend took a step closer, then stopped. "Felyra, I—" She glanced around.

"You want to mutiny?" the captain taunted. "You want all of you to end up hanged? Go ahead. Try it. We'll see how far killing your instructor gets you in your Soulbinder quest."

The other initiates did nothing. Several looked at the ground, avoiding eye contact with either of them. Felyra understood the spot they were in. Most of the initiates hated Janduan, but he was the gatekeeper to getting what they wanted.

Ruane stepped again and opened her mouth.

"No." Felyra shook her head, stopping her friend. "You don't need to go down with me. None of you do. It was my action." She lifted her chin. "But that doesn't mean I won't go down without a fight."

She turned to Janduan, raising her weapon. Dropping into a crouch, she bared the staff toward the hated man, ready to bat away any stones that hurtled toward her. "You want to kill me, Captain?"

Her friend's voice reached her back. "Felyra."

"Not now, Ruane. I've got to do this." She narrowed her eyes and tightened her grip. The captain had a strange grin on his face, made macabre by the blood and missing teeth. Felyra stepped toward him.

"Felyra, you need to—"

"I've got this!"

The captain's shoulders bounced as he chuckled. She lifted her staff, readying to strike him again.

"Felyra!"

A jolting thud bounced her head. She didn't even feel the pain, only a hollow sensation as if she'd dunked her head underwater. She tried to follow through with her attack on the captain, but her body tilted. Her sight grew blurry and dimmed. She hit the ground, only recognizing what had happened when Grax bent down in her face and smirked. With that, she passed out.

A SHARP STING jolted Felyra awake. Her eyes flew open, and she startled.

Ruane crouched before her, pressing a finger to her lips. She held a rag that glistened with red after being pulled back from her face. A deep shade of night bathed their surroundings. The fire in the center of camp, where most of the initiates sat, was the only remaining source of light. A few of the other young men and women looked their way, but most pointedly ignored them.

Felyra could move a bit, but bonds of rope held her arms behind her back, pinching her skin. Her shoulders pressed against the smooth bark of a dead tree. Her arms and face hurt with sharp, prickly pain while her head throbbed with a deeper ache.

"Grax knocked you out," Ruane whispered.

She nodded. "Yeah, I figured."

"I got permission to clean up your cuts, but—" Ruane paused as if unable to complete the sentence.

"But, what?"

"The bind-cursed, power-hungry—"

"What, Ruane?"

"You're to be hanged when you wake." She nodded toward the bare branch above them. "Right here."

"That's pleasant." Felyra managed a nervous laugh. "Maybe I should go back to sleep."

A half-smile showed on Ruane's face. She extended the damp rag to Felyra's face and pressed.

The sting radiated through her, but she fought to remain still. "I was such an idiot. I shouldn't have attacked him."

"He was the idiot," Ruane insisted, working the rag along the cuts. "I tried to turn back for you—on the run, when he pushed you down. I stepped out of line to let the others pass, but Janduan grabbed my shirt and dragged me along. He threatened to do the same to me if I didn't keep going." Her words grew thick. She wiped at her eyes. "I'm so sorry, Felyra. I should have done something."

Felyra shook her head. "You'd be tied up here with me if you had."

"Thank you for stopping Grax."

"Of course." Her eyes flicked through the camp. "But Janduan was the real monster. Where is he?"

"He went to the river to clean himself." She lowered the cloth and smirked. "You should have seen him. His face was nasty, and the missing teeth . . . I could barely avoid laughing when he spoke."

Felyra managed a smile, but the reality of her situation kept her from enjoying the thought. "I guess it's fitting."

Ruane frowned. "What do you mean?"

"I wasn't going to make it as a Soulbinder, and that means I would be common infantry. We both know how well that would have worked out for me. My family is gone. My dreams are quashed." She shrugged. "Hanging for standing up to a bully is about the best *realistic* way I can imagine going out. I hope you make it, Ruane. I hope you become a Soulbinder, defeat the Kalshians, and kick people like Janduan out."

Her friend forced a smile. "I'll do my best."

"Looks like she's awake," a whistling voice said from the darkness.

Felyra turned her head to find Captain Janduan walking up from where sounds of the river rippled. He patted a rag against his mouth. Reflected in the firelight, the blood on his face was gone, but it still stained the top half of his tunic. To her delight, the conspicuous gap in his teeth remained. He stopped and stood before her, sneering.

"In my time at the academy, I've never met a fool as great as you," Janduan said. "Delusional about your abilities and insubordinate to authority. You would never make it in the Thravian army. Now we can be rid of you once and for all." He pointed at Ruane and flicked his finger between the two young women. "That's enough from you. You've cleaned her, now back off."

A knot tightened in Felyra's chest.

Her friend nodded as if accepting the captain's words. "I'm so sorry, Felyra."

Under the captain's watchful eyes, Ruane wrapped her arms around her in a last embrace. Felyra's shoulders felt like fire from the contact on her scrapes, but she didn't care.

"I hope you will work fast," Ruane whispered.

Felyra nodded, also hoping to not hang for a lengthy period as the rope slowly choked her to death. The message repeated in her head. *You will work fast?* The wording felt odd.

When Ruane released her hold and retracted her arms, an object slid against Felyra's back and landed in her bound hands. Felyra quelled any reaction to tip off the captain. "I hope it will be quick, too," she said as Ruane backed away.

Appearing satisfied, Janduan turned to the crowd around the fire. "Get the rope ready," he called. "I'm going to change."

Ruane backpedaled toward the crowd, but her eyes held an intense stare as if willing her friend into action.

Felyra wriggled her hands to explore the new object they had received. A smooth wooden handle gave way to cold metal. When she rotated the grip, the metal turned into a sharp edge. *A knife!* Her heart pounded.

Ruane had turned around and walked to the far side of the fire. A few of the initiates glanced her way, but most avoided eye contact. Grax stood, pulling a knot tight that formed a noose at the end of a length of rope. He moved toward Felyra.

Captain Janduan bent over on the far side of camp and lifted a fresh shirt from a pack.

Forcing her face to remain impassive, Felyra worked behind her back, sliding the knife back and forth across the ropes that bound her. The sound it made was faint, no louder than the crackling of the fire. The snap of the strands reverberated through her arms as the braided fibers cut free. Straining against the knots, her hands felt looser with each passing moment.

"Sorry about this," Grax muttered. His usual condescending demeanor was gone. He tossed the noose at the branch above her. His first attempt fell short, and the rope hit the ground.

"Why do you hate me?" Felyra asked.

He paused before gathering the rope in his hands again. "I don't hate you."

"What is it, then? Am I a *threat*? Does a crippled orphan make you nervous?"

"I lost my parents, too, you know."

Her knife paused its work. She didn't know. "I'm—I'm sorry."

"I just don't wear it on my sleeve like a badge of pity."

Her eyes narrowed. "I don't—"

"You don't belong here, Felyra. Soulbinders need the best, and you can barely walk."

"Then why am I still here?"

He scoffed. "Because the headmaster was your father's buddy. That's why."

*No. It's not true.* The thought had plagued her mind all year. She wasn't physically gifted. She could barely keep up with the others. That's why she tried so hard: extra conditioning, extra weapons practice. She needed all the help she could get.

"They want someone like me," Grax said. "I was born like this. I was made to be a Soulbinder."

"Is that why you don't try?"

His eyes bored a hole through her.

"It comes easily so you put in the least effort you can."

He tossed the rope again while muttering, "You don't know what you're talking about." It took two more tries before he slung it over.

"Don't tie it off yet," Janduan called. "Once you lift her, I'll fix it taut. Get her ready."

Felyra moved the knife quicker, ignoring the danger of cutting so near her wrists. Another strand of rope snapped clean. With everyone else near the fire, no one could see her hands feverishly working.

Grax pulled under her arm, lifting her to her feet. She cried out, not from the shock of being lifted but from the horror of dropping the knife. It clanked on the roots of the tree, lost in the darkness.

Grax worked the noose over her head and slid it tight around her neck.

On the far side of the fire, Ruane's eyes were as wide as orbs. Felyra gritted her teeth and wrestled her wrists. The looser they got, the more slack she had to work with.

Janduan's heavy steps thudded in their direction. "Thaylor, help him lift her."

The black-haired initiate jerked to attention. After a moment's pause, he left the fire ring and walked forward.

*Not yet. Not yet.* Nearly free, Felyra strained her hands. Rope burned her wrists as the knots pulled apart. The coil around her neck chafed.

Janduan arrived and grabbed the free end of the noose. He stepped beside the next closest tree, holding the end beside a free branch. "Lift her high so I have enough slack."

Grax stood at one of Felyra's sides. Thaylor arrived at the other. They nodded to each other, then squatted. Their arms wrapped around each of her legs, and then they stood. Felyra struggled for balance as she lifted in the air.

The rope was slack for only a moment until Janduan wrapped it around another limb, pulling it tight. "Give me a second," the captain said, working on a knot.

Felyra's pulse pounded. She would drop at any moment. A final yank of her hands pulled them free, earning gasps from the watching crowd.

"Okay, drop her!" the captain called.

Felyra ripped at the noose, pulling it off the instant before she fell. Her neck didn't yank on the coil of rope. Her legs jolted as they hit the ground, but she remained upright. Grax and Thaylor stumbled back, stunned. They both looked up as if wondering what had gone wrong.

Felyra didn't give them a second. She turned away from the fire and bolted toward the darkness, sprinting as fast as she could go. Stones whistled by her head, close enough for her to feel the air. One collided into a tree trunk as she passed it.

Captain Janduan's shouts propelled her forward. It took a

moment for her eyes to adjust. When they did, she found rolling ground with few obstacles, lit by the scant moon. Her limping gait limited her speed, but following her through the night would be a challenge for anyone. She ignored the pain in her leg and hip. The scrapes across much of her body were a distant memory. She focused on her steps, keeping her body upright. Over her heavy breathing, she strained her ears for any sounds of pursuit. She even snuck glances back but saw nothing.

"Come back here!" The faintness of Janduan's call gave her hope. "You'll regret this! If you don't return . . ."

When the captain didn't complete his threat, she hoped that meant he came up with nothing. She worked up an exhausted grin until he finished his thought.

"If you don't . . . your *friend* will take your place!"

The distant words chilled her bones. *Ruane?* Her pulse somehow beat even faster. *He wouldn't do that. She hasn't done anything. He's only bluffing.* It made no sense, but Janduan didn't always do what she thought made sense.

She didn't stop, but her pace slowed. Her legs continued forward as her mind warred over the dilemma. Going back would mean her death, but she couldn't be sure she wasn't trading Ruane's life by fleeing.

Her internal debate felt like it took hours, but it could have been minutes. She had lost all sense of time. She tried to stop, but fear drove her onward, far away from Janduan and the other initiates. Her legs were stumps. Her body was numb. Sweat made her clothes stick.

*No.*

The thought was clear and powerful. Her struggling pace ground to a halt. She stood for a long moment, giving her breath a chance to settle. The burbling sounds of the nearby Lagrash River reached her ears.

*I can't do it to Ruane.*

She pivoted, preparing to head back when a voice in the darkness made her jump.

"Who are you?"

A shadowy form stood next to a tree. She strained her eyes in the dim light. One man sat on guard while five others slept. She had stumbled into a camp of some sort. The sleeping men roused at the man's greeting and rose to their feet as well.

"Me? I-I . . ." She struggled to form words. Exhaustion impaired her ability to think through the situation.

"What's the matter? You don't know who you are?"

"I'm Felyra." Her weak voice died on the wind.

"I'll tell you who she is." The newly wakened man had a deep voice. In the moonlight, she made out a brown goatee and a bald head. "She's the last one for our chain."

The men's laughs shook a nerve inside Felyra. Filled with malice, their intention was difficult to mistake. At the edge of their camp, she spied something she had missed. Four more bodies—women—lay on the ground, huddled together. Two lifted their heads with resigned curiosity. Felyra gulped. Their bare ankles had metal clasps affixed to them, connected by chains. The last woman in the row had a bundle of metal links next to her. A shackle lay open on the ground—restraints with no one to restrain.

"You're-you're slavers," she croaked.

The men laughed again. "We prefer the term merchants," the man said, "and we're always happy to acquire new goods."

Summoning every ounce of energy she had left, Felyra turned to run. Her first step propelled her into a hulking body that arrested all momentum—a man who had snuck behind her. His rough hands grabbed her wrists while another man latched on to her from behind. The remainder of her spark was dead. Her legs would no longer move. Her arms didn't respond. While she stared helplessly at the man's thick beard, a single thought ran through her head.

*Now I'm a slave.*

## CHAPTER THIRTY-TWO

# OUT ON PATROL

*hrust. Hook. Slash. Circle thrust. Jab.*

*Thrust. Hook. Slash. Circle thrust. Jab.*

Kaleth switched feet, repeating the moves with his left hand. Drops of sweat fell down his forehead and dripped off his nose. His arms glistened. Exhaustion told him to stop, but he pushed through.

He worked on pivoting and attacking in all directions, then practiced a takedown on an invisible opponent, pausing after his final thrust. He panted, resting with his knee in the grass. His pulse thudded through his body. The handle of the knife was slick in his clammy palm.

Six months of training had transformed his body. Defined ripples ran down his arms and knotted his legs. His chest and stomach were flat and hard as if armor of leather covered him. He took pride in being able to keep up with the others in both conditioning and strength training. The other initiates marveled at his progress, but none knew the true source.

Touching the grass, Kaleth breathed in, sucking a trickle of energy from the healthy growth. His exhaustion faded. His rapid breaths settled. Fatigue in his limbs dissolved. Removing his hand, he frowned. Lit by the early morning light peeking over the surrounding buildings, the grass he used faded a shade. No one would notice unless they were looking, but he still wanted to do better.

He pulled two more knives from sheaths and took a deep breath. His chin lifted, locking his eyes on the target against the wall. The concentric circles taunted him as if they contained a magical barrier that pushed his weapons away. He sucked in a slow, deliberate breath. Once filled, he jumped to his feet.

The first knife twirled through the air. He knew it would miss from the moment it left his fingers. *Rushed. Sloppy.* It thunked on the edge of the target before falling to the ground. The second throw felt better. It stuck in the target, albeit off center. The third landed true in the middle but hit with the wrong end. It landed in the grass, too.

He took an extra moment with the final dagger. Another breath flowed through him as he sighted the smallest ring. *You can do this.* His arm felt strong. His form was solid. He exhaled as he loosed the weapon. It flung across the courtyard, flipping end-over-end. The thud of it embedding in the target made his heart jump. It was solid, stuck in the center.

*Two out of four. Not bad.*

He glanced at the common room window where lanterns lit the inside space. The initiates had gathered. It was about time for the planned announcement. Time to wrap up his early-morning practice session.

A nervous energy filled the Lightbinder common room as he entered. The twenty-six other initiates gathered in groups, mumbling in conversations that created a simmering commotion. Dragon Squad stood together with Rayd and Roselle keeping to the side.

"Where've you been?" Jovi asked as Kaleth approached.

"You were training again, weren't you?" Lainn chuckled. "Trying to make us look bad."

"I'm not trying to make anyone look bad. Just trying to get better."

"Well, I've been impressed. The turnaround you've made since the strength test has been dramatic. Running, lifting, fighting . . . you look like a new person." A line dug between his brows. "Unless you *are* a new person." Jovi pinched Kaleth's arm.

"Ouch! Stop it!" Kaleth wiped his friend's hand away. "I'm still me, and it's not like I'm *that* different."

Jovi's suspicion appeared to fade. "Okay, you may be you, but you *are* different."

Kaleth looked at the ranking board. The proud feeling his squad's words had given him deflated at the reminder that he was still ranking twenty-seventh. He had hoped his skill in the classroom would have counted for more, but so far, it had not impacted his rank. *Even with magical strength abilities and great class results, I'm still the worst out of everyone here.* The prospect of making the top six and earning enough money to save his family felt even more impossible now than it had at the beginning of the year.

"You have any skills signed off yet?" Jovi asked.

The question turned his stomach. He had asked Rayd to sign him off on ironball carry—both for distance and weight—as well as poison types, but the squad leader had something to nitpick about each time. So far, he had refused to sign anything for him. Meanwhile, Jovi already had eight completed. "No, nothing yet."

His friend leaned closer. "They're gonna use those logs as part of the final selection. Keep at it. He *has* to sign you off. If not, go to Aurik."

Kaleth nodded although he had no desire to bring down the wrath that would come from going over Rayd's head.

"So why do you all think they called us here?" Lainn asked. "What do you think this is going to be?"

"Birthday party," Jovi quipped. "For sure."

"You really think Aurik's going to celebrate someone's birthday?" Chyla asked.

Jovi shrugged. "Maybe a scavenger hunt?"

Chyla rolled her eyes.

A new cadence of mutters drew their attention toward the front of the room. Aurik had arrived. The principal raised a hand, bringing the crowd to silence. "There will be no conditioning or classes today."

An excited hum rolled through the room.

"You will leave shortly, and for the next week, you will participate in town visits. We'll divide you into eight groups of three or four initiates each. You'll visit nearby towns and partner with the constables. The purpose is to learn the challenges of law and how to deal with disorderly behavior. Some of the roughest citizens of Kalshia can be found in the smaller towns that dot the countryside. Ask questions. Learn from their wisdom. Do whatever they tell you to do. This is a unique opportunity few get to experience."

Jovi raised his hand. "Can we pick our teams?"

Aurik shook his head. "To vary your interactions, groups will be formed across squads and assigned in order of rank."

Kaleth's eyes flicked to the board, along with the rest of the room. He tried to count backward from spot twenty-seven but kept losing his place, distracted by Aurik reading the names out loud. His stomach twisted. He half expected it from the start, but when the names finished, hearing confirmation that he was the fourth person on Rayd's team felt like a knife twisting in his gut. The squad captain glanced sideways at him and frowned.

"Headmaster Genoris," Aurik said. "Welcome."

Kaleth turned to find the headmaster standing in the doorway.

Looking bright despite the early hour, Genoris waved a hand. "Don't mind me. Please continue."

Aurik nodded. "You'll each receive a stipend for expenses. Those visiting farther towns will travel with horses so you don't spend all your time getting there and back. Leave your academy jackets here. You're meant to work, not parade around as Lightbinder initiates. Sorene, would you read out the town assignments for each team?"

The blonde instructor with tight braids lifted a sheet of paper and read town names, consulting with the ranking board to see which team it corresponded to. "Rayd-il-Stonne's team will go to . . . Fairdre."

Kaleth frowned. He'd never heard of it. When the assignments were complete, the room dispersed, initiates given only thirty minutes to pack their gear.

"Good luck on your travels, Kaleth," Headmaster Genoris said, pausing as he moved through the crowd. "What was your assignment?"

"Fairdre," Kaleth replied. "Wherever that is."

"Ah, yes, southeast of here. Just past Twainford, the road forks and passes through Belforth Gap." The headmaster nodded with a distant gaze, as if his mind were elsewhere. His focus snapped back toward Kaleth. "Fairdre's a rough town. Look sharp while you're there, and good luck."

"Thank you, sir. I will."

As the headmaster wandered off, Rayd's snarling face arrived. "Pack your stuff, Grunny. I'm not waiting for you if you're late."

Kaleth swallowed a lump. Memories of the wilderness test flooded his mind. He would need to keep a sharp eye open. It was going to be a long week.

South of Kalistor, off the plateau, the road was shady and pleasant. It was late morning, but the elm trees lining either side of the path blocked the still-rising sun. To the left, the North Lagrash tributary gurgled happily. The fresh breeze from atop his horse helped Kaleth work through his nerves.

He had ridden horses before, but rarely and not well. The brown mare he rode now kept moving into a trot, jostling his teeth and hurting his rear. When he pulled back to ease her into a walk, her neck flung side-to-side. The other initiates laughed.

Donzil-il-Pergil, ranked eleventh, had brown hair and a thick beard to match. His sleeves were pulled up high, revealing bulging arms that looked like they could crush a rock. A member of Raven Squad and filled with as much confidence as muscles, he and Rayd seemed a perfect pair. They rode together, laughing and commenting on the people they passed.

Number nineteen, Orion-il-Sunnigan, was from Iron Squad. Having shaved before they departed, the young man with his coiffed blond hair looked the youngest of the group. His chiseled jaw and thick neck bore the look of a Lightbinder, but his lack of sense gave Kaleth the impression he was two knives short of a kamak set. He rode on Rayd's other side, leaning in so he didn't miss any of the other two boys' conversation.

"You even ridden a horse before?" Donzil asked, looking back over his shoulder.

Riding behind the other three, Kaleth pulled the reins again, trying to get his mare to settle. She whinnied, then stamped the path. Finally, her stride matched the others, giving his jostling body relief.

"Kaleth's never even *seen* a horse before," Rayd quipped.

Orion spun around, jaw drooping. "You've never seen a horse?"

"Yes, I've seen horses," Kaleth spat back. "And I've ridden them. Just not often."

Rayd laughed at his own joke. "People who live in Grunwind can barely afford clothes, much less a horse."

Kaleth's ears burned. The jibe hurt even though it was true. Few of their neighbors owned horses because of the cost of keeping them. He decided against reminding Rayd that his father grew up down the street from where Kaleth now lived.

"I would think someone trying for Lightbinder would be better prepared," Donzil said. "But then again, twenty-seventh place explains that."

Kaleth wanted to be angry but, again, admitted the truth of the words to himself.

"What do you think we'll do in Fairdre?" Orion asked.

Rayd shrugged. "Probably stupid stuff like break up bar fights and watch over the jail. My father says these town visits are pointless. He tried to convince the academy to give them up. Our time is better spent in combat training than babysitting constables."

While the other three initiates complained about what was to come, Kaleth calmed his mind by turning his attention to the greenery they passed. Tree limbs stretched over the road, passing just above his head. He reached up and let his hand drift across the leaves. A glance ahead confirmed the others were lost in their own conversation.

Balancing in the center of his saddle, he grasped the horn with one hand while letting the other arm rest against his hip where his father's tattoo hid beneath his clothes. Pressing against the glyph didn't help summon the power, but it made concentrating easier.

He focused on the verdant life surrounding him, breathing slow and steady. The other initiates' conversation faded away. The rhythmic steps of his horse lulled him into a state of calm. He sensed the energy surrounding him. Like a simmering desire, it waited for him. He blew out a slow breath, and on command, it responded to his call.

Strength flooded through his limbs. His sight seemed brighter. His hearing grew sharper. He sensed every nerve in his body, lit up with awareness. His muscles rippled with potential. Although his body wanted him to continue, he forced himself to stop pulling. He cut the invisible thread of life streaming to him. An involuntary gasp escaped his mouth, but he covered it by clearing his throat.

Bottled energy filled him to the brim, threatening to spill onto the road. He kept his eyes forward, holding his breath. Trying to act casual, Kaleth turned around. The branches of green that dangled over the road hadn't faded a bit. He grinned.

Curious about how long it would last, he continued riding, holding the unbridled energy inside. Even when he breathed, the power remained. The world felt sharp and promising. It seemed there was nothing he was incapable of doing. He estimated seven minutes before he sensed it fading.

The first sign that they drew near North Twainford was the smell. The odor of sweat and latrines permeated the air a mile before they caught sight of anything. After cresting a small rise in the road, the full extent of the permanent army encampment revealed itself.

Between the road and the river, a mixture of tents and crude wooden structures spread between the few remaining trees, stretching as far as he could see. A wooden bridge spanned the Lagrash, ending at a similar encampment on the far side. *South*

*Twainford.* Thravia's answer to the Kalshian military presence looked smaller and in more disarray. Their camp layout had little discernible order, as if it had sprawled over time as need demanded.

"It's crazy," Donzil said. "Both camps just sit there, staring at each other from across the river."

"They threatened us first," Rayd said. "Kalshia responded by posting a larger army. Then Thravia added more. Then Kalshia added more. And so on."

"You'd think one would attack the other."

"They have. Every few months someone tries infiltrating with spies or some new method. Thravia's too afraid of our Lightbinders to commit to a full assault."

*And apparently, we're too afraid of their Soulbinders,* Kaleth thought.

"I wonder how many Lightbinders are posted here," Orion said. "Maybe hundreds?"

"Sixty-two, last I heard," Rayd said.

A guttural shout drew Kaleth's attention to a cleared field amidst the camp. On one end, a row of targets looked like pincush- ions with all the arrows stuck in it. Bow men and women lined up a good distance away and loosed a fresh volley. Behind them, hundreds of young men and women wearing black-and-green uniforms ran through sword drills.

"It's the Blade initiates," Rayd said. "I see Julas, and there's Meriden."

"You want to say 'hello?'" Orion asked.

Rayd scoffed. "To those idiots? No. They'll be lucky if they're not demoted to Grunts."

The crowd of fighters impressed Kaleth. Their sword work looked similar to what the Lightbinders had worked on, although they lacked the confidence and poise he was used to seeing. Still, it was intimidating.

"Are those binder cannons?" Donzil pointed toward the close side of the bridge where a stone gatehouse controlled access to the crossing.

Mounted atop the gatehouse, four iron cylinders pointed across the river, each with glowing boxes affixed to the sides. Kaleth spotted more, organized in pairs every fifty yards along the riverbank.

"Of course," Rayd said. "We could blast the Thravian army into dust anytime we want."

Donzil chuckled. "I'd love to see that."

"My father designed that model. The old ones didn't have the feeder trough, so the Bows manning them had to load after each round."

The group of four arrived at the main entrance to the camp. Two Blade guards stood at alert on either side of a dirt path between buildings. They each took a half-step forward and rested hands on their sheathed hilts as the mounted initiates drew closer.

"Halt, riders. What is your business on the road?"

Kaleth, Donzil, and Orion pulled their horses to a stop, but Rayd didn't slow.

Both guards drew their weapons and jumped forward. "I said, halt!"

Rayd turned only his head toward them. "We're not heading to your camp."

"Rayd," Kaleth said. "We can take a second."

The guard grabbed the reins of Rayd's horse and pulled. "I told you to stop! And I don't care if you—"

"Jorace," the other guard uttered in a sharp hiss of air. He squeezed the man's shoulder, pulling him back from the horse. "Rayd? You're Rayd-il-Stonne, aren't you?"

The man named Jorace's eyes opened wider. He dropped the reins and stepped back. The tip of his sword lowered. "I'm so sorry. I didn't realize it was you. Your father was just here a few weeks ago. He's a great man. I'm sure you will be, too."

"I'll be even better," Rayd said. He called over his shoulder, "Come on, you three. We still have hours to go."

Kaleth kicked his horse into motion, following the others. He nodded at the two guards as he passed, wishing his squad leader wasn't such a jerk.

## CHAPTER THIRTY-THREE

# ROAD OBSTACLES

Just east of Twainford, they reached an expected intersection. The road that turned north looked narrower and overgrown, but a crooked wooden sign confirmed it was the path to Fairdre. The party of four took the new route, riding two abreast.

Before long, the landscape changed. Sharp hills rose from the earth, causing the road to meander between them. On a downhill section, the road grew even narrower as two cliffs emerged on either side. All four riders craned their necks to gawk at the bluffs rising around them. Rocky ridges loomed overhead. Despite the lack of vegetation atop the cliffs, their road cut through the center, deep in cool shade.

"This must be Belforth Gap," Kaleth said.

"What's that?" Orion said.

A cart blocked much of the path ahead with a horse standing at its front. Beyond it, three men bent over a tree that had fallen across the path. The men looked up at the new arrivals, sweat dripping from their brows. One man stood and arched his back, pressing a hand against it in a stretch. "Good afternoon," he called.

Kaleth echoed the greeting, but the other initiates remained quiet.

"It seems we're stuck," the man said.

"Where are you headed?" Kaleth asked.

"Fairdre. Trying to, at least. This tree is blocking our cart."

Walking his horse in single file, Rayd squeezed by the side of the cart. Kaleth looked over the wooden rails as he passed, noticing a faded canvas stretched across its cargo. When Rayd arrived at the tree, he coaxed his mount over the obstacle and continued on the road. Kaleth frowned.

"If it's not too much trouble. Would you—" He gestured toward the tree. "Could you give us a hand? My name's Lofkei. We'd appreciate the help."

"We're in a hurry," Rayd said.

"Hey," Kaleth called to his fellow initiates, waving them to come to him.

Rayd groaned, turned around, and walked his horse to join the others.

"What do you think?" Kaleth spoke softly enough to where the men couldn't hear.

"I say we move on," Rayd said.

"You're afraid it's a trap?"

The squad leader screwed up his face. "What? No, I'm not afraid. I just don't want to stop and help."

"How would this be a trap?" Orion asked. "We don't have anything valuable."

"Yeah, I guess not." Kaleth frowned. "Well, they could use a hand. If it's safe, we should try to help."

"Fine," Rayd muttered.

Kaleth turned to the men, keeping his senses on full alert. "Of course we will help."

"Thank you all so much," Lofkei said. He pointed toward the side of the path. "We were planning to move it over there—raise the small end and pivot. If you three could help us lift, I think we should manage it."

Kaleth ran his eyes down the trunk. It wasn't too thick, but trees were deceptively heavy. The three men were well built, so he imagined it shouldn't be too difficult. "Sure." He and the others spread out, positioning themselves around the tree. Kaleth patted the men's horse on the neck when he passed it. "What's your business in Fairdre?"

"Supplies from Lynharbor." Lofkei motioned toward the cart.

Kaleth stepped over a small branch to an angle where he could lift better. He kept the men in his peripheral, noting how they moved and positioned themselves. "What sort of supplies?"

Lofkei shrugged. "Odds and ends to trade. Nothing special. You all ready?"

The response sounded odd, but nothing appeared out of place. Kaleth reached out to the tree, sensing it for energy. Only a faint glimmer of life answered him back. *Dead limbs don't work. Noted.* He glanced around and spotted moss and weeds growing in the cracks of the cliff. Acting as if he took a moment to stretch his muscles, he reached out and inhaled power from the surrounding vegetation. He didn't need much, so he cut himself off before anyone grew suspicious. His body radiated with energy, hidden where no one could see.

"I'm ready." He squatted next to the trunk. While Donzil and Orion adjusted their positions, Kaleth's brow tightened. He cocked his head and stared at the tree. Then he raised his eyes to the top of the cliffs. Not a single tree peeked over the brink, and nothing more than a vine or a scrub brush grew along the walls. "Strange that a tree like this would end up here. You all just . . . rode up to it?" He felt his pulse beating faster. Something was wrong.

"Let's go," Lofkei said, crouching next to him with perspiration beading on his forehead.

Kaleth wrapped his hands around the trunk. His muscles tensed, ready to work. His alert mind was ready to respond.

"Lift together."

A glint caught Kaleth's eye. A layer of woven metal peeked out from the end of Lofkei's sleeve.

*Chain mail!* The hairs on his neck prickled.

Lofkei counted down. "Go in three . . . two . . ."

The pieces came together in a flash. *The tree blocking the road. Hidden mail. Suspicious cargo.*

"One . . . go!"

Kaleth took his hands off the tree. Lofkei had already drawn a dagger from a hidden sheath and lunged toward his chest.

"No!" he shouted. The power flooding his limbs heightened his reflexes and bolstered his strength. He leaned forward, blocking Lofkei's arm with his own before the blade could find its target.

The man's eyes flared when his attack ended. Kaleth grabbed his wrist with his other arm and wrenched it in a circle, spinning him and yanking the arm behind his back. Lofkei yelled. Kaleth wrested the knife out of his hand. The man spun with wild eyes and lunged at him, bare hands clawing toward his face. Kaleth moved without thinking. He swatted the arms away and slashed the knife across Lofkei's chest.

Despite the prodigious force behind his attack, the edge of the blade failed to progress.

*Chain mail!* He muttered a curse for forgetting it so soon.

Shouting around him drew his attention. Rayd, Donzil, and Orion each grappled with attacks of their own. The canvas over the cart flung back, and four more men jumped over the railing.

Kaleth's throat went dry. Giving him a second to think filled his body with dread. His muscles tightened. *Push the fear back. Don't let it take over. I can stop these guys.*

"Kill them all!" Lofkei shouted before lowering his shoulder and surging forward.

Kaleth planted his feet and pushed back. With his extra energy, he felt like a stone wall, stopping the man in his tracks. The unprotected skin of Lofkei's neck stuck out. Kaleth gripped the handle of the knife. He knew what needed to be done. Before he could react, thick arms wrapped around him, clasping across his chest and pinning his limbs against his sides.

"Get him now," a gruff voice yelled in his ear.

The memory of his father draining energy from Jairus came to him. He reached out to draw from Lofkei, but nothing happened. It was as if he tried to suck water from a stone.

Unaffected, Lofkei sneered and pulled a second knife. "It's the end for you."

Groaning, Kaleth used his reserve of power to lift his arms. The iron grip that held him crumbled. The man cried out when his clasped hands broke. Kaleth flung his head backward. The back of his skull collided with an object that made a sickening crunch. The man with the gruff voice howled. Kaleth spun and kicked his chest. The power behind the effort sent the man reeling. He tripped over a limb and tumbled backward, clutching a bloody nose.

Lofkei's next jab nearly got him, but Kaleth had enough speed to block him again. Sorene's instruction ran through his mind as he hooked his arm to move the blade out of the way. The bare neck showed itself again, and Kaleth didn't hesitate. He struck hard and fast, plunging his knife into the man's neck.

Lofkei's eyes bugged and his body twitched. Blood gushed from the wound, running down his neck and covering his tunic. Kaleth held on to his weapon, pulling it out as the man collapsed in a heap.

The sounds around him faded. His pulse thudded in his ears. Body frozen, he stared at the bloody knife. *That could have been me.* His body trembled. An overwhelming urge to flee filled him. *No! Ignore the fear. It doesn't exist!*

Surrounding noise snapped him back into focus. The man he had kicked away was back on his feet, knife in hand and approaching with another. Kaleth kept his eyes on them but bent to pick up Lofkei's second weapon. Armed in both hands, he spun the blades into reverse grips and raised them to a ready position. While the men hesitated, he sucked in more energy from the nearby plants.

Their attacks were predictable and slow. Kaleth marveled at how easy it was to fend them off. He dodged around blows and knocked away jabs. He struck a few hits to arms and bodies, but again, mail prevented them from doing much harm.

A man grabbed one of his arms.

Kaleth shouted while slamming the butt of a knife onto the backside of the assailant's upper arm, using a surge of energy to give it extra power.

The yell that tore from the man's lips echoed off the cliff walls. He tottered backward, clutching his arm that bent in the wrong direction.

Kaleth ran toward the other attacker, swinging knives with both hands. They swished in a figure-eight pattern, creating a fearsome display.

The other man's confidence had fled. He backpedaled for a second until turning to run.

Kaleth spun toward his fellow initiates. Donzil was double-teamed with an attacker on each side and a gash across his arm. Kaleth lowered his shoulder and barreled forward. He hit one of the attackers in the side and felt the man's ribs snap. The force of the blow knocked the man against the rocky wall, where his head struck with a thud.

Left with only one man, Donzil landed a punch in his assailant's side, causing him to curl inward. Kaleth followed with a powerful kick to the side of his leg. The blow bent his limb, and a *crack* filled the air. The man yelled and grabbed his leg as he toppled.

"Help!" Rayd yelled. On the far side of the tree, he lay on his back, grappling with a man. The attacker groaned as he pushed a knife toward the squad leader's chest. Rayd held the man's wrist, pushing against it, but gravity and the man's bulk moved it inexorably lower. Open wide with rings of white, his eyes found Kaleth's.

*There's nothing I can do*, he thought. He couldn't get there fast enough. The truth was, he didn't want to. The boy who had ruined his life was about to get what he deserved.

Rayd shouted an extended groan as his muscles rippled, straining against his attacker.

A cold feeling swept through Kaleth. *It could have been me.* He imagined the knife coming toward his own chest. His body again told him to run—leave Rayd. He would celebrate the justice. A shudder ran through him. The pull on him to flee was strong. *No! I am not afraid! I am confident!* I can save him if I want to.

The tip of the blade reached Rayd's clothing.

Kaleth's jaw tightened so hard his teeth hurt. He flipped one of his knives and caught it by the blade. After cocking his arm back, he slung the weapon forward. It spun end-over-end until the tip arrived at its target. A wet squelch accompanied the knife entering the man's head above his ear. His groaning quieted. His body went rigid. Rayd's pushing had a greater effect, and the lifeless body rolled away.

*I did it!* Kaleth thought.

The rest of the injured fighters took off down the road, one at a time. They limped and yelled as they ran away from Fairdre.

Orion traded blows with the last man standing, who had already lost his knife. When Kaleth arrived, the attacker stepped away. He glanced at the two lifeless bodies and then his fleeing partners. The light in his eyes dimmed as his resolve faded. Spinning on his heels, he took off in a dead sprint after the other men.

The sudden chaos faded with the trailing footsteps of the fleeing men. Kaleth's heart pounded. An icy wave ran through him as his body trembled. He balled his hands, flexing, then stretching them out. A rush of dizziness threatened to overtake him. *I am not afraid. I am not afraid.* He pushed the fear deeper and deeper, but it wouldn't go away. Like a spring that had been coiled too tight, dread sprang back, overwhelming him.

He fell to his knees, pulling his arms tight to his body. His eyes grew blurry as they filled with tears. Breaths came rapidly, failing to fill his lungs. Terror rendered him helpless. He couldn't stand. His body shook while silent tears fell.

He allowed himself a moment. No more pushing it back. No longer hiding from fear. Gradually, he recognized that the danger was over. The attackers were either dead or gone. His breath steadied. His lungs began to fill with oxygen. He wiped at his eyes and nose, trying to keep the others from hearing him sniff. After a final full breath, he stood. The fear had passed.

Orion looked bruised but in overall good shape. Donzil grabbed his own arm where a stain of blood had spread over his sleeve. "It's not bad," he told Orion. "Just a scrape."

Rayd stared at the corpse with the knife in the side of its head as he stood.

"You all right?" Kaleth asked, trying to keep his voice sounding normal.

The squad leader turned to him, his eyes vacant. He blinked several times before glancing over his own body. "Yeah, I think so."

"Nice work, Kaleth," Donzil said. "Don't underestimate a weakling if he has a knife in his hand, huh?"

Kaleth forced a smile at the backhanded compliment. The gravity of what he'd just done sank in. *Seven men attacked us. I killed two and caused the rest to run off.* His pulse continued to beat rapidly, but it was quickly settling. He noticed Rayd's continuing empty stare, so he stepped closer. Part of him wanted to turn his knife on the squad leader for what he'd done to his father's book, but concern gave him surprising restraint.

"You sure you're all right?" Kaleth rested a hand on his broad shoulder. "No injuries?"

The physical touch snapped Rayd out of his stupor. He pulled his body away. "I said I'm fine!"

Donzil crouched next to Lofkei's body. "Who do you think these guys were? Road bandits?"

"Probably," Rayd said. "They're common the farther you get from Kalistor."

"But why us?" Kaleth asked.

Rayd's brow furrowed. "Why rob us?"

"Yeah. We don't have much."

"Don't forget our stipends," Orion said. "They could have wanted that . . . or the horses."

"They wouldn't know we had a stipend, Binder-Brains," Rayd said. "They couldn't have known it was going to be us coming down the road. What? You think they scouted us out, then tossed that tree down at the last second?"

Kaleth shrugged. "I don't know. They *could* have."

"Hey, guys," Donzil said. He pulled his hand away from Lofkei's pocket, jingling a leather pouch.

"What's that?" Rayd asked.

Donzil untied the top and dumped the contents into his hands —heavy gold coins.

"Whoa!" Orion shouted.

Donzil counted them. "This is forty gold."

A stunned silence lasted only a moment until all four initiates burst into excited laughter.

"Forty gold! Wow!" Orion pointed at the bleeding corpse by Rayd. "Check to see if he has any."

The squad leader was already rummaging through the man's pockets, but a thorough search revealed nothing more of value.

Kaleth frowned. "Why would road bandits have forty gold in their purse?"

"Who cares," Donzil said. "It's ours now."

"If they're robbing several parties, they could have this," Orion added as he leaned over the sideboard of the wagon and started rummaging.

"But if that were the case, it wouldn't comprise eight five-gold coins," Kaleth said. "It would be coppers and singles."

Donzil pointed up the road. "If you want to run them down and ask, be my guest. I'm content to keep the loot and move on."

Rayd extended his hand and beckoned for the coins. "Give it here."

Donzil took a step back and clutched the prize to his chest. "I found it. That means I get to keep it."

"I'm the only squad leader in this group. That makes me in charge."

"Kaleth's the one who killed him," Orion said as he returned empty-handed from the wagon. "Maybe he should keep it."

The reminder of killing the man set his nerves on edge. Keeping forty gold seemed too good to be true, so he harbored little hope of it happening.

Rayd frowned. "Fine. We'll split it."

A grumbling Donzil handed out two five-gold coins to each of them.

"Come on," Rayd said after pocketing his money. He walked toward where their horses had settled a short ways up the road. "We still have a bit to go, and I want to get there by nightfall."

Kaleth pressed his coins together and marveled at the sudden fortune. Besides the six he'd already given his family, he had another nineteen gold coins back home. The bonus ten brought him officially one-third of the way to his goal of one hundred.

The animal hitched to the abandoned cart caught his eye. "What about their horse?" Kaleth asked.

"Leave it. Bring it. Whatever you want," Rayd said. "I don't care. I just don't want to deal with it."

He walked to the horse and patted it on the neck. The animal seemed calm and unfazed by the fight that had occurred. "All right, buddy. Why don't you come with us?" Kaleth bent over and pulled the pins that hitched him to the cart. He found a saddle in the wagon and tossed it on the horse's back, then led it by the reins to join the others.

CHAPTER THIRTY-FOUR
# FAIRDRE

An hour later, the road widened and the trees thinned. Wooden buildings popped up, and a weathered "Fairdre" sign announced they had arrived at their destination.

Kaleth looked forward to dismounting. After a rough start earlier that day, he managed well atop his horse. Even so, his legs and back were ready for a break, and he dreaded the soreness that would soon follow. He glanced over his shoulder, content to see the other horse followed, tied by a long lead to the back of his mount.

"Where are we supposed to go again?" Orion asked.

"The constable's office," Kaleth answered. "They know we're coming and are supposed to assign us work."

A man labored at the edge of a field on the side of the road. He stopped and looked as the initiates passed.

"Excuse me, sir?" Kaleth called. "Can you tell us where the constable's office is?"

The man squinted as if he didn't trust the question. After a moment, he pointed ahead. "Center of town. Look for the dragon."

Kaleth waved in thanks. Next to him, Rayd stared ahead as if oblivious to everyone else. On the opposite end, Orion and Donzil launched into a conversation about what they would do with their newly acquired gold.

His undesired compassion prompted him to lean closer to his squad leader. "Hey, Rayd." The semblance of a friendly greeting stuck in his throat and left an unpleasant taste.

Rayd turned to him, then narrowed his eyes. "What?"

Kaleth shrugged. "I just wanted to—" He failed to verbalize what he wanted to express. "You've been quieter than normal."

"So, what?"

His gut twisted. "So, I wanted to make sure everything was all right."

When Rayd didn't snap back, Kaleth was convinced there was a problem. The clopping of hooves on the hard-packed dirt continued for a moment.

"My father's the exal general," Rayd said.

Kaleth nodded.

"If he were with us back there, he would have bathed the road with their blood." He paused with his mouth open. "Kind of like you did."

Kaleth forced himself to keep from grinning.

"If he would have seen my contribution . . ." He exhaled a long breath and didn't finish his thought. "Respect," he whispered after a moment. "I work hard, too."

Kaleth's brow pinched as he waited on Rayd's unseen internal conflict to resolve. "None of us were ready for that," he finally said. "They ambushed us. There's nothing you could have done."

"You managed." The bitter words hung in the air. "Father would have *loved* to see that."

*I did manage*, Kaleth thought. His pulse quickened. *I took them down when my squad leader couldn't.* "Do you, uh . . . think I could possibly get signed off on my skill log?"

The softness on Rayd's face snapped into hard lines. "For what? Incompetence?"

The knee-jerk retort didn't carry the same bite it usually did. "I was thinking knife throwing. That and, um . . . disarming an opponent?"

Rayd's heavy frown pulled down at the sides of his face. He rode in silence for a moment before he extended a petulant hand.

A surge of excitement ran through Kaleth. Remaining in the saddle, he fumbled with the clasps of the saddlebags. In a moment, he passed his skill log and a stylus to his squad leader. Rayd flipped to the knife section and initialed on two separate pages.

"Thank you," Kaleth said.

Rayd slapped the log into Kaleth's gut.

"Oof!"

"Let's get something straight. You're weak, out of shape, and you'll never be better than me. I said it when you started, and I still insist you have no business trying for Lightbinder. I want you off my squad. I don't care what you did back there in the gap."

The familiarity of the harsh words refreshed Kaleth. They didn't carry the same conviction as they usually did. Not rising to the bait, he tucked his no-longer-empty skill log back in his bags. Having caught his squad leader in a chattier mood than normal, he pressed his luck. He lowered his voice. "Where did you learn about glyphs?"

Not taking his eyes off the road ahead, Rayd stiffened. "Glyphs?"

"Yeah. Like you used to trap me in my room. Who taught you?"

The squad leader didn't take his eyes off the road ahead. The steps of their horses' hooves filled the air. "I learn all sorts of things."

"Yeah, but it's a lost art. I didn't think many people knew about it. How did you—"

"That must be it!" Orion interrupted, pointing ahead to where a carved wooden valsic dragon stood in the center of a town square.

Rayd kicked his horse into a trot to take the lead and leave Kaleth behind.

"Fine," Kaleth muttered to himself. "Keep your secrets."

The town square had buildings on four sides with three dirt roads leading into it. Two sides contained a variety of shops— clothing, food, and supplies. The rundown storefronts and their streaked thatched roofs didn't promise that quality products lay within.

A long wooden building dominated an entire side of the square. Men sat around tables on a covered porch while women lingered around the entrance to the building. The sign above the door read

"Vice House." Opposite, a smaller building had metal bars displayed in its windows. "Fairdre Law" seemed a likely candidate for who they sought.

All four initiates dismounted. Kaleth groaned, arched his back, and shook out his tired legs.

Rayd nodded toward Fairdre Law. "Orion, check it out."

The initiate hopped up the steps and opened the door. He was inside for only a moment before he reemerged, shrugging. "No one's here."

A woman walking the street passed between them.

"Is this the constable's place?" Kaleth asked.

She flinched, jumping out of range as if subverting an attack.

"It's all right. We're not here to harm you."

Looking ready to run, she paused and narrowed her eyes. "Yes," she said after a moment. "This is the jail."

"We're looking for him. Do you know where he'd be?"

Her shoulders bounced as a single chuckle escaped. "Sure." Turning, she pointed across the square. "You can usually find him in Vice House."

"She sure is skittish," Orion said even before the woman was out of earshot.

Rayd led the way across the square to hitching posts where they tied up their horses. When Kaleth wrapped the reins, a shout drew his attention.

"Thief!"

A young man burst from a shop with a glittering necklace trailing through his fingers. He smirked as he ran across the square. Men and women moved out of his way without trying to stop him. An older man emerged from the shop, shaking his fist but stopping just outside the door.

Kaleth watched with an elevated pulse as the young man disappeared down an alley. "Should one of us do something?"

Rayd huffed. "Our job is to find the constable. Come on."

Kaleth frowned but followed the other three to the doors of Vice House. He nearly tripped on the steps when he caught sight of the women at the entrance.

A dark-haired beauty in her mid-twenties stood on the right side of the door. She wore a tight crimson dress that left little about her body to the imagination. The blonde on the opposite side stared at him with a crooked grin. Her hair curled around both sides of her smooth face. She couldn't have been more than a few years older than him. "You're a cutie," she said. "What's your name?"

His throat felt dry. "K-Kaleth," he managed.

She giggled and covered her mouth with her fingers. "My name's Sugar." Her finger worked its way down until it stopped at the neck of her dress. She teased it lower, emphasizing her cleavage. "Don't forget about me, all right?"

Heat crept up the back of his neck. "Um . . . all right." Someone pushed against him.

"Come on," Donzil said. "Keep moving."

Kaleth snapped his mouth shut, which seemed to have been hanging open. It took effort to tear his eyes from Sugar and her parting, playful wave.

The moment he stepped through the door, the new environment assaulted his senses. The space inside was massive. Two men worked behind a long wooden bar, pouring ale and cleaning glasses for the patrons sitting on stools. Past the bar, dozens of tables filled the room. They weren't tables covered with food but with cards and dice. A few even had lips around the edges of the tables where men leaned over and poked sticks at something inside. In a town the size of Fairdre, Kaleth couldn't imagine where all the people had come from. Women dressed like Sugar and the dark-haired woman from the door mingled with the men. Their outfits made him blush. Short dresses ended high on their legs, and plunging necklines displayed an abundance of skin.

The laughter and chaos of voices left his head spinning. It was difficult to make out anything over the uproar. A sour, musty smell filled his nose, like spilled ale and men who had gone too long without bathing. The miasma was so thick he could taste it.

When a pleasant smell teased his nose, his senses lit up. He turned, trying to find the source as an older woman arrived in a long red dress. Dark liner rimmed her eyes while her crimson lips curled in a warm smile. A thick layer of powder tried to hide age lines, but some stubbornly remained. Black hair piled atop her head in an elaborate display of curls. "Welcome, young gentlemen. What are you interested in today? A drink? A game? A bed?" She winked. "A woman?"

The others were silent, presumably dumbfounded by their options. "We're looking for Fairdre's head constable," Kaleth said. "Do you know if he's here?"

"Clagorn. Yes, of course." She pointed to a table where a group cheered, looking down at something Kaleth couldn't see. "The bald man at Ring Two."

Kaleth nodded. "Thank you, Miss . . ."

"Miss Ruby." Her eyes sparkled. "Let me know if there's anything you desire."

Kaleth led the way across the room, motioning for the slack-jawed others to follow.

The commotion at Ring Two drew them forward. Three men watched the ringed table, shouting and pumping their fists while one in a uniform stood impassively. Two women hung on the spectators, cheering with them while rubbing their shoulders and backs. Outside the one-foot-high barrier that circled most of the table, mugs of ale sat next to each man while stacks of arranged coins sat before the man in uniform.

When he arrived, Kaleth leaned closer to peer past the table's ring, and his curiosity turned to horror. Two scorpions circled each other in the small ring. Each around nine inches long, they held their pincers forward and dangled their stingers above their jet-black bodies. One contained a yellow "X" on its back while the other had a red one.

*Realm: Animalae. Category: Arachnill. Group: Scorpion. Strain: Paratill Scorpion.*

Kaleth felt the blood drain from his face. A sting from a paratill scorpion wasn't only an annoying pain to deal with. It would kill a man in minutes. Endemic to Terrenor—across the sea—they were rarely seen in Verdalyn.

The arachnid with the red mark jabbed with its tail, but it

missed, making a *thunk* as it struck the wooden table. Men around the ring cried out, some in excitement and some with disappointment.

The yellow fighter snapped its pincers, keeping the other at bay. They circled again. Pincers grew closer until the red one snagged the other, holding it tight. The attack was so quick that Kaleth barely noticed it happen. Its tail lashed forward, striking the other on the head, cracking the shell, and embedding its stinger. The yellow one attempted a move of its own, but the red scorpion was too quick. In a flash, it had released its grip and scurried backward.

Bald-headed Clagorn shouted and pumped his fists in celebration, while the man next to him dropped his face into his hands.

The yellow-marked arachnid staggered forward, but its moves grew erratic. Its pincers dragged, and the tail curled tight. In a moment, the entire body slowed to a halt. In its last act, the tail uncurled, flattening against the ground behind its body. The red scorpion skittered around as if celebrating its victory.

The man in uniform counted out copper coins and passed piles to Clagorn and to another man on the opposite side of the table. He swept a remaining stack of losing bets into a pouch tied around his waist.

"Are you Clagorn, the head constable?" Rayd asked.

The bald man didn't look like any constables Kaleth had seen in Kalistor. His meaty arms and plump body weren't from an excess of muscles. Rather, he appeared to be someone whose diet comprised nothing but sweets and ale. A thick beard grew down to the middle of his neck. He continued to grin as he counted his newly acquired coins, leaning his body into the buxom young woman attached to his arm. "Who's asking?"

"We're initiates from the academy."

"The academy?" He turned, frowning.

"In Kalistor," Rayd clarified. "Lightbinder Academy."

The man's frown grew more prominent. "Why are you here? I told them I didn't want anyone."

Kaleth felt his brow furrow. He and the other initiates exchanged glances. Rayd's mouth opened, then closed again.

"They assigned us to come to Fairdre," Kaleth said. "We were supposed to find you when we arrived."

"All four of you?"

He nodded.

The frown on Clagorn's face softened. A chuckle rumbled in his throat, growing and shaking his robust belly. "Well, you did your job. Yeah, I'm Clagorn, the head constable. And you four are the luckiest of the bunch. There's no work for you to do in Fairdre. You get a week of doing . . . whatever you want." He punctuated the sentence with another laugh while his hand rubbed his attendant's outer thigh.

"What do you mean?" Kaleth asked.

"The academy wants you to learn about law and order. They think observing what goes on in a smaller town will give you perspective and wisdom. Bah!" He swatted with his hand. "It's all rubbish. And I don't have anything for you to observe."

"You are the constable, right?"

Lines formed on his forehead. "I am."

"Surely there are things that need to be done." Kaleth pointed toward the door. "Only a moment ago, we saw someone rob a shop on the square."

"We do things differently here. We let people work their issues out."

"You mean you let people steal?"

Clagorn's smile evaporated. "Don't come here and tell me how to run my town."

Kaleth swallowed. "I didn't mean to—"

The bald man waggled a finger in his face. "The people of Fairdre will engage if necessary, and if not . . . so be it."

His blood felt heated, and his breath came rapidly. "So, we come here to help you, and our job is to sit by and do nothing while people commit crimes?"

Rayd touched him on the shoulder. "Cool it, Grunny. Our job is to do what he says, and he's telling us to drop it."

Clagorn smirked. "Yeah, *Grunny*, listen to the smart one. I know they work you hard at the academy." He spread his arms wide.

"Well, congratulations, you just received a free week of drinking, gambling, and—" He turned to the woman with him. She smiled and rubbed her hand across his chest. "And anything you desire."

Rayd, Orion, and Donzil nodded and smiled, but Kaleth couldn't get the thief out of his mind. The skittish woman also made more sense as he considered what life in the town must be like.

"You have money?" Clagorn asked.

"They gave us a stipend for food and lodging," Rayd said.

Donzil grinned. "And . . . we picked up a bit more along the way."

"If I were you," Clagorn said, "I'd stay here at Vice House."

The thought of staying a week in the noisy, smelly gambling hall turned Kaleth's stomach.

"If you spend time at the gambling tables, Miss Ruby will comp your rooms. You'll only need to pay for food and drinks, and who knows . . . you may make it all back from cards and dice."

"Are there any other places to stay in town?" Kaleth asked.

Rayd shot him a withering look. "Why?"

Kaleth shrugged. "In case we wanted to stay somewhere less . . . raucous."

"You can sleep in the woods if you want," Rayd said. "I'm staying here."

"Yeah, me too," Orion added with a goofy grin.

Donzil nodded. "Yeah, this isn't so bad for a small backwoods village."

"There's the Fairdre Inn." Clagorn ignored the disparaging remark about his town. "Keep traveling down the main road. It's at the far edge of town. It's run down and boring, and they only have a handful of rooms. Nowhere near as fun as this place, and you'll have to pay for lodging."

"Did I hear you four might stay with us?"

Kaleth turned to find Miss Ruby arriving with Sugar and the other young woman from the entrance.

The older woman smiled. "We have rooms and drinks aplenty. We'd love to host you."

Sugar slid next to Kaleth and trailed her fingers down his arm. Goosebumps raised on his skin.

"Yes, we will," Rayd said. "At least us three. Don't know about Grunny over there."

"Kaleth, do you want to go somewhere else?" Sugar gave his arm a gentle squeeze.

He cleared a catch in his throat. "I-uh . . . it's a bit chaotic here. I might check out the other place."

Sugar scrunched her face up into a pout.

"Suit yourself." Rayd turned to Miss Ruby. "What can we do to get some drinks?"

Donzil clinked the coins together in his pocket. "And maybe a dice game?"

"Why don't we get you settled in? Then I'll set up a table for you." Miss Ruby waved another young woman over. "Girls, would you show these three young men to their rooms? Numbers sixteen through eighteen at the end of the hall should work."

"Have fun doing whatever," Rayd said to Kaleth. "You know where to find us." He walked away, letting the dark-haired beauty lead him by the hand.

Sugar waggled her fingers at Kaleth as she walked away with Orion.

Alone in the center of the room, Kaleth sighed. *I must be an idiot.* He couldn't see himself spending a week in a place like that, though. His legs felt heavy as he walked toward the exit.

## CHAPTER THIRTY-FIVE

# THE AUCTION

Kaleth's two horses clopped behind him as he led both by the reins down the main street. After what Clagorn had told them about the way the law worked, details held more significance. Street vendors cast suspicious glances when he passed. Other people walking kept their distance from him. He could imagine the allure of no law if he were a criminal, but it seemed to create little but fear for the common person.

The prospect of having a free week grew more exciting the longer he considered it. He could train at his own pace, and most importantly, he could venture into the woods and experiment with his new power. There was much he didn't know, and his control could use more work.

He fiddled with the coins in his pocket. The two gold he'd received as a stipend now made twelve after the bounty they'd received from the bandits. Finding a room and board should be a breeze.

The buildings thinned out the farther he walked from the square. Porches sagged and some ceilings even showed holes. A small square contained a stage that looked as if it would collapse if anyone stood on it. As he continued along, the thicker woods drew near, and only a handful of buildings remained in his path.

He spotted the Fairdre Inn by the sign hanging outside. It was a decent-sized property with wooden walls and two stories of windows. A planter box of flowers attempted to give the place some cheer, but wilting blossoms resulted in the opposite effect.

A bell shook overhead when he opened the door, but nothing rang from inside its casing. The common room he entered contained a half-dozen tables. Two older women sat around one in quiet conversation while a man read at another. A fraction of the size of Vice House, the quiet atmosphere was a refreshing contrast.

"Hello?" he called.

The three patrons looked at him but didn't respond.

Shuffling feet preceded a crook-backed woman with gray hair and a heavy burden of wrinkles rounding a corner. "Welcome. Sorry, dear. I didn't hear you arrive."

He pointed over his shoulder. "I guess the bell didn't sound when I came in."

She waved a hand. "Oh, that thing hasn't worked for years. My name's Agnes. What can I help you with?"

"I'll be in town for the week, and I'm hoping to get room and board. My name's Kaleth. I hear there are only a couple of inn options."

"Sure. Sure. I can help with that. Is it only you? Because I only have one open room at the moment."

"I'm with three others, but they're staying at Vice House."

She raised her eyebrows. "And you're not? A young man like you?"

He shrugged. "It felt like . . . a lot."

She nodded, the corner of her mouth curling up. "Yeah, it does. A week of room and board for one will be one gold and two coppers."

"I also have two horses. Is there a stable nearby?"

"Two more coppers, and I can board them in ours."

He handed over his stipend and received six coppers in return.

"Supper's at seven. Welcome to Fairdre, Kaleth."

•   •   •

Kaleth closed the door to the inn behind him. With an hour until supper, he thought a stroll through the town would be what his legs needed after riding all day. The air smelled fresher than it did in Kalistor. The trees looked greener.

A short way up the street, he reached the smaller square he had passed before, but people filled it where it had been empty. Men, women, and children stood facing the ramshackle stage, waiting as if a show would soon begin. Kaleth looked around for a sign to announce what was about to take place, but nothing clued him in.

A man in his fifties with a graying beard sidled next to him. "You looking for your wife?"

Kaleth's brows pinched together. "Um . . . I'm not married."

The man had an eager look in his eyes. He raised on his toes and glanced around the crowd. A crooked grin showed a conspicuous gap in his teeth.

"Are *you* looking for your wife?" Kaleth asked, unsure if that was the right question or not.

"Already got one of those. Looking for someone to do the things she won't. Someone with some spirit. You know what I mean?" He poked his elbow into Kaleth's side and cackled, whistling through his teeth. "Eh . . . you're too young. You probably don't know. I can lock her in the basement at night, and she can clean or do something during the day. Wife might even thank me." He laughed again, but the tone left a bad feeling in Kaleth's gut. The man nodded toward him. "I'm gonna head up for a closer look."

When the older man disappeared into the crowd, Kaleth leaned toward the next closest man. "Excuse me."

The short man had greasy hair and yellowing teeth. He raised an eyebrow and leaned away.

"Can you tell me what's happening here?"

The man's eyes narrowed. "The weekly auction." Spoken matter-of-factly, the scoff that followed emphasized the intended judgment.

*Auction?* He frowned, considering the old man's comments.

A chorus of mutters got his attention. Men parting the crowd headed toward the stage. Between them, a line of five women trudged along with their heads bowed. Links of chain jingled in the air.

Kaleth cocked his head.

The men mounted the steps on the side of the stage and dragged the line of women to the center. The bald man at the front with a goatee addressed the crowd. "Men and women of Fairdre, we are here to fulfill your greatest desires. We have searched far and wide to bring what you need—what you cannot find on your own. Ever since King Rhinean outlawed taking slaves from Kalshia, it has made our goods rare. But we have prevailed. We braved danger and threat of death to bring you these five exotic and wild beauties, straight from the heart of Thravia."

Kaleth's stomach turned. *It's a slave auction.*

The first four women looked similar. They kept their heads bowed and eyes down. Despite smudges on their faces and greasy hair, they looked to be young and attractive. The last in line was a mess. She jerked against the grip of the man who stood next to her. Her wild, curly hair dangled in front of her, but each time she struggled, it waved it back and forth. Cuts, bruises, and dirt marred her disaster of a face that peeked through the swishing strands.

"They are strong and hard workers. Don't let their appearances dissuade you. They will clean up nicely. Maybe you need a cook—someone to clean. Some of you men might want a wife. Or some of you might be looking for new escorts. I'm looking at you there, Miss Ruby."

The crowd chuckled.

Kaleth spotted Miss Ruby standing near the stage.

"First up, we have Diamond."

A man pushed the first woman's hair behind her ears and lifted her chin.

"She's nineteen years old. She has the skin of a baby, the strength of a smith, and the hands of a queen. I'll start the bidding at five gold."

It was difficult to tell from his distance, but Kaleth guessed the woman was closer to thirty years of age than she was to twenty.

Miss Ruby raised her hand.

"Five gold. Do I hear eight?"

A man with a crisp hat raised his hand.

"Eight, do I hear ten?"

Another man joined in. Miss Ruby shot him a withering look. She took the next bid of twelve. Hands raised and lowered, bringing the bids to fourteen, fifteen, then to seventeen, where both men bowed out.

"Seventeen gold it is, and Diamond is sold to Miss Ruby."

One of the men on stage kneeled to fiddle with the irons that clasped around the woman's ankles. When released, they dragged her to the opposite end of the stage where one of Miss Ruby's assistants handed over a small coin pouch, then dragged the woman toward the town's main square.

"Next, we have the beautiful Tulip."

The next girl in line looked up with wide eyes. Her brown hair was already pulled back. Even from his distance, Kaleth noticed her legs trembling.

"Beautiful inside and out, Tulip smells as nice as her name implies. Only eighteen years of age, she expressed her greatest desire is to be a loving wife for a strong man. Who will start the bidding at five gold?"

The man with the crisp hat raised his hand.

"Five gold, great. Who will give me eight?"

A new man by the far side of the crowd raised his hand. "I'll take ten!"

"Twelve!" the man in the hat shot back.

After a few more bids back and forth, the man with the hat won her for nineteen gold.

The next two girls continued similarly, fetching ten and thirteen gold.

Nervous laughter rippled through the crowd when the last girl was all that remained.

"And now we have . . ." the auctioneer laughed as well. "This one has . . . spirit."

A man smoothed her hair and lifted it behind her ears. Kaleth gasped along with most of the crowd. The cuts were much worse than he had glimpsed. Yellow and purple bruising covered half her face as if she'd been beaten.

Kaleth's heart hurt at the sight. He pictured his sister. If she were taken from home, beaten, and sold by slavers, he wouldn't rest until the people who took her had paid for it. He imagined that one had a family, too. *Surely someone out there loves her.*

The man next to her licked his thumb and tried to touch it to a cut on her face. She jerked back and snarled, "Don't touch me!"

A chorus of oohs sounded through the crowd.

"See, there's that spirit," the auctioneer quipped.

The young woman glared at the people in the square.

A recognition rushed through Kaleth. He tilted his head. *She looks familiar.*

The man on stage maintained a positive grin despite the malevolent looks being hurled from his final product. "She's strong. She has energy all day. Possibly even more than some of you men can handle." His exaggerated wink drew chuckles from the crowd. "The bruises will heal. The cuts will mend. And once they do, she will be a bargain of a woman to have around."

"What's her name?" an older man with a graying beard shouted from the crowd.

"She's a young sixteen years old, and her name is Jasmine."

Through gritted teeth, the young woman said, "That's not my name."

The crowd was silent. The auctioneer's eyebrows raised. "Haha. She has a sense of humor, too."

"Call me by my name." Her voice carried over the crowd.

The auctioneer paused. He took a moment to compose himself, then forced another smile. "Very well. Her name . . . is Felyra."

The name hit Kaleth like a thunderclap. *Olive skin. Curly black hair. Green eyes.* The dingy and torn clothes weren't familiar, but past the cuts and bruises, he made out the scar that ran across her jaw. His breath quickened, and his pulse thundered in his ears. *The Thravian who saved my life.*

"Let's start her at three gold. Who will bid for her?"

Kaleth scanned the crowd, hoping no one would take a chance

on her. His heart fell when the man with the graying beard and whistling laugh lifted his hand.

"Three, thank you. Do I have five?"

*No!* His stomach twisted into a knot at the thought of her going to the man and his locked basement. He touched his pocket. The coins pressed hard against his leg. Ten gold and six coppers. *No, my family needs this.* He stared at her defiant green eyes and could think of nothing but her killing Tyron and then pulling him from the frozen river.

*I've been working all year to save gold. I can't throw it away, now. I can't.*

"No one? Last chance for five?"

Kaleth swallowed a lump in his throat and lifted a shaking hand.

The auctioneer pointed at him. "Five, thank you. Do I hear seven?"

The bearded man responded.

"Seven. Very good. How about Nine?"

He lifted his hand again, pressing through the force that tried to hold it down.

"Nine gold to the young man. How about ten?"

Kaleth glanced at the bearded man. The older man stared at the stage, pursing his lips.

"Ten? Last chance, sir."

"Ten," the bearded man said.

Kaleth tried to breathe, but his lungs wouldn't work. "Ten gold and six coppers!" he called out, lifting his chin.

"Very well. Ten gold and six. How about you, sir? Will you wager more?"

The bearded man opened his mouth.

*Don't do it.* His heart pounded in his chest. He pressed his sweaty palm hard against his pocket.

After a pause, the man's jaw snapped shut.

"Sold, for ten gold and six to the—"

"Eleven!" the other man called, shooting his hand in the air.

Kaleth felt as if his breath had been sucked away. He stared at the stage with a limp jaw.

"Splendid, will the young man go eleven and five?

He looked at Felyra with an empty feeling in his gut. *I don't have it.* Her thrashing had settled. She hadn't looked at him and only stared past the crowd with a clenched jaw and a fierce gaze. He didn't know what to do. She had saved his life.

As if acting of its own accord, his hand lifted into the air.

"Eleven and five. Incredible! Would anyone bid twelve?"

The other man shook his head with finality.

"Eleven gold and five coppers takes Jasmine—er . . . Felyra, sold to the young man."

Kaleth couldn't move. He didn't have the money. What was he supposed to do? The people around him nodded in recognition of his winning bid.

On stage, a man standing behind Felyra held her by the shoulders while another unclasped her irons. When the chains hit the floor, her feral cry ripped through the square. She snapped her head backward and smacked into her captor's face. He cried out and reeled backward, holding his nose. Felyra yelled as she ran. The crowd near the stage jostled to get back while the six slavers scrambled to grab her.

Kaleth broke his inertia and hurried forward. He pushed through the crowd, heading toward Felyra.

When she reached the auctioneer, she sped up and lowered her shoulder. The man took the blow in the gut but wrapped his arms around her at the same time. As he fell over, he pulled her with him. They both hit the wooden stage hard.

A great crack rent the air as the wood split. The boards of the stage erupted at the collision of bodies, sending a plume of dust and debris into the air. The crowd was in chaos. Kaleth battled against fleeing bodies to make forward progress.

He spotted Felyra under the stage. On her hands and knees, she wriggled on, pushing broken boards out of her way. She scurried for a gap at the edge of the platform. From there, it would be a brief run to the closest alley.

Kaleth found him cheering for her. Despite him having been the winning bidder, all he wanted was for her to be free from the slavers.

Arriving at the gap, she extricated herself from the crawl space.

*Run*, Kaleth thought. *You can do it!*

A slaver landed in front of her after jumping off the stage.

*No!*

The man's fist cracked across her face.

"No!" Kaleth shouted.

Felyra fell to the ground, stunned by the blow. The man bent over. "No one gets away from us!" he shouted, hitting her again and again.

"Stop it! Leave her!" Kaleth slung bystanders aside and rushed forward. He caught the man's cocked arm and pushed him over. "Stop it!"

The man stood over Felyra, chest heaving and arm cocked. The other slavers gathered, eyeing him. "She defied us," the auctioneer said. "She must be punished."

"I won her. I'll take care of her." Kaleth fished in his pocket and pulled out all his remaining coins. He tossed them at the man. "Now leave her be."

It took the auctioneer a moment to calm, but his smile soon returned. "Very well." He scooped to pick up the coins that had fallen in the dirt. The smile faltered as he counted. "This isn't eleven and five."

Kaleth balled his clammy hands to keep them from shaking. His throat felt like he'd swallowed sand. "Ten gold and six copper is all she's worth now."

The man's eyes narrowed. "You're reneging on your bid?"

His pulse thundered in his ears. "She was mine at eleven and five, and then you damaged her."

"This is only ten gold and six copper."

"She'll need medicine. It will take her time to heal. She may even have a broken nose now."

"That doesn't matter. You owe us what you bid."

Kaleth swallowed hard. "I'm not paying it."

The tension hanging between them was thick. Tendons in the man's neck flared.

"I *will* pay ten and six."

"Slaton!" the man called over Kaleth's shoulder. "You want her for your bid of eleven?"

Kaleth held his breath. He didn't turn around lest the move might encourage the other man.

A whistling laugh cut through the air. "After what she just displayed? No, thanks!"

The man frowned. The coins clanked as they dropped into his pocket.

"She's all yours."

Kaleth exhaled, letting his shoulders relax. Content that the fight was over, he turned to Felyra. Fresh cuts marred her face, which lay against the ground. Her eyes were closed. Her lips moved, but only muttering sounds escaped. "Felyra." He crouched next to her, resting a hand on her arm. "Are you all right?"

Her eyes didn't open. After a moment, the struggling head relaxed and her lips stopped. Her chest still moved in measured breaths, but she had passed out.

The man named Slaton loomed over his shoulder. He chuckled. "I guess I should thank you, huh?"

Kaleth didn't even turn to acknowledge him.

"You saved me from having to deal with that. The man wasn't lying about her spirit. Good luck to you."

The man shuffled away, and the rest of the crowd dispersed. Kaleth remained in his crouch with a hand on her arm. His heart hurt seeing her broken and bruised. *Captured and taken from her home to be sold.* He shook his head. He didn't regret his empty pockets. It gave him great joy to return the favor she extended to him months before.

Working his arms behind her back and under her knees, he lifted her body and struggled to his feet. Her limp body was awkward and bulky to carry. He cradled her against his chest, leaning back to keep the weight centered. Taking short steps, he made his way back to the Fairdre Inn.

## CHAPTER THIRTY-SIX

# NURSING TO HEALTH

K aleth wrung out a rag over the basin that sat on the end table. While the water had started clear, it had morphed into a deep shade of pink. He sat on a stool beside the bed —the one he had rented for the week. A candle burned on the table, providing flickering light for the room. The sun had set hours before, but he remained vigilant. Felyra sat propped up on the mattress, bolstered by the multiple pillows Agnes had found. She continued to breathe but had yet to open her eyes.

Kaleth leaned forward. He pressed the damp rag against a gash on her forehead. The wound already looked partially healed, so it wasn't something she received during her escape attempt.

Each touch of the rag and gentle wipe reduced the blood and grime covering her face. He worked down her cheek, taking care not to aggravate the discolored bruises. A cut on her chin looked better after he ran over it with his rag. His eyes caught on the old scar that had been there long before he met her.

*I wonder what that was from?*

He touched the white line. The surrounding skin was smooth, but the scar contained a raised ridge that pressed against his finger. He recalled saying something about her scar and her lashing out in response. His eyes flicked to hers as a sudden fear of her waking rushed through him. She didn't rouse, but he still removed his touch.

A gentle knock turned his head. He crossed the room to open the door. Agnes held a fresh basin of water.

"Thank you," he said. "Here, let me move the old one."

He returned to the bedside and lifted the bowl of stained water so she could set hers down.

"I brought a fresh rag, too." She pulled a piece of cloth from a pocket and draped it over the side of the bowl. "Nothing yet?"

He shook his head. "She tossed her head a few times but hasn't woken. I imagine the sleep is good for her."

"With all the injuries she has, rest is exactly what she needs." Agnes nodded toward the bed. "You've done nice work. She's looking much better."

"Thanks." He managed a half-smile. "It's difficult to not scrub too hard. I don't want to wake her up with fresh pain."

"Would you like me to try a bit?"

He shook his head. "I can do it. Thanks, though."

She nodded. "I checked with the other patrons before they retired for the night. None of them were interested in giving up their rooms. I'm sorry."

"It's fine. I'd rather not leave her alone right now, anyway."

"Very well." She pulled a fresh candle from a pocket and set it on the table. "If you're going to be up, you might need this."

"Thank you, again."

Agnes took the old bowl and rag from his hands and stepped toward the door. "If you need anything, come and get me. I'm in the room at the bottom of the stairs. Once she's awake, perhaps she might like some soup. The charge to feed her would be minimal."

A sinking feeling filled his gut. "I—uh . . . I imagine so, but I'm actually out of money. I spent it all on her."

At his mention of purchasing Felyra, Agnes frowned. "If you're going to buy a woman from the slave auction, you should at least take care of her."

"I will," he blurted. "I am. At least, I'm trying. But I'm not *buying* her for me. I just didn't want her to fall into that other guy's hands.

I'm not planning on—" He paused and looked at Felyra. "I have no idea what I'm planning."

Agnes stepped through the open door. "I'll bring the meals you paid for up here if you can't come down. What you choose to do with them is up to you."

"I have an extra horse. Any interest in buying that?"

"I don't need another horse, but I'm sure you could find a buyer in town. Plenty of horses here, though. You won't get much."

Kaleth closed the door behind her, then returned to his stool. He dunked the new rag in the fresh water, then wrung it out. With delicate care, he resumed cleaning.

The candle burned lower as the night progressed. When he'd done all he could to rinse her wounds, he turned his attention to the bare wooden planks above the bed. A loose nail he'd found would work. He leaned over her, steadying his balance with a hand against the wall. His chest hovered a few inches off her face. He took in a deep breath.

*To knit together her wounds and speed up recovery.*

The scratching of the nail was loud. Although he'd been wishing she would wake for most of the night, he now hoped she would hold off a bit longer. After forming a circle, he drew the backward S and the vertical line that formed the healing glyph. As he completed the design, he felt the telltale sign of energy leaving his body—the sign that it had worked.

*That should help*, he thought as he returned to his stool and leaned his back against the wall. He considered blowing out the candle, but worried about her waking in the dark and being disoriented. With her eyes closed and curly black hair framing her face, she looked more at peace than he'd yet to see her.

*She'll be okay*, he told himself. *She just needs to rest.*

SHIFTING GRAVITY JOLTED HIS BODY. Kaleth's eyes flew open. The stool underneath him had slid, and his body had begun to fall, tipping his seat. A kick of his legs and a flail of his arms regained the balance he needed. The legs of the stool regained their places on the floor, and he held out his arms, poised and still.

A creak turned his head. Light streaming through the window illuminated Felyra standing with the bowl raised above her head. With bared teeth and a twisted face, her growl filled the room as she readied to hurl the object at him.

"Whoa! Whoa!" he shrank back and raised his arms to block his face. "Felyra, it's me. It's all right."

The growl stopped. Her gritted expression softened as the bowl lowered. Her forehead wrinkled. "How do you know me? Who are —" She leaned her head closer and squinted. "Kaleth?"

"Yes." He lifted his hands to take the bowl from her. "Here, I'll take that." He took the basin and set it back on the side table.

Without a target to attack, she wobbled on her feet. Backpedaling, she attempted to sit back on the bed.

"Here. I can help."

He took her hand to steady her. Her skin felt clammy and cold, trembling as he helped her back onto the bed.

"Where am I?"

Kaleth pulled up the blanket. "You're at an inn. You've been asleep since yesterday."

"What happened?"

"Do you not remember?"

She shook her head. "I remember the auction. Someone bought me, then I ran." Her eyes opened wider. "It was you. You won the auction."

"I couldn't let that other guy win. He was awful."

She sat up straighter, leaning farther away while her eyes darted around. "What are you planning to"—She swallowed—"to do with me?"

Kaleth's eyes widened. "Oh, no! I'm not doing anything. You're free."

She blinked several times. "You paid money for me just to free me?"

"Yeah."

She looked at the pink-tinged basin of water, then back at him. "And you've been taking care of me?"

He shrugged. "I figured I owed you one, right?" He chuckled. "For saving my life?"

"Owed me *one*?" She lifted four fingers. "You owe me *four*." She smirked, then winced, jerking her hand to her face. "Ooh. That hurts."

Kaleth rushed forward. "Are you all right?"

Holding her jaw, her forehead furrowed. "It's okay." A long moment of silence filled the room. The corners of her eyes glistened. She mouthed, "Thank you," but it wasn't more than a breath.

Kaleth fidgeted. The more she watched him, the more he tried to figure out what to say next. "Anyway," he said, "when you tried to escape, that guy caught you and beat you."

She frowned. "I don't remember that at all."

"You were pretty fierce. Silvertail, right?"

Her brows pulled tighter as if she didn't get his meaning.

He pointed at her chest. "Your necklace. The silver-tailed ermine. You're fierce."

She puffed a laugh through her nose and fished under her shirt, stopping when she confirmed the thin chain was still there. "That's right. Yes, that's me."

"The man stopped when I arrived. You passed out, so I carried you back here."

She looked over at the basin. "And you've been cleaning my wounds."

He shrugged. "Yeah. Well, there's only so much I could do. They'll heal though. You look much better already." The wounds still had a long way to go. He hoped there wasn't a mirror anywhere around. She'd do better to not see her current state for a while. He noticed the healing glyph over the bed had faded overnight, having done all it could.

Footsteps sounded in the hall. Kaleth looked at the door before a light knock sounded. He opened the door to find Agnes outside, holding a bowl. The scent of warm, salty broth wafted in, making him salivate.

"I brought your breakfast." Agnes' neck craned around his body, and her eyes lit up. "Oh, she's awake. How are you feeling, miss?"

"I'm . . ." Felyra paused. "To be honest, I'm in a lot of pain."

"I'm sure you are. This one was up late into the night caring for you."

Kaleth felt his face flush.

"That's a good sign, but you never know with people who buy slaves." Agnes narrowed her eyes at him as she scooted by. She traded the soup for the old basin water. While she was near the bed, she leaned over and whispered to Felyra just loud enough for Kaleth to make out. "If he starts to treat you poorly, you let me know. My name's Agnes and I'm just downstairs. Yell for me."

Felyra smiled. "Thank you." She nodded toward Kaleth. "This one and I go back a bit. I think I should be all right with him."

Agnes' eyebrows raised. "Really? Well, that's good."

"Agnes." Kaleth stopped her when she was at the door. "Do you have any feldsthorn, by chance?"

She frowned. "Feldsthorn? No, why would I?"

"It can be mixed in a tea to lessen pain."

"I didn't know that. Sorry, no I don't. There's an apothecary near the main square. I imagine he might have some."

Kaleth's shoulders sank. *If only I had money.* "Thanks."

Agnes closed the door behind her.

Both Kaleth and Felyra turned to the soup. "Are you hungry?" he asked.

Her eyes grew wide, and her tongue peeked from her lips to wet them.

"I wonder if she'd bring us a second bowl," Felyra said, her eyes not leaving the soup.

"No need," Kaleth lied. "I ate while you were asleep, so I'm not hungry. This was for you."

His stomach rumbled, but his shuffling feet covered the growling as he moved closer. "The men who had you, did they feed you?" He sat on the side of the bed and lifted the bowl of soup.

"Only enough to keep me alive."

"How long has it been?"

"I'm not sure. Several days."

Kaleth grasped the spoon. "Would you like me to help?"

"You don't need to. I can do it." She sat up straighter and winced at the movement.

"I don't mind."

She looked at the spoon, then eventually nodded.

Kaleth leaned closer. His side rested against her leg. He lifted a spoonful of broth, holding the bowl under it as he moved the spoon closer. Her lips parted and took in the mouthful. Swallowing appeared to take great effort. She closed her eyes, pressing them together.

"Does it hurt?" he asked.

She shook her head. "It's okay. Just warming my throat back up. It's good." Her lips parted again, waiting for him.

He lifted another spoonful and fed it to her, watching her lips and her face as he repeated the motion. Seeing her injuries while she was awake brought a new level of sorrow to his heart. Before long, the soup was gone. His own stomach growled again as he fed her the last bite. The spoon clanked in the bowl as he set them both down.

"Thank you," she said. "I needed that."

Kaleth looked at the deep purple bruise on her jaw. The edge faded to green then yellow before it disappeared into a long gash.

"What is it?" she asked.

"Nothing."

"No, you're thinking of something."

He paused, unsure if his curiosity outweighed what was appropriate. "Your injuries. Not the ones from the auction, but the others. They look several days old. I wondered what they were from."

She didn't respond.

"It's fine," he said. "You don't have to talk about it."

"No, it's all right. It was from—" Her lips froze.

He gave her a moment before filling in, "From the slavers?"

Her eyes flicked to his. "Yes. Yes, it was from them. They knocked me in the dirt and beat me."

"How'd they catch you?"

"I happened across their camp. I would have run but . . . but they grabbed me before I could get away."

"Up in the mountains? Where we met?"

Her throat undulated as if swallowing hard. "Near there." She offered no more details.

"Well, I think you'll be in luck. The bruises will heal for sure. I think the cuts and scrapes will mend well. A week from now, I wager you'll be as good as new." The scar on her chin came to his mind, but he didn't dare mention anything about it.

"Kaleth," her hand covered his with a gentle touch.

He froze. Fighting the urge to pull it away, he stared at her, trying to appear as natural as possible.

"No one has ever done what you did for me. Who knows where I'd be now, had you not been there?" A light squeeze pressed his hand. "Thank you."

His heart pounded. He wanted to say something brilliant in return that showed his kindness. Instead, he awkwardly stood and pulled his hand away from hers. "Great." He emphasized the word with a single clap. Stumbling over his feet, he hurried his way toward the door. "I'm, uh, going to take the—" He stopped and returned to the side table to pick up the empty bowl. "Guess I need this, huh?" His nervous laugh wavered. "I'll take it down to Agnes. Then, I'm going to go to the uh—who's the guy with the—the pother—no . . . potha—" He shook his head. "That's not it, either."

"The apothecary?"

He snapped and pointed at her. "Yes. That's it. I want to see if he has some feldsthorn. Will you be okay if I go? Do you need anything?"

She smiled. "I'll be fine. Thank you."

"And I thank, too. I mean—you, too—to thank, that is."

Her forehead creased.

*"I thank, too?" Come on, Kaleth, what are you doing? And why can't you remember the word apothecary?*

A light knock snapped him away from his awkward conversation. He crossed to the door and opened it. No one was there. About to step into the hall, he noticed something on the ground. His mouth pulled up at the corners. It was another bowl filled with broth.

## CHAPTER THIRTY-SEVEN

# FELDSTHORN

The town center was less busy than it had been on the previous day. Shopkeepers were up and out, but only a few patrons perused their goods. Kaleth found the apothecary shop with little trouble. On the corner of the main square, advertisements for herbs, medicines, and tinctures displayed in the windows.

A tug pulled on his pant leg. "Excuse me." A young girl who couldn't have been over five grasped the fabric of his pants in her tiny hand. She looked up with expectant eyes. Her brown hair fell back in curly waves, and a smile covered her face. "I finished my art. You wanna see it?" She held up a sheet of parchment that was folded over on itself, showing nothing but the blank backside.

"Um—" He looked at the apothecary shop, then back at the girl. He was mid-step in pulling away from her grip when he paused. Crouching down to get on her level, he smiled back. "Yes, I would love to see your art. What do you have?"

Her eyes lit up. She released his pants and used both hands to unfold the paper and raise it closer to him. Scribbled colors covered the page. Reds and yellows looked like flowers, and two objects made of sticks could pass as people.

"This is my mother and father. They're working in our garden, growing flowers. See, here's our house, and this is my dog, Patchy." She pointed to a ball of brown scribbles that looked nothing like a dog.

"Yes, I see Patchy. Are you two good friends?"

She nodded with her entire head and neck. "Patchy's my best friend. What do you think of my art?"

Kaleth took another moment to look at the picture. He nodded as if deep in thought. After a moment, he settled on the back of his heels and looked at her. "What's your name?"

"Charlotte." She lifted her eyebrows.

He looked back at the picture and pointed at the center. "This is one of the most beautiful pictures I've seen in a long time, Charlotte."

She beamed. Her eyebrows raised. "Really?"

He nodded. "I mean it. I think you have a genuine talent. I hope you keep it up and make even more."

She held the picture in front of herself and stared at it. Her mouth hung open as her eyes skipped across the image. Glowing with delight, she wandered away.

Kaleth chuckled to himself as he stood.

A sharp smell hit him when he stepped inside the apothecary shop. Bottles of colored liquids and powders filled shelves, and a wrinkled man with wisps of gray hair watched from behind a counter.

"Good morning," the man said. "You must be new in town."

"I am. Just here for the week." Kaleth scanned the shelves.

"What can I help you with?"

"What medicine do you have for pain?"

The man folded his hands on the counter. "That depends on what you need. What sort of pain are we dealing with?"

"A beating. Lots of bruising and cuts."

The man turned and reached for a clear jar with a pile of brown roots inside. "For something like that, I'd recommend filibous root."

"Filibous dulls the pain, but doesn't speed up the healing,"

Kaleth said. "How about a tincture of varicilin or maybe some feldsthorn?"

The man's eyebrows lifted. "Well, someone knows their medicines." He chuckled as he put the jar of roots back. "Sure, I have both. Varicilin is the best, but it isn't easy to come by."

"How much?"

"One gold coin for a bottle."

Kaleth winced.

"Of course, feldsthorn is readily available in the riverlands. Ten thorns would only be three coppers."

Kaleth nodded. "All right. That's not too bad. Let me see if I can get the money. I'll be back."

KALETH INSPECTED each door as he walked down the hall of Vice House, stopping at number sixteen. He rapped on it, then paused. No one responded. The result was the same after a firmer attempt. He tried the knob, but it didn't turn. *Locked.*

Door seventeen had the same result. He frowned as he stepped to the last door in the hall. To his surprise, the knob turned. The creaky hinges announced his presence, but nothing stirred inside.

A sour, pungent odor hit him as he stepped through the doorway. He screwed up his face and gagged, covering his nose with a hand. The curtains shaded most of the sun, casting only a sliver of light across the space. The room was cozy, with a bed, a wardrobe, and a small table covered in empty bottles.

On the far side of the bed, a full head of dark hair faced in the opposite direction. A blanket covered the woman's body, leaving a hint of bare shoulders and her upper back exposed. A tight crimson dress that Kaleth remembered well draped over the footboard at the end of the bed.

The blanket on the other side of the bed had been disturbed, and the pillow was empty. Kaleth stepped closer until his foot tapped something on the floor.

"Mmm. What . . . ?" A mumbled sound revealed the second person in the room.

Kaleth squinted in the dim light and bent closer. Rayd lay on the floor, covered by nothing but his underclothes. When he lifted his head from the wooden board, a squelching sound turned Kaleth's stomach.

"Where am . . . who are . . . ?"

The smell grew worse as Rayd pushed up to a sitting position.

"Rayd," Kaleth whispered. "Are you okay?"

The other initiate's head settled, looking in his direction. "Kaleth? What are you—" He looked up to the bed, then back at him. Chunks of something stuck to the side of his face.

"I think you might have . . ." He pointed at the squad leader's face. ". . . vomited."

Rayd's voice grew more forceful. "What are you doing here? Get out!" He struggled to his feet.

Kaleth took a step backward. "I'm sorry. I just need to borrow three coppers."

"What?" Finally standing, Rayd's feet staggered in a triangle pattern. "I'm not giving you money. Use your own."

"It's not for me. It's for—"

"Get out!"

"Rayd, please. I need—"

"Leave, Kaleth, and don't come back!" He pressed a hand against his chest.

Kaleth stumbled backward. He was about to leave when Rayd's body convulsed. The squad leader lifted a hand to his mouth and bent over. A guttural heave bellowed from his lungs as the upper half of his body undulated and a sharp retch filled the air.

Fresh vomit splattered onto the floor. Rayd bent forward with his hands on his knees, gagging and coughing. The woman in the bed rustled.

Kaleth stepped forward again and rested his hand on the lintel. "Rayd . . ." he said softly when the retching quieted.

The other initiate snapped his head in his direction and wiped his mouth with the back of his hand. "I said, get out!"

The door slammed shut in Kaleth's face, rattling the walls and booming down the hall.

. . .

Kaleth inhaled deeply when he stepped outside the front doors of Vice House. The odor of ale and vomit clung to his nose, but fresh air and the scent of nearby trees helped mask it. Pressing against his empty pockets, his shoulders slumped as he crossed the square. The apothecary shop taunted him from where it loomed on the corner. Avoiding the door, he passed by, continuing toward the far end of town.

"No luck?"

The question stopped him. He turned to find the apothecary standing in the doorway to his shop. Kaleth shrugged. "I thought I could get money from someone, but it didn't work out. I've got a horse though. I think I might need to sell it."

The old man nodded. "You know . . . I've been in Fairdre for sixty-two years. Over time, you get used to the attitudes and selfishness. It doesn't mean it's right—just expected. So when my granddaughter goes on and on, beaming because of the young man who appreciated her picture, that makes me think that young man is someone special.

Kaleth raised an eyebrow. "Charlotte? She's your granddaughter?"

The man nodded. "Tell you what . . ." He pointed toward the far side of town. "At the end of the road, there's a path that leads to the river. I suggest you check it out. It might be just what you're looking for. Just watch where you step." He flashed a wry grin before waving and heading back into his shop.

When Kaleth reached the Fairdre Inn, he continued farther until he found the promised path. Packed dirt cut through the undergrowth, making a serpentine path into the woods. The river gurgled nearby. A breeze rustled the leaves. He watched his feet as he walked forward.

Before long, the path ended at the river. Ten feet across, water flowed over rocks and trickled past mossy logs. The flat, packed ground on the bank indicated it was likely a common area for washing, bathing, or drawing water.

Kaleth spun, checking the ground. He stepped toward the foliage and kicked at the thick greenery. He stepped into its midst, sweeping his eyes. "Ouch!" Something pricked his leg. He extricated himself from the thick vegetation, then pulled up the hem of his pants to find a spot of blood where something had pricked him.

He leaned closer to the ground and brushed the plants aside. A clump of five oval-shaped leaves contained a flowering yellow seed at the center. He bent the leaves over to look at the stalk, and a grin formed on his face. Three sharp thorns decorated the side of the plant. He looked around, noticing dozens of identical stalks hiding amongst the foliage.

*Feldsthorn. Just what I need.*


Kaleth knocked before opening the door to his room. When he pushed it open, Felyra lifted her head, then rubbed her eyes.

"I tried to sleep," she said, "but it's tough with the pain. Any luck?"

He smiled. "I got what I needed." He returned to his stool, then set down a teapot and a small stone mortar bowl filled with broken-off thorns.

"Is that feldsthorn?"

"Mmm-hmm." Kaleth selected a thorn, then pulled a rag from a pocket. He pressed the flat side of the thorn into the cloth and squeezed. It resisted for a bit until the right amount of pressure forced the sap to evacuate the plant. He dropped the shell of the thorn in the bowl and repeated the act with the next one.

"What does that do?" Felyra asked.

Kaleth continued his work, squeezing thorn after thorn. "The sap is great for healing open wounds. In nature, the thorn serves as a natural deterrent to keep animals from getting to it. It's best when they're fresh, but dried thorns also work well."

When he finished the last of nine thorns, he set the rag down and picked up a pestle. Grinding it into the discarded shells, he mashed the objects into a fibrous mess.

"And what is this for?"

Kaleth lifted the lid from the teapot. Steam escaped, fogging the air above the table. He dumped the ground mess inside, then replaced the lid.

"The leftover thorns brew into a tea. Rather than topical healing, it helps with the entire body. Also, it makes you sleepy, which you need."

Giving the tea a moment to steep, he picked up the cloth. The faint-green gel clumped together in the center of the fabric. Kaleth moved to the side of the bed, then raised the cloth. "Are you all right if I . . ." He circled the cloth in the air. ". . . with the wounds?"

She nodded. "If it will help, sure."

He leaned closer.

Felyra lifted her chin and focused across the room.

Kaleth used his free hand to hold her chin, careful to touch an uninjured area. He pressed the gel against a cut that ran down her cheek.

She sucked air in through her teeth, hissing.

"Sorry," he said, trying to keep the cloth still.

"It's all right." She pressed her eyes together. "Just do it."

Slowly, he wiped the cloth along the wound, spreading the healing sap across her skin. When a thin layer of gel coated the wound, he moved the cloth to another.

She hissed again but didn't pull away. "Keep going. It's fine."

Kaleth worked across her face, touching up each injury. Soon, each wound glistened. "Can I see your arms now?"

She extended her arm, showing off scrapes. The wounds themselves looked several days old, but an infection had turned the skin an angry red shade.

Kaleth held the back of her hand, keeping her palm up. Her skin was tough, like someone who grew up in the wilderness, but touching it, and his nearness to her, still quickened his pulse. He wondered if she could hear the heavy beating of his heart. Cleaning the scrapes on the arm was easy. He wiped the cloth along them, cleaning and disinfecting the wounds. Once that arm was finished, he took the next one in his hand. His heart skipped a beat.

"It feels cold now," Felyra said. "On my face. Cold and tingly."

"That's good. That means it's fighting off germs and speeding up healing. Soon it will go numb."

When both arms had been treated, his eyes moved to the cuts peeking out from under her neckline. "Are you okay if I clean your shoulder?"

She stretched to see where he meant, then nodded.

Kaleth repositioned closer. He touched the neckline of her shirt and tried to pull it to expose the scrapes he'd cleaned with water the night before. Pulling with one hand pressed the fabric against other scrapes, making him pause.

"Here," Felyra said. She shrugged and lifted the neckline, giving it more slack. When she pulled it to the side, it exposed her shoulder, down to her upper arm. A long gash and multiple smaller scrapes stared back at him across her bare skin.

Warmth creeped up his neck to his ears. Ignoring her bruises and cuts, she was quite pretty. The more skin she showed, the more he couldn't avoid the thought, but he pushed it away. She wasn't in any condition to be dealing with that.

With his heart beating even harder, he leaned closer. Although he wanted to use his other hand to steady his work, he didn't dare touch her unclothed shoulder. He brought the rag closer. It hovered beside the long gash, but a tremble in his arm shook it.

"If it makes you uncomfortable, I can try it," she said.

"Oh no, it doesn't make me uncomfortable." He pressed the rag against the wound, but the motion was more of a jab than a delicate touch.

She winced, pressing her eyes closed again.

"Sorry." He moved his other hand closer. "It might help if I—" He rested his hand on her collarbone. "It's easier with the support."

"That's fine." She blew out a slow breath.

Kaleth worked the rag along the wounds, cleaning the cuts as best he could.

"Perhaps you'd be more comfortable if you were—" She took in a breath. "Naked and freezing to death."

His muscles locked. The rag felt caught where it touched her. *Surely, she doesn't want me to . . .*

"After all, I've known you longer without clothes than I have when you've had them on."

His jaw hung limp. He scrambled to think of what to say. Sweat prickled on his forehead as his hands grew clammy.

When he didn't move, she eventually opened her eyes. "I'm joking, Kaleth." She closed them again, her lips curling into an amused smile.

A nervous chuckle bubbled from his lips. She joined him, louder, causing his laughter to grow in intensity. When they both finally settled, Kaleth wiped his eyes and continued the job. He didn't hesitate to support his hand by touching her shoulder, and soon the cleaning was complete.

Felyra still had a crooked grin when she lifted her shirt back to its original position. "It's already feeling a lot better. Thank you."

He couldn't think of what to say in response, so he remained quiet. Finished with the sap, he balled up the rag and set it aside. An aromatic, herbal scent wafted from the pot. He lifted it by the handle and filled a cup with tea.

"This will help even more," he said as he handed it to her.

Felyra held the cup up. Steam curled off the liquid. She tipped it to her lips and sipped. Her face puckered. "Ugh."

"Yeah," Kaleth said. "It's not tasty, but it's good for you."

She lifted it again and drank more. Screwing up her face, she downed the rest of the cup before handing it back. She smacked her lips as if trying to push the taste away from her.

Kaleth set the cup by the pot. "You should get sleepy in a few minutes. If you're up for it, you should get some rest and let the medicine work."

She nodded. When Kaleth stood from the bed, she reached for his arm. "Will you stay?"

The question combined with the touch of her hand made his heart skip. "Of course." His response sounded more breathy than he intended. He pointed to the stool. "I'll be right here. You rest, and don't worry about anything."

He settled into his seat as she closed her eyes. The faint smile on her face lingered. The wounds and bruises on her face already looked better than they had the day before. His pockets may be empty, but being able to return the favor and care for her made it all worth it.

## CHAPTER THIRTY-EIGHT

# RECOVERY

Felyra blinked her eyes open. Her tingling senses told her something was wrong. A surge of adrenaline rushed through her. She looked at the stool; no one was there. And that was the problem. For the last four days, Kaleth had been there every time she woke.

A sloshing of water made her jump and jerk her head to the other side of the room.

"Sorry," Kaleth said, pausing with a steaming bucket perched on the side of a basin.

"It's all right," she said. "It just surprised me. What is this?"

He grinned. "It was Agnes' idea. She has this bathing basin she said we could use. She's been helping me heat buckets." He poured the water in.

The definition in his arms caught her attention. *I don't remember him looking that strong last time we met.*

"This should actually be enough," he said, "so I'm glad you woke."

She pulled her gaze away from his arms. "This is for me to take a bath?"

"I thought you might enjoy it. If you feel up to it, that is."

She had gotten used to the grime of sweat, dirt, and blood ever since she'd left Revalle. Thinking about the clean water made her acutely aware of her state. "That would feel great. I would love it."

His face lit up. He lifted a finger. "I'll be right back. I have one more thing for you."

The empty bucket jostled at his side while he exited the door.

Felyra pulled back her blanket and slid her legs to the side of the bed. She gave herself a moment to ensure she wasn't dizzy before she stood. One hand remained on the side of the bed until she took three unsteady steps to make it to the basin. A light steam lifted from the water inside, the humid scent filling her nostrils. She breathed it in, imagining it cleaning dirt and dust from the inside. Her hand dipped in, and she waved her fingers. Her eyes flared, and her mouth pulled up at the corner.

*It's warm.*

Beside the basin, a short table held a scrubbing brush, a bar of soap, a hairbrush, and a towel.

The door opened again, and Kaleth entered, out of breath as if he'd been running. A green-and-white dress draped over his arm.

"What's that?" she asked.

"This is from Agnes," he said. "It was her daughter's, but she passed away last year. She said she doesn't need it, and I'm guessing—" He indicated to the clothes she wore. "I was thinking you might not want to wear that anymore."

She glanced down at herself and laughed. The shirt was dirty and torn. The pants were ripped in several places. They hadn't been washed in so long that she assumed they didn't smell the best. It had been a while since she'd worn a dress, but anything would be better than what she had on.

"An outfit change would be welcome," she said.

Kaleth grinned again, then stepped back to the door. "Are you all right to bathe yourself? Or do you need . . . ?"

She cocked her head and raised an eyebrow at the bold suggestion. "Do I need . . . what?"

"Should I get Agnes?" His earnest expression proved he hadn't jumped to the same conclusion she had.

She smiled. "I'll be fine. Thank you, Kaleth."

He bobbed his head and backed out the door. "I'll just be down-stairs. Shout if you need anything."

She crossed to the door and turned the lock. Alone and safe, the warm waters begged her to enjoy them. Removing her clothes felt freeing. The rips and blood on them reminded her of both Captain Janduan and the slavers, and casting them off felt like sloughing off the memory. She was now free to be someone different, to forge a new Felyra. She left her ermine necklace on, not wanting to remove that part of her past.

When she eased her body under the water, an involuntary sigh escaped her lips. It felt like a warm hug of one hundred blankets wrapping and healing her at the same time. Taking the final plunge, she submerged her head. The injuries on her face didn't even sting.

*That feldsthorn sure did the trick.*

She rubbed her hands through her hair, feeling the caked dirt and grime release their hold on her. Suspended underwater, she held her breath and let the strands of hair float around her. Every inch of skin celebrated the restoring touch of water. She didn't want to leave. When her lungs begged for new oxygen, she lifted her head above the surface.

She lay in the water, soaking until the warmth had long fled. Not wanting to miss the chance to get clean, she picked up the bar of soap from the table and scrubbed her body until her skin glistened its natural olive tone.

She took more care with her face. She dunked it under the water and lathered with soap. Her fingers dabbed the skin, noting any unhealed cuts and remaining tender areas. Most of her newer wounds seemed to have mended. When she ran her fingers along her jaw, the scarred ridge she'd had for years remained as it always had. She chided herself for the unrealistic thought that the feldsthorn could have somehow healed it, as well.


Felyra left her room for the first time in several days. When she first entered, she was passed out, bruised, and bleeding, and now she was bathed, partially healed, walking under her own power, and wearing a clean dress.

The dress from Agnes fit well. The white sleeves poofed up over her upper arms. Agnes' daughter must have been shorter because the hem ended a few inches shy of what she would have worn. But she wasn't about to complain.

She grasped the railing at the top of the stairs and descended. When she reached the bottom, an eager Kaleth jumped up from where he sat at one of the community tables.

"Felyra," he said. "I didn't know you were going to come down. Are you—" He stopped mid-sentence as she stepped into the common room. His jaw hung slack, and his eyebrows lifted. "Felyra. You, uh . . . you—"

"I . . . what?" she prompted.

He continued to stare, muttering occasional words but forming no complete sentences. "You are—um, you look . . ."

"You look wonderful, dear," Agnes said, arriving at the front door to the inn. "Quite the progress from when you first showed the other day. Let me see you." Felyra stood still as Agnes craned her neck to inspect her face. "Yes, much, much better. I can barely tell there were any injuries at all. Fascinating."

Felyra thought of the chin scar but bit her tongue from making a disparaging remark.

"Are you okay to stand?" Kaleth finally made words.

She nodded. "I feel good. It's nice to move a bit. If you were interested, I was thinking it might be nice to walk through town a bit."

Kaleth frowned. "Oh, no. We're not doing that. You don't want to do too much too quickly."

"I'm sorry. I don't think I explained myself well." She pointed her thumb over her shoulder. "*I'm* going to go for a walk through town. If you're interested in joining me, I would love to have you along."

Again, Kaleth's words didn't seem to work as his face reddened. After a few moments of fumbling, he managed, "Sure, I'll join you."

. . .

THE BREEZE in the street was a welcome change from the stuffy room where she'd been recovering. At first, she took slow, purposeful steps, but soon she abandoned caution. Her leg hurt, causing a slight limp, but that was nothing different from what she was used to.

Kaleth walked next to her. He looked ready to pounce should she misstep or topple like a felled tree. It wasn't just his arms that looked stronger. His whole body seemed thicker and more capable. Either her memory wasn't as good as she thought it was, or he'd bulked up in the last half year.

"I've spent the last four days being cleaned and fed by you," Felyra said, "but I still don't know anything about you. When do I get to know the *real* Kaleth?"

He took a few more steps. "What do you want to know?"

"For starters . . . Kaleth what? What's your surname?"

"Kaleth-il-Valorr."

"Valorr . . . your father?"

He nodded. "What about you? Felyra Silvertail?"

She smiled. "Felyra Nightwind."

"Nightwind. I like it."

"My parents let me pick it."

"Why do Thravians choose their surnames and not use their father's names?"

She chuckled. "You know . . . I've never really considered it. Maybe as a way to distinguish from Kalshian tradition, I guess. I think it started after the Rift."

"It's getting more common in Kalshia. My friend Jovi changed his name to Strapper when he was eight. His father wasn't the best, and I think he was ashamed to bear the name. Some do it to hide where they come from, but I think most just like the freedom of expression."

"Tell me about your father. What is he like?"

His smile faltered. "He was wisdom. Love. He was present and kind."

"He passed?"

Kaleth nodded. "Earlier this year. I'm proud to bear his name."

Her thoughts shifted to her own father and how losing him had gutted her.

"I'm sorry."

"My sister is younger than I, and my mother is ill. I've been trying to take care of them since Father passed, but there've been setbacks."

"Do they live here?"

He shook his head. "Kalistor."

"Then what are you doing here?" She held up a hand. "I'm sorry. That sounded wrong. I meant—"

"It's fine. It's a valid question. What they need is money, actually. We have a debt I'm working to pay back. I'm here because—" He seemed to waver over what to share. "It's what had to happen."

She waited for him to elaborate, but he offered nothing more. "So, to save up money, your plan is to purchase slave women and then set them free. Seems like a solid strategy."

He chuckled.

"I feel awful to have put you in this spot. As soon as I can earn it myself, I'll repay you."

"You repaid me more than enough the time you saved my life."

"You mean the four times?"

They laughed together.

She touched his arm with both hands, bringing their stroll to a stop. "Regardless . . . I thank you."

Her pulse quickened at the physical connection. His soft eyes returned her gaze while a genuine smile set her at ease. Her fingers slid down his arm until they grazed his hand, and before they disconnected, his fingers caught hers.

Felyra's stomach swooped. Her breath felt short as if she'd sprinted. She couldn't take her eyes from him or release the tenuous hold between their hands. Her lips parted, but she didn't know what to say. "It was the rabbits," she blurted.

His forehead wrinkled. "It was what?"

"In the mountains. You had asked why I saved you, and I said I didn't know. It was the rabbits."

His wrinkles smoothed. "The rabbits? In the snow?"

She nodded. "You spared the mother when the babies came along. For someone who had to have been starving, it couldn't have been easy to give that up. That made me wonder what type of person cares more about a small animal family than his own well-being? I thought a person like that might be nice to keep around—even if they are a Kalshian."

The corners of his mouth pulled up, but he said nothing. For a long moment, they stared into each other's eyes. The connection between their fingers sent a buzzing sensation through her body. She felt both hot and cold at the same time. After what felt like an eternity, unable to take the intensity any longer, she let go.

She turned away and continued walking. "So, um . . . what's next for you?" She spoke loud to be heard over the intense thumping of her heart.

"I'd, um, been meaning to tell you." He rubbed the back of his neck. "I need to leave Fairdre—tomorrow, in fact, to head back to Kalistor. I was only supposed to be here for a bit."

A sinking feeling ran through her. She tried to mask her disappointment. "That's too bad."

"I've been worried about you, though. I'm glad you're able to get up and around now, but what will you do next? Can you make it back to your family?"

Her forehead pinched. "Family?" The memory of telling him about her family in the mountains returned to her. "I've moved on since then. I've been living in Revalle."

"So, you'll return there?"

The question seemed simple, but Felyra hadn't thought that far ahead. *Where should I go?* Janduan would kill her if she tried to return to the academy. Her family was gone. She had nothing. She tried to avoid thinking of Ruane and whether the captain had done anything to her as a penalty for her running.

"Would you mind if I write you?" Kaleth asked.

"Write me?"

He nodded. "In Revalle. Would it be all right with you if I sent you letters? Our kingdoms are at war, but letter porters are still cheap."

"You would do that?"

His genuine smile and bright eyes gave her butterflies. "If you would like it, it would be my honor."

She tried to keep her smile from growing too large, but the corners of her mouth seemed to have a mind of their own. "I would love that." Unsure of what to do, she turned her attention to her feet and watched them as she walked.

Before long, the road led them to a large square with a wooden carving of a valsic dragon in the center. The door of a nearby shop burst open, and a young girl with curly brown hair rushed out.

"There you are," the girl called in a squeaky voice. "I've been looking for you all week."

A smile formed on Kaleth's face. "Charlotte!"

She grasped a folded piece of parchment in her hand. It trailed behind her, along with her hair, as she ran. "I made more like you told me to." She lifted the paper toward him. "This is for you."

"For me?"

Felyra stared at Kaleth's face. The look of shock and excitement appeared to be genuine, not put on to placate the girl.

He opened the folded sheet, and his jaw dropped. "This is even better than the last one. You must have been working hard this week."

The picture didn't look impressive to Felyra. A scribbled forest with a river that looked too blue to be real. An animal stood beside a tree, but she couldn't decide if it was a bear or a frog or even a bird.

The girl grinned, showing off a gap where a tooth used to be. "I have been. This is my fourth picture this week. My older brother says it's not good, but what does he know? I told him what you said, and I think he got jealous."

"I'm sure that's what it is," Kaleth said. "And I get to keep this?"

"Yep!"

He folded the paper and held it against his chest. "Thank you, Charlotte. This is just what I needed."

Appearing content that she accomplished her mission, the girl waggled her fingers, then turned and ran back to the shop.

"Who's that?" Felyra asked.

"Charlotte. We met the other day." Kaleth unfolded the paper to look at it again. He angled it toward her. "Pretty cool, huh?"

Her eyes couldn't pull away from the smile lines on his face. She chuckled. "Yeah. Pretty cool."

"How are you feeling after walking? Would you like a rest?" He pointed to a bench next to the dragon statue.

She felt fine but liked the idea of sitting for a moment. She nodded. "Sure."

They crossed the square to the bench where the shade sheltered a few weeds peeking out from the dirt. Felyra smoothed the back of her dress as she sat, angled toward Kaleth.

"I have a question to ask you."

Felyra held her breath. The tone in his voice was more serious than she expected.

"You don't have to answer if you don't want to."

"All right."

He paused and leaned closer. His voice dropped to a whisper. "Would you rather . . . be able to fly or never have to sleep?"

She blinked multiple times. "That's the question?"

"That's the question."

"Sorry, I was expecting something—"

"More lighthearted?"

She chuckled. "Yeah, that's it. Um . . . I would have to say flying."

"Me, too!" His eyes lit up. "I mean, it would be amazing to have all that extra time if I didn't have to sleep, but . . . flying would be incredible. Okay, next one. Would you rather have to always wear a mask so no one could ever see your face or always have to wear a hat that—"

"A mask," she answered, cutting him off.

"Oh—okay. The hat was going to have a huge brim that got in everyone's way."

"Mask. For sure."

Kaleth's brows knit together. He stared for a long moment as if trying to read her. "Are you . . . self-conscious?"

Heat flushed up her neck. *Does he need to be so obvious about it?*

"I guess I've never thought about it, but I can imagine how it might get annoying."

"Maybe we could discuss something else," she said, frustration building.

He didn't seem to hear her. "Do you wish you could hide to blend in with the crowd?"

"I'd rather not talk about it."

"I never get attention like that, so I wouldn't know what it's like."

"Kaleth, can we—"

"Do most pretty women feel the same way?"

"Do most—" She cocked her head, lips frozen. "Pretty women? You—you think I want to hide because I'm . . . pretty?"

He shrugged. "Is that a thing? I don't know." His raised eyebrows didn't mock. Not a trace of guile filled his face.

"You're serious."

"Of course." Kaleth's brow softened.

She averted her eyes and looked at her hands. "I've never seen myself as pretty."

"Then you've never really seen yourself."

She wanted to look at him, but fear of overwhelming emotions forced her to focus on her hands. The corner of her mouth pulled up. Her sight blurred at the edges until she wiped the beginnings of a tear away. Her fingers brushed the scar on her chin, but she didn't tense.

"I asked two," Kaleth said. "Now it's your turn."

"Me?"

"Yeah, ask me a question."

"All right." She looked around the square, searching for something to spark an idea. "If you could have a redo on one thing in your life, what would it be?"

"Redo for one thing? Hmm . . ." Kaleth grew quiet until he nodded. The playful tone in his voice was gone. "When my father was alive, he asked me to do something for him. It was simple—deliver something across town. I would love a do-over of that night."

"The delivery didn't go right?" she asked.

"You could say that."

"And he was disappointed?"

He was silent for a moment until he issued a soft laugh. "No, he wasn't. But I disappointed myself." He exhaled a long breath. "What about you?"

She swallowed a thick lump. "Years ago, my mother and I both got sick. I came out of it with surgery scars and pain when I walk, but she, uh . . . she didn't make it."

"So, your redo would be . . . that she would get better?"

She sighed and stared at her hands again. She held them so they wouldn't shake as a thick sorrow threatened to take over.

"It's okay," Kaleth said. "You don't have to talk about it."

She forced herself to speak. "Mother had told me to stay out of the alley by the market. It's where they toss all the rotten food, and I had hoped to find something fresh that had been overlooked. I didn't tell her about the rat bite because I was afraid I'd get in trouble. When my fever began, she took care of me. By the time we were both in the throes of the wasting disease, it was too late to do anything about it. My redo is . . . I would stay out of that alley. If I had, perhaps Mother might still be alive."

Kaleth nodded, not saying anything for a long time. "Thanks for sharing," he said finally.

He had the look of someone with a question on the tip of their tongue. "What is it?" she asked.

His brow furrowed, then he shook his head. "It's nothing."

"Ask me."

After a pause, he sighed. "In the mountains, you—" He looked unsure how to word his thoughts. "I thought your parents were alive."

A sinking feeling registered in her gut. Her lie about her parents had fallen through. She drooped her head, then shook it. "That was a lie. They're both gone."

"I'm sorry."

"I don't know why I lied. I think it's easier to pretend."

Kaleth reached his hand out and rested it on hers. She turned to face him. His eyes were soft and held a comforting kindness. "It's all right. I'm sure it is."

Her heart fluttered as she moved her other hand. When she placed it on top of his, his mouth tweaked into a grin.

"Hey!" a slurred greeting called from the doors of a seedy-looking inn called Vice House. A tall, young man with thick black hair and a full beard stumbled out of the doors. He looked over his shoulder back into the building. "You were right, Orion. It's Grunny!" Two other young men emerged with him.

"Oh, great," Kaleth mumbled.

"Who's that?" Felyra asked.

"His name's Rayd, and unfortunately, those are the guys I'm here with."

"Whatever you've been doing this week, you've been missing out." Rayd arrived and stood in front of the bench. His eyes looked glazed, and he swayed on his feet. "You should have seen the streak I was on last night."

"Yeah," one of the other guys said. "He won twelve hands in a row. It was incredible. Three girls were literally hanging on him, begging for his attention."

"My ten gold is up to twenty now."

Kaleth's eyebrows lifted. "You seem better than when I last saw you the other morning."

Rayd flinched. "I've been doing great all week." His eyes flicked to Felyra, and a smirk formed on his face. "I guess you haven't been doing too poorly, either. Looks like you found yourself some local tail to weave limbs with, huh?"

Felyra's jaw tightened after she sucked in a quick burst of air.

Kaleth jumped to his feet. "Felyra isn't *local tail*," he said, standing in Rayd's face. She caught a waver in his words. "And we're just talking."

The bearded young man outweighed Kaleth by fifty pounds of solid muscle. His full chest and thick arms seemed to grow the closer Kaleth got to him. Despite being physically outmatched in every way, Kaleth stood with fierce resistance.

"Whoa!" Rayd held up his hands and laughed. "Looks like I hit a nerve, boys." He turned back to Felyra and hiccuped.

She narrowed her eyes and stared back, meeting his gaze with a furious glare.

Rayd chuckled, covering his mouth.

"Do you have a problem?" Kaleth asked.

"Oh, no. It all makes sense though."

"What makes sense?"

"For you to find a girl who will trade two sentences with you, she would have to be deformed and scarred like this bind-cursed dog."

Felyra felt as if someone had kicked her in the gut. Her sight turned hazy, and a buzzing built in her ears. She struggled to breathe. Before she had time to think, a loud crack snapped the air. She blinked to clear her vision.

Rayd staggered with one hand on his knee and the other against his face where he'd been punched.

Kaleth stood over him with his arm cocked. "Never call her that again," he growled with a cold fury.

Rayd straightened. His mouth formed a grim line. He lifted his fists. "Are you sure you want to do this, Grunny?"

"Kaleth, it's fine," Felyra said. "Let's go."

The other two guys snickered. "Let's go, Kaleth," one of them mimicked.

Kaleth's face shifted between fear and determination. He stood his ground but looked like he could bolt at any moment. While appearing to battle internally, he bent his knees and readied both hands to fight the other young man.

Rayd shook his head. "Fine, then." His fist lashed forward, pounding against Kaleth's stomach.

The force behind the blow would have knocked a hole in stone, but Kaleth barely even winced. He didn't flinch or back down. Rayd's eyes flared. He shook out his fist as if the punch took a toll on him. He tried again, going for the face. Kaleth reacted that time, blocking the arm with his own. He followed with a counterblow to Rayd's stomach.

The larger boy gasped upon impact. He leaned over, wheezing and clutching his gut. He staggered away, breaking the tension between them. The other two observers stared with wide eyes, glancing between the two fighters.

"Come on," Kaleth said, breathing heavily as he held his hand out to Felyra.

She took it and stood. His arm trembled. Rayd continued to stagger in pain as Kaleth led her away from the bench. She stepped on clumps of brown weeds, curious at how quickly they had withered in the sun. As they walked away, her heart pattered with pride. It was the first time anyone had ever stood up for her like that.

## CHAPTER THIRTY-NINE

# PLANNING WHAT'S NEXT

Felyra chewed a hunk of bread while sitting up in bed. She was strong enough to stand or sit in a regular chair, but Kaleth insisted she rest in the bed as long as she could. With it being their final day, that was only going to be a few more minutes, so she relished every moment. Soft rays of morning light filtered into the room, and the cracked window let in a fresh breeze.

Kaleth sat on the end of the bed, one leg tucked underneath him while the other dangled over the side. On the floor, the pillow and blanket he'd been using had been folded and set to the side. He held a faded leather book called "Whispers of the Soul" that Agnes had lent him. To pass the time, he'd been reading it to her over the previous several days.

After he wrapped up reading a ten-line verse about a tree in the middle of a field, he frowned. "I don't get it. So . . . the tree turned into a person after it was struck by lightning?"

She smiled, puffing a laugh through her nose. "No, the tree was always a person. The field represents his world, and the storm is life's challenges. It's beautiful, really."

"Ohhh." He nodded. "So chopping down the other trees was like friends dying."

"Mmm, not really."

Kaleth closed the book and sighed. He crossed the room to return it to a shelf. "Poetry's hard. How are you so good at it?"

"My mother used to read to me. We had a book Father got from a trader in the market. The binding was cracked, and some pages were stained, but I didn't care. It had two hundred poems. I could probably still recite every one of them." The wistful memory brought a smile to her face.

He returned to the bed and sat on the corner.

The pillow and bundled-up blanket on the floor caught her eye. "Thank you, Kaleth, for this week and all you've done."

A shade of red washed over his face as he averted his eyes. "It was nothing."

"I mean it. I can only imagine where I would be if you hadn't been here. Plus, how you defended me in the square—with your friend."

"He's not my friend, just someone I'm stuck with."

"No one has ever stood up for me like that, and I'll never forget it."

His eyes found hers. A kind smile covered his face, melting her heart.

After a long moment of silence, she cleared her throat. "When will you leave?"

"Whenever the horses are ready. The ride to Kalistor will take all day, so we need to get going. How about you? Are you sure you're good enough to ride?"

The question was valid. She was unsure, herself. She moved her legs over the side of the bed and slid her body down the mattress until her feet hit the floor. Her old torn pants peeked out from under the dress as the fabric rode up. Agnes had cleaned them and patched up what she could, but they remained in rough shape.

"Sorry I couldn't afford to get you something new."

She waved a hand. "They're fine. A bit worn, but they'll work. And riding with just this dress would have been painful." Her legs felt solid. Her vision didn't spin. She stood, keeping one hand on the bed. After giving herself a moment to determine how her body felt, she determined she was solid. She nodded. "I'll be good."

"And you're still okay if I write you?"

She fought to keep the corner of her mouth from pulling up. "What will you write about?"

"I can tell you about what I've been up to. Maybe even try my hand at poetry. You can tell me if it's good or not. And you can share . . . whatever you like."

Her pulse grew quicker, but she willed it to remain calm. "That sounds great."

His broad smile left her insides aflutter. Thoughts of her own scarred face disappeared as she lost herself in his eyes. Leaning in, he extended his arm and touched the top of her hand. A jolt ran through her, racing her pulse. His fingers curled around her hand. She wanted to respond but wasn't sure what to do, so her hand remained motionless.

He smiled for a moment, but then his forehead wrinkled. "Or . . . I had another idea."

The hopeful tone of his voice left her somewhere between excited and terrified.

He pulled his hand away from hers. "Come to Kalistor?"

The statement phrased as a question took her breath away. Kalistor, the home of the enemy, filled with killers and oppressors. *I could never live there.*

His eyes settled on her. "You could stay with my family. My mother and sister would adore you. They would love having another person around."

His hopeful smile settled her nerves, but not enough for her to feel good about the suggestion. She felt short of breath. "I'm not sure, Kaleth. I can't just come and live with you."

"Well, it wouldn't be with me. My family has an extra bed now that I'm gone."

She cocked her head. "Where do *you* live?"

His brow furrowed as if he hadn't been ready for the question. His lips readied to speak until a knock on the door made him turn.

Agnes opened it a moment later. "The horses are ready. They're tied up out front." She nodded between both of them. "It was a pleasure hosting you both this week. I hope you have safe travels."

Kaleth grabbed his pack off the floor. "I'm going to load this up. I'll be back in a moment."

"I'll come down, too, but . . . give me just a moment."

He nodded before ducking through the door.

Felyra exhaled a long breath after he left. *Move to Kalistor?* The idea sounded ridiculous, but the more she thought about it, the more reasonable it sounded. *I don't know what Kaleth's mother and sister are like, but if they're anything like him . . .* Her mind sparkled with the thought. Nothing was left for her in Revalle. Her family was dead. Soulbinder Academy had tried to kill her. *Maybe I could be a spy for Thravia, living behind enemy lines.* The idea piqued her interest, but she quickly pushed it away. *I couldn't do that to Kaleth.*

A whinny drew her eyes to the window. She stepped next to it and looked down at the street where Kaleth stood next to a horse. He patted its neck, speaking softly.

She breathed in the crisp air, smiling as she watched. *Am I an idiot for considering this?*

He set his pack on the horse's back and attached it with two straps. Another horse was saddled and ready to go—the extra one he had offered to her.

She bent over and picked up the burlap sack of dried rations and a waterskin Agnes gave her. Her heart beat so hard, she felt it might burst. With a smile, she turned away from the window and headed for the door.

"You ready, Grunny?"

The familiar voice sent a ripple of fear through her. *Where do I know that from?* The answer rushed back as she returned to the window. Rayd, the young man from the square, arrived on horseback with the two other young men who had been with him. Prickles formed on the back of her neck.

"Did you enjoy your week of boredom?"

"It was fine," Kaleth replied.

"We spent it drinking ale and chasing women," one of the other young men said.

"Don't forget the tables," the final rider added. "Kaleth, you should have seen Rayd last night. He blew his entire winnings betting on the scorpion matches." The other two laughed, but Rayd only shrugged.

"Who cares? It wasn't even my money to begin with." Rayd nodded toward Kaleth. "You probably spent the whole time pounding that girl with the cheese-grater face, didn't you?"

Felyra's stomach dropped.

Kaleth lunged toward the mounted boy. "She's not—" he stopped, halted by a gleaming dagger the mounted boy angled in his direction.

"Watch it, Grunny."

Kaleth paused, easing out of his attack stance. "She was just a girl. She wasn't anyone."

Felyra frowned. Feelings of betrayal warred with common sense. *He tried to stand up for me. He doesn't need to fight over me again.* Despite the words she told herself, she couldn't escape the disappointment.

Rayd sheathed his weapon. "Come on. We need to hit the road."

"I need to get one more thing. You three start; I'll catch up in a minute."

"Suit yourself." Rayd nodded to the other two, then turned his horse around. "But when Aurik asks where you are, I'm going to tell him you weren't ready to go—as if he needs a reason to cut you from Lightbinder training."

Felyra gasped, her involuntary breath cutting through the air. She spun away from the window. Her breath felt sucked from her lungs as if she'd been punched in the gut. She pressed her hand over her stomach, but the ache didn't leave.

*He's a—he's a—*

She couldn't bring herself to finish the thought. Her greatest enemy. The people trying to destroy her country. The fighters responsible for her father's death. Kaleth was training to become one.

"He's a Lightbinder," she whispered.

The words curled her toes. Her legs trembled. She wanted to scream and run, but there was nowhere to go. Her bag was ready.

She was dressed and ready to leave. With dead legs and heavy shoulders, she opened the door and headed downstairs.

Kaleth looked up as she stepped out the front door. His eyebrows raised, and a beaming smile covered his face. What would have warmed her insides only moments before now left her cold and empty.

"You look good," he said, moving toward her. He reached to take her bag but hesitated when she flinched.

"Sorry," Felyra said, leaning away from him. "I like to pack my stuff." She continued to the other horse.

"I understand that. You want to make sure it won't fall off." His eyebrows raised. "So, what do you think? Come with me to Kalistor?"

Her heart felt conflicted. His genuine smile tried to set her at ease, but the knowledge of who he was—what he trained for—went against everything she stood for. Felyra shook her head. "No." She turned away from him and busied herself strapping her bag to her horse. It took all her effort for her hands not to shake. She tried to relax her clenched jaw. "I appreciate the invitation, but I can't."

"I understand. It was a crazy idea, anyway." His words sounded laden with letdown. "I'll have to content myself with letters then. Felyra Nightwind . . . in Revalle."

*Revalle*, she thought. *Where my execution awaits.*

"I guess it's time for me to head out. I hope your travels are safe."

"I'll be fine."

He took her hand. The touch of his fingers sent an unwanted jolt through her body. She wanted to rip it away but found herself pressing in return. Kaleth lowered his head. His lips touched the back of her hand. Frozen in time, the touch was tender. Prickles raised the hairs on her arms, and a flush raced through her body. It took an incredible effort for her to pull her hand away.

Kaleth stepped into the stirrup and mounted his horse. "I hope we meet again, Silvertail." He settled into his saddle and looked sideways at her. The quirky grin on his face softened the hardness threatening to encase her heart. "Judging from our history, let's wish for it to be under better circumstances next time."

She puffed an involuntary laugh through her nose. "Agreed." As his horse stepped down the road, she lifted a hand and managed a wave. Her body felt pulled in multiple directions while he grew smaller down the street. She had never met a young man like him—someone who looked past her exterior and saw her for who she was inside. But he trained to become the very thing she hated—the group she wanted to destroy.

When she pulled her eyes away, she gazed at the Fairdre Inn. She'd spent a week there recovering and finally felt whole again, but her stay was complete. There was nothing left for her here.

She imagined a noose waiting for her in Revalle, through the gates of the fortress, with Captain Janduan waiting beside it. She pictured Grax and his friends waiting to toss rotten fruit at her, laughing as they executed her. If Ruane hadn't been killed or tortured, she would be glad to see her, even if it were only for a moment. She imagined a stack of envelopes sealed with wax and addressed to her—letters from Kaleth, her enemy.

She grabbed the horn of the saddle and raised herself to the seat. The worn leather felt hard, but so was she. Despite the beatings and injuries, the threats, and the danger, there was only one place for her to go. She pulled her horse's reins and coaxed it into a walk—not toward Kalistor, not following Kaleth, but heading toward the only place she knew . . . Revalle.

## CHAPTER FORTY

# SEARCHING FOR CARRICK

The green-handled ironball jostled on Kaleth's shoulder as he ran down the central corridor of the academy. He kept pace with Jovi, only a few steps behind Rayd and Roselle. Lainn and Chyla trailed after them, unable to match their speed.

On the last lap of morning exercise, Kaleth felt his strength waning. Despite his slight figure and smaller muscles, he had kept up with the pack, but it wouldn't last much longer. The muscles in his legs tired. His lungs ached from lack of oxygen.

A green vine climbed up the wall, spreading its tendrils across the stone. Flat leaves were large near the ground but grew smaller the higher up they went. When Kaleth jogged past, he pulled at its energy. The leaves trembled. A few curled and faded from a vibrant green to a sickly color. Before the change grew obvious, he stopped. The energy he had borrowed from the plant filled him with strength and speed. His senses sharpened, and his body felt alive.

A few minutes later, the initiates jogged into Binder Court and tossed their ironballs down in a pile. Kaleth pretended it was nothing to lose the weight, but his body thanked him for the reprieve. His borrowed plant energy only lasted so long.

"I'm still amazed," Jovi said, his chest puffing in and out as he recovered from the work.

"At what?" Kaleth asked.

"At you! How did you—" He paused to enjoy another deep breath. "From where you were, how did you get to"—he gestured at Kaleth's body—"*this*?"

Kaleth grinned. He wasn't the only one who had noticed his physical transformation. After using his father's ability for months, his muscles had developed rapidly. He had transformed from the scrawny specimen he used to be. While still not nearly the size of the other initiates, his arms and legs contained definition. His neck was thicker. When he ran a hand across his stomach, he felt the hard lumps of muscles under his skin.

"It's probably the meat. Maybe I just needed some real food for a change."

Lainn arrived, breathing heavily. "Meat? Ha! Must be magic meat or something."

Jovi's brow furrowed. He leaned in and spoke in a mock whisper. "You need to cut me in on this magic meat."

Kaleth chuckled. "I don't have magic meat."

"Magic potion? Magic beans?"

Kaleth swallowed a lump. The lighthearted questions were hitting too close to the truth. Jovi's fingers extended in an attempt to pinch his arm until Kaleth swatted it away. "Stop it! I'm still me. I'm out here doing the work like you all. I guess I just had a lot of room for improvement."

Instructor Sorene arrived, wearing her blonde hair in her trademark tight braids. "Pull out your daggers," she called. "You get a moment to rest, but then grab a suit. You're going to pair up and spar."

Kaleth walked to the shelf where dozens of heavy, leather chest protectors hung on hooks and arm guards rested on shelves. He grabbed what he needed, then moved to an open area of the courtyard with Jovi. He took his knives from their sheaths, then draped the chest piece over his shoulders.

"It's not just the training though," Jovi said, pulling the straps tight on his armor. "Ever since we returned from those patrols, you've been different. Did something happen in Fairdre?"

Jovi was his best friend, but Kaleth wasn't sure why he had said nothing about Felyra. A part of him was embarrassed about needing her to save his life in the mountains. Not to mention the fact that she was from Thravia, the land of their sworn enemies.

Jovi's eyebrows hovered high on his forehead. "Well?"

Hiding something from his friend when he sensed something was up was impossible. "I met someone in the village."

"Someone . . . ?"

Kaleth fit his arm into one of the arm sleeves. "A girl."

A broad grin covered Jovi's face. "I knew it!"

"You didn't know it."

"Well . . . I knew *something*. What's her name? Does her body burn like a hearth in winter?"

"Does her body . . . what?"

"Is she as fair as a fire is fierce? Does the sun tread in her footsteps?"

"Jovi, ugh! This is why I didn't say anything."

Jovi held up a hand to stop him. "I just need to know the basics." He emphasized each word separately. "Does. She. Have . . . a gorgeous body?"

Kaleth sighed. "Her name is Felyra."

"Felyra. Sounds like a hearth-burning sultress. Did you—" Jovi leaned in and waggled his eyebrows. "—weave the limbs?"

"We hung out for a few days, and that was it. Nothing happened between us. We agreed to write to each other though. I sent a letter yesterday, in fact."

"Oooh, that's something. Who knows . . . maybe we'll go on more patrols and you can get back to Fairdre."

"She's actually—" Kaleth paused, taking a moment to pull the straps on the second arm guard. It felt good to talk about Felyra, but admitting where she was from felt like a bigger step. He leaned closer and lowered his voice. "She's from Revalle."

Jovi's mouth dropped. "Revalle?"

Kaleth nodded.

"As in the Thravian capital? As in the home of the enemy?"

He nodded again.

"Does she know her people are a bunch of bind-cursed traitors who keep attacking us for no reason?"

"We didn't talk about it. It felt like an awkward subject, so we both avoided it. Don't say anything to the others about it, will you? I don't want them getting the wrong idea. She's really cool and has been through a lot."

"Wow, you're smitten, aren't you?"

Kaleth shrugged.

"So let me get this straight. While I was in Dairling, nearly all the way to Valisti, cleaning up prison bedpans, mopping out stalls, and repairing thatched roofs in the blazing sun, you were hanging out with girls?"

"It wasn't like—" Kaleth paused and cocked his head. "Actually . . . yeah that was pretty much it. I got some skills signed off, too."

"Oh, yeah?"

"Disarming an opponent and knife throwing," Kaleth said. "You're up to, what? Ten, now?"

"Twelve," Jovi confirmed. "Although one was ironball hold for time, and it was Garod who actually did it, back before he . . . you know. Rayd signed my log by mistake."

"Jovi!"

"What? I was gonna say something, but . . ."

"But you didn't."

A sheepish grin covered his face.

"That's enough rest," Sorene called. "Pair up and begin sparring. I want to see those elbows up. Keep your jabs tight, and slash with power."

"Keep working on your log," Jovi said. "Two is not gonna cut it at the end of the year."

Kaleth nodded. The leather coverings felt snug against his skin. He pretended to stretch his neck while he took a moment to glance around. The grassy courtyard was a verdant green where he stood. He continued to stretch while he paced, spreading the effect of the energy he pulled over a wider space. His body replenished with power, but the effect on the grass was negligible.

"You ready for a dagger in the chest?" Jovi asked. He held up his weapons with a grin.

Kaleth patted the leather armor. "Bring it on."

Jovi stepped in, but Kaleth maintained the measure between their bodies. Feet shuffled back and forth as if a rod attached to their hips. Kaleth kept his thumbs tight around the end of the handles. Jovi attacked first, but he was too far away. His thrusts stopped short. Kaleth stepped in and jabbed, but a quick step back took Jovi just out of range. They both smirked, circling.

"You're not dancing, you're fighting," Sorene said in their direction. "Get in there!"

Jovi lunged forward, stepping close. Kaleth blocked the resulting jabs with his quick reflexes, stopping the brawny arms at the wrists. He spun away from the following slashes, keeping his body and arms free from injury. Jovi was on him again. A thrust nearly caught him unaware, but he raised an arm just in time.

Jovi grunted as their arms labored against each other, with daggers pointed at each other's chests. Kaleth strained, using his borrowed energy to amplify his weaker muscles. Jovi's arm shook as he pressed his much larger body forward.

"How do you . . . do that?" Jovi said, straining through his teeth.

Kaleth wrapped his wrist and pulled Jovi's hand down. His friend's arm pivoted, taking the blade out of danger. With nothing to stop him, Kaleth swept his dagger across Jovi's arm guard, raking the dull metal against his protected forearm. Before Jovi regrouped, Kaleth jabbed forward like in their drill. His brimming energy heightened his instincts and reaction time. The blunted end slammed against his friend's chest, making a deep thud against the leather.

"Nice work, Kaleth," Sorene commented.

He relaxed, letting his arms droop as a surge of pride swept through him.

Jovi stepped back and rubbed his chest. "Oof. That's gonna hurt."

"Then block it next time."

His friend raised his eyebrows at the taunt. He lifted his daggers in ready position and took a deep breath. With a twinkle in his eyes, he stepped in again.

"Pathetic," Rayd said, stopping both fighters. The squad leader stood casually. At his feet, Roselle picked herself up from the ground where he'd just knocked her over. He sneered at Jovi. "And you're supposed to be one of the best in our squad."

Jovi pointed toward Kaleth. "You might not have noticed, but he's pretty good."

Kaleth welled with pride. Of course, it was his oldest friend speaking kindly of him, but the compliment felt nice.

Rayd scoffed. "He's ranked last, his arms and legs still look like twigs, and he fights like an eight-year-old."

"An eight-year-old who saved your life," Kaleth said.

The searing look Rayd leveled in his direction could have melted iron. Kaleth gulped, regretting his words. He had no interest in riling up his squad leader.

Rayd stepped toward him. "With a lucky toss."

"You're right." Kaleth tried to ameliorate the tension as nausea built in his gut. "It was lucky."

"Are you mocking me?"

"No."

"You think you're better than I am?"

"I don't. I—"

Rayd's knives came toward him like a tempest of twirling steel. Unsure if his squad leader was actually trying to kill him or not, Kaleth backpedaled. He tried to stay out of range, but the larger boy pressed forward. Soon, the wall loomed at his back. His heart pounded. The strength of his arms had waned. His reflexes felt sluggish. A cold wave of terror washed over him. He checked in each direction, but there was nowhere to run. *Hide the fear. Push it away. I can do this!*

What he needed was energy. He reached with his senses to pull in strength from the grass, but Rayd was on him, breaking his concentration. Kaleth stepped forward, blocking the massive arm. He deflected a second jab with his opposite hand. With both arms tied up, he tried to knee his leader in the gut, but it felt like hitting a stone wall. Rayd only laughed. He pushed Kaleth away, like a bear flinging a rag doll.

"Not so cocky now, are you? Working hard only gets you so far, Grunny. You should respect natural ability more than you do."

He spun, heart pounding. His squad leader advanced like a charging bull. A jump to the side dodged a jab at his chest, but the following elbow knocked his breath away. He bent over, gasping for breath when the knife came again. With his energy drained, Kaleth was too slow. The tip jabbed through his regular jacket, piercing his upper arm where the protective brace ended.

"Gah!" Kaleth dropped his own knife and clutched his arm. Searing pain reached his brain.

Rayd stopped his attack and stood tall. "Sorry about that." The smirk on his face told a different story than remorse.

"What are you doing?" Jovi yelled. "This is practice."

Rayd looked down his nose. "Even practice can be dangerous."

"You did that on purpose!"

"Excuse me? Are you questioning your squad leader?"

Kaleth was peeling off his jacket as Sorene walked up. "That's enough, you two. Are you hurt?"

The argument died. The fear clawing for his attention rapidly faded. Kaleth winced as he pulled his arm through the sleeve. "Just a scrape."

Sorene stepped closer to inspect the wound. Blood ran from a puncture wound below his shoulder. The instructor didn't even flinch at the sight of the blood. "You need a Mender. See Carrick. He'll stitch you up. In Central Tower, take the stairs down to his office."

A dizzy spell washed over Kaleth. He pressed one hand against the injury and lifted the other for balance.

Jovi glared at Rayd as he passed. "I'll go with him."

The two young men left Binder Court. Jovi stood at Kaleth's side, keeping his hands up as if he expected him to topple at any moment.

"I'll be okay," Kaleth said. "Thanks for coming with me, though."

"Does it hurt?"

The thought of acting tough lasted only a moment. "For sure. It's like a throbbing jolt pulsing from my arm into the rest of my body."

When they exited the Lightbinder building, the weeds growing in the outside corridor caught his eye. He pulled energy from them, using little restraint. Fatigue faded. The throbbing pain subsided. His shoulders relaxed, and his steps felt solid again. He lifted his hand and cringed at the bloody mess. Although the pain was better, the gaping wound still needed to be stitched. *I guess Father's ability can only do so much.*

"You know, I used to think you were crazy for choosing Lightbinder," Jovi said as they walked. "Figured you had snapped or something after your father and his—well, his uh . . ."

"Death?"

"Yeah. 'Why would Kaleth try for Lightbinder?' That's what I kept asking myself."

Kaleth chuckled. "You and me, both."

"I'm realizing it's because you had a whole lot more in you. Strength I didn't even know about. I guess you wanted to show everyone what you could do, huh?"

Kaleth didn't reply. Their boots plodded down the corridor, scraping against the pebbles in the path. The silence between them thickened.

"Was that it?" Jovi prodded.

A heavy knot settled in Kaleth's throat. He couldn't continue hiding it from his friend. *He deserves to know.*

"It wasn't that," he admitted. "It was more like an act of desperation."

"What do you mean?"

He exhaled a long breath. "You know how Jairus killed my father over his debt?"

"Yeah."

"Now it's on me."

Jovi's feet caught the path, causing him to stutter-step. "On *you?* Are you serious? How much?"

"One hundred gold."

Jovi froze in his tracks.

Kaleth stopped and looked back.

"You're kidding. That's . . . that's . . ." His eyes glimmered with recognition. "That's why you chose Lightbinder."

Kaleth nodded. "Jairus gave me one year to repay the debt."

"Let me help."

"No! Jovi. That's why I didn't tell you."

"I'm making a gold a week just like you. I could—"

"And you've sent it all to your mother already. Haven't you?"

Jovi's face fell. He nodded.

"As you should have. She needs it. You need it."

"But—"

"It's *my* debt. I'm over halfway through the year already. I can make it the rest of the way, and I *will* make it in the top six. That's all I need."

Jovi swallowed hard but eventually nodded.

"For now," Kaleth gestured to his injured arm, "I'm about to die from blood loss, so can we keep moving?"

Jovi's feet dragged as he resumed walking.

Thirty yards from Central Tower, a patrolling Blade and Lightbinder duo stopped them with a raised hand. "Where are you two going?" the Lightbinder asked.

"To the Mender—Carrick." Jovi indicated toward the tower. "He's supposed to be in there."

The guard pointed at Kaleth's shoulder. "Show me."

Kaleth removed his hand from where it pressed against his arm. The blood that covered his skin made it look even more grisly than it felt.

Both guards leaned closer. After glancing at each other, the Lightbinder waved them on. "Head straight back once you're done with Carrick. It's not safe to wander the corridors."

"Yes, sir," Kaleth answered. "We will."

They entered Central Tower, where clanging dishes from the kitchen greeted them. Grunts in brown labored over what would be their next meal.

"Do you know where this Mender is?" Kaleth asked.

Jovi shook his head, then called out, "Hey!"

A Grunt looked their way.

"Do you know where Carrick's office is?"

His eyes grew when they tracked to the messy wound on Kaleth's arm. He pointed. "The far hall. Take the stairs."

They crossed the dining room to enter the back hallway. Three doors lined a corridor that eventually turned at a hard angle.

"Stairs, huh?" Jovi muttered. He moved to the first door.

"I don't think that's it," Kaleth said.

"Maybe it's a secret party room we never knew about."

Kaleth expected it to be locked, but a click sounded, then the door swung open. A spiral staircase of inky blackness gaped behind the threshold.

"Or, it's our stairs," Jovi said, grinning.

Kaleth frowned. "I'm not sure . . ." His words faded. It *was* a set of stairs that headed down. He glanced in each direction along the hall, but nothing gave him more information. "I guess we try it."

Jovi touched a darkened binder lamp on the wall. It burst alight, illuminating a set of ancient stone steps. A second lamp lit up somewhere below, throwing light back up the stairs. As they descended, moss grew thicker at the edges of the steps and on the walls. Weeds peeked out of cracks in the stone. They circled downward, passing eight lamps in total.

"This seems silly," Jovi said. "I would hate having to climb these every day."

When the circular stairs ended, another hallway stretched along a new corridor. The ceiling was short, not so much that Kaleth had to duck, but it felt cramped. They tried the two doors on the hall, but they were both locked.

Jovi knocked. "Hello? Carrick?" No one answered.

When they reached the far end of the corridor, the passage ended in a blank wall. Both boys stopped.

"I guess you were right," Jovi said, turning to backtrack. "Ugh. Back up those stairs."

Kaleth didn't follow. "This is odd."

"What?"

He felt his forehead scrunching. "Why would this passage be here? It goes nowhere."

"There are doors back there. Maybe this part is . . ." Jovi faded out as if he couldn't think of a valid reason for the dead-end section.

Kaleth rested a hand against the wall. The smooth stones tickled his fingers as he let them drift across. A break in the mortar caught his eye. "They wouldn't make this unless they planned for it to go somewhere." He pulled at the edge. The seemingly solid wall split along a faint crack. A small door pivoted, and a gaping blackness waited beyond. After a moment, a binder lamp flicked on, illuminating another spiral staircase descending into a new dark realm.

"Whoa!" Jovi breathed.

"Interesting," Kaleth said, "but I don't think this is right."

Jovi shrugged. "They said down the stairs." He pointed through the doorway. "I can jog down and check?"

Kaleth shook his head, then touched the binder lamp at the entrance to the new stairs. "We'll both go."

Kaleth counted ten more binder lamps as they wound down into the unknown. The moss that used to be patchy now covered each step. Verdant walls absorbed the padded sound of their feet. The lack of noise made the hair on his neck stand on end.

After descending for what felt like forever, they exited the stairwell into a square chamber with a short ceiling. It looked like an abandoned stone room lost in time in the center of a forest. Multiple binder lamps attached to each wall, keeping any portion of the chamber from hiding a shadow. What struck Kaleth wasn't the bright light the room contained but rather the lush vegetation. Vines clung to the walls, draping them in a tapestry of leaves. Moss covered most of the floor with a soft blanket of green. A cold fireplace cut into the wall, with a mound of ash at the bottom and a stack of dried wood piled next to it.

At the far side of the room, two Lightbinders stood at attention with daggers in sheaths and swords on their hips. They blocked a large mahogany door behind them. Upon their arrival, the guards sprang into action. One pulled two daggers out, and the other unsheathed his sword. "What are you doing here?!"

The Lightbinder guards looked every bit of what Kaleth expected. They were each four or five inches taller than him. Massive arms and legs looked like they tried to burst from their uniforms. They both appeared how he expected Rayd would look after another ten years of steady strength training. The tension in their limbs and dark expressions told Kaleth they were not welcome.

"Are you . . . Carrick?" Jovi asked with a shaking voice.

"We're sorry," Kaleth said. "We were trying to find the Mender, Carrick."

Both daggers hummed to life, lit by a glow that seemed to come from nowhere. The guard carrying them stepped forward, raising the weapons as if preparing to attack. The other Lightbinder's sword followed suit. Its glow surrounded the weapon, but the man stepped farther away, stopping next to a red box that was fixed to the wall. He watched Kaleth and Jovi but raised his hand, hovering next to the box as if deliberating over his need to touch it.

"Whoa!" Kaleth held up his hands. He pictured the weapons moving as impossibly quick as he'd seen his instructors demonstrate. "We're Lightbinder initiates. We're not here to do anything. Just looking for Carrick."

"You're in the wrong place," the guard with the dagger said. He nodded toward the stairs but kept his eyes on Kaleth. "You need to leave."

Kaleth had a hundred questions, but he held them back. Jovi was the first to the stairs, but Kaleth was right on his heels. Before rounding the first spiraled corner, he glanced back. The guards continued to stare, remaining in their alert stances.

They hurried up the spiraling path without speaking. The steps drained his energy, but the abundance of plant life in the passage allowed him a steady supply of strength. Jovi was dripping with sweat and panting when they spilled out into the original hallway of Central Tower.

"What . . . was that?" Jovi puffed between breaths.

Kaleth was barely winded. "They're guarding something."

"But, what?" He rested his hands on the tops of his knees. "Treasure? Gold coins? A pile of gems?"

"Was that box an alert of some sort?"

"What box?"

"The one on the wall."

Jovi looked up with a blank stare.

"The guy with the sword. He stood by a red box like he deliberated over touching it."

"How would that sound an alert?"

"Can binder powers do that?" Kaleth asked. "Touch something and raise an alert?"

Jovi shrugged. "It can make lamps, shoot projectiles, and raise lifts. I imagine it could."

"I wonder if there are prisoners in there?"

"Behind the door? This isn't the dungeon. That's over by the castle."

*Why would they hide prisoners in the academy?* Kaleth wondered.

"And why is it a forest in that room?" Jovi burst as if the ridiculousness of it had just come to his mind. "There's no sunlight. There's no water."

A thought ran through Kaleth's brain. "Do you remember back at the beginning of the year? In strategy class when Instructor Beram asked us how Thravia could infiltrate this fortress to steal something?"

"Yeah."

"Something buried in a chamber, deep underground, behind a locked door with two Lightbinder guards."

"Whoa! Do you think that was a real scenario?"

"Maybe they're actually guarding something Thravia wants to steal."

"I think I know what it might be. What would Thravia want more than anything?"

Kaleth racked his brain, but no obvious answer came to mind.

Jovi's eyebrows raised comically high. "The source of the Lightbinders' power!"

Kaleth frowned. "You mean the rings?"

Jovi's face fell. "Oh, yeah. I forgot about those. Well, what else would it be?"

No other ideas came to mind. Kaleth shrugged. A fresh twinge of pain made him wince. He had forgotten about the gash in his arm and the bloody mess covering half his body.

"Is it hurting?"

Kaleth nodded. Leaving the door they'd just gone through, he stepped farther along the hallway, stretching his neck forward to see around the bend. Only a few steps from the door they'd left, a wide staircase showed itself around the corner. He chuckled.

"Yeah, I guess that's probably the one they were talking about," Jovi muttered. "Sorry about that."

Halfway down the wide flight of steps, a door that said "Carrick - Chief Mender" greeted them. Kaleth shook his head and laughed again before rapping the knuckles of his free hand on the sign.

Freshly bandaged, Kaleth entered the common room as the rest of the initiates returned from late-morning conditioning. He sat in a chair and nodded to Jovi and Lainn, who made a beeline for him.

"Everything okay?" Jovi asked. "Sorry to leave you, but Carrick didn't seem to want me there."

Kaleth tapped his arm where his scrubbed jacket covered a clean bandage. "Feels okay for now. I'm supposed to take two days off from conditioning."

"Lucky." Jovi fell into the chair next to him.

"You call this lucky?"

"Eh." He shrugged. "I could go for a break. I'm exhausted."

"Isn't that the idea of conditioning?" Lainn asked. "Tire you out so you get stronger?"

"I'd rather condition myself with lunch." Jovi rested his hand on his stomach. "Prepare my body to be ready for its next meal by practicing."

Kaleth's stomach growled at the thought.

A murmur filled the room. Lainn nodded toward the wall. "Hey. The board is updated."

Kaleth's eyes drifted to the list of names and rankings. He had to blink several times to ensure he was seeing clearly. Jovi's elbow in his ribs helped him to consider that what he saw was real.

He stared at his name, Kaleth-il-Valorr. It occupied slot twenty-four on the board. Twenty-four out of twenty-seven.

"Come on!" a frustrated Iron initiate with a thick beard shouted, pointing at the board with disbelief. Kaleth recognized him as taking slot twenty-seven.

"Nice showing, Kaleth," Lainn said.

Jovi grabbed his shoulders and jostled him with a celebratory shake.

"Congrats, Kaleth," a familiar voice said.

Kaleth forced himself to tear his eyes away from the board to where Donzil and Orion stood.

"I talked with Aurik yesterday," Donzil said. "I may have mentioned something about how you handled yourself with those road bandits. While you may not be rank-eleven material, we would have been dead if it weren't for you, and he needed to know."

Kaleth nodded. "Thank you." He cleared his voice to fix the breathy catch in it.

When Donzil and Orion had left, Jovi leaned forward and opened his mouth. His expectant eyes indicated something important was coming, but his pause lasted a long time. Kaleth and Lainn both leaned forward with him.

"Road bandits?" Jovi finally said. "This is the first we're hearing of this?"

"Seriously," Lainn added. "What did you do?"

Kaleth felt his neck growing red. "We, um, met bandits on the road. They ambushed us, and we fought back."

"And . . . this was your first chance to tell us about it?" Jovi asked.

"I mean. There wasn't really a—"

Jovi hit the table with a playful thud of his fist. "You've been back a week! We're left to hear about this from some random Raven you're now buddy-buddy with."

Kaleth shrugged. "It felt awkward. And it wasn't just me, it was all of us fighting."

"Sounds like you handled more than your fair share. You saved their lives." Jovi leaned in and lowered his voice. "Even Rayd?"

A rumble of disgust came from deep in Kaleth's throat. "I know. I don't know what I was thinking. It all happened so fast. But since then, he's been . . ." His thoughts drifted through all that had happened since then. "Well . . . he's been about the same as usual."

"Nice work, number twenty-four." Roselle stood with a hand resting on a cocked hip. Her lip curled in a wry smile. The red hair that was usually pulled to one side was loose, falling haphazardly in all directions.

"Uh . . . thanks." The friendly comment disarmed him. "What's your deal by the way?"

"My deal?"

"Why do you hate me so much?"

She laughed. "I don't hate you." She sauntered forward, eyes locked onto his. When she passed the generally accepted distance two people kept from each other, his body stiffened. "It's fun to have friends, but it's even more fun to have enemies. Rayd was the obvious choice to align with, and you were the easy choice to loathe. Sorry about that. You're growing on me though. Who knows . . . I may come to like you one day."

She leaned toward his ear. Her hair tickled his neck as she whispered, "You wanna go up to your room for a quick round before lunch?"

He gulped. "A round of what?"

She laughed. "Bind me. You're an idiot."

His neck felt suddenly hot. She waited, raising an eyebrow.

A raised hand from Aurik turned the room's attention to where the principal stood in the entryway. Conversations died. "I know you're probably hungry after this morning's conditioning. Unfortunately, lunch will be late today."

A rumble of discontent grew in the room.

"We told you to always be prepared for the next Lightbinder test because you never know when it will be time. Today is the day."

The playful expression on Roselle's face disappeared.

"The test of knowledge," Jovi whispered.

The rumbles silenced. A dropped pin could have been heard in the deafening silence. Kaleth's stomach twisted in a painful knot. He barely lived through the wilderness test, thanks to Felyra. He had only survived the strength test because of his father's secret. He wasn't sure how many more close calls he could handle.

"I recommend you spend the next hour studying because this is the knowledge test. Hopefully, you've been paying attention in your classes and absorbed the information, but this next hour will be your last chance to cram. The test of knowledge is about . . ." He paused, letting the minds in the room scramble to anticipate. "Poisons."

## CHAPTER FORTY-ONE

# THE POISON TEST

A medicinal scent permeating the dining hall overshadowed the lingering smell of discarded food. Tables had been rearranged in the previous hour, forming a large square with twenty-seven individual stations.

Headmaster Genoris stood in the center of the arrangement. He held his hands together, greeting them with a grim smile. "Spread out. One initiate for each collection of vials."

Kaleth followed Jovi around the edge of the tables until he lined up in front of a station. A cloth covered an object that sat on each table. A faint hiss reached his ears, and a stream of smoke curled through the fabric from the left side of the covered object.

"Poisons," Jovi said. "This is all you, Kaleth."

Kaleth turned to his friend, who wore a confident smile.

"The wilderness was tough. The strength test was hard. This . . . you were made for this."

Despite his friend's confidence, his guts felt twisted in a knot. "Thanks. I wish I felt it. How about you?"

Jovi shrugged. "It's not my strength, but we'll see." He wore a smile, but beads of sweat glistened on his forehead. "Just watch out for berries, right?"

Across the way, Rayd settled behind an identical station. His shoulders were pulled back, and his chin was raised, but the slight furrow in his brow showed he might be less than confident about the upcoming trial. When he found Kaleth watching him, he blinked hard and the hesitation vanished.

Headmaster Genoris strolled the space in the middle of the room while the young men and women chose their places. He stopped on the opposite side of Kaleth's table. "How are you feeling?"

"Um . . . okay, I guess."

The headmaster lifted a corner of the cloth that covered the object. A mischievous glint reflected in his eyes. "You knew your poisons better than anyone, even before you arrived. I'd like to think you'll be okay, but still, it's not meant to be easy."

Kaleth felt a lump growing in his throat. He nodded.

"Keep in mind, I'm the one who mixed what's in these vials." Genoris leaned over the table and lowered his voice. "Remember what I have in my greenhouse."

Kaleth waited, but the headmaster said no more. He only stared back with raised eyebrows. After the whispered word of warning, the man moved along, appraising the other initiates who continued to find their stations.

Jovi leaned toward him. "What was that about?"

Kaleth frowned. "I don't know. I think he was trying to help me, but . . . I'm not sure what he—"

"Silence from now until the end of the test!" Genoris called, raising his hands and spinning to take in the entire hall.

The heavy doors to the hall closed with a deep rumble. A nervous energy hummed in the room.

Kaleth racked his brain to think of the greenhouse. The man grew a wide variety of plants there. Most were common, but some were—

*Yellow-hearted vetril.* He recalled Genoris pointing out the rare and dangerous plant. *A subverter.* His heart pounded.

"Please remove the cloth from your stations," Genoris ordered.

Kaleth pinched the corner of the fabric and lifted the end. The coarse brown cloth slid off, revealing a wooden rack with five glass vials.

"When it's time, you will all drink the vial on the left. They are poisons. Make no mistake, they *will* kill you."

A lump formed in Kaleth's throat. He surveyed the glass container. It contained a blue liquid and had a trail of steam curling from the top.

"Your job is to analyze the contents of the middle three containers. One of them will counteract the poison, rendering it inert and harmless. The other two will not. You each have flakes of shock nettle in the final container. When you've made your choice, drop a bit into your chosen vial and drink the contents. The nettle accelerates the reaction —good or bad. If you choose correctly, you will continue your journey, one step closer to becoming a Lightbinder. If you cannot remember what you've learned and choose wrong, you will be dead within ten seconds. And don't bother letting your eyes wander. The stations have a mixture of poisons and antidotes, giving each initiate a unique test."

Kaleth scanned the hall. Jovi's left-handed vial was brown and thick—likely lincerric acid. Lainn's, just past him, looked like death-bloom. Rayd caught his eye from across the room. The squad leader bent over and inspected his vial. It was inky black, but the smoke rising from the tube had a greenish tint. *Black tiger.* Kaleth shuddered. He instantly spotted the milky-white vial of ashroot elixir that would be its antidote.

"Remember, you are not only trying to survive—you are trying to impress. Speed can help do that. It shows a mastery of knowledge, but don't choose wrong. If you drink the incorrect vial, you will die. If you deliberate too long, you will die."

The room sat a moment in the heavy words.

"The top twelve initiates on the ranking board receive an advantage. Instructors will remove one of the incorrect antidotes. This will leave you with only two vials to choose from."

Across the way, Rayd turned to Roselle, who had taken the station next to him. They exchanged smug expressions as an instructor removed a vial from each of their stations.

"Does anyone have a question?"

Genoris turned in a slow circle, checking all initiates. Principal Aurik, Sorene, and the other Lightbinder trainers paced around the outside. The mood was grim. No one spoke. People shifted their hips and stared at the vials before them.

"In that case, it's time," Genoris said. "Take a moment to inspect the vial on your far left."

Kaleth felt as prepared as he could be. He had grown up learning about poisonous plants and medicinal remedies. Everything new he'd learned since arriving at the academy had made sense and stuck with him. Still, his hand shook as he reached for the object.

The glass was hard under his fingers. A faint sizzle grew louder as he brought it closer. The liquid in the container was a deep blue —a common color for poisons, so he couldn't base its identity on that alone. He swirled the object. The liquid clung to the sides of the glass before it trickled back down.

He lifted the opening to his nose and inhaled. A sharp tang seemed to sharpen his senses. It reminded him of a blackberry bush in the middle of summer. *Berries, ha. Good call, Jovi.* He snuck a glance at his friend who had his nose buried in his own poison. Kaleth brought his vial back and breathed in slowly. Past the presence of berries, he inspected the scent for a sign of juniper. It wasn't there.

*Can't be bellick*, he thought. *No juniper, and it's too thick.*

The one identifiable trait that came through clearly was a musty residue that lingered in his nose.

*Fermented berries and valis moss.*

When mixed and strained into a thick concoction, it left the berryflayer poison—common for putting down animals or sneaking into an enemy's wine goblet. *And a poison subverted by yellow-hearted vetril.*

"Then, when you are ready . . . drink."

Kaleth's pulse sped at the command. Holding the vial up, light shone through the blue liquid, displaying a beautiful substance filled with deadly consequences. He turned to his side and found Jovi looking back.

His friend lifted his own brown container as if about to give a toast. "Cheers."

Kaleth tried to laugh, but the gravity of the situation prevented him. He bounced his vial in return, then brought it to his lips.

The liquid clung to his throat, thick and viscous. It trickled down his tongue, testing his tastebuds with sweet berries and earthy undertones. He imagined the poisonous contents closing his throat and stopping his heart.

"Don't take too long to choose an antidote," Genoris said. "Best of luck to you all."

Kaleth's eyes flicked to the three vials in the middle. *Need to be fast. I have to impress them.* His heart raced as he lifted the first one. It was murky brown and gave off a faint odor of bad eggs. *Adrenophan*, he thought, lowering the container. *Used to rouse an unconscious person and would exacerbate the effect of yellow-hearted vetril.*

He shook his head as he lifted the second option. *Cruel.* The mixture of heartsoothe was unmistakable with its green coloring and apothecary-shop scent. Kaleth held his breath and looked around the room. Most initiates still inspected the first container. *Anyone else would be fooled by this. Heartsoothe would be the obvious answer, but vetril takes something else to work.* He racked his brain, which had gone blank. When he looked at the third vial, the name of the substance flooded back. The deep-red coloring of the next container jostled his mind.

*Redroot.*

He lifted the vial. It looked like a thinned-out container of blood. A citrus scent wafted from the top. *This must be it.* He had never encountered an antidote made of redroot, so he had little experience to measure it by. All he knew was that heartsoothe was the obvious fake.

His pulse beat hard as he took a sprig of the shock nettle. Fingers trembled as he dropped it into the container. A light hum reached his ears. The red liquid danced as the green leaf agitated it.

Pricks of sweat dotted Kaleth's forehead. He was the first to mix the nettle leaf with a choice. It was bold and decisive. A tightness formed in his stomach. It wasn't painful yet, but something was wrong. He imagined the poison inside his body, preparing to tear it apart. Taking a breath grew more difficult with each second he delayed.

He raised the vial to his lips, heart pounding. His clammy hand gripped the glass. *Either I'm going to be right or I'm going to be dead.* The thought was sobering. *Dead.* His eyes flicked around the room. *Do they all have yellow-hearted-vetril in theirs? They would all take the wrong antidote.*

Kaleth lowered the vial a bit as his forehead scrunched into a tight wad. *They can't kill everyone. They don't want to kill everyone.* But in class, they had talked about heartsoothe and how it was the antidote to berryflayer among other poisons. It was the safest choice, even if someone couldn't identify what the poison was. *He never even*—a faint gasp escaped his lips. *Genoris has never even mentioned vetril in class, or redroot. How would he expect anyone to choose it?*

The answer sobered him. He lowered the red vial even farther. *He wouldn't. I had been expecting it to be there, but . . . I don't even know how to identify its use.* He looked again at the green container he had discarded. *Heartsoothe counteracts berryflayer, and outside of the headmaster's words, there's no reason to think the poison was anything different.*

Other faint hums sounded through the room as initiates made their selections. A glance around the room revealed a handful of vials in various colors being tipped into mouths. The tightness in his gut grew sharp as if a knife was being pressed into him as the poison worked its way through his system. Each breath felt like a struggle.

*So much for moving fast and making an impression,* he thought. He tried to push Genoris' words out of his mind. *If I were any of the other initiates . . . If he hadn't whispered anything, what would I have done?* The exercise was easy. His answer was clear. He would have identified the poison as berryflayer, and he would have chosen the second vial the moment he'd seen it.

Kaleth set the red vial back and dropped a fresh sprig of shock nettle into the green one. He swirled it a moment to allow the object to mix with the liquid.

As he lifted the vial, he noticed Rayd from across the way. The squad leader stared at a raised green vial with his forehead pinched.

Kaleth held his breath. *Heartsoothe is not what he needs for black tiger. He's going to choose wrong.* Conflicting emotions ran through him: revenge for what he did to his father's book, payback for all the times he'd made fun of him and been mean.

Rayd tipped the vial and touched it to his lips. As he poured it into his mouth, his eyes found Kaleth's.

He hadn't decided if he cared or not, but a tight shake of Kaleth's head worked its way past his indecision.

Rayd's eyes widened. He balked. Midway through his pour, green liquid dribbled against his face and fell to the table. He choked, sputtering and drawing the attention of the room. He dropped the half-empty vial. It crashed against the table, sending shards of glass and the rest of the green solution in all directions. The squad leader scrambled to drop a bit of shock nettle into the milky-white vial. Barely giving it a second to mix, he raised the solution to his lips and downed it in a desperate gulp.

With less urgency, Kaleth drank his own container. The familiar taste of heartsoothe potion coated his throat. The scent reminded him of a ferny glen, and the grassy flavor brought back memories of illness when he was young.

After drinking the potion, his heart rate lowered. While his body couldn't react that fast to the actual ingredients he'd drunk, his mind told him he could relax.

Jovi caught his eye. His friend smiled, looking at him while nodding. "You had me nervous there for a second," he whispered. "Yours was berryflayer, right?"

"Yeah, I think so."

A commotion sounded as an initiate hit the floor. The young man who fell made a garbled, choking noise while he writhed, mostly hidden by the table. The sound turned Kaleth's insides to water. Two other initiates followed soon after. Anyone still deliberating made a hasty decision, downing whichever vial they had been considering.

Rayd clutched his chest. He bent over, alternating between dry-heaving and making hideous gasping noises. Roselle backed away, giving him room to thrash his limbs while the various concoctions warred inside him.

The pain in Kaleth's gut receded. He imagined the potion working through his body, counteracting the poison. Each breath grew easier to take. *I can't believe I almost drank the wrong one.* He looked up to where Headmaster Genoris stood on the far side of the table enclosure. The man had an appraising eyebrow raised. The furrow in his brow smoothed, and a smile worked across his face. He nodded.

Rayd's thrashing lessened. He had kept his feet but braced a hand against the table to stay upright. Roselle leaned toward him and said something, but he waved her away, then wiped the sweat from his pale face. The more time passed, the more solid he looked.

Six initiates fell to the floor and didn't rise again. Six victims to test number three, but none of them were from Dragon Squad. Their group had been ready. Kaleth had drilled them well. Still, the presence of death cast a pall over the room.

"Nice work, Kaleth," Headmaster Genoris said as he wandered past his table. "If there was one person I knew was going to pass, it was going to be you."

Kaleth kept his voice down. "Why did you tell me to think about your greenhouse? Were you talking about yellow-hearted vetril?"

Genoris' forehead wrinkled. "What? No, I was—" The headmaster's eyes widened. "You thought I was—oh, I'm so sorry, Kaleth. No, I was talking about the sporadicus fern. You noticed it when we were there. I was trying to remind you."

Kaleth blew out a long breath. "We talked about vetril and how it was a subverter of berryflayer and needed redroot to cure it. I figured you were pointing to that."

"Oh, no. I'm sorry. I didn't mean to confuse you. I guess I shouldn't have said anything. I'm glad you still got it."

It was an understandable confusion. As the headmaster wandered off, Kaleth was left with an appreciation of his quick thinking and the fact that it had worked out. His arm trembled. He gripped his fist into a ball to gain control of the muscles. The tremor wasn't residue from the poison, but adrenaline still coursing through his veins.

He thought of his mother and sister. They waited in the city, trusting he could cover their debt. A debt he was one step closer to managing. A hesitant grin pulled at his face. *Three tests down. Only one more to go.*

## CHAPTER FORTY-TWO

# FAMILIAL PRESSURE

"Seriously?" Jovi asked

Kaleth looked up from his book to find half his squad crossing the common room.

"Studying? The poison test is done. Surely you can take a night off."

"Take a night to do what?"

Jovi grinned as he brought a bottle of dark liquid out from behind his back. "I nicked it from the kitchen."

"Jovi," he chided.

Lainn and Chyla produced a handful of glasses. They clinked as they were set on the table.

"We all lived through another test," Jovi said as he unscrewed the bottle and poured a generous portion into each glass. "We worked hard to get here, and sometimes you need to recognize that work."

"Not to mention . . ." Lainn allowed his words to fade as he pointed to the ranking board.

"That's right," Jovi said. "We all moved up."

Kaleth found his name. Despite his near-disastrous performance in the test, thanks to those who didn't make it, he moved up to slot nineteen out of twenty-one remaining initiates.

"Rayd! Roselle!" Lainn called.

Their squad leader and his female shadow crossed the far side of the room but stopped at the call. They turned toward them and paused.

Lainn lifted his glass, holding carefully to keep it from spilling. "Come and celebrate with us."

Kaleth fought to keep from groaning aloud.

Rayd looked equally bothered, but he crossed the room, nonetheless. Two more glasses materialized from somewhere, and Jovi filled them.

"Three down, one to go," Lainn said. "This year, at least. How are you feeling, Rayd?"

Their squad leader bristled at the question. "I'm fine."

"It looked rough there for a bit." Jovi had a playful sparkle in his eyes as if he relished teasing their leader. "Did you swallow a bit of the wrong antidote? What did it feel like?"

"I said I'm fine!" Rayd's red face looked ready to erupt with steam out of his nose. He lifted the offered glass and threw back the drink in a large gulp.

"It's a good thing you changed your mind," Jovi continued. "That was a close one. I wasn't sure about the . . ."

While still talking, Jovi's words faded in the background of Kaleth's mind when Rayd's gaze flicked in his direction. The anger was a front. The eyes were a glimpse into his inner self, where a softness lived. *He would be dead if it weren't for me*, Kaleth thought. *Twice. And he knows it.* Rayd's chin lifted as if acknowledging the unspoken appreciation he was too proud to speak.

The reality vexed Kaleth. His enemy—the person who had ruined his life—was alive because of his moment of kindness. *Was it kindness? Or was I wanting to prove I knew better than him?*

Rayd said nothing. His eyes returned to the group as Jovi wrapped up his prattle. Muffled voices traveled into the room from down the hall.

Lainn nodded toward the entrance to the room. "Looks like someone's here for you."

All of Dragon Squad turned as Exal General Stonne entered the room with two other men trailing him. Dressed in his crisp black uniform decorated with medals and ribbons, he cut an imposing figure. His thick neck and sharp jaw were taut. The crowd-winning smile he usually wore was nowhere to be found. His eyes cut through the room and locked on his son. Their merry squad grew silent. The other lingering candidates who dotted the common room joined them in their sudden reticence.

"Rayd-il-Stonne," he said, enunciating each word. "My son."

Rayd stood at attention with his chin lifted. He held his hands behind his back, but a tremble shook his fingers.

"I hear the test today didn't go well. Is that true?"

Rayd's lips parted, but he failed to form any words.

"It was embarrassing enough that you limped along in slot number three, but now you're—" He turned to the ranking board and took a moment to scan the names. "Seventh?"

Stonne remained quiet for a long moment. The silence filling the room was so thick it would take a knife to cut it. When he moved, a father filled with vitriol had replaced the composed general. He spun toward his son and stormed forward.

"The son of an exal general! Seventh? Amidst a field of rabble and drooling idiots! What are you thinking? Do you not care about your name? About who you are?"

Rayd flinched as his father got in his face. "I care, Father. I'm trying."

"Trying?" The exal general's laugh bounced off the stone walls. "Trying, are you? You're taking those lessons I arranged—the years of privilege—the endless advantages. You're using those, and you're *trying*? And you're left with—" He glanced at the board again. "Seventh? Bind-cursed seventh!"

Stonne grabbed his son by the face, wrapping his massive hand over the younger man's jaw. He pushed his head backward. Rayd stumbled, knocking over the table and chairs as Kaleth and the others jumped out of the way. Glasses tumbled, shattering and spilling as they hit the ground. Rayd's back collided with a bookshelf. His father pressed his head against it, squeezing his son's cheeks.

"I *told* you not to choose this, but you wanted the glory. Well, you're an embarrassment to your family! What happens if you're demoted, huh? Get in line and turn things around or you can find your way home with someone else." He looked around at the others. "I'm sure one of them ranks higher than seventh. Maybe I should adopt them instead."

Conflicting feelings warred inside Kaleth. "Sir." He spoke but lacked the conviction to commit with volume.

Principal Aurik and two other Lightbinder instructors stepped into the room but froze at the sight of the exal general.

"I'm sorry, Father." Rayd's words muddled as he spoke through his squished face.

"You *are* sorry!" Stonne pushed harder.

Rayd's face contorted against the bookshelf. A cry of pain built from deep inside, filling the room with an agonizing groan.

"If you can't move yourself up this board for the sake of your family, you don't deserve to be part of it. Now get yourself together and stop embarrassing me."

"Sir!" Kaleth's shout was forceful enough to get the exal general's attention.

Stonne eased up on his son as he turned to Kaleth. His glare softened.

Rayd wrenched free of his father's grip and staggered to the side, rubbing his face.

"Kaleth-il-Valorr." His anger looked tempered but not gone. "I wouldn't expect you to be here. Do you have something to add?"

Kaleth could barely speak, both terrified of the man and shocked that the exal general knew his name. "Your son is our squad leader, and he's doing well. You should be proud of him. I think—" Terror halted his words. His legs told him to run—to flee out the door. He clenched a hand to keep his arm from shaking.

Stonne raised an eyebrow. "You think . . . what?"

His voice was breathy. "I think you should go, sir."

The man said nothing for a long moment. Finally, he scoffed. After another hard look at his son, he backed away. Running both hands down the front of his jacket, he pressed out invisible wrinkles. With a glance around the room at the unmoving people, he made his way toward the exit. "Let's go," he said to the men he had arrived with.

"So this is what you've been up to?" one of the men said.

Kaleth hadn't looked at the other men until then. He sucked in a breath when he noticed the wide neck, bald head, and scar in place of his right ear.

"The Night Saber," Jovi breathed over his shoulder.

Kaleth swallowed the lump in his throat. "What are you doing here, Jairus?"

The vile lender walked to him. "You think lenders only live in the shadows of the kingdom? I told you I have connections all over. Even armies need money, and they want to work with the best. I'd ask you the same question, but the answer is obvious. You're here because you think you can earn my money by becoming a Lightbinder."

"I'm almost there."

"One more test, right? After that, you get the bonus, correct?"

Kaleth didn't answer.

He chuckled. "Well, I hope you make it. But if not . . ." He leaned closer and whispered. "A brutal end to your family will do wonders for helping recover my reputation."

The words sent a chill down Kaleth's spine.

"And don't even think about running to the constables or to your Lightbinder superiors. You won't find a sympathetic ear." Returning to the arched opening, Jairus nodded to the exal general. "Ready when you are."

Stonne looked back to where his son remained pressed against the bookshelf. "You know . . . I almost wish the poison would have done its job. At least then I'd be done with the humiliation that comes with claiming you as my son."

When the men disappeared, the room was silent. All heads turned to Rayd, but the squad leader continued staring toward where his father had left. Concerned lines etched into his forehead. His body hunched forward. The arrogance he generally portrayed was long gone.

Kaleth's gut felt like it had been punched. His own father had been nothing but kind and supportive, so the idea of experiencing what he'd just observed felt impossible. Despite his enmity for the squad leader, he didn't wish the rejection on him.

The corners of Rayd's eyes welled with tears. His lower lip trembled. It took Kaleth a moment to register what was happening since he had never seen him show emotion in that way. No one moved as their resolute squad leader broke down before their eyes.

Kaleth stepped forward. He wasn't sure what to do about Rayd, but he knew what he would want if their positions were reversed. Each step felt like an eternity. He set his glass on the table, then moved in front of the young man. Rayd's welling eyes hadn't moved from where his father had exited the room. Kaleth stepped closer, bringing their bodies together. He extended an arm and set it on his squad leader's shoulder. He wanted to share words of comfort—something to make it all right, but nothing good came to mind.

The muscles in Rayd's shoulder tensed. For an instant, Kaleth thought it was shock from being comforted, but the jerk of his arms confirmed he was wrong.

"Get off!" Rayd yelled. His hands lifted and pushed against Kaleth's chest, making him stumble backward. The squad leader's soft eyes had grown alert. His shoulders lifted, and his body hardened. "I don't need your sympathy. I'm seventh on the board. I'm better than all of *you!*" He focused on Kaleth. "Especially you. You stumbled your way through the tests but are still the worst one out of all of us. You're ranked nineteenth . . . out of *twenty-one!* You think you have a shot at making Lightbinder? A poor kid from Grunwind earning that respect? It doesn't matter how hard you work. I'll be dead before I see you make it." Not giving anyone a chance to respond, Rayd stormed off.

Kaleth watched after him, stunned. He had wanted to comfort the other initiate, but what he got back were insults and a harsh dose of reality. The fresh reminder of Jairus' threat didn't help.

*He's right. No matter how much I improve, I still have no chance. And that means my family is doomed.*

# CHAPTER FORTY-THREE
# FACING JUDGMENT

Felyra didn't see anyone from her class when she entered the courtyard of Soulbinder Academy. The elderly attendants scuttled around as they always did, carrying crates of laundry, food, and supplies, but none paid her much heed. A grizzled man with wispy hair took the reins of her horse and led it to the stables.

Her heart pounded. She didn't know what the response would be to her return, but it was all she knew to do. She craned her neck around each corner, hoping a friendly face would be the first she found.

She nicked a fresh uniform and changed in the supply room. While she appreciated Agnes' dress, it was no longer suitable. The bunk room was empty. Her old bed remained untouched from when she'd last left it, when she had been filled with adrenaline from the anticipation of the Expedition. It turns out she'd had every right to have been worried that morning.

The classroom was also vacant, but movement out the window caught her eye. When she approached the panes, the muscles in her chest tightened. Her class gathered around the Blockade field, and Ruane stood on the platform that kicked off section two.

A rush of relief filled her at seeing her friend alive, but the purple-and-green bruises marking her face turned Felyra's stomach. *Because of me.* Her friend began, stepping around the rotating boards of the narrow path.

Felyra left the window and hurried out of the classroom. Weeks of worry sloughed off her shoulders knowing Janduan hadn't killed Ruane. She hoped her friend would forgive her for turning the wrath of the captain in her direction. A hard swallow attempted to clear the dryness in her throat. *Earning Ruane's approval is the least of my worries.*

Her heart pounded as she exited the stairs. When she left the corridor to enter the yard, she heard nothing but her pulse beating in her ears. Ruane stood frozen before a swinging ironball at the end of the section. *Come on, you can do it.*

Her friend rocked back and forth as if practicing the timing. When she moved, it was a moment too early. Her leg caught the back of the swinging object, throwing off her balance. She yelled as the heavy object rocked back in her direction. A quick twist of her body sent her tumbling off the platform and crashing to the ground in a puff of dirt. A mixture of groans and laughs filled the crowd of spectators.

"You all are pathetic," a voice projected through the crowd.

Felyra's gut felt punched as her eyes tracked the voice. Captain Janduan paced at the far side of the initiates, glaring at them while twirling a staff.

"Not one of you has made it through," he said. "You're the weakest class I've seen in years. You might as well all quit now and save yourselves the embarrassment."

*He wants to kill me. What am I doing here?* Felyra thought, her legs weak. Seeing Ruane alive was a great relief, but she wasn't sure what her plan was to convince the captain to go easy on her. The instinct to hide was strong. *No one has seen me yet. I could run again.* The truth hit her hard. *But where would I go?*

While she stood in indecision, some heads of nearby initiates turned her way. Muttering voices reached through her muffled hearing.

*Run or fight?*

She couldn't come up with an answer. Her body decided for her when her legs propelled her forward. She pushed through the crowd. Each step took forever. The starting platform seemed to grow more distant with each second that passed.

"Who's next?" Janduan taunted.

Felyra climbed the ladder with numb limbs. The mumbles around her grew louder, but all she heard was the thudding of her pulse.

"Who wants to—" The captain stopped, staring at her.

"Felyra Nightwind," she called out with a steady voice. "First year."

The crowd erupted in commotion. Along the battlements, instructors jumped to their feet.

"Felyra," Janduan growled. "Grab her!"

The nearest initiates looked up at her, but no one moved to do anything. Grax stood amidst the crowd. He glared with a furrowed brow, a mixture of contempt and curiosity. Ducking under the edge of the course and holding her shoulder where she'd fallen, Ruane joined the group. A beaming smile covered her bruised face.

"Someone stop her!" the captain cried, more desperate than before.

Felyra heard shuffling bodies at her back—the captain pushing through the others to get to her. If she waited, she would be caught and killed. She eyed the narrow, wooden path—the course no one had completed. With one chance to impress, she rushed forward.

The world around her faded. All she focused on was her steps. A leap, then a duck. Balance check with her arms. A heel stretched over the side, but she kept moving before she lost it. The small platforms and angled purchases kept her moving. She wasn't fleeing danger, but running toward hope. She wanted to prove herself. The initiates at the swinging bags stared with wide eyes when she arrived. They held them back as if ready to toss but ambivalent about what to do. She didn't hesitate. The bags swung toward her much too late.

Section one complete.

"Get her down from there!" Janduan cried.

Her heart beat faster as she started the next section. The twirling ironballs and sandbags danced in her vision. She grew dizzy looking down the length of the course and focused on only what was in front of her. She dodged around a wooden board, then ducked under a swinging ball. Her periphery warned her of the next board sweeping toward her legs from behind. When she was about to step back over it, a sandbag rounded the corner, aiming for her head. Without thinking, she rolled forward, avoiding both the board and the bag. The rest of section two was a dance between objects, but she found the exercise refreshing. She moved from instinct, trusting her gut, and soon found herself atop the platform that started section three.

The shrieking of metal cut through her focus as she stared at the stabbing blades and swinging axes. The end waited on the opposite side of a gauntlet of death. Janduan's words came to her mind, *"Freezing is a fail."* Fear wouldn't stop her. Sucking in a breath, she began.

The first few obstacles weren't as bad as they looked. She took them one at a time, noting the rhythm of their movement. A swinging axe gave her pause. The pendulum was easy to dodge, but just past it, a grinder of blades twirled and stabbed from each direction. She couldn't discern the pattern. There were too many to keep track of. *Take them one at a time.* Eyes alert and body tense, she lunged past the axe into the maw.

Her eyes took in each threat, processing the angle and speed. She limited her scope to only what was an immediate danger, factoring in the new arrivals when she'd passed the previous. A spiked club grazed her arm, pulling at the fabric of her sleeve but leaving her skin unharmed. She sucked her stomach in as a vicious dagger thrust toward her midsection.

Passing the weapons one by one, she noticed the noise of the crowd. At first, it was only a murmur, but the farther she traveled, the louder they grew. The end of the section called her forward. Only a few more swinging weapons to pass. She could do it. Her fellow initiates clapped and cheered, shouting her name. She tried to ignore them.

Her mouth curled up at the corners. She ducked under a sword. The platform was so close. After passing another axe, she held her breath. *One more to go.*

*Smack!*

A sturdy object crashed into the back of her feet, knocking them clear of the platform. With nothing to grab, Felyra fell flat on her back, hitting the wood hard. The impact knocked the wind from her lungs. Before she could surmise what had happened, the axe she had just passed swung into her vision. Its double-sided blade traveled on its repetitive arc, but she was in the way. With the weapon a breath from her face, she rolled. The wooden slats below her disappeared. Her stomach jumped into her chest as she fell. A moment later, she hit the hard dirt.

She struggled to suck in a breath, and what she managed was tainted with dust. Her back ached, but falling so close to the end hurt the most. Groaning, she opened her eyes.

Clear sky lay above until Captain Janduan stepped into view. He sneered as he held his open hand in the air. A moment later, a floating wooden staff flew into it—the staff that had just taken her out. His fingers tightened around the weapon, blue ring sparkling in the light. "I can honestly say I'm glad to see you've returned. You and I have some unfinished business, Cripple."

FELYRA WAITED on a hard bench outside the headmaster's office. Her back still ached from when she fell. A Soulbinder guard stood nearby, preventing any hope of her fleeing down the corridor. She didn't mind. She had arrived on purpose, knowing the moment of judgment would come.

She lifted her head when the door opened. Grax exited the office. He glanced her way and narrowed his eyes. She felt his gaze explore her face and the wounds there that had yet to heal. He smirked but said nothing. She squirmed under the scrutiny.

When he was halfway down the hall, another person arrived.

*Ruane.*

Felyra smiled. She jumped to her feet, but the guard at her side pulled a sword, forcing her to hover over her bench. She had worried for weeks about her friend. The bruises on her face looked worse up close.

"I'm sorry he hurt you," Felyra said. "I was about to come back when slavers took me."

"Slavers?" Ruane's eyes widened. "I had no idea. We just thought you ran off. I'm fine. Just some bumps." A smile pulled at her lips. She lowered her voice. "You should have seen how mad he got after you left. It was worth it just to see him lose it."

"Ruane," the headmaster's voice called through the door.

The guard nodded, then motioned as if herding her through the door.

Ruane gave a meek wave of her fingers before she disappeared inside. The guard closed the door, and Felyra returned to her bench.

She strained her ears but discerned nothing more than muffled words. With a sigh, she leaned her head back against the wall and waited.

After a lengthy interval, the door opened again. Felyra jerked upright as her friend emerged. Her eyebrows lifted as if trying to ask how it went, but Ruane only shrugged, turning up her hands. She opened her mouth to say something, but arriving footsteps caused her to pause.

Captain Janduan said nothing as he approached, but the sneer on his face spoke volumes. His boots clopped against the stone floor. One hand rested on the sword at his hip. He brushed past Ruane, knocking into her as he entered the office.

A rush of cold moved through Felyra. Being so close to the man who had almost killed her left her hands tingling.

"Move on," the guard ordered to Ruane. "Don't speak about it."

The softness in her friend's eyes helped it all feel okay. "Good luck," was all she said. She walked down the hall, leaving Felyra alone with the guard.

The wait seemed to take twice as long as the previous meetings. She couldn't even make out muted talking. She thought through the ways it could go, but few of the realistic scenarios felt positive. She had assaulted an officer. She disobeyed him. That was rebellion.

*What was I thinking in coming back here?*

When Janduan left the office, he didn't even glance in her direction. The look on his face suggested smug satisfaction, but he was hard to read. Her knotted stomach pulled even tighter.

"Felyra."

The sound of her name stopped her heart. She knew it was coming, but that hadn't prepared her for it. Her palms felt clammy as she stood. Her pulse returned, redoubling its volume in her ears as she approached the door.

She had never been in the headmaster's office before. Floor-to-ceiling shelves lined the back wall, filled with leather books. Where the shelves ended, a large window opened the room to share the city of Revalle and the battlements of the fortress. In the center of the room, two leather chairs faced a dark-brown, wooden desk. The desk was tidy, containing little more than organized stacks of paper, a writing stylus, and a fresh, unlit candle. Headmaster Baloran stood behind the desk, resting his hands on its surface. A finger flicked, and the door she had just entered through closed on its own.

The headmaster frowned, piercing her with his gaze as she stood in front of the chairs. "Sit."

Felyra gulped. The command was not a request. She complied.

"I heard troubling things after the group returned from the Expedition—things I didn't want to believe. The fact was that you did not return. You ran away."

"Sir, I—"

He held up a finger to stop her. "We are at war. Our enemy is out there, training and plotting to defeat us. They want what we have, and we want what they have. The stakes are not small, Felyra. The only way we'll be able to defeat them is if we work together as a unit, and Captain Janduan is part of that unit."

"I know that, sir, but—"

"Did you interrupt a training session during the Expedition, circumventing the direct order of a commanding officer?"

A lump formed in her throat. She tried to think of something to answer other than the truth, but there was no way around it. "I only did it because—"

"Did you or did you not disobey the captain's order?"

She swallowed, but the lump remained. "I did."

"And did you *then* assault your unarmed commanding officer in the face with a staff?"

Her heart beat wildly. "I was—I was—" Nothing she could think to say sounded right. The fact that Janduan had been mean wouldn't justify her actions to the headmaster. She sighed and lowered her eyes to the floor. The nod of her head felt heavy, as if resigning herself to death.

"Armies cannot survive if orders are not followed. Kingdoms will crumble if we turn on ourselves and against our commanders."

She said nothing in reply.

"Do you understand why Janduan sentenced you to be hanged?"

She nodded.

"Order must be maintained. Commands must be followed. Insubordination leads to insurrection." He paused, letting a long moment of silence fill the room. "Now that I'm demoting Janduan from the lead trainer position, hopefully, we'll have less disobedience."

Her head snapped up to see a mischievous smirk on Baloran's face. "Now that you're . . . ?"

The headmaster chuckled, his eyes sparkling. "I knew there was more to the story after they returned from the Expedition. Your return today was a good reason to dig further. Grax and Ruane helped me piece together more of the puzzle."

"Grax spoke up for me?"

Baloran waggled a hand side-to-side. "I wouldn't say 'spoke up,' but he did shed more light. Ruane told me how the captain treated you on the run." He inclined his head forward and raised his eyebrows. "It's still not justification for striking an officer, but it helps me understand."

"I know it's not. I'm sorry, sir."

"I'll bet it felt good though, didn't it?"

Her eyes widened. "Felt . . . good?"

"Janduan's been . . ." He paused as if carefully choosing his words. ". . . *troublesome* for as long as I've known him. We only have so many Soulbinders, so we need him, but his orders were—" He stopped again. "We're making a change, so let's just leave it at that. He'll still be around, just not in charge of training."

*Oh, he's really going to hate me now*, she thought. "So . . . what's to happen with me?"

"You assaulted an officer and disobeyed orders."

Her stomach tightened.

"Normally, that is punishable by death, but I see it as having extenuating circumstances. Cleaning duty—two hours daily for the next four weeks."

A weight felt lifted from her shoulders. It was as good as she could hope for.

"We made cuts after the Expedition. We're down to twenty, now—twenty-one with you." He leaned in and lowered his voice. "Soulbinder selection is coming in a few months. Be ready. We need all the help we can get."

Two weeks after returning to Revalle, Felyra's injuries were noticeably better. Her bruises and cuts had all but disappeared. The pain in her leg remained as it always had, but its familiarity felt easier to deal with.

The sparring room was her favorite place in the academy. While sword training exhausted her, the simple discipline of repeating movements allowed her to tune out doubts and fears. Alone in the room, she was one with her blade, distracted by nothing but dripping sweat and aching muscles.

*Strike. Block. Strike.*

*Move your feet.*

*Block. Strike. Strike.*

*Keep your balance.*

Her hand tightened to compensate for the slippery grip on the leather hilt.

"This is supposed to be rest time, you know."

She spun to find Ruane standing in the doorway.

"You realize we have sword class in an hour, don't you?"

Felyra shrugged. "I'm warming up. You wanna join me?"

Ruane shook her head. "If you didn't wake up before the crack of dawn to do your cleaning duties, you could do those now and actually get some sleep at night."

"I get sleep. I'm fine."

Ruane held up an envelope with Felyra's name written in crisp penmanship. "This came for you."

"Who would send me a letter?" She couldn't imagine why the academy would write to her when they could summon her to talk.

"It came via letter porter, which is odd."

The truth came to her with a start.

"What?"

She reached for it. "It could be . . ."

Ruane jerked the letter out of reach when Felyra tried to take it. "Could be, what?"

"Kaleth," she breathed.

Ruane frowned. "Kaleth?" Her eyes popped open wide. "The boy from the mountains? The Kalshian who saved you from the slavers and nursed you back to health?" She passed the letter willingly.

Felyra ran her finger under the flap and ripped the wax seal. She pulled out a card covered with tight lettering. Her heart skipped a beat, but receiving a letter from the enemy also terrified her. She read the letter to herself.

*Silvertail,*

*I hope this letter finds its way to you. If you're reading it, then I trust you made it safely home, and that makes me grateful. I'm sorry I couldn't have been there to escort you, but I'm not sure I would have been welcome as a Kalshian. I think what our kingdoms need is to spend some time together freezing in the mountains. Maybe then, there would be less animosity.*

*The week I spent in Fairdre was one of the best I can remember in a while. My last year has been a difficult one, and it was nice to have some peace where all I had to do was be with you. It was calming and restful. I felt safe in a way I'd forgotten was possible. I know the experience must have been less enjoyable for you, so I'm sorry about that. Regardless, I have great fondness for the time we shared.*

*I've got a test coming up soon that honestly has me a bit worried because I don't know what will happen. I promised to write to you, so I wanted to do it before the test. I know very little of what it's about, but I like to think I'll be ready. Before my father died, he taught me a lot, which should be helpful.*

*The other day, I saw a girl with curly black hair from behind, and I had to double check to make sure it wasn't you. That would have been wild— running into you for a third time. Wild . . . but welcome. I still owe you a few rescues, so hopefully those meetings will work out somehow.*

*Please write back . . . if you wish. I'd love to know you're safe and hear what you're up to.*

*Kaleth*

Ruane snatched the letter from her hand when Felyra's eyes finished working.

Felyra stared at nothing. Her mind raced through a bevy of feelings. She felt threatened that a Lightbinder in training was contacting her. He could be a spy, having marked her from when they first met, but the idea of that being true seemed absurd. He had been about to die when they met. Surely that wasn't staged.

She also felt thrilled. Despite being her enemy, he had saved her and taken care of her. He was kind, and she felt comfortable talking with him. The fact that he took time to write her a letter released butterflies in her stomach.

"Whoa," Ruane said. "Fondness for the time you shared? He wants to know you're safe? Felyra, this guy is *into* you!"

Felyra scoffed but couldn't stop a smile from pulling at her lips. *He really is, isn't he?*

"It sounds like something is going on between you two. And who's 'Silvertail'?"

"It's nothing. No. Nothing's going on."

"I don't believe it. Why would he write to you, otherwise?"

"There's nothing between us." She sighed. "There can't be."

"Why not? Because he's from Kalshia? Is that so impossible to get past?"

"It's not that. It's because—" Her words caught in her throat. Admitting out loud that he was training to be a Lightbinder made it real. She'd rather ignore it and pretend it wasn't true. "We just can't."

Ruane seemed to catch the heaviness in her resignation. Her friend stopped teasing and let it be. She returned the letter. "Will you write him back?"

Felyra tucked the letter back into the envelope. She stared at it for a long moment as her insides warred. She opened her mouth several times, but no words came out. "I don't know," was all she could manage.

"Come on. He wrote to you. Write him back."

"No." The word sounded final, but a hesitation pricked at her. She crumpled the envelope, squeezing it into a ball. "No, I won't write him." She walked to a waste bin at the edge of the room and tossed the paper in. Her heart ached as it hit the bottom.

THE BUNK ROOM was quiet when Felyra entered at the end of the day. The lanterns on the wall had been dimmed but still gave off enough light to see by. She used the basin in the washroom to clean her face, wiping off the grime and dried sweat that had accumulated during the day.

Ruane sat on the top bunk when Felyra approached. Her friend shot her a smile. "Nice job today." She lay down but kept a mischievous grin on her face. "Don't forget your writing before you sleep."

"My wri—?" It took Felyra a moment to remember, but then she spotted the crumpled envelope on her bed. She sat slowly as if sudden movement would disturb it.

"Good night," her friend whispered from above.

She didn't reply, lost in staring at the object. *No. I can't.* She pulled her legs underneath her, crossing them while avoiding touching the letter. Her breath grew quicker. A tremble worked its way up her arm. She shook her head. *I don't need this. I have enough to worry about as it is.*

An urge to burn it pricked at her mind. A personal letter from the enemy would be suspicious if anyone else knew. But what he'd written was innocuous. Nothing mentioned who he was. It wouldn't hurt to keep it. *Or even to send a letter back.*

*No! I will not write him!*

She grabbed the ball of paper and tossed it on the shelf of the cubby next to her bed, releasing it as quickly as she could, as if a longer touch would affect her resolve.

A stack of sheets in her cubby caught her eye. The writing stylus beside them stared back at her. She frowned. *There's no point in writing him back. It's not like I'll ever see him again. Even if I did, I—* How would she feel if they did meet again? Lightbinders were the enemy—cruel and heartless. Yet she recalled how Kaleth cared for her—how he paid to rescue her from slavery.

A whisper drifted down from the bed above her. "If you don't write him, maybe I will."

She let out a breath that began as a sigh, then morphed into a groan. Breaking her body's reluctance, she grabbed the stylus and a sheet of paper.

# PART FOUR

## CHAPTER FORTY-FOUR

# TRUTH ABOUT THE PAST

Genoris held the binder lamp close to his body. He covered part of it with his hand, allowing only the light he needed to illuminate his path. Just past midnight, few people would be up. No one would question the headmaster, but he still wanted to avoid attention. His raised hood would keep anyone from recognizing him at a distance.

The Central Tower was empty when he pushed open the doors. The bare tables and vacant chairs felt conspicuous as he passed them, heading toward the hallway on the far side. He stared at the first door he passed. The latch begged him to open it. He pictured the staircase beyond that circled deep into the earth. *Just go there, now. Stop putting it off!* The idea had merit. They wouldn't suspect it. But it was far too risky. He shook his head and continued.

When he arrived at the staircase around the corner, he checked over his shoulder to ensure no one followed. Content, he headed down the stairs, passing Carrick's office. He continued down two windowless floors until it opened to an underground chamber where two binders lamps hung on the wall. Four hooded figures turned his way—two Blade guards and two young Lightbinders.

The headmaster lowered his hood, showing his face. The other men relaxed the visible tension in their shoulders and dropped their own hoods.

"Meeting like this is dangerous," a Blade with a black beard grumbled. "You can explain your presence to anyone who asks, but any of us just look suspicious. We can't do this anymore."

The other three nodded and mumbled in assent.

Genoris waved his hand as if dismissing the comment. "It's minimal risk. You all knew it was dangerous when you signed up, besides . . . any suspicions in the academy come to me to deal with."

"What happened with Kaleth back at the poison test?" one of the young Lightbinders asked. "I thought you said you would handle him, but that was months ago."

The headmaster's jaw tightened. "He should have been handled. He didn't take my bait, though."

"And those bandits you paid to attack him on the road failed, too."

Genoris whipped two daggers out from sheaths at his side and infused them with light. The lamps on the wall dimmed as his weapons shone brightly and emanated a low hum. "Watch yourself, Zaric."

The other Lightbinder pulled a knife of his own. It sprang to life, illuminating the green gem in the ring on his finger. He bent his knees and readied his arms as if preparing to fight.

Genoris leaned forward, narrowing his eyes. The shining tips of his blades pointed at the younger man. A rumble formed in his chest. He would not be intimidated by a recent graduate.

Zaric's throat constricted from a hard swallow. No match for the headmaster, his feet shuffled backward. He lowered his hand. "I'm sorry, sir. I didn't mean disrespect."

Genoris lowered his weapons and allowed the light in them to fade. "Kaleth has been more trouble than expected. I'll keep looking for opportunities."

"I still say it doesn't matter," the Blade with the beard said. He pointed at the solid wall behind him. "It's waiting for us one hundred feet in that direction. They only keep two guards at any time. You three have Lightbinder skills and both of us can handle ourselves. It would be easy. No one would ever suspect us until it was too late."

"Have you ever fought a Lightbinder, Garran? One who's trained and capable of harnessing the power of the sun?"

Garran frowned.

"No, you haven't. It's not just a numbers game. If we storm the vault and fail, our shot will be gone . . . and so will we."

"What if we recruited more people to our cause?" Zaric asked. "Surely there are others who are sympathetic."

"And what if we misread them? What if they warn the other instructors? No, we cannot take that chance. I have been thinking though. Our culling has not scared them off as I anticipated. The initiates are down by half, but it's not enough. It's time for something bigger."

Garran's eyebrows lifted. "Bigger? Like what?"

The initiates stared at Genoris as he weighed how much he wanted to share. "Those who were going to be run off are gone. Dealing with everyone remaining needs a fresh approach. Rather than chipping away bit by bit, I will eliminate them all at once."

"Everyone?"

He nodded. "The entire academy—initiates and instructors—at the year-end banquet on Highsummer's Jubilee, three weeks from now. In the chaos that follows, it should be easy to take what we need."

"What about Kaleth?" Zaric asked. "He seems to have a knack for foiling plans."

The headmaster blew out a heavy breath. "Leave him to me. This time I won't fail."


Staring through the window of his dorm, Kaleth inspected the red and orange light trailing across the sky as the sun's early rays reflected against the wispy clouds. They formed a blanket, reminding him of the fateful day after he and his father had climbed Shilvan Peak. So much had happened in the months since then, but the sky remained the same, like nothing had changed.

*Everything has changed.*

He thought of the mark on his hip, the abilities he had gained, and the skills he had learned. He was so close to saving his family.

The academy attacks had continued in the second half of the year. Bodies kept showing up in gruesome displays or disappearing altogether. Three more Lightbinder initiates died, one of which was found gutted in the common room one morning. A handful of Grunts had even been killed. Two more Lightbinders self-demoted to Grunts just so they could be transferred to Twainford. The number of patrolling guards kept increasing, but their presence didn't seem to have any effect.

Kaleth pulled open his desk drawer and heard the faint clink of metal coins. He glanced at the other bed in the room to ensure Lainn hadn't roused. Fishing his hand to the back of the drawer, he pulled down the false wall he'd propped up. The leather pouch behind clinked with ten gold coins. A thrill rushed through him at the thought of what he'd accumulated—thirty-seven gold coins he'd already delivered to his family and ten more in the bag. The total was nearly enough to cover half of his family's debt. All he needed now was the year-end bonus for surviving a year of Lightbinder training. And all that took was surviving one more trial.

*Surviving* and *rising to the top six on the ranking board.*

He tried to push the depressing thought away, but he couldn't stop picturing the board. A lump formed in his throat. They were down to sixteen initiates, but he had only worked his way up to number fourteen. Despite his skill in the classroom and dramatic physical improvement, everyone else had started from a much better place. He also suspected Rayd's constant disapproval of him might be a factor in holding back his ranking.

*Eight more to move past. I can do this.* His stomach turned. The confidence was forced. *I really can.*

His skill log caught his eye. Having started with only two skills months before, he was up to thirty. Most initiates had around twenty—Roselle apparently had all forty-five—but he felt proud of his thirty. His goal was to get the final fifteen in his last few weeks.

Lainn rustled in the bed next to him, and Kaleth slid the pouch back into its hiding place. Before he pushed the drawer closed, the pile of a half-dozen letters with his name on the front caught his eye. He grinned as he pulled them out and sat back on his bed.

The first letter had arrived via letter porter several weeks after he'd sent his. He had been worried that his letter never made it to her or that she had changed her mind about writing. He could still remember the elation he felt when the first one showed up.

He selected the bottom letter from the stack and opened it up to read the familiar words.

*Kaleth,*

*Why am I writing? I don't know. Maybe I'm a fool. We come from such different worlds, yet I feel drawn to you in a way I can't describe. I've never known a Kalshian who cared. I laughed after I wrote that because I've never actually known a Kalshian until I met you. Until that day in the mountains, you were only an idea, a shadow, a face I assigned to every frustration or pain.*

*Something changed. Was it the way you spared those rabbits? Was it because you rescued me from that auction? Was it because you called me pretty? Can I even believe those words? Somewhere between my childhood of hating Kalshians and now, my worldview shifted. You are different. I am now different. Everything in the world around me tells me I can't trust you, but still . . . you're all I think about.*

*How did your test go? I hope you passed. In response to your letter. Yes, I am safe. I've been busy, settling back into my life in Revalle.*

*Given our circumstances, I'm sure this could never be more than it is. We're just two people prone to saving each other's lives, who grew up with opposing situations. My sincerest wish is that we can keep what we have, but please don't hope for us to run into each other again. I worry our luck of saving each other may have run out.*

*Silvertail*

Whenever Kaleth reread the letter, he ignored the part about their relationship never becoming more than it is. He rationalized her hoping they wouldn't run into each other again as fear of her experience in slavery. His eyes always settled on, *"you're all I think about."*

He imagined the curls of her black hair bouncing as she bent over a desk to write. He pictured her olive skin glowing warmly under the light of a candle.

After the first letter's delay, the wait for future ones had grown shorter. The last few had each arrived around two weeks apart. He counted the days until the next one would arrive, which would hopefully be in a day or two.

"Surely you have those memorized by now," Lainn said.

Kaleth jerked his head up with a start. "Hey. Morning."

Lainn pulled his blankets back and grabbed a shirt from where it hung next to his bed. "When are we going to get to meet this girl? She's from Fairdre, right?"

"I, uh . . . yeah, that's where I met her. I'm not sure that she's planning to come and visit here, though."

"Are you going to visit her over the break?" He pulled his blanket taut, laying it flat so that no wrinkle showed.

*Break?* Kaleth had never allowed himself to think that far. The initiates got a two-week break before the next year of training kicked off. He had always expected he would die before then. "Um, maybe. We'll see."

He pushed the letters back into his drawer and closed it smoothly so he wouldn't jingle the hidden pouch of coins. The thought of visiting reminded him of his family. It had been a couple of months since he'd been home. He longed to see their faces and know they were okay.


THE INITIATES GATHERED in Binder Court, preparing for morning conditioning. Kaleth kept an eye on the door while he stood on one leg, pulling his foot up to his rear to stretch. When Aurik stepped through the arched passage, he dropped out of his stretch and jogged to meet him.

"Sir," Kaleth said.

The principal raised his eyebrows and stopped walking.

"After class today, I would like to visit my family again. Just wanted to make sure that would be all right." It pained him to be so deferential to the man he'd hated for so long.

Aurik frowned. "The year-end break is coming soon. Can you wait until then?"

"I don't know that I will survive the next trial."

"You're doing well and have made enormous improvement. The instructors and I have all noticed. You passed the other three. I think you have a good shot at this one."

"Yeah, but this is the fear test." He hadn't intended to empha-size the word "fear" but stressing it revealed more than he had intended to share.

Aurik raised an eyebrow. "You struggle with it?"

Kaleth didn't want to share with the man, but he found his words spilling out, unbidden. "I've always wanted to be brave like my father, but fear holds me back. I'm getting better though. I'm working on hiding it—pushing it away. But sometimes, I—"

"Hold on." Aurik frowned. "Hiding it?"

"Yeah. Fear tells me how I'm going to fail, but I don't want to listen to it, so I try to ignore it. If I'm going to be brave, I can't have fear. I'm getting there, I promise, but—"

Aurik's shaking head stopped him. "Bravery isn't about not having fear, Kaleth."

"What do you mean?"

"Fear is a healthy feeling. Pushing it away will not make you brave, it will hide part of yourself. It's never truly away, and it's going to pop back up when you least want it to."

"I don't understand. How can I be brave if I'm afraid?"

"Bravery isn't the *absence* of fear. It's action while in the *presence* of fear. You choose to do something dangerous, knowing the possible outcome is worth the risk. A dangerous action *without* fear isn't bravery. It's ignorance."

The perspective was new to Kaleth and contradicted Genoris'

advice. The idea of not fighting fear was freeing, but he still wondered if he would be capable of taking action.

"As far as visiting your family goes. Think how proud your mother will be when you show up having completed the fear test. Why don't you wait?"

Hearing Aurik refer to his mother heated his blood. He had held in his unspoken anger too long. "After what you did to my mother, you owe me this."

Aurik's eyes widened at the change in tone. After a beat, he sighed and let his shoulders fall. "One of the worst days of my life."

Kaleth pinched his brows together. "You remember?"

"Of course I do."

The revelation gave Kaleth pause. "When did you recognize me?"

"From the moment you called 'Lightbinder' at the Selection Ceremony. How could I not remember you? The look in your eyes when we spoke at the mill. I could never forget it. You still blame me for what happened to her, don't you?"

The hesitation Kaleth felt was gone. "Of course I do. You are the reason she was injured—why we fell into debt—ultimately, the cause of my father's death. I wouldn't have to be here today if you hadn't done what you did."

The principal lowered his eyes. For an extended moment, he bobbed his head with pursed lips as if deep in thought. "We had a Lightbinder initiate named Jasper. When he joined, he had the eagerness of a gambler on a winning streak, but he had the body of a—well . . . like you. It was immediately apparent he was in the wrong school, but he wouldn't see it."

Kaleth wasn't sure where the story was going, but another initiate like him choosing their school intrigued him.

"He survived the wilderness test by the skin of his teeth but then struggled during training. His exuberance faded quickly. I spoke with him early on. I gave him the option of changing schools, but he wouldn't do it. I think he knew he had chosen wrong, but he wouldn't admit it. Pride got the best of him. The week before the strength trial, he was in a terrible place. He barely trained. He sat on his own and wouldn't talk to anyone or look them in the eyes. I didn't know what to do. It was clear he was going to fail the trial, and we figured that would sort out the issue." A faint grimace turned his face down. "The day before the test, something snapped. Are you familiar with binder orbs?"

Kaleth cocked his head. "Headmaster Genoris had some. He didn't say what they were for, though."

"You'll learn how to make and use them next year. It's a round object that explodes when detonated. Jasper took one from the lab. He threatened to blow up anyone around him if we didn't let him leave. I talked with him. I tried to convince him to stop, but he wouldn't listen. His mind was addled. He prattled on about the downfall of Kalshia and the inevitability of ruin. My fear spread past the academy to the rest of Kalistor. When he ran, I had to follow." Aurik's eyes drifted as if looking past the academy's walls.

"He didn't have a plan; he just wandered the city. Whenever I got close, he held up the orb and shouted that he was going to throw it. I told him he could go if he'd just set the binder orb down, but he wouldn't do it. He grew more and more agitated as he got deeper into the city. He railed about conspiracies like . . . how butterflies were working together to poison our food supply and how all the city's blacksmiths were spies for Thravia. Finally . . . his circuitous route led him to the mill."

Kaleth felt his pulse beating in his head.

"Jasper paused outside its entrance. Once more, I pleaded with him to set the weapon down. He responded by shaking his head. He stared at me with wild eyes while an unsettling grin took over his face. The last words he said were, 'The people of Kalistor need to pay.' I lunged after him, but he got a jump on me. As soon as he crossed the threshold of the mill—" Aurik didn't finish the sentence.

Kaleth knew what happened next: an exploding building, falling walls, and a collapsing roof. Bodies blew apart and limbs were crushed. Grain ignited, filling the area with searing heat and dangerous smoke.

"The blast blew me back, hit by a stone block. It broke my arm and cut up my face."

Kaleth spotted two scars on Aurik's face he'd never noticed before.

"As soon as I could stand, I ran inside the mill. All I heard was the roar of flames and screaming voices. I lifted fallen stones to drag out trapped workers. I burned my arms. When all was done, I had pulled twelve people from the rubble, one of them being—"

"My mother," Kaleth gulped.

Aurik nodded.

"I had always thought—I assumed you caused the explosion. I thought you accepted blame for it."

"It *was* my fault . . . in a sense. Jasper snapped because of our training program. We pushed him to his breaking point and gave him access to the weapon he used. If that doesn't imply blame, then I don't know what does."

Longstanding grudges and deeply seated anger felt shaken. The person who injured his mother was an initiate—someone not too different from himself.

"I'm sorry about your mother, Kaleth. I hurt for everyone who was killed or injured in that explosion. I constantly relive that day, thinking of something different I could have done."

Kaleth swallowed a lump. "Thank you for telling me."

"Go and see your family."

He lifted his chin and opened his eyes wide.

"Just make sure you return by tonight."

"I will, sir."

"And make sure you're ready for the last exam. It won't be easy."

His moment of excitement was replaced by a pit forming in his stomach. He forced a nod. "I will."

CHAPTER FORTY-FIVE

# DANGEROUS VISIT

It would be his last visit before his mother and sister's fate would be sealed—for better or worse. The heavy thought weighed on him as he walked the streets of Grunwind. The sun had already set. A trace of lingering light gave the neighborhood a hint of a glow. He shook the leather pouch in his pocket.

A happy bark drew his attention over his shoulder. A dog trotted toward him. It took him a moment to place the white face and rust-colored fur, but the smile on the dog's face confirmed it was his old friend, Charlie.

"Hey there, pup! How are you doing?" He stopped and crouched, letting Charlie catch up. The dog nuzzled into Kaleth's chest as he scratched on both sides of its body. The wagging tail thumped against the side of his leg. After a moment, Charlie looked up and licked Kaleth in the face. He sputtered and playfully pushed him away. The dog seemed more encouraged by the light shove. He crouched and hopped side-to-side.

"I'm glad you're doing well, Charlie. Watch out for thorns, and watch out for Rayd-il-Stonne."

When Kaleth stood, the dog must have sensed playtime was over. After one more pass to rub against his legs, he scampered off with a smile on his face.

The encounter left Kaleth feeling encouraged. With so much danger and most things out of his control, it was nice to know he had a positive impact on something.

When he passed the path that led to the mill, conflicting emotions ran through him. He had always blamed the Lightbinders. Aurik's perspective provided more background to what had happened, but it didn't change the impact on his mother and her health. It didn't bring his father back from death. But he did find it easier to cope with knowing it was from a lone initiate rather than the Lightbinder organization as a whole.

The sight of his family's house brought a smile to his face. With the sun having set, it meant dinner time. His mother and sister would be cooking or already eating. But as he drew closer, his smile faltered. The red door was cracked—not propped open as if intentionally done, but slightly askew. No smoke rose from the chimney. No light came through the window. He picked up his pace. Jogging the final steps, he burst through the door.

"Mother? Sora?"

The small room was dark. No fire burned in the hearth. No one lay in the beds. He crossed to the stove and hovered his hand near the metal. Cold. His pulse pounded.

*Where could they have gone? Would they have fled?* He dismissed the idea. His mother still wasn't mobile. He surged toward the entrance to check with Silvia next door, but he froze before he made it outside. An envelope sat in the center of the table. The sight made his heart skip a beat. He stepped toward it.

The envelope was white with crisp edges. On its face, blocky letters spelled his name—not the handwriting of Sora or his mother. His brief hope had soured. With a trembling arm, he picked it up. He lifted the flap on the back and pulled out a letter. He had to lean toward the window to read.

*Kaleth,*

*Your mother and sister are not here. The idea of running away can be dangerous if left to fester, and I'm sure you wouldn't want them in danger. They needed somewhere to stay for a while, for their own safety. I'm sure they will be kept secure, at least until your deadline. Good luck at the academy. I will be watching.*

*Jairus*

His vision blurred. The room spun. He dropped the letter and braced himself against the wall. Bent over, his breath came in ragged spurts. The threat was nothing new, but he had always hoped they could run off at the last moment if needed. Now that hope was gone.

The walk back to the fortress felt interminable. For a moment, he entertained the thought of fleeing. After all, he had little chance of succeeding. But the thought of his mother and sister held by that man firmed his resolve. He would make it as a Lightbinder or die trying.

Leaving Ramble Square behind, he trudged along the narrow path to Sky Fortress. His steps felt heavy on the uphill climb. The greenery on the cliff walls reminded him of his ability, so he pulled energy from the plants as he continued up. His insides came alive. He felt light on his feet and capable of anything. His instincts sharpened. He pulled more until a tingle grew inside him. A mixture of pleasure and pain filled his limbs as they struggled to restrain themselves. He tried to bring in more energy, but his body pushed back. It was as if he had filled a waterskin full and it threatened to burst.

Holding the unbridled power inside, his steps were light. The effort to climb was negligible even though he had sped up his ascent. Oxygen filled his lungs, fueling his effort. The energy filling him eased the physical weight he felt, but it could not touch the heaviness in his heart.

At the top of the path, he turned to the south, looking toward the darkness that stretched into the distance. Revalle lay somewhere out there, hiding in the night. A smile crept across his face as he thought of Felyra—her spirit, her grit, and the softness he noticed when she let down her guard.

*Will I ever see her again?*

He hoped so, but couldn't imagine how it would happen. He trained to fight against Thravia. *What if I have to attack and she is caught in the crossfire?* His stomach turned at the thought until he pushed it away.

*Let's hope it doesn't come to that.*

The two guards posted at the gate differed from the ones who had been there when he had left. When he drew close, one of them looked at him. The move seemed stiff, as if forced.

"Name?" the guard prompted.

"Kaleth-il-Valorr."

The other man glanced at a sheet of paper and nodded. Both men took small steps to the side, allowing a gap between them that led to the cracked gate behind.

"Welcome back," the guard said, returning his gaze to the city.

Something about the interaction gave him pause. It could have been the way they avoided looking at him or their stiff postures. A tingle ran through his body. Something felt wrong. Initiates had been captured and killed all year, and there he was walking alone at night.

He took in a slow breath as he drew closer to the men. His enhanced senses lit up, trying to help him make sense of his unease. He checked over each shoulder, but nothing was there. He glanced at the battlements high above, but nothing looked out of place. He nodded toward the men as he stepped through the gap between them, aware of how close they were.

His muscles were ready to run, brimming with energy borrowed from the plants he had passed on the climb. Academy guards should be the least of his worries, but something told him to be cautious. He glanced at the empty sheaths on his jacket and thought of his training knives sitting on the desk in his room. He had no weapon, and both guards had swords on their hips. His eyes tracked to the side as he passed them. Each step toward the gate felt exaggerated in length. Trying not to look suspicious, he chanced a quarter-turn of his head, using his peripheral vision to monitor the guard. He hadn't moved.

Kaleth rested a hand on the cracked gate, pausing a moment to look back. Both guards remained in their stiff poses, staring toward the city.

*I'm only days away from completing my first year. Of course, I'm nervous.* He chuckled to himself, then stepped through the opening.

Binder lamps glowed on the walls down the long corridor ahead. The moon lit up the Grand Courtyard and Kalistor Castle behind it. He released the tension in his muscles. The energy filling his body remained, keeping his senses alert.

*Relax, Kaleth. There's no danger here.*

Despite telling himself to take it easy, his body wouldn't listen. The hairs on the back of his neck prickled. His ears detected a change in pressure as if something moved. His mind whirred, putting it together.

The whooshing of a knife sounded odd at first, but his body reacted before he had time to think. He ducked, then spun, turning as a sharp point slid past the top of his head. The man wore black, blending with the shadows in the corner. His arm seemed to move in slow motion. Kaleth reached up, pressed against the man's wrist, and jerked the knife handle with the other. The man gave a strangled cry while the weapon popped from his grip.

Kaleth snatched the hilt of the freed blade and turned it on his attacker. His arm moved so quickly that the man in black didn't have time to react. He plunged the knife into the man's chest, over his heart. The moment happened so fast. He released the hilt and blinked several times.

The unfamiliar attacker staggered backward, looking down and gaping at the dagger sticking out of him. He tried to say something, but blood burbled from his lips.

The two guards from outside stepped through the cracked gate. Their eyebrows raised as they took in the scene—not what they had expected to see. Their visages turned hard, and they pulled swords.

The moment caught up with Kaleth. A gut-wrenching shudder shook him. *Push it away! Don't be afraid!* The fear felt as present as ever. He recalled Aurik's words and refocused his thoughts. *Take action despite the fear.*

He eyed the knife sticking into the attacker's chest as the two guards drew closer. Kaleth was fast. He was strong. He could fight off the two men. *But what if I fail? If they get me, what will happen to Mother and Sora?*

The guards cocked their swords, ready to strike. Kaleth hesitated a moment longer, frozen with indecision. Energy filled his body, warring with the desire to flee. He was ready to act. He was brave.

His wish for bravery couldn't sway his need for safety. His shaking body lurched away from the guards just before they arrived. Filled with energy, he sprinted in the opposite direction. He abandoned caution as he hurtled down the passage, moving at speeds no man could match. He chanced a glance over his shoulder as he crossed the Grand Courtyard. The guards had already given up. He navigated a few more turns and passages for good measure. It was only once he entered the Lightbinder quadrant and closed the door before him that he stopped.

His pulse surged through his body, pumping blood with vigor. His lungs heaved, trying to keep up. After a long moment, an extended sigh trickled out of his mouth. His shoulders fell and his muscles loosened. The reality of what had just happened crashed over him.

*Someone wants to kill me.*

## CHAPTER FORTY-SIX

# PUZZLE TEST

Felyra and the rest of the initiates packed the hallway outside the Grand Hall. Most sat on the floor with their backs to the walls. Some stood and leaned. Several paced its length, traveling between where the hallway turned a corner and the window at the far end. The air was thick with tension as they waited on the trial that would decide their fates.

Felyra kept one foot on the ground. The other leg was cocked, propping her boot against the wall. Her back rested against the stone. She switched legs and adjusted her position every few minutes. Her heightened anxiety wouldn't allow her to stay still.

"This is gonna take forever," Thaylor moaned, knocking his head against the stone as if on a loop. His silky black hair swung with each motion.

"I hope he kills his brain cells doing that," Ruane whispered.

Felyra's mouth curled up on one side. They *had* been waiting for a long time. She felt the same impatience, but there was nothing to do except wait.

"Something funny, Cripp?" Grax asked.

Thaylor turned at his side and joined in staring.

Ruane stood straight. "Her name's Felyra, you bind-cursed idiot, and you should know better than to mess with her."

"It's fine," Felyra said, waving her friend down. "No. Nothing funny. Just waiting like everyone else."

The double doors to the Grand Hall opened, and all waiting initiates looked up with mixtures of excitement and fear on their faces.

Felyra's shoulders tensed.

Peveral, the new lead instructor, poked his head into the hall. His gray hood was back. His expression was hard—nothing but business. "Ruane Nimble."

Her friend stiffened by her side.

"You've got this," Felyra said, trying to bolster her with confidence.

Ruane crossed the corridor and passed through the opening, disappearing when the door closed behind her.

"Do you know what it is?" Grax looked at Felyra from across the way with a raised eyebrow.

"The trial?" She shook her head. "Awareness, focus, and puzzles —that's what they said to be ready for. Outside of that, I don't know."

"Puzzles," Grax scoffed. "It's ridiculous. What, do they want us to out-puzzle our enemies?"

"Um . . . maybe. Isn't that kind of what a battlefield is? A puzzle where we need to put the pieces in the right order?"

He frowned but didn't answer her retort. After a moment, he averted his gaze as if engrossed in the stone blocks on the wall.

The waiting continued for what seemed like forever. Other initiates were called one by one until only a handful remained. By the time Peveral poked his head through the door and called her name, Felyra's nerves were frayed, and her stomach ached.

The Grand Hall was empty of furniture except for a round dais in the center. Flickering lanterns lit the room, illuminating the previous initiate who was being escorted out a door on the far side. Soulbinder instructors stood in a wide circle, facing in.

Headmaster Baloran motioned toward the center. "Take your place at the dais, Felyra."

Standing by a table, a man had his back turned to her. He

fiddled with something before he turned around. Felyra's blood turned cold. *Janduan.*

It had been four months since the headmaster demoted him from the lead trainer role. The change was welcome for her, but he still always seemed to be around. The man's face twisted in a sneer. His lip pulled up so high, a deep crease formed along his cheek. When Felyra passed him, the fury he displayed eased into an amused exhibition.

*Curious*, she thought, stopping as she arrived in the center of the room.

"Another round of cuts in the Soulbinder selection process will follow today's trial," Baloran said.

A lump formed in Felyra's throat.

"What we test for today embodies an attribute we look for most. A Soulbinder is a master of control—yes, control of yourself—but more specifically, control of other objects. You must be able to think quickly and act decisively. But you must be able to do it while splitting your focus in several areas. For today's trial, you must assemble the puzzle on the dais."

Felyra turned to the platform and frowned. A dozen wooden blocks in various cuts and shapes lay strewn across the surface. *Assemble a puzzle? That's it?*

"When complete, it should form the shape of a pyramid. Of course . . . it's not quite so simple."

A click from the side of the room drew her attention to where an instructor had pulled a lever on the wall. Once activated, the dais turned in a slow circle.

"Besides the movement, you'll need to be aware of what's going on around you."

A rumbling noise surrounded her. She swept her gaze to find stones the size of her fist lifting in the air next to each of the other men and women.

"If you take a rock in the head, completing the puzzle will become much more difficult. An initiate well suited to soulbinding will solve the puzzle while also being aware of and tracking multiple threats around them. Taking too long will reveal your lack of potential." He gestured behind her. "Whenever you're ready, you can begin."

Felyra turned back to the wooden blocks. She took a deep breath to steady her pulse. It didn't work. A nervous glance at the floating stones around her increased her urgency. Grabbing two pieces, she got to work.

The intended flow of the puzzle was easy to grasp. The pieces that formed the square base were quick to identify, and moving them into place didn't take long. The rotating dais required her to shuffle her feet. Having to move increased the difficulty, but it also allowed her to watch every direction. Her eyes flitted up, keeping a watch for hurtling rocks. So far, none of the observers had done anything.

With the base complete, she worked on the next level. Her hands felt clammy, and her underarms grew damp. A whizzing of air caught her attention. She looked up with only a moment to spare before a stone nearly crushed the side of her face.

"Whoa!" she cried as she ducked. Another projectile came toward her, but moving with the rotating surface kept her clear of it. Her eyes danced up and down. The threat of obstacles continually interrupted the focus it took to place the pieces. She fit a few more, narrowly avoiding more rocks that flew her way.

Staring at the five unused blocks, she frowned. She needed an angled piece, but nothing that remained fit. *I must have something wrong.* She dodged a stone, then replaced one of her set blocks with a new one. She frowned even deeper. *That doesn't work either.*

The flying obstacles came more rapidly. Felyra spent more time watching and dodging rocks than she did looking at the puzzle. The longer she took, the quicker they came.

*How am I supposed to do anything while dealing with this?*

Needing to focus, she diverted her attention long enough to look at the pieces. She spun them in her hands and shook her head. Ducking under a large rock, she caught a glimpse of the base of the dais. A wooden piece peeked out from a shadow, hidden under a lip. She crouched and reached for it. A rock she hadn't noticed crashed into the dais where she had stood a moment before.

The angled piece was small and made of wood, just like the others. She held it up, her heart surging. A step to the right dodged a flying rock. With no more projectiles on track to hit her, she turned her attention to the puzzle on the dais. The new piece was exactly what she needed. It slotted perfectly into the puzzle. Once it was set, the others fell into place. She had to dodge a few more obstacles before she was complete, but after fixing the top of the pyramid, she stepped back with her hands raised. A final whizzing rock rushed past, inches from her face.

"Done!" she shouted. Any floating stones that had yet to be hurled dropped to the floor. It was only when she let her muscles relax that she realized how tense she had been. Her jaw ached from how hard she had clenched it. She wiped the sweat off her forehead with the back of her arm. Her racing pulse slowed.

"Thank you, Felyra," Baloran said. "Exit out the side, please."

She scoured the faces of the instructors, looking for any sign of approval. The headmaster seemed pleased, but his smile looked no different from when she had entered. As she walked to the side door, Janduan approached the center of the room. His dour look made her feel like she had done something right. He avoided making eye contact. When he arrived at the dais, he disassembled the puzzle, preparing for the next initiate.

"Let's go," a woman at the door urged, pulling it open and motioning for Felyra to leave. "The rest of the afternoon is free. Convene back here after dinner for the cutting ceremony."

*Cutting ceremony.* The thought both thrilled and terrified her. She had been working all year and it all could end that evening. Failure to be selected wasn't an option. Anytime she had considered it, she pushed the thought from her mind.

The back corridor led away from the Grand Hall. Felyra followed the passage, thinking about the others who waited by the main entrance. A smirk crossed her face when she imagined Grax being hit upside the head by the flying rocks.

When she entered the bunk room, Ruane's feet dangled from the bunk above her bed. Her friend pushed off the edge, landing on her feet. "How did it go?" she asked.

Felyra shrugged. "Good, I think. I completed the puzzle. You?"

Ruane smiled and nodded. "Me, too. Two stones hit me. The second got me on the side of the head." She rubbed her temple where a circular red mark covered her skin. "That almost took me out, but I kept at it."

"I managed to not get hit, somehow," Felyra said. "I almost missed the hidden piece. The stones were coming so fast, it was almost too late."

Ruane's hairline lowered while her forehead wrinkled. "Hidden piece?"

"The one on the ground? At the base of the dais?"

Her friend's expression didn't change.

Felyra sighed. "Janduan."

"He hid one of your pieces?"

"Yeah, I guess so."

"But you still completed it?"

Felyra couldn't stop the grin. "Barely."

"That's incredible. I bet you make it."

"As a Soulbinder? After my result on the Expedition?" Her friend's confidence encouraged her, but the reality of how she'd done during the year was difficult to ignore. "I guess we'll find out soon."

THE GRAND HALL had been returned to its regular state. The circular dais had been removed, and the ominous ring of instructors was gone. Fellow initiates mingled through the room, chatting. They wore forced smiles as if trying to look casual, but Felyra spotted the lines etching their faces. She smelled the nerves, an understandable feeling she shared.

All the training. All the pain. The abuse from Grax and Janduan. Everything she had worked for could be gone that very day. She didn't have a plan for failure. There were no backup ideas. She had focused on nothing else since her father died, so the thought of not making it terrified her. The world was cruel to scarred women with limps.

Ruane's hand found hers, squeezed, and then let it go. "You'll be fine."

Felyra turned to her friend and forced a smile. "Thanks. I wish my brain would hear that. *You* surely will. You're great at everything, not just a few things, like me."

"You're good at what matters."

"It all matters. If I make it through, I will probably be the first Soulbinder who can't run."

"You can run; don't sell yourself short. But there *are* other things you do better, which are even more important. I think you'll be one of the greatest Soulbinders we have."

Felyra let the thought fill her mind. She pictured herself wearing the gray uniform with the hood, fitting in with the rest of the elite force. She imagined walking through Revalle, turning heads and generating respect. In battle, standing next to a force of Soulbinders would feel unstoppable. Working together, manipulating the world around them to stop the Lightbinders.

Her skin prickled with sweat. *Stopping the Lightbinders.* What if she had to face Kaleth? What if one of them had to live and the other had to die? She clenched her teeth.

Instructors arrived, snapping her from her thoughts. Felyra faced the front of the room, standing next to Ruane while the other initiates gathered, the air simmering with anticipation. Headmaster Baloran took the center of the room, flanked on each side by a row of instructors and army leaders. His crisp, gray uniform with its silver pockets and folded back hood gave him a commanding presence that increased the longing Felyra felt to be chosen.

"You have all trained hard." Baloran's projected voice filled the room, bouncing off the stone walls and high ceiling. "Soulbinders form the heart and soul of Thravia's army and give us a chance in the fight with Kalshia. I wish we could take you all, but our resources are limited. Every one of you has given sweat and blood to get where you are, but only a handful can be chosen. Only the best can be added to our ranks." He rubbed his hand over the blue ring on the middle finger of his opposite hand.

"A week from now, on Highsummer's Jubilee, you will have the final test of the year. You have all worked hard to get where you are. You've proven yourselves capable in several disciplines, but we can only take a portion of you into this next test. Only a dozen will continue forward. The rest will enter the army in other roles."

A knot tightened in Felyra's chest at the thought of being placed with the rest of the army. She'd spent so long focused on this one goal. Missing it when she was so close would devastate her.

"The initiates chosen to move forward in their Soulbinder training are . . ."

Felyra focused on the headmaster's lips, looking for the telltale sign of teeth on the bottom lip that could pronounce the letter "F". Ruane squealed when her name was called. Felyra managed a smile and spared a glance for her friend. Other young men and women celebrated, one at a time, as the list continued. Grax's name was called, turning her stomach. He caught her attention from the corner of her vision as he lifted his chin and flashed a smug grin. He was the seventh name. The thudding of her pulse in her ears was deafening. She could barely hear the names as Baloran read them off. Names that weren't hers continued to be called. Time was running out. Her dream slipped away with each word he spoke.

"And the final name is . . ."

She held her breath. The collective crowd of young men and women leaned in. The moment dragged out forever.

The headmaster's teeth pressed against his bottom lip for a split second. "Fenris Wardragon."

Her heart jumped at the F sound, then plummeted. She stared forward, her jaw drooping. An attempt to breathe felt like tugging on a locked door. *No. No.* Everything she had focused on—all her dreams—were gone in a moment, drowned by the cheers of the surviving initiates.

## CHAPTER FORTY-SEVEN

# REJECTION

"If you didn't hear your name, I'm sorry," Headmaster Baloran said. "Grab your gear from your bunk room, then follow the instructors to the army barracks."

A squeeze on Felyra's shoulder brought her out of her stupor. Her body twitched.

"I'm so sorry," Ruane said. "I thought for sure you'd make it."

Tears threatened to burst from Felyra's eyes. She held them back by staying quiet.

"I'll talk with the headmaster. I'll let him know how great you've been doing. He can still change his mind."

"It doesn't matter," Felyra whispered. "They don't want me. I'm a liability because I can't keep up with everyone else."

"Sounds like we have another test in a week. I'll probably be cut then, anyway."

Felyra forced a smile. "You won't get cut. You're going to impress them, and you're going to get one of those rings."

"Time to leave, Cripple," Janduan said in her ear as he walked by.

She glared at him, but his gloat was more than she could take. "I've gotta go," she mumbled.

"Felyra," Ruane said.

She ignored Ruane's protest and tromped out the door, leaving her friend and her dreams behind.

Slumped shoulders marked the bunk room as the nine cut initiates packed their belongings. Felyra stuffed her few changes of clothes into a travel sack, then paused at the sight of Kaleth's letters. She'd received seven over the last few months and knew them all by heart. She picked up the stack of envelopes and tucked them into her sack.

"Let's go," an instructor said, standing in the doorway. "Army barracks are on the other side of town. I want to get there before the sun sets."

Thaylor slung his sack over his shoulder, his thick, black hair flinging in sync. Even though he was cut at the same point as she was, he still wore a haughty grin as if he were better. His stiff shoulder slammed into hers as he passed her bunk to exit the room.

"I need to speak with the headmaster before I leave," Felyra told the instructor.

He shook his head. "Impossible."

"I only need a few minutes. I've trained here for eleven months. Surely, he can spare a few minutes."

"We need to leave. Plus, Headmaster Baloran is busy. He's meeting with the Soulbinder initiates. You can't be there." He pushed her through the door. "Keep up with the others."

Felyra stumbled along. Her legs felt like stumps, numb and heavy. Her fellow rejected initiates walked in front of her, but none looked as dejected as she felt. Becoming a Soulbinder was everything she had worked toward, and now she had nothing.

When they passed the double doors of the Grand Hall, she heard muffled words through the thick barrier. She slowed and leaned in. The rest of her group continued forward, not even appearing to realize she had paused. When she was about to move to catch up, the group rounded a corner and disappeared. She angled her ear toward them. No feet shuffled to come back. No one called out, asking where she was. Not feeling motivated to hurry after them, she turned back to the doors. The speaking remained garbled, despite her proximity. Holding her breath, she pulled a door. It opened. When it was just wide enough, she stepped through the crack.

The entry was dark. The lanterns around the room barely reached where she stood. She slunk against the wall, tucking her body in its shadow. The atmosphere in the Grand Hall felt different than before. No longer were the chosen initiates celebrating. They stared at the headmaster with fixed attention.

"What kind of dangerous?" Fenris asked.

The word "dangerous" perked her ears.

"The kind that some may not come back from," Baloran said. "Don't worry, though. You'll be with fully-trained Soulbinders—myself, Peveral, Janduan, and five more from Twainford—and you'll have army infantry mixed in with you. We'll be near their castle, but our focus is the Central Tower of their Lightbinder Academy."

*Lightbinders!* Felyra thought. *That's where Kaleth will be.*

"And we're going inside the fortress? How do we get past the walls?"

"You'll learn soon. Our goal is to infiltrate the fortress while they're distracted. This mission will test your fighting ability and your stealth skills. You will see firsthand the danger of war and the power of their Lightbinders. We've lived too long squabbling and fighting back and forth. This mission, while serving as a test for you, will also change the trajectory of the war."

Grax raised a hand. "How do we know they'll be distracted?"

"Our source confirmed they'll have their usual ceremony on Highsummer's Jubilee. Not only will everyone be busy, but if all goes well, most Lightbinders will be dead when we arrive."

Felyra's hand covered her mouth before a gasp could escape. Her body trembled. *Kaleth!*

"Our Soulbinders and soldiers should have little trouble achieving our objective when we arrive at their depleted forces."

"Taking their rings?" Grax guessed. "Is that the objective?"

Baloran shook his head.

"What then?"

The headmaster paused. After a tense moment of silence, he continued as if no one had asked the question. "We depart in the morning. We'll rendezvous with the rest of our troops, then sneak through the hills to Kalistor. The main army will cause a distraction at Twainford while our smaller force infiltrates Kalistor. Then, we return to Revalle as heroes. Not only will it give our city hope once more, but we will rid Kalshia of its next generation of Lightbinders."

Felyra tried to stifle her cry, but failed. Heads turned in her direction.

Janduan closed the distance before she could move. There was nowhere to go. He squinted into the dark entry until his face hardened. "Cripple, why am I not surprised?" He pulled her by the arm, dragging her forward.

"Felyra," the headmaster breathed. "What are you doing here?"

Her eyes flitted between the initiates and the instructors. "I'm sorry, sir, but I needed to speak with you."

"This information was not meant for you. You should—" He stopped, seeming at a loss for words. After a moment, he turned to the others. "That's all for now. Pack your things. We'll leave in the morning. Felyra, come with me to my office."

She locked eyes with Ruane, who grimaced.

The headmaster made for the double doors, leaving the rest of the room to disperse. Felyra followed. The walk down the hall seemed like it would never end. Their boots echoed off the walls of the empty corridor while disappointment oozed off the headmaster.

When they arrived at his office, he gestured to the chair opposite his desk, then sat with a sigh. "What am I supposed to do with you, Felyra?"

The casual familiarity caught her off guard, which allowed her frustration over being cut to seep back into her mind. "For starters, you could let me back into Soulbinder training."

"What?" He shook his head. "I'm sorry about that, but—"

"Are you?" she blurted. "You called me a highly capable young woman."

"And you are."

"You said no one tried as hard as me."

"I also said, 'I'm not the only one who chooses.'"

"Does that mean you would have chosen me?"

"I did. I pushed for you. You aced the focus test. I still feel you're one of our top initiates. If it's helpful to hear . . . it was close."

The realization that she had just missed the cut did not help.

Baloran massaged his fingers into his forehead. "You weren't supposed to hear those plans in the hall. It's not that I don't trust you, but no one outside of the parties involved can know." He blew out a long breath. "I'll have to lock you up until it's over."

"What? No! I'm not the enemy."

He frowned as if he lacked conviction at his sentencing of her.

An idea came to her mind and gave her a flicker of hope. "Take me with you."

"Felyra, we can't—"

"You said you're taking infantry, right? That's technically what I am now, so I could be one of them. Also, you said the cuts were close, so I could just as easily be one of the twelve Soulbinder initiates going." He didn't immediately refute the idea, which gave her hope. "You told me I had focus, intelligence, and a strong work ethic. You said you needed me. Please, sir. I just want to help. If you truly think I have value for this army, don't lock me up. Use me."

The resolve plastered on his face crumbled. "I can't look at you without thinking of your father."

"Don't do it for him; do it for Thravia. Do it because I can help."

"Janduan will be on the mission."

Her eye twitched, but she swallowed a lump in her throat. "I'll do it. Let me come."

After a long pause, he nodded.


BALORAN MADE her sit outside his office while he called in Peveral. They spoke for a quick moment until the head instructor left, then Baloran joined her in the hallway. "It's settled. You will join the Soulbinder initiates for this mission, but you are still cut from the selection process. We agree it is better to use you than to lock you up."

Although it was what she expected, confirmation that he hadn't changed his mind about the academy disappointed her. Still, she nodded and smiled.

"Head to your old bunk room and get ready with the rest."

"Thank you, sir!"

When she entered the bunk room, Ruane squealed and ran toward her, knocking Fenris onto his bed. "We heard! You get to join us!"

The glowering faces behind her weren't lost to Felyra. Not everyone was glad she was there. "I'm not back in the program," she said loudly so that all in the room could hear. "But they asked me to join this mission."

Ruane shrugged. She walked back toward her bunk while she continued talking. "I'm just glad you're here. Did you hear what we're doing?"

Felyra followed. "Going to Kalistor, yeah."

"We're supposed to pack now."

Felyra lifted her pack from over her shoulder. "Already set there." She tossed the pack on the bed, then sat next to it.

"Oh, yeah. Nice. Well, give me a bit. I need to finish up."

Grax stopped beside her bed. He sneered, then shook his head. "Ridiculous."

"You're ridiculous, Grax!" Ruane snapped. "You can take your lazy attitude and shove it up your bind-cursed butt!"

"I missed you, too," Felyra called to the initiate as he walked away.

Her thoughts drifted to the mission. *Infiltrating the Lightbinder Academy.* Her stomach twisted as she remembered what the head-master had said. *Most of the Lightbinders will be dead.*

Her fingers tapped against her leg as she stared at her pack. *They deserve it. Kaleth is one of them. He's just another—* She couldn't finish her thought. He wasn't like the others. He couldn't be. He was kind and gentle. He saved her life and saw her as a person, not a monster.

Her pulse beat fast. Ruane was busy on her bunk. The others in the room focused on gathering their things.

She held her breath as she undid the clasp on her pack and pulled out paper and a stylus. She turned to her cubby. No one paid attention to her or cared about what she wrote. Putting the stylus to paper, she scribbled quickly.

## CHAPTER FORTY-EIGHT

# SKILL LOGS

Kaleth's leg bounced underneath him. He stared at the bookshelf on the opposite end of the common room, but his eyes remained unfocused. An elevated pulse ran steadily through his body despite not having moved.

"For the love of everything good, would you *stop?*"

Kaleth turned to find Jovi staring at his shaking leg. He stopped bouncing it. "Oh, sorry."

"We're all nervous, Kaleth," Lainn said.

"I'm not nervous," he lied.

"It's Highsummer's Jubilee," Jovi said. "We should all be celebrating, but here we are, anxious wrecks."

The three of them sat around a table with Chyla. Rayd and Roselle were the only Dragon Squad members not there. Initiates of other squads milled around the space, pacing or talking in groups.

"Did I tell you I got another skill signed off?" Kaleth said.

"Nice," Lainn said. "Which one?"

"Poison Creation, just yesterday."

"How did you not already have that one?" Jovi asked.

"Rayd wouldn't sign me off. He always said I had done something wrong. This time, I did it while in chemical sciences. Genoris commented on how they were perfect, so Rayd couldn't turn me down."

"So, that makes . . . forty?"

"Forty-three, actually." A grin forced its way across Kaleth's face. "I've been busy the last couple of weeks. I couldn't get Rayd to sign off on Stealth or Incapacitation. He always said my choking technique was wrong."

Jovi lowered his voice. "You should have choked the life out of him to prove you could do it."

Kaleth and Lainn chuckled.

"That's great, Kaleth," Chyla said. "I only ended with twenty."

The group quieted. Chyla ranked fifteenth, one behind Kaleth. Twenty skills wouldn't impress anyone enough to move her up.

"Don't worry," Kaleth said. "You're still ranked near me."

"Which isn't saying much," Lainn said.

Jovi punched his arm. "Come on. Don't be a bind-cursed jerk."

"Ow! What? It's not." He pointed at the ranking board. "He's *literally* fourteenth. This isn't a surprise."

"You don't have to point it out, though. He was just trying to help her feel good."

The reminder of his ranking twisted a knot in Kaleth's gut.

Lainn paused a moment, then nodded. "Sure." He looked at Chyla. "I'm sorry. Hey, there is still one more test. Who knows what might happen?"

A Grunt stepped into the room. "Mail," he called, waving a handful of envelopes in the air.

Kaleth looked his way. The Grunt flipped through envelopes, calling out names of other initiates.

"How do you test fear?" Jovi asked.

The question tightened a knot in Kaleth's stomach. The fear trial would begin soon, just before the special year-end academy banquet. Despite his training and confidence from his special ability, the unknown trial gave him pause.

"Heights," Chyla suggested. "Walking a high wall. Or maybe navigating a pit of serpents or spiders."

"Being underwater. A dark room. Fire." Lainn pointed to the window. "It *is* dark outside."

Jovi chuckled. "Maybe we have to escape from a dark room filled with serpents and spiders that's slowly filling with water."

"Ahh!" Chyla shuddered. "Don't even say it."

"I bet there will be some sort of combat involved," Kaleth said.

"You think?" Jovi asked. "Like . . . fighting each other?"

A thick silence hung for several moments around their table.

"Maybe. I don't know. But we haven't tested any combat yet, and it's a key part of being a Lightbinder."

"Well . . ." Jovi clapped his hands and rubbed them together. "I hope I live through the test because I hear the celebration banquet is worth it."

A dark cloud continued to hover over Kaleth. "It will only be a celebration for those who make it up to sixth." He knew what his odds looked like.

Jovi leaned closer to Kaleth. "Seriously though, don't count yourself out. You've moved up from fiftieth, and fourteen is not that far back from six."

Kaleth nodded.

"If it *is* combat, your knife skills are better than most all of us, so you have a great chance of doing well. You're a genius in class, and you nearly have all your skills filled out. Wait until the instructors find out. That's huge! Everyone's ranking must be close, so I think you've got a great shot."

His friend's words supplied a spark of hope, something that had eluded him most of the year. He chuckled to himself. "Yeah, I guess it is possible. Thanks, Jovi."

"Kaleth-il-Valorr," the mail Grunt called.

Kaleth turned toward him and lifted his eyebrows. "Here!"

"This came in via expedited porter," the mailman said.

He took the envelope addressed to him, written in a familiar script.

"Is that from *her*?" Jovi asked.

"Nice timing," Lainn said. "She probably wrote to wish you good luck."

Kaleth ran a finger under the flap, held closed by the tension of the wax seal. He paused as the three Dragon Squad members leaned in, watching. Rather than break the seal, he tucked the envelope in his pants.

"Aw, come on," Jovi said. "You're not going to read it?"

"Not with you all looking over my shoulder!"

Lainn spun his body away. "We won't look, will we?" He motioned for Jovi to turn away in the same manner.

"It's fine," Kaleth said. "I'll read it later."

A silence grew around them. All heads faced the entrance. Kaleth followed suit to find Aurik standing in the archway. "Initiates! It's time. Your year is complete, and the final trial is all that awaits. Fear is inevitable. Even the strongest Lightbinders will face overwhelming odds, so this test is not to avoid fear, but rather to see what you do during it. Do you freeze, or do you overcome? For those who survive, we will wrap it up with the Highsummer's Jubilee banquet. Please gather your skill logs and knives, then come to the Grand Courtyard."

In a chorus of mumbling conversations, the initiates dispersed.

Kaleth blew out a slow breath. He already had his knives in their sheaths. Ever since the attack at the gate, he hadn't left his room without them, but his log was in his dorm.

"This is it," Jovi said. "Good luck, you all."

Kaleth hopped up the stairs, taking them two at a time. He and Lainn both entered their room and grabbed logs from their respective desks.

Holding his book of skills bolstered Kaleth's confidence. The signatures inside proved the hard work he'd put in and the progress he'd made. His open window allowed a fresh breeze to waft through the chamber, lifting his spirits as a smile worked across his face.

*Jovi's right. There's a chance I can do this.*

While descending the steps, he rifled the pages of his book. His brows twitched. Something felt off. He came to a stop near a binder lamp on the landing of floor three.

"Is something wrong?" Lainn asked.

Kaleth's pulse quickened. "You go ahead. I'll catch up."

As Lainn left, he flipped to the front where "Kaleth-il-Valorr" was written on the top. But as he turned the pages, a pit grew in his stomach, and it deepened with each passing sheet.

Disarming an Opponent. Blank.

Ironball Carry. Blank.

History Recitation. Empty.

All the skills he'd worked for were nothing but bare sheets. His hand began to shake, and he struggled to breathe.

He flipped to Poison Creation and gawked at the page below it, where Rayd's signature marked it off with the date of the day before. It was the only page with anything on it. "What happened? Did I—"

"What's wrong, Grunny?" Rayd stepped through the door to his room on the third floor.

Kaleth held up his skill log. "Where did my skills go?"

Rayd frowned. "What do you mean?"

"I had forty-three that you signed off."

His frown deepened. "I signed off the poison one yesterday since you finally got it together, but . . . I've been telling you all year that you needed to work on your log. Leaving it until the last minute wasn't a wise move, especially given your place in the rankings." A hint of a smirk quirked his mouth. "I don't *remember* signing any for you other than that one."

A rush of anger flooded through Kaleth. "Liar!" He surged toward the squad leader, leading with his fists. He hadn't taken the time to pull in extra energy, so his movements felt slow and weak.

Rayd dodged the first punch and blocked the second. He returned a fist to Kaleth's belly.

"Oof!" His knees hit the floor. Kaleth bent over, sucking air through his gaping mouth. "You. Switched my." Heaving breaths interrupted his words. "My log."

A blow struck the side of his face, turning his vision white. Kaleth collapsed to the floor. Spots of red and black dotted his vision. He held his jaw, which felt like it was on fire. The inside of his mouth tasted of warm copper.

"You're fourteenth, Kaleth. You have no business in this school.

Skill log or not, you will never be a Lightbinder. You will never be higher than me."

His vision returned as a blurry Rayd headed down the steps. The parting words stung him to his core. Rayd was right. Even if he had filled out all forty-five skills, that wouldn't be enough to move him up eight slots. Kaleth groaned as he rolled over and propped his back on the wall. He rested his head against the stone. *This is ridiculous. Who was I kidding in thinking I could make it?*

He had no chance. His mother and sister had no hope. Taken by Jairus, they had no way out. They would join his father in death and it would all be his fault.

*I should have tried to work a regular job. Perhaps it could have ended differently.*

He worked his jaw in a circle, wincing. His stomach hurt as much as his mouth. He considered casting a healing glyph until he remembered the one already on his hip. A glance down the hall found a clump of weeds in the corner. They curled and faded to brown as he looked at them. The effect was immediate. His stomach no longer hurt. His breath had settled, and his jaw no longer throbbed. Unable to be healed, the blow to his pride and loss of hope felt as demoralizing as it ever had.

*What if they die and I'm the only one left?* He hadn't even considered what the cost of failure would look like, if he even lived through the year. He'd be alone. Alone and indebted to the army as a Grunt. He'd have Jovi, but his friend would be off leading as a Lightbinder or at least as something more useful.

*I could seek out Felyra.*

The idea sparked a flutter in his heart. He had wanted her to leave everything to join him, but there was no reason he couldn't do the same to join her. Surely he could find work of some sort in Revalle. The backup plan gave him hope until he remembered his family. *I can't give in so soon.*

*I can't give in.*

He considered how far he'd come. His strength had grown over the year. His ability to fight was actually quite impressive. His knowledge was as good or better than anyone else in the class. Rayd had his opinions, but he wasn't the one who decided anything. Kaleth shook his head. *Why do I let him get in my mind? I'm actually doing well.*

His eyes settled on Rayd's door. *And why does he hate me so much?* Rayd had every advantage Kaleth didn't. His family was rich and powerful. He had been training ever since he was young. The presence of a last-place initiate shouldn't bother him. *He trapped me in my room at the beginning of the year. He injured me on purpose while sparring. And he took my—*

His sinuses cleared. *What did he do with my old log?*

The idea spurred him to action. He jumped to his feet and stepped to the door of the squad leader's room. *If I'm lucky, maybe he forgot.* He looked toward the stairs and strained his ears. *No one.*

His hand trembled as he reached forward. The handle looked identical to the one for his room. He touched the cold metal, then held his breath and listened again. *Nothing.*

He turned his hand, expecting resistance, then gasped. The handle turned freely. The door creaked as he pushed it open. Focused on beating him up, Rayd had forgotten to lock it.

His pulse pounded as he stepped inside. The stroke of good luck felt too good to be true, but he still needed to find the log before anyone came by and found him. He closed the door behind him.

Kaleth touched on the binder lamp. Rayd's original roommate, a Claw initiate, had died during the poison test, so it was easy to tell which bed was Rayd's. The window above it was open. The shelves contained a handful of books on military strategy, but Kaleth's log wasn't among them. He pulled open the desk drawer and rummaged through its contents. No log again. As he was about to close it, a note caught his eye. He took out the piece of paper and unfolded it.

*Rayd,*

*I'm sorry for all the pressure on you. I want you to know that it will be over soon. As your mother, sometimes I struggle to know when to support and when to challenge.*

Kaleth had never met Delphine, Rayd's mother. Reading her words humanized him a bit from the arrogant bully persona he'd known.

*But remember, you brought this on yourself. You chose your path against our advice. Now you must live with the consequences. As the exal general's son, there are expectations. It's critical that you make it. Our reputation depends on it. If you determine you cannot avoid demotion, do not be the one who brings shame to this family. You must find a way out. There should be plenty of opportunity in the final test. Your father and I are counting on you.*

*Mother*

He put down the letter. *Maybe she's not too different from the exal general after all.* "A way out?" *What's that supposed to mean?*

Remembering why he was there, he spun to take in the rest of the room. There were few places to hide a log. The mattress caught his eye. He lifted the edge and grinned. A skill log had been shoved between the mattress and the frame. His hand shook as he opened to the first page. He exhaled when he found "Kaleth-il-Valorr" written across the top. Flipping through the pages revealed signatures by each of the skills.

A sound outside the door made his heart stop. *Footsteps.* He tucked the log into his jacket and held his breath. The steps halted. *It could be anyone. Other people live on this hall.* The doorknob rattled as it opened. The sight of Rayd's wide eyes was almost worth the terror Kaleth felt.

Rayd's shock twisted into a hard expression in a second. "When you didn't show in the hall, I wondered. I didn't think you'd be this stupid, though."

"Switching my log, Rayd? Really? Am I that much of a threat to you?"

"You're nothing to me! I don't care about you! You have no strength, no skill, no rich family. There's nothing to respect about you!"

Kaleth took a hesitant step to get around, but Rayd moved his body to block. His fists formed into balls. "Let me by, Rayd."

"No! Leave the log." His jaw was set like stone, but moisture glistened in his eyes.

Options were limited. The doorway was the only way out unless he wanted to jump through the window. *My room is directly above. Potentially, I could . . .* Kaleth let his senses wander outside to where he sensed vines crawling up the walls. He pulled in a fresh batch of energy. His sight grew sharper, and his muscles felt like rocks. He moved more deliberately, pushing Rayd to the side. The mountain of muscle barely budged, even with his augmented strength.

A punch came for Kaleth again, but his reflexes were faster than before. He dodged and threw a jab of his own that connected with Rayd's face. The larger initiate groaned and tottered farther back into the doorway. He rubbed his jaw, then leveled a look of irritation in Kaleth's direction. Both his hands raised into fists. He started to charge until Kaleth directed a kick squarely in his chest, using as much strength as he could. Feet off the ground, the other initiate flew into the hall and collided with the door opposite his room.

Kaleth was stunned. He stood, gawking at the result of his power. His urgency and the need to run escaped him.

Rayd rubbed his chest and winced. It only took a moment to regain his balance and square his stance. The hatred on his face could have curdled milk. He ripped two knives from the sheaths on his jacket.

"Whoa!" Kaleth held up a hand. "We have an entire test coming up. We don't need to do this."

Rayd pointed at Kaleth's sheathed blades with the tip of his knife. "Pull them."

Kaleth shook his head. "I read your mother's letter, Rayd."

The squad leader flinched.

"I'm sorry your parents are putting you through so much pressure. Was she telling you to . . . ?" He leaned forward, trying to avoid saying it. "To kill yourself if you can't make it?"

"Pull them!"

He shook his head. "Don't listen to them. You don't need to do that."

The air was thick with tension. Rayd wore a hard exterior, but his eyes contained a mixture of anger, sadness, and terror. His raised knives were as still as stone. With every second that passed, Kaleth felt it more likely he would back off.

"Fine," Rayd finally said. He charged.

Kaleth panicked. Rather than stand and fight, he turned toward the window and ran. One step brought him by the bed. He pushed off with the next. Heavy boots thudded after him. Rayd was only a breath away. At any moment, he expected a dagger to tear into his flesh.

Brimming with stored energy, his foot reached the sill of the window. He didn't pause. He didn't wait to gain his balance and sight his target. His momentum carried him outside. With power filling his legs, he leaped. The stone exterior flew past him. He craned his neck and stretched his arm. His own window on the fourth floor came into view. He reached the apex of his jump as his hand grasped the inside of the sill.

Dangling by an arm, he looked down. Rayd and a knife appeared out the window below. Kaleth pulled up his feet, keeping them out of reach. After grabbing the window with his second hand and scrabbling with his feet, he worked his way through the window until he spilled into his room.

*Gotta move! Don't freeze!* He wouldn't make the mistake of letting Rayd collect himself again.

Kaleth hit the door hard, then crashed into the hallway. Using all the energy he had, he sprinted down the stairs in a tight spiral. When he passed the third floor, the expected sight of Rayd hurtling toward him awaited. The knife couldn't have missed by more than a hair. Kaleth continued running, ignoring the harsh sound of the blade colliding with stone behind him.

With his father's ability and a head start, Kaleth couldn't be caught when he hit the ground floor. He sucked in fresh life from weeds in the main corridor. His fatigue was gone and his limbs felt fresh. Running toward the Grand Courtyard felt easy despite the frantic squad leader puffing at his heels. He slowed when he reached the end of the corridor.

A makeshift barrier blocked the wide passage to the Grand Courtyard, and a set of stairs climbed to the top of the wall next to it. The air over the wall glowed with binder light and echoed with spirited conversation. Instructors, city officials, and even fortress guards mingled in the corridor. Some were making their way up the stairs, but many continued to talk in groups.

Kaleth blew out a long breath and allowed himself to relax as he slowed to a walk. Surrounded by everyone else, Rayd would be too smart to try anything. Proving his theory, the other initiate arrived a moment later. Kaleth's muscles grew taut, but his squad leader's fury seemed to have abated. He glared at Kaleth but took no action.

Standing at the front of the crowd, Instructor Sorene held out a hand. "Skill logs please."

Kaleth fished the recovered log out of his jacket. He locked eyes with Rayd while handing it over. His squad leader's gaze narrowed, but he didn't say a word. He followed by handing over a log of his own.

"You're the last two." Sorene dropped the logs on a table, then grabbed two pairs of gleaming knives. "Trade me for these, then take the door on the left."

Kaleth exchanged his old, dull blades for the fresh, sharp ones. The metal looked freshly polished. The wooden handles shone with fresh lacquer.

*Why would we need sharp knives?*

He gulped, then tucked the weapons into his sheaths.

Sorene lifted her chin and raised her voice. "Final initiates are here! Observers, take your seats!"

The crowd of people jostled and moved toward the steps. Kaleth pushed through. "Excuse me. Sorry. Excuse me." He squeezed past men telling stories and women laughing.

A knock of an arm preceded a splash of wine across his jacket. Kaleth froze and splayed his hands as if not moving would help the red liquid to roll off him.

"Kaleth!" Headmaster Genoris held the spilled glass. "I'm so sorry about that. I didn't see you coming through."

Rayd walked around him, laughing under his breath.

Kaleth brushed his jacket, letting the excess wine drip to the floor. "It's fine. Sorry for spilling your drink."

Genoris snapped at a Grunt who hurried over with a rag to blot the spill.

"At least that's black and red, right?" Genoris pointed at the jacket. "No one will even be able to tell. Good luck, Kaleth. I'm rooting for you."

When Kaleth continued, a dank scent reached his nose. He looked around, but nothing appeared nearby that would give off such a smell. He lifted his arm to smell his jacket where the wine had spilled. *That's it.* It was faint but distinct—an interesting aroma for wine.

The guard by the left door held it open, and Kaleth followed Rayd into the dark passage beyond. When it slammed shut behind him, his stomach sank. *I'm in the fear trial.*

## CHAPTER FORTY-NINE
# INFILTRATION

Felyra's company of Soulbinders and initiates pushed hard to get to the Lagrash River, walking day and night with only a few hours of rest. They skirted Twainford to the west to avoid running into any Kalshian patrols. After leaving their pack horses on the south bank, they waded across the exposed river at night, porting their gear on their heads before ducking into the sparse tree cover on the opposite side.

On Kalshian soil, they moved slower. Not only did they carry their supplies, but the trees grew thicker as they traveled farther north. Janduan pushed them hard. While the speed was fast, Baloran's presence tempered the captain's anger toward Felyra.

Felyra's bad hip screamed from days of travel without end and the heavy weight of her burden. Her toes blistered. Her limp grew more pronounced. She panted along with the others.

On the fourth day of travel, Janduan grew more testy. It was Highsummer's Jubilee, but they had yet to arrive. Their speed picked up. As night fell, they pushed forward, stumbling through the dense path in single file by the light of the moon. A silhouette of the looming Verdal Plateau drew closer every minute.

After an endless slog, they approached the ruins of a stone structure. Men in nondescript plain clothes stepped out from behind ivy-covered walls. "They're here," one of them called into the bowels of the collapsed building. Janduan and Baloran led the way inside.

Men and a few women milled around inside the gloom of the collapsed building. Felyra counted twenty in total. A tall man with thick silver hair and a beard approached. Ruane gasped.

"That's Celedar Wardragon," Grax whispered.

Felyra's eyes opened wider. *Old Silver Hair.* Every adult and child in the kingdom knew him.

The legendary leader greeted Baloran, Peveral, and Janduan, pausing extra long to grin at the captain. Finally, he turned to address the initiates. "Welcome to our camp. Soon you will get your first taste of action in our battle against Kalshia. From what I understand, your instructors will be watching to see who deserves one of our rings." He stepped again and stopped in front of Fenris. "Good luck to you." The words seemed directed just toward the young man.

Fenris nodded. "Thank you, Father."

Felyra sucked in a breath.

Baloran gestured toward an empty area of the ruins. "You all can set your packs down and rest. Get some water and food. We've got a few hours until it's time."

"What will we do then?" Grax asked.

"Be patient. You'll find out soon."

Felyra groaned as she dropped her burden to the ground. She sat on a rock and stretched her aching leg. Her hip felt like it wanted to pop. She angled it in multiple directions but couldn't find relief.

"Father?" Grax said. "Celedar Wardragon is your *father*?"

Fenris nodded.

"Fenris Wardragon," Ruane said. "I never put the names together. I guess I should have been nicer to you all this time, huh?"

"You better not get special treatment," Grax said. "We all earned our spots here."

"So did he, Grax," Felyra said, shutting him up.

"I don't know about the rest of you, but I slipped the headmaster a gold coin to be chosen," Ruane said.

Felyra chuckled, but the other initiates didn't seem to find the joke funny. She took a moment to look at their remains of a shelter. The roof had collapsed long before. Some walls had crumbled, but most remained standing. Vines and moss grew over the stones, which felt camouflaged in the surrounding vegetation of the dark forest.

"I didn't know it was so tall," Ruane said.

Felyra followed her gaze to a towering shadow jutting from the plateau a half-mile to the north. She could barely make out dark spires and walls at the top.

"Do you think they have a secret passage to get in?"

"I'll bet someone is going to let us in," Fenris said. "An inside spy."

"We have eight Soulbinders," Grax said. "We could blast their gate to shreds with floating battering rams."

Felyra chimed in, "Or have a Soulbinder merely unlock the gate and open it."

Grax frowned. "Blasting it would be more fun."

"But I'm not sure we'll do either. The front gate will be guarded. We only have thirty-six people in total. I'm sure they'll have Light-binders ready to go as soon as there is an alert."

"We can take them," Grax insisted.

"You can, can you? Are *you* going to take them, Grax? With your finely honed ability?"

"Shut up, Cripp. You shouldn't even be here."

"Well, I'm here!" Felyra's neck felt hot. A stern look from a group of soldiers reminded her to watch her volume.

"She's part of this army just like we all are," Ruane said.

"Hey," Fenris said, craning his neck after his father and the other leaders. "What do you think that is?"

Felyra looked past the walls to where the Soulbinders gathered. They all looked at where four large wooden platforms rested on the ground. She stood and walked closer with the rest of the initiates close behind. The square objects had low wooden rails that ran around each edge.

"Each lead will support the one to their right," Celedar said. "Except me, I'll manage the far one."

"Have you tested it at capacity?" Baloran asked.

"Of course, but we should practice with your group, to make sure you're ready."

The headmaster nodded. "Let us know what we need to do." He looked up and motioned for the initiates to come closer.

"Everyone take positions," Celedar called so everyone could hear. "Each ascender should have two Soulbinders. One will take center, and the other will be ready for when we arrive in the fortress. Infantry, take your place around the edges . . ." He stepped onto one of the ascenders, crouched at the edge, and gripped the wooden rail with both hands. ". . . like this. It's imperative that you don't move. Keep your head down, arms locked, and body still. Don't move a hair until we've landed."

"Landed?" Grax blurted.

Felyra echoed the same incredulity in her mind.

"That's right," Celedar said. "Welcome to the world of Soulbinders."

Felyra moved to the farthest ascender, away from Janduan. She crouched next to Ruane and gripped the wooden rail.

Ruane whispered, "So they're going to *fly* us over the walls?"

Felyra fought to keep her voice steady. "I guess so."

"Is that possible? If they can do that, how have we never seen people flying around before?"

She didn't have an answer. She didn't relish the idea of flying into the air, but it didn't appear they had any choice in the matter.

A man she didn't know took the center spot of their ascender and crouched. Baloran filled in one of the edge positions as the second Soulbinder of their group. Felyra wasn't prepared for what to expect. She pictured flying through the air and then tumbling over the side just before they arrived atop the high fortress walls.

"We'll lift together," Celedar said. "Hold fast to the rail and keep your body as still as possible."

Felyra gripped tighter. She looked at her feet, terrified to flinch. A rocking motion forced her to tighten her core in order to steady her body. Her locked arms kept her stable, but a breeze fluttered her hair. They lifted off.

The sensation sent a swoop through her body. Her eyes closed out of instinct, but she forced them open. Over the railing, the dim ground around the ruin grew smaller. She lifted her eyes as much as possible without moving her head. They approached the top of the nearby trees but slowed to a stop. For several seconds, their ascender hovered in midair. Her arms shook from how hard she gripped. Finally, they moved again, easing back to the ground. The landing jostled everyone, causing them to mutter and sway together.

Felyra exhaled and lifted her head. The ground had returned. She stood and stepped off the ascender.

"That was incredible," Ruane said.

Felyra smiled. "Yeah. Terrifying but incredible."

Men grabbed gray, hooded uniforms from behind the partial walls, then passed them around. The ones given to Felyra and the other initiates had the crossed-sword patches of infantry. She spotted a few uniforms that contained a Soulbinder emblem.

Celedar projected loud enough for all to hear. "Put on your uniforms now so you'll be ready. In one hour, we will fly over the walls and attack. Silence is paramount. Having your swords ready and mind sharp is critical. Take a moment to rest. Soon . . . the Lightbinders will be dead."

CHAPTER FIFTY

# TEST OF FEAR

The grassy surface of the Grand Courtyard lay before Kaleth, but it was only a fraction of its full size. Walls sectioned off what felt like one-fourth of the space. In the center, barriers of wood and metal formed tunnels and obstacles. Standing back-to-back, Jovi and Orion turned in a slow circle. They each held both of their daggers up and ready in a reverse grip.

Jovi was the first to spot the new arrivals. "Finally!" He jogged to them, continuing to look over his shoulder. "Did you get lost? Taking time to read your love letter?"

Forgotten in all the action, Kaleth pressed against his hip to ensure the letter remained. "No, I just . . . forgot something. Got it sorted, though."

"Ugh, what's the smell?" Jovi asked. "Is that you? Did you roll in a dragon den or something?"

Orion leaned toward him and inhaled. "Yeah, that's him."

"It wasn't me." Kaleth pointed toward the top of the wall. "Genoris spilled his wine on me."

"Not like any wine I've had. It smells like animal musk." Jovi chuckled.

Kaleth was eager to change the subject. "Do we know what we're doing yet?"

"They divided us into four groups," Orion said. "We're supposed to work together to survive."

"Work together?" Rayd groaned. "And we ended up with Grunny in our group. Great."

Kaleth ignored the barb. "Survive what?"

"I hear we have to fight a monster," Jovi said.

Kaleth rolled his eyes.

"What type of monster?" Orion asked.

"He doesn't know," Rayd said. "He's just making things up."

"Well, it makes sense! We've got knives. We're in this arena. We've got to survive *something!*"

Kaleth's eyes lifted to the top of the surrounding wall, where a crowd had gathered. Lit by a long row of binder lamps, the spectators extended along the walls surrounding the Grand Courtyard. He spotted Aurik, Sorene, and Falmouth watching intently. Instructors of the other classes mixed in with guards he didn't know. Headmaster Genoris nodded in his direction, then shook his fist in a show of encouragement.

A hissing shriek cut through the air over one of the dividing barriers. The four initiates spun toward it, but nothing was there.

"That's the section where Lainn is," Jovi said. "Roselle, too."

Orion's voice wavered. "Do you think that was one of them?"

"That sound wasn't human," Kaleth said, pulling his knives out.

"See," Rayd said. "Monster."

"Rayd, did you know your father was going to be here?" Orion asked.

In the observation area nearest them, Kaleth spotted Stonne-il-Malthus. The exal general cut a charismatic figure. His barrel chest filled out a pristine army uniform. His winning smile stretched from ear to ear as he conversed with other dignitaries.

"Yeah, I knew," Rayd grumbled.

Kaleth froze as his eyes traveled farther. Jairus, the Night Saber, watched him. The man's bald head stood out in the night. The wide neck and scar in place of his ear were impossible to mistake. His stomach twisted in a knot as he pictured his mother and sister locked away somewhere.

Kaleth walked closer until he stood under the post where the man watched from. "Let them go, Jairus," Kaleth grumbled.

"Kaleth," the Night Saber greeted. "I'm glad you made it. I was getting worried you wouldn't show. You realize that your family's safety depends on your performance. Instead of ordering me around, perhaps you should focus on your own situation."

Kaleth gestured toward the other instructors and guards. "I'll tell everyone here what you're doing."

Jairus chortled. "What I'm doing? Be my guest. Should we start with my friend here?" He gestured to Stonne-il-Malthus, who spoke with someone on his other side. "The exal general has been one of my closest allies since I was young. I'm sure he'll be eager to side with the lowest-ranked initiate who's doing even worse than his own disappointing son."

Kaleth squirmed.

"That's right. I know about the rankings. I know you have little chance of making it."

The man's words cut into him like knives. "If you hurt them—"

"What?" Jairus pulled a blade. "If I hurt them, you'll do what? Do you want to climb these walls and fight me? I'd love to see it."

Kaleth appraised the twelve-foot-tall walls with a new light. He never would have been able to mount something that high before, but with his father's ability . . . A thug next to Jairus raised a crossbow just enough so Kaleth could see it.

"You recognize that crossbow?" Jairus asked. He waved his knife in the air. "Or perhaps this knife? If you don't, I'm sure your *father* would."

Kaleth's veins felt ablaze. He gripped his knife handles harder until his hands hurt. He considered the odds of being able to land one on Jairus' forehead but decided they weren't good.

"Make sure you excel in this test. If you're going to get that bonus and be able to pay your debt, this is your last chance. If you can't . . . I'll have no choice but to follow through with my terms."

Kaleth's breath came quicker.

"If you come down the ramp to the city without my money, you'll find their two bodies hanging in the square—their entrails dragging in the dirt. Although . . . your sister is quite attractive. Maybe I'll keep her around awhile. I'm sure I can find a use for her at my place that might pay off the debt."

A firm hand clasped his shoulder.

"Kaleth."

His name sounded muddled and thick. He couldn't take his eyes off the Night Saber.

The hand pulled against him. "Kaleth!" Jovi turned him around and set both his hands on opposite shoulders. "You can't fight him right now, but you *can* do it out here. Something is coming, here in this courtyard—soon. And we need you. Your family needs you . . . to be here, now. This isn't over."

Kaleth cycled through several breaths. His anger didn't dissipate, but a cooler head prevailed. Finally, he nodded. After a last glance at Jairus, he followed Jovi back to the others.

"Everything all right?" Orion asked.

"Orion," Jovi scolded. "Not now."

A new shriek sounded closer, spinning them toward a corner in their field of battle. A wall hid whatever made the noise.

"Bind and break me," Orion breathed.

"It's coming," Jovi said.

Kaleth wrapped his thumbs around the butt of each knife and held them with cocked arms. *The final test. My last chance to prove myself.* His body trembled. Hiding wouldn't help. Running would accomplish nothing. He needed to be brave. *Action through the fear.* The idea resonated more than his old strategy of pushing the fear away. Aurik was right. It never went away.

"We must work together." His words sounded strong—deeper than his normal speech. "This test is about us battling what's about to round that corner, not each other. We're going to need every one of us to survive. Are you with me?"

Jovi and Orion mumbled affirmations, but Rayd was quiet.

"Rayd, are you with us?"

The squad leader still didn't answer.

"Forget about the letter. Forget about your parents. This is your chance to make a difference. You need to be present, and *we* need you."

"Convenient," Rayd scoffed. "But, yes, I'm here. I'm with you."

The words of support from Kaleth's enemy somehow brought a faint smile.

The spectators on top of the wall quieted. Clicking and pattering noises came from behind the barrier. A breeze blew toward them, bringing with it a foul odor of decay.

"That's pleasant," Jovi said.

Kaleth blew out a slow breath, but his nerves didn't ease. He sucked in energy from the grass at his feet. His muscles were ready —his senses primed.

*I need to prove myself. I have to stand out. Action through fear.*

Despite the wobble in his legs, he stepped closer, leaving the other three at his back.

"What are you doing?" Jovi asked.

"Getting ready." He lifted his knives higher. The reverse grip felt natural after a year of drilling. He was quick and powerful—capable of keeping up with anyone or anything.

Rayd pushed past him. "Warriors are forged, not born," he said to himself.

Orion came next, passing Kaleth but staying just behind the squad leader.

Part of a black leg stepped out from behind the barrier. Kaleth tensed. It was the width of his arm, but the wall hid its full length. Covered in a hard, glossy shell, it reflected the light of the binder lamps.

"I see it," Orion whispered.

"But what is it?" Jovi asked.

Another identical leg joined it. The new one measured about five feet off the ground before it angled down and out of sight around the corner. When a third leg came into view, Kaleth's stomach dropped. His studies with his father covered animals and plants from all over. They focused on learning those native to Kalshia and Thravia, but they didn't neglect the unique species of East Verdalyn. In particular, the island of Zynthara fascinated him.

The sheltered, mountainous land held some of the most unique and terrifying animals in all of Verdalyn.

*Realm: Animalae. Category: Arthroskel.*

Another leg came into view, followed by its head at eye level. Eight black eyes—orbs the size of Kaleth's fists—were laid out in two rows of four. Below the eyes, two fangs the color of ink extended a foot out of its mouth. The other teeth formed a line of razors that dripped saliva.

*Group: Arachni. Strain: Mammoth Soldier Spider.*

Kaleth's body felt clammy as if blood had drained from his face and limbs.

The massive spider crept forward, bringing its body out from around the barrier. Its torso was fat and covered with coarse hairs. Its skin bulged as if squeezing it would cause it to burst. When it walked, it used the back six legs. The front two were raised and cocked. Their tips came to a point, hardened with a needle-sharp carapace.

"Oh, I hate being right," Jovi said.

Orion's voice shook. "What in the bind-cursed earth is that?"

"It's a giant spider," Rayd said.

"Mammoth soldier spider," Kaleth said, not taking his eyes off the monster. With the animal free of the barrier, the putrid smell amplified. Kaleth fought not to gag.

"It's big, so it will be slow," Jovi said. "Right?"

"No." Kaleth's heart pounded. "It will *not* be slow."

The spider flexed its jaw, repeating a loud clicking sound. Rayd and Orion stepped back in unison until they passed Kaleth.

"That saliva is acid," Kaleth said. "Don't touch it or it will eat through your skin."

"Noted," Jovi said.

"And avoid the front legs. Soldier spiders first skewer their prey to incapacitate them. Then they will sink their fangs into your skull and let the saliva eat through your brain."

"How do we fight it?" Rayd asked. "Does it have a weakness?

Kaleth nodded. "The back legs. We need to surround it. Its

danger is in the front. If we can keep it focused on one person, the other three can take out the legs from the back."

The spider lifted its head and bellowed a shriek that sent ice down Kaleth's spine.

*Action through fear. I can do this.* He swallowed a lump. "I'll take the front."

"Kaleth," Jovi breathed. "No."

"I can do it. You three be careful. It's still fast. Watch out for it spinning on you. As soon as it turns, those front legs will impale you."

"I'm gonna do it," Rayd said. He glanced up at the spectator area where his father stood. The exal general still didn't watch but remained in deep conversation with the man next to him. "I'm the squad leader. The front is my job."

"Rayd, I'm serious. I—"

The spider moved again.

"Go," Rayd ordered.

Kaleth sighed but nodded. He and Jovi moved to the right side and Orion took the left. Rayd stayed in the center. He scraped his knives together which caused the monster to perk up, lifting its body a hair.

Kaleth stepped as smoothly as possible. He kept his eyes on the spider, crossing his legs as he moved sideways. The clicking returned, its teeth clacking together. He reached its right flank but kept out of striking distance. One quick spin toward him and he'd be gone.

Rayd crouched, holding his knives forward. "Come on, you monster!" His arms bulged. His perfect hair and full beard made him look like a veteran warrior.

Despite his hatred of the squad leader, Kaleth couldn't help but be impressed. He continued farther, coming in line with the back leg. Through the six ambulatory appendages, he spotted Orion nearing the matching place on the opposite side.

*Almost time.*

Having left the downwind area, the monster's putrid odor grew faint. He gave thanks for the reprieve until he caught a whiff of the wine on his jacket. He was now the one downwind. The thought stopped his feet.

*I doubt it would care about wine. It already knows I'm here.*

Rayd stepped closer. His knives kneaded the air, waiting to strike. He was close. Too close. *We need to act. Now!* He tried to catch Orion's eye, but the other initiate hadn't cleared line of sight yet.

The breeze picked up, tussling Kaleth's shaggy hair, blowing it and his musky scent toward the spider. The bulbous body that had been bobbing froze as if turning to stone. The legs that had been creeping forward flexed, straining the confines of their hard shells. Coarse leg hairs poked through cracks. They stiffened as one.

Brimming with energy from the grass, Kaleth couldn't wait any longer. He spotted a joint in the back leg that would be his target. He clenched his muscles, ready to strike.

*Mother. Sora. This is for you.*

Before he could move, the spider spun toward him as fast as snapping a finger. Its jaws flicked open, extended far past what he imagined possible. Rows of razor teeth filled its mouth and glistened with acid. The leg he had been about to attack was long gone, replaced by eight fist-sized eyes and a maw of death.

CHAPTER FIFTY-ONE
# TEAMWORK

The roar that bellowed from the spider's gullet was deafening. Kaleth's insides felt like they liquified. He kept his knives up, but his arms shook.

The beast rushed at him, closing the ten feet that separated them in an instant. Thinking fast from his enhanced energy, Kaleth dodged one stabbing appendage, then blocked the next over his head with crossed knives. He deflected another attack with an arm, then ducked under the next. The strikes came one after another with lightning speed. Fueled by his surplus energy, he avoided over a dozen life-ending attempts.

A scream ripped from his throat when a stabbing limb finally caught him under his shoulder. The pain was like nothing he'd ever felt before. He fell backward, hitting the ground hard. The spider leaped forward, hissing as it flew—fangs bared.

Kaleth watched as the beast fell toward him. His life was over. His family would die. He could stab into its face, but there was no stopping the momentum of its fangs and deadly saliva. The monster's underside caught his eye. Flinging his feet up, he caught the spider just before it collapsed its heft onto him. He used all the energy he could muster to kick up. The spider was heavy, but the muscles in his legs managed. When he kicked, the beast flew into the air, flipping as it careened over him. The screech that came from it pierced his ears.

Free again, Kaleth jumped to his feet. He ran in the opposite direction, toward the other initiates, who windmilled their arms, beckoning him to run. He pulled fresh energy from the grass beneath him. A quick burst of healing eased the pain in his wound. A glance over his shoulder revealed the soldier spider on its back with its legs flailing in the air. Kaleth slowed.

*This could be our best chance to attack it. Maybe we should—*

The giant arachnid flipped over, springing to its feet. After a fresh shriek, it lowered its head and charged toward Kaleth with the speed of a sprinting deeling.

Kaleth scurried around a wooden barrier just as the monster slammed into it. Legs splayed over the top and around the side. Dripping fangs clacked against the wood. Using a jab he'd practiced thousands of times, he plunged his knife into a leg. The monster roared and scrambled backward.

Keeping the obstacles between him and the animal, Kaleth moved farther away. The other three initiates met him next to a passage of debris that formed a wide but short tunnel.

"What happened?" Jovi panted. "Did you insult its parents or something?"

Kaleth shook his head. "No idea."

"How are we supposed to kill something like that?"

Orion craned his neck around the edge of the barrier. "We could try Kaleth's idea again. We almost had it."

"Until Grunny hogged all the glory," Rayd grumbled.

Kaleth's jaw dropped.

Jovi stepped between him and their squad leader. "Excuse me? You think he's *hogging* glory?"

"It's clear he didn't want me taking the lead," Rayd said.

"You think I *wanted* that to happen?" Kaleth asked. "I didn't do *anything.*"

"Oh, sure. You didn't just—"

"Stop it!" Orion pushed each of them in the shoulder. "What do you think of trying it again?"

Kaleth shook his head. "It's too fast. We need to do something new."

Jovi looked at the tallest obstacle in their arena. The wooden structure stood six feet off the ground. "If we got up there, maybe we could—"

"You'd be skewered like a trapped rabbit," Rayd said.

"Well, we've got to try something!"

Kaleth rubbed his hand against the debris wall. The passage it created was as tall as him. *Trapped!* "I've got it!"

The others turned to him, eyebrows raised. His heart pounded. "We'll need all of us, especially you, Rayd."

The squad leader frowned.

Kaleth pointed to a pile of loose wooden beams. "Orion and Jovi, each of you grab two of those and be ready by either end of this passage. Rayd, hide out near this end. I will lead the spider through the tunnel. Once I'm clear, cap the ends."

Holding one of the wooden boards, Jovi frowned. "That thing will just push these over. Even if they were mortared into place, it could snap them like twigs."

"Trust me. Just be ready."

"And what am I doing?" Rayd asked.

"Once Orion puts the beams in place, have your knife ready." He leaned closer and set a hand on Rayd's shoulder. He whispered, "Be ready to cast a containment glyph."

The squad leader's eyes grew wide.

Kaleth grinned. "This is your chance for glory, Rayd."

"Guys," Orion's hand shook as he pointed over their shoulders. "It's coming."

Jovi and Orion split in each direction, hiding behind the sides of the passage while Rayd stumbled after them. Gripping the handles of his knives, Kaleth left them and walked toward the spider.

The beast moved cautiously. The leg Kaleth had stabbed stepped with an abbreviated cadence, but it seemed otherwise unaffected. Still some distance away, the monster paused. Its eyes flicked in different directions. The front legs hovered in the air, waving the hardened points at Kaleth. Its teeth clacked again.

Kaleth glanced over his shoulder, judging the distance to the passage. He stepped farther. *Come on.* He waved his knives in the air, but the spider didn't budge. "Come and get me!" Nothing.

The wind picked up, blowing against the back of his neck. As if triggered by a switch, the spider tensed. Its fangs extended as it unleashed a fresh roar. Kaleth backpedaled. *Not too fast. Don't lose it.* Like a mad boar, the monster charged.

Kaleth turned and sprinted. He used every bit of energy he could muster to propel him faster. At the edge of the tunnel, he glanced behind to make sure he hadn't lost the beast. His heart stopped. It continued to close, only feet away. "Get ready!" he shouted, rushing through the passage as fast as possible.

The spider didn't stop but had to slow when it reached the tighter confines of the narrow tunnel.

"Orion! Rayd! Do it!" Kaleth exploded out the far side and turned as he slid on the grass. "Jovi! Now!"

His friend draped the wooden planks across the passage's opening as soon as he cleared it. "I hope you know what you're doing, Kaleth!" While there was plenty of space for legs and jaws to reach through the gaps, if the boards could hold, they would prevent the spider from escaping.

The monster moved slower through the passage. Bent over, Kaleth scraped hastily in the grass.

*Focus. Intention. Action.*

He barely had time to think through the steps. Ferocious shrieks assaulted his ears, drawing closer with every second. Jovi held the loose planks in place. "Kaleth! Hurry!"

Sweat dripped, stinging his eyes. When he scratched the third arched line of the glyph, he scurried backward. "Done! Back off!"

Jovi jumped back as the spider's bulk slammed into the boards. What had been loose moments before held fast. Dripping jaws chewed against the wood. The front two legs flailed, trying to skewer Kaleth, who sat on his knees just out of reach.

"Nice!" Jovi yelled.

The spider turned its attention to Jovi, and one of the stabbing appendages grazed his leg.

He spun and fell to the ground. "Argh!"

Kaleth jumped up. "Are you all right?"

Jovi winced, pressing on the wound. He pulled his hand away and whistled. "It's okay. Just a scrape." He struggled to his feet, pressing against the wound again.

"This won't hold long," Kaleth said. "We need to stab it through the sides." He hurried down the outside of the passage, looking for a gap wide enough to reach through with a knife. Rayd and Orion remained at the far end. "Come on, guys! Stab it from the opposite side!" He turned his attention back to the walls.

"What are we supposed to be doing back here?" Orion shouted.

Kaleth tried to reach his knife-wielding hand through a gap, but it was too tight. He released a frustrated sigh. "Keep trying," he said to Jovi, who limped to him. Kaleth jogged to the far end.

Orion held the loose wooden boards against the end of the tunnel.

"Let it go. They'll stay." Kaleth pointed to the opposite side of the tunnel. "Go around and—"

When Orion released the boards, they fell to the ground, clattering against each other.

Kaleth turned to Rayd, who stood dumbly beside Orion.

"Did you cast it?"

The squad leader's jaw moved, but no sound came out.

Kaleth scanned the ground for a containment glyph but saw nothing. "You didn't." The letter from Rayd's mother burst into his mind. "Was this on purpose? Did you—"

"I don't know how."

"What?" Kaleth's jaw dropped. "But, my dorm room door? I thought you—"

"I don't know!" Rayd shouted. "I can't cast glyphs!"

A piercing shriek bellowed from the tunnel along with a wave of rotting air. Kaleth's stomach jumped into his chest as he looked down the passage. The mammoth soldier spider had turned around and was already halfway back toward the opening.

Kaleth dropped to the grass. "Hold the boards!" he shouted to Orion.

The other initiate trembled as he lifted them in place. Rayd backed away.

Kaleth frantically worked on another glyph. His circle looked like an oval.

Clacking of teeth grew closer.

The arched line of his glyph was crooked.

Still looking down, the animal's front legs entered his peripheral.

The second line looked better.

*One more!*

A shriek tore through the air. Kaleth glanced up to find Orion with an armored point sticking out his back.

*No!*

The loose boards at the end of the tunnel exploded as the spider blasted through them. Kaleth rolled away. A stabbing leg jabbed into the ground where he had been a moment before. He jabbed his knife into the leg, cracking the chitinous shell as it punched through its armor.

Free of the enclosure, the spider howled, rearing on its back legs with the front four churning the air. When its body landed again, its eyes all turned toward Kaleth.

"Run, Kaleth!" Jovi's distant call barely cut through the horrific noise coming from the monster.

After jumping to his feet, he obeyed his friend and sprinted in the other direction. He rounded an obstacle which was blasted into pieces by the monster crashing through it a moment later. Leaping with light feet, he bounded up a pile of rubble. The spider made quick work as well, barely missing Kaleth as he scurried down the back side. After a few more quick steps, he skipped to a stop. *Dead end.* He spun to find another route, but the spider blocked his way. He tried to run, but the animal skittered sideways, blocking his path. It hissed and wailed, thrashing its legs toward him. Bubbling green pus leaked from the appendage Kaleth had just injured. It filled the air with a fetid reek.

Jovi and Rayd both approached the monster from opposite sides, Jovi dragging his injured leg behind him. They closed in as if trying to attack its back legs, but the animal knew they were coming. It kicked, knocking them back and flinging them across the ground.

Kaleth's heart pounded. The sweat on his hands made his knife handles slick. Pausing a second allowed fear to creep back in. But he didn't fight it, and he didn't push it away.

*I'm doing this for Sora. I'm doing this for Mother.*

He absorbed fresh strength from the grass, not caring who might see its effect. His jaw was set. Rock-hard muscles filled his arms. He tightened his grip on his knives and wrapped his thumbs over the ends. Jittering nerves bounced inside him, but he allowed it to motivate rather than hinder. The wound in his shoulder didn't hurt at all. Taking in a deep breath, he flooded his lungs with oxygen.

The spider flinched as if it could sense his intensity. For the first time, it stepped farther away. Rayd and Jovi still floundered on the ground where they had tumbled.

The only one left standing, Kaleth ran forward.

The spider crouched. It lifted its front legs in warning.

Each step propelled him nearer. He stepped on a black mark in the grass where dripping green ooze had charred it.

The teeth clacked again. Fangs spread. A shrieking hiss filled the air.

Inside the monster's striking distance, Kaleth bounded toward the injured leg, missing a jab from the healthy limb. The spider didn't strike out with its bad leg, and Kaleth raked the blade of his knife across the spot where he had punctured the shell. The knife severed the remainder of the hard protection and the meaty flesh beneath it. Before the beast could respond, Kaleth leaped into the air. His left foot braced against the closest leg and bounded off, sending him flying in front of the spider's face. The foul hiss preceded snapping jaws, but he passed by before the fangs touched him. When his right foot connected with the spider's opposite leg, he pushed off again, sending him into the air.

The eight eyes tracked him as he soared above the spider's body. Its rows of teeth gaped, giving sight down its throat. Kaleth fell to his knees on the monster's back, plunging both hands into its hide. The blades punctured the skin. He dug deep into the top of its head, tearing through sinew and spilling green liquid across its back.

The response was swift and violent. The monster's legs spasmed. It jerked its head to shake Kaleth. The effort only pulled the gash wider. His knives ripped the wound down the side of its head before he was flung to the grass. Kaleth tucked and rolled as he hit. The massive spider jerked with violent contortions until its legs curled. The movement grew slower until the mammoth form tipped over, rolling onto its back—still.

Cheers boomed off the top of the wall, where guards and instructors applauded.

Jovi limped to him. "That was amazing!" He sidled to him while keeping his body facing the inert spider. "Are we sure it's dead?"

"I'm not sure of anything," Kaleth admitted. "But it seems pretty dead."

"You were incredible! Must have been those early mornings of extra knife drills you've been doing."

Rayd's lack of enthusiasm contrasted Jovi's. "Um, nice work, Grunny."

He pulled a light dose of grass energy to combat the effect of the adrenaline crash. While taking in a deep breath, he recalled the fourth member of their group. "Orion!"

The three initiates rounded a barrier to find the Iron Squad member lying face up next to the tunnel, still with lifeless eyes. His chest was a mess of blood and shredded leather. Kaleth bent over to check for a pulse.

*Nothing.*

A lump formed in his throat, but the adrenaline surging through him tempered the remorse. He shook his head before turning to Jovi. "How's your leg?"

Jovi shrugged, keeping a pressed hand against the wound. "It hurts, but I'll live." His pale face belied the bravado of his words. His body teetered. "What happened to that spider? It was as if it had a vendetta against you."

"I have no idea." He looked at the curled-up carcass as an

odorous dank smell reached his nose. It was strong. Familiar. He touched his jacket where the remains of the wine still stained it. He sniffed and curled his nose at the musky scent. "The spider smells a bit like this wine."

"The wine?" Rayd said. "Maybe it thought you were a rival."

Kaleth stiffened. *Is it a coincidence?* He glanced up at Headmaster Genoris, who was already looking at him. The man's tight jaw changed into an affable smile. He gave an exaggerated nod as if to congratulate Kaleth on surviving. *Did he spill it on me on purpose?*

Kaleth brushed his palms down his jacket, trying to wipe any residue away, hoping his suspicion would leave with it. "Well, we survived the final test. I'm not sure what it will do to the rankings, but—" He stopped, staring at his hands. They were still red. He moved them close to his nose and sniffed. The scent was even more powerful than before.

"It's not coming off?" Jovi asked.

Kaleth redoubled his efforts, scrubbing hard against the grass. "No, it's not." When he stopped, he checked again. Still the color of blood.

Jovi pointed at the curled-up spider. "Well, I don't think he's coming back to life. I think you'll be fine."

"What about the other groups?" Rayd asked. "Do you think they're fighting the same spiders?"

The binder lamps lit their arena of battle, but they couldn't see into the other sections. Kaleth scanned the tops of the barriers, but all was quiet. "What are the others doing? I don't hear any fighting."

"Um, Kaleth." Jovi's voice shook. He lifted a finger and pointed at the farthest wall. "What's that?"

A silhouette of a thin, black object stuck up into the air from the far side of the wall.

"I don't see it moving," Jovi said. "Maybe it's just—"

A second silhouette joined it, followed by a large black body. Eyes gleamed in the light of the closest binder lamp.

"Bind me," Jovi whispered.

Rayd pointed across them. "There's another."

The spider from the next section was already atop its wall. It perched like a grotesque statue meant to scare off crows.

"Bind me," Jovi said again, louder.

A shriek over the closest wall turned their attention. The third spider scrambled over the barrier in one frantic motion, landing in their arena with a thud that shook the ground.

Jovi backpedaled. "Bind and break my cursed body!"

Shrieking wails sounded from all three directions. The two that were on the wall jumped down in unison. The three initiates backpedaled until the wooden obstacle stopped their progress.

"We need to get out of here!" Kaleth shouted.

As if reacting to their plan, the first spider scurried into the open area, putting itself between them and the exit door. Kaleth blanched. They moved away from the obstacle, but the other two monsters herded them into the open space.

"This couldn't have been part of the test." Jovi's words slurred as his steps grew more erratic.

Kaleth looked at him. "Hey, are you—"

His friend toppled.

"Jovi!" Kaleth bent over, but a hiss from the nearest spider made him freeze. The monster lifted the front two legs in the air and bared its teeth. The other two animals approached, forming a semi-circle around the initiates.

"I'm fine." Jovi sounded drunk. He waved a knife in the air while remaining on the ground. "I can fight."

"How do we fight three of them?" Rayd asked.

Kaleth had no idea, but one thing was clear. He ripped at the buttons down the front of his Lightbinder jacket and pulled it off as fast as possible. The spiders stamped at the ground and hissed even louder at the disturbance in the air. After one twirl over his head, Kaleth flung the jacket as far as he could. It sailed through the air, flapping and waving. The spiders followed the object with their multiple eyes until it disappeared over the lip of the balcony above.

One spider rushed after it, stopping under the spectator area. It shrieked as it flailed its piercing legs in the direction of the jacket. The other two beasts were not as easily deterred. They crouched and crept closer, angled to block any attempt at running. Saliva dripping from their fangs hissed as it hit the grass. Clacking teeth made Kaleth's jaw ache.

He pulled in fresh strength from the grass at his feet. Despite his renewed vigor, his confidence had fled.

The spider on the left paused. It opened its jaws to unleash a hideous cry, then bent its legs as if ready to pounce.

Kaleth gripped his knives harder. He reached out to sense the spider's energy, searching for anything he could touch with his father's ability.

Before the monster leaped at them, the other one bellowed a shriek of pain. It reared on its hind legs and scrabbled in the air. When it came down, it had pivoted to face the other direction. Kaleth's heart leaped when he spotted a knife sticking into its back. Past the monster, Roselle walked toward them, crouched and holding her other knife in one hand.

"Come here, you bind-cursed bug!" she shouted.

Lainn stood next to her with Donzil just behind. Seven more initiates either stepped out from behind obstacles or dropped from the boundary walls.

Rayd whooped in celebration. Kaleth grinned until noxious breath turned his attention back to the one remaining in front of him. Its front appendages cocked. The other legs contracted.

Kaleth gasped. Like a hidden treasure buried in the earth, he sensed raw energy. It wasn't soft and bright like he had found in vines and weeds. Rather, it was dark and shifting. Hoping it was what he needed, he yanked on the power with his mind.

The spider jerked. Aborting a leap halfway, part of its body lunged while the rest collapsed beneath it. It wailed as if confused and struggled to get its feet back beneath him.

*I did it!* It felt too good to be true, but he didn't let go. Filled with power, speed, and honed senses, he ran along its length, raking his knife across the ineffective legs.

The spider howled. The sluggish jostling of its body grew less pronounced with each sliced appendage. By the time he had cut through all six of the ambulatory limbs, the beast had no fight left.

Kaleth leaped on top of the collapsed monster and finished it with a knife plunged into its brain.

Rayd stared, gaping. He spun between the one Kaleth had killed and the poor beast that was surrounded by ten initiates who all tried to prove themselves to the instructors above. The gang made quick work of the already injured monster.

A scream pulled his attention above him as the trailing ends of black legs disappeared over the edge of the balcony with the spectators. A hideous shriek filled the air, chilling his bones. A guard flailing his arms flew through the air to crumple on the field below. Another flipped grotesquely over the wall, trailing blood from where an arm used to be.

"We need to help them!" Kaleth jumped off his recent kill and landed next to Rayd.

Humming sounds rang in the night, corresponding with a dimming of the mounted binder lamps. Glowing knives in the hands of four Lightbinders closed on the spider. The piercing wails of the monster were quick. When it fell, it tumbled over the edge, landing on the grass in a heap of twisted limbs. The legs twitched for a moment until they grew still. The last of the four mammoth soldier spiders was dead.

## CHAPTER FIFTY-TWO
# HIGHSUMMER'S JUBILEE

The mood in the dining hall was a dramatic shift from the killing field of the Grand Courtyard. Festive bows and flowers decorated the room. People laughed and talked with a merriment that seemed to ignore the horror the initiates had just gone through. Four stringed musicians even sat in a corner, filling the room with a lively tune.

After getting patched up by Carrick, Kaleth and Jovi were the last to find their seats. A white bandage now wrapped around Kaleth's shoulder, under his tunic. Jovi leaned on a crutch as he eased into his place at the table.

"They sure do this up right," Kaleth said.

"It's Highsummer's Jubilee," Jovi said. "And we just lived through the entire training year, including those spider monsters. Two substantial reasons to celebrate."

"They even have the fortress guards here," Kaleth said. "I wonder who's guarding the walls."

"They're supposed to come in shifts," Lainn said. "That way everyone gets to eat."

Dozens of Grunts entered with platters of bread and cheese. They moved through the room, depositing the food on the tables.

"I'm going to eat too much," Jovi said. "I just know it."

The initiates, instructors, and guards around the congested room helped themselves to food. Kaleth grabbed a roll and tore it in half. The flaky insides gave off a puff of steam. *Still warm.* He smiled as he took a bite.

"So, what happened with that last spider you fought?" Lainn asked, looking at him.

Kaleth's muscles tightened. In the chaos of the trial, he had freely used his father's ability without considering who might see him and get suspicious. He swallowed. "What do you mean?"

"It looked slower than the others. Do you think it was sick or something?"

"Hey!" Jovi punched Lainn in the shoulder while biting into a hunk of cheese. "Don't take away from his feat of awesomeness!"

"No, sorry, I didn't mean that. It just looked like it moved slowly."

"Actually, I think you're right." Kaleth forced a chuckle. "It was moving slower than the others. It must have been sick or maybe injured. Otherwise, there was no way I would have been able to do what I did."

Lainn seemed to accept the explanation, allowing Kaleth to blow out his held breath.

The relief at surviving the test was palpable at the initiates' table, but tension still hung over it. All Kaleth could think of was whether or not he'd done enough. Thirteen initiates lived through the trial. Orion, Chyla, and Aarin were all killed by the spiders, two of whom were above him. By default, that would put him ranked twelfth, but he felt good about his performance. It might have been enough to move him up.

A forced clearing of a throat drew his attention to the wall below the stairs. Headmaster Genoris stood with his back to the wall, holding a glass of wine. "Welcome, Lightbinder initiates to the end-of-year feast on Highsummer's Jubilee!"

Cheers and applause filled the room. Kaleth wanted to be excited, but he couldn't shake his suspicion of the headmaster.

"Congratulations to you thirteen for outlasting thirty-seven of your peers."

The grim reminder cast a pall over the crowd.

"The test you faced tonight was your most difficult yet, and even though the trial didn't play out as intended, you all showed incredible bravery and skill. I promise we will ensure the walls are higher next year."

A few chuckles filled the room.

"After tonight's meal, we will announce the top six initiates—the six of you who will receive Lightbinder rings and will continue your training to become the most elite warriors in all of Verdalyn."

The simmering laughs ended, filling the room with a palpable silence. Kaleth's stomach churned in nervous anticipation. The lives of his sister and mother depended on that outcome.

"A year ago, all of you were different people—unskilled, weak, and lacking discipline. But look how you've grown. I'm proud of you all and your hard work. Year two will look different. The remaining top six will learn lightbinding skills here at the academy. Then, you will head to Twainford and join the Blades, Bows, and Menders who left here earlier in the year. But rather than reuniting as the inexperienced initiates you were when you last saw them, they will look at you with awe. The strength of their jealousy will turn their eyes green." He smiled. "Before we bring out the main course in today's feast, I want to unite our schools in a toast—a batch from my own stores. Servers!"

Grunts entered the hall carrying oversized flagons. They spread through the room, pouring a small amount of wine into empty glasses at each seat.

Jovi leaned into the center of their table and whispered, "I hope it's not Kaleth's musk wine."

A Grunt leaned past him, filling his glass, then Jovi's. Kaleth touched the stem and frowned. He couldn't ignore the idea that the wine from earlier was intended to draw the spiders.

Kaleth lifted his glass to his nose and sniffed. To his surprise, it contained a fruity scent, quite different from what had spilled on him.

When all the glasses around the room had wine, Genoris raised his own higher. "To the academy!"

A mumbled echo answered back, "The academy!"

"To the Lightbinders!"

Grins filled the initiates' table as they answered louder than the others, "The Lightbinders!"

"And most importantly—" Genoris' face grew serious. "To Kalshia."

The crowd echoed the name of their kingdom.

The headmaster raised his glass one final time, then took a deep drink. Initiates, instructors, and guards followed his example.

Having grown up on water, milk, and the occasional ale, wine was a new experience for Kaleth. An aroma of cherry and chestnut teased his nose as he raised it to his lips. He sipped, letting the wine roll over his tongue. It was earthy and tasted of honey—not altogether unpleasant. As he swallowed, an odd aftertaste clung to his taste buds. He frowned. *It tastes . . .* He couldn't place it.

Rarely having alcohol at official functions, the instructors, guards, and initiates fully enjoyed the opportunity. Glasses tipped in long swallows. Immoderate doses ended with smacking lips and hearty chortles.

Grunt servers entered the room again but with platters of food instead of drink. They spread through the room, placing food on the tables. Kaleth rolled his tongue around his mouth. It reminded him of the blood in his mouth when Rayd had hit him earlier. *It's almost as if . . .*

A Grunt set a plate of roasted boar in the center of his table. Its savory aroma banished all thoughts of the wine.

"That's what I'm talking about," Jovi said, leaning forward and inhaling.

A bowl of potatoes sat next to one of cooked carrots covered in butter. Kaleth salivated. Distracted by the food, he almost missed Genoris heading up the stairwell. The headmaster looked focused as if he planned to skip the rest of the feast.

Conversation picked up as the meal was laid out. Initiates, instructors, guards, and Grunts alike dove into the food spread across all the tables.

Despite Kaleth's watering mouth, nerves over the impending

ranking announcement killed his appetite. A crinkle in the waist-band of his pants reminded him of the letter he had yet to read. He rose from the table. "Excuse me."

Jovi already had a mouthful of boar. "You're leaving *now?*"

"I'll be back."

He walked to the edge of the room and stepped into the hallway that led to the Chief Mender's office. He caught sight of the other door—the first one that led to the secret underground room. Away from prying eyes, he pulled out the envelope he'd been eager to read. He broke the wax seal and lifted the flap. His mouth pulled into a smile as he unfolded the letter inside, but it faded as he saw the contents. It wasn't Felyra's usual writing about dreams and poetry. She wasn't asking how he was or relating funny stories of animals she'd seen. The letter was only one line, and she didn't even sign her name.

*Kaleth,*

*Beware Highsummer's Jubilee. Stay alive.*

His mind jumped to the spiders. *She's wishing me luck. But how would she have known about that?* It was possible but seemed unlikely. Even if she knew about him being in the academy, she wouldn't know of the test. *If it's not that, then what? Genoris and the wine?* He shook his head.

He strolled back into the main hall, tapping the paper absently. *And why would she not sign her name?* She wouldn't sign if she was worried about the letter being intercepted and traced back to her. That meant she knew something important . . . and secretive. Something important enough to risk warning Kaleth about. She was from Revalle, warning Kaleth. And it was some-thing dangerous enough that could kill him. The pieces came together.

*It wouldn't be about the fear test. She's warning of an attack! An attack on Highsummer's Jubilee!* He scanned the hall, looking for the headmaster. After a second, his brow pinched together. *I don't know that I can trust him.* An unsettled feeling in his gut warned him to be cautious.

Around the room, men and women laughed and drank, gorging on food and wine. The danger from the spiders was a distant memory. The challenge from the previous year was no more. It was even as if everyone had forgotten the killer who had been murdering initiates during the year—the person trying to scare everyone into leaving.

The memory of Genoris heading up the stairs came back to him. *Why did he leave?* It felt odd. He had left in the middle of a celebration—during a party to commemorate the final day of *his* academy. He had even supplied the wine for the toast. The wine that—

The thought blazed in his mind, sending a shudder through his body.

*Copper!*

He felt dizzy. He pressed a hand against the wall to keep upright. The taste reminded him of blood, but also of something else. A rare red mushroom that hinted of honey and left a unique coppery aftertaste.

*A reaper morel.*

Killing initiates. Scaring them off. Likely an instructor. Danger on Highsummer's Jubilee. Reaper morels were rare to find in the wild, but anyone could grow them in a greenhouse.

He shook his head. *No! It can't be Genoris.* The headmaster had been kind since he'd started. Surely he couldn't be a murderer. Kaleth argued with himself but couldn't come up with a better explanation. He forced a laugh. *I'm being silly. Reaper morels are supposed to pass through your body. It wouldn't do anything. There would have to be something to speed up the digestion. But there was nothing that—*

Another dizzy wave rocked him. His breath came in spurts.

*There is something that could do it.*

He ran for the stairs. Still in his seat, Jovi had his glass tipped to his lips. When Kaleth ran past, he smacked the drink away, sloshing its contents on the table.

"Hey!" Jovi shouted.

"Don't drink anymore!" Kaleth yelled without stopping his run. He gestured to the entire table of Lightbinder initiates. "Any of you! No more wine!"

Rayd's appraising eyes followed him.

"Where are you going?" Jovi asked. "Come and eat with us!"

Kaleth ignored his friend and sprinted up the stairs, leaving the feast behind.

## CHAPTER FIFTY-THREE

# ROOFTOP CONFRONTATION

He pulled life from any weeds he passed. His legs strained to run as fast as they could. The wind from him flying down the hall slammed shut a door that had been left ajar.

He skidded to a stop in the binder lift and yanked on the lever. The room shuddered and rose.

*Come on! Come on!*

The lift moved agonizingly slow. He thought of the reaper morel working through his system. He pictured the initiates, instructors, and guards downstairs who had unwittingly ingested it. All it took was a shock of lightning to expedite the poison's efficacy. If that happened, then they would all be dead.

He gasped. *Most of the fortress' potential defenders would be gone, clearing the way for an attack!*

When the binder lift stopped, Kaleth's stomach dropped, not from motion but from the humming noise that hit him from down the corridor. He pulled out his knives and hurried down the hall, treading as quietly as possible. He pushed down the terror of facing a Lightbinder.

The headmaster's office was empty. The lamps were on, and a

cluster of binder orbs sat on his desk, but no one was there. The door to the balcony was open. A crackling sound mixed with the hum coming from outside the door. His nerves heightened the closer he got to the source. He raced out the door and looked down the steps toward the flat part of the roof.

Headmaster Genoris faced away from Kaleth, looking at the large decorative stone. His hands hovered above his head with fingers curled. His thick gray hair stuck out in all directions. Snapping and buzzing sounds filled the air while what looked like miniature bolts of lightning jumped in each direction. The air seemed to shake while the oppressive humming sound made him grit his teeth.

Kaleth started to run down to confront him, but the sparks of lightning grew more intense. They coalesced in a ball above the stone as if directed by the headmaster's hands. The zapping and crackling were so loud and bright that Kaleth held up a hand to block the intensity.

*No! There's no time!*

Lowering his hand, Kaleth squinted while aiming with a dagger. He stepped forward and hurled it at Genoris' ring hand.

It missed.

The knife struck the stone. The impotent spark it gave off and any sound it would have made were lost in the tumult that dominated the roof.

A groan built in Genoris' throat, oblivious to the knife. His hands lifted higher, drawing even more lightning from the stone. It grew somehow brighter and louder. Kaleth's hair prickled all over his body, even at his distance. He lifted his last weapon. Any second, the headmaster would release the charge. In a moment, it would be too late.

Kaleth didn't have time to hesitate. He flung the dagger, then watched as it spun through the air. He didn't dare breathe as if it would throw the blade off course. Everyone in the Jubilee feast below depended on him. After what felt like an eternity, he gasped when the second knife buried itself into the back of Genoris' hand.

"Gah!" the headmaster yelled, audible even over the cacophony.

Without him corralling the lightning, it made its own path. The static charge released into the sky, shooting up with a thundering crack. Kaleth shielded his eyes from the blinding light moments before he was knocked onto his back.

His body ached as he sat up. It took several blinks to clear the residual whiteness from his vision. Everything was quiet. The humming was gone. When he made it back to his feet, he looked down the steps to see the outcome his lucky second throw had achieved.

The ball of lightning was no more. The stone looked like nothing more than a large rock. Having been knocked over, Genoris struggled to stand. He waved his arms for balance. When he stabilized, he stared at the knife that pierced his hand. A quick turn brought his wide eyes to bear on him. "Kaleth? Why did you do that?"

Taken aback by the headmaster's address, Kaleth second-guessed everything. "I—um—I thought . . ." He sputtered as he began down the steps. "What were you doing, sir?"

"I was releasing the lightning." Genoris motioned to his hand. "Why did you do this?"

Kaleth narrowed his eyes. "Now? During the Jubilee feast? You thought this was the best time to do that?"

"I grew worried. It had been so—"

"What about the wine?"

Genoris cocked his head. "The wine?"

"'A batch from your own stores,' huh? You encouraged everyone to drink. If I go through your greenhouse, will I find the reaper morel you used?"

Genoris didn't move. He stared for a long moment, doing nothing but blinking.

"And the spill from earlier. That was on purpose, wasn't it? Meant to draw the spiders to me."

The headmaster's shoulders relaxed, but the tension moved to his face. Keeping his eyes on Kaleth, his free hand wrapped around the hilt of the knife. With a rapid pull, he jerked the weapon free, fighting the wince that followed.

"Kaleth-il-Valorr." His voice had dropped to an eerie tone. "I always had a feeling you'd be trouble."

His suspicions were confirmed. He thought it would be a relief to know, but it only amplified his nerves. "Why do you want everyone dead?"

"So we can get what we need."

"We?"

"Thravia, of course."

"So you're a spy."

"I hardly think that's the right word. Try, Deliverer of—"

"Murder?"

"Justice."

Blood dripped from Genoris' injured hand. He tossed Kaleth's knife to the ground. It settled next to the greenhouse where the other blade lay. In a swift motion, he pulled his own knives. Longer than Kaleth's, they gleamed in the light of the binder lamps.

"What is it Thravia needs?"

"What was taken from us."

"Taken? I thought Thravia took the Soulbinder rings to begin with."

"I'm not talking about rings. Thravia took those in a foolish attempt to stop *him*."

"Him? Him, who?" Kaleth's stomach turned.

Genoris grinned but didn't address the question. "What Thravia *needs* is the return of their Stones."

Kaleth frowned. *Stones?*

Genoris' face turned hard. "And now you've *ruined* it!" Spittle flew from his lips. He looked to the dark sky, checking in multiple directions—agitated.

Kaleth flexed his muscles. They brimmed with energy, ready to spring into action. He glanced around for nearby foliage to draw additional power from, but the rooftop was bare. The greenhouse teemed with life, but it was too far. "Why would you tell me all this? Are you . . . wanting me to join you or something?"

Genoris paced. "I would like that. You're smart and capable—able to do much more than your body implies. But that attempt would be pointless."

A tightness registered in his gut. He pressed against his stomach. "Because you know I'd never do it?"

The headmaster shook his head. "Everyone has a price." He stopped pacing. "What if I offered to save your mother and sister in return for helping me?"

Kaleth gasped. He pictured Sora and his mother bound and held by Jairus' thugs.

"They're being held by the Night Saber in exchange for a debt of gold." With a flick of his wrist, his daggers sprang to life, emitting a metallic thrum. The glow coming from them surrounded his hands, illuminating the green ring on his finger. "I could find him and kill every one of his men. Your mother and sister could walk free, spitting on the corpses of Jairus' men. Or . . . I could give you the gold you need."

Kaleth's eyes widened.

"One hundred, right?" He pointed up the steps. "I have that and more tucked away in my office. How about . . . both?"

The pounding of Kaleth's pulse distorted the headmaster's words. "You'd-you'd give me the gold *and* help them escape?" It was everything he could have dreamed of. All he had worked on for the previous year was his for the taking.

"We're not that different, Kaleth. I told you my parents died when I was fifteen. That was true, but we weren't from Lynharbor. We lived in Highburn."

"Highburn. In Thravia?"

Genoris nodded. "I made ends meet for a couple of years, then I crossed the border and forged papers to enter the academy. Like you, I wasn't the biggest or the strongest, but I worked hard. Let me teach you, Kaleth. We can save your family. You can give them the gold, then I can teach you what it means to be a Lightbinder." He pointed to the glowing knives. "How to do this."

His jaw shook. He tried to answer, but nothing came out. *Would it be wrong? This was all about saving Mother and Sora.* Tears pooled in the corner of each eye. *It's all I want. It's all I want. It's* . . . It wasn't all he wanted. "What about the people below us?"

"What's more important to you? Your family or them?"

A tear ran down his cheek. It took all his effort to shake his head. "No." The word sounded like the croak of a frog. "I can't do it."

Genoris chuckled. He straightened as the glowing daggers returned to normal. "You're a fool."

A stronger pinch tugged at his stomach. "Why did you say it was pointless? You knew I'd never turn on the others?"

"Oh, no. That shocks me, actually. I pictured you kissing my ring and promising me anything. I thought you cared for your family more."

"I do! I—I just can't save them by condemning the others." A queasy feeling ran through him. It turned sharper as if something cut into him. He grimaced and pressed hard against his gut. "Why is it pointless?"

The headmaster stared but didn't speak.

Kaleth tottered. He lifted his arms for balance, trying to combat the dizzy spell and blurred vision that attempted to knock him over. "Gah!" He bent at the waist, wrapping both arms around his stomach. The pain was intense, like needles stabbing into him. The truth of what was happening hit him. He had been so focused on saving the others, he'd forgotten about himself. The hard surface of the roof rushed to meet him.

Genoris strolled to come alongside the prone Kaleth. "While you may have temporarily saved the others, you bathed yourself in the lightning's effect. It was *pointless* to convince you to join me because no one comes back from an activated reaper morel poison."

Pain permeated every part of Kaleth's body. His legs curled toward his chest. He squeezed his eyes shut in a futile attempt to dull the pain.

"It's too bad, Kaleth," Genoris said. "We could have been good together." He resumed his agitated pacing of the roof.

Kaleth racked his brain for anything his father had taught him about reaper morel poison, but he came up blank. He rolled and twisted but nothing helped. He thought of trying to cast a healing glyph, but he'd never get it done in his state.

*Healing!*

What he did have was his father's ability. Hidden amongst the agony, his body hummed with borrowed energy. He didn't need it to fight or run. He needed it to heal. Flexing his gut intensified the pain. He focused all his body's healing power on the poison within his veins. His breath came in spurts. He kept his eyes shut. He sensed his body working hard to fight off the foreign presence that battled within. His arms shook. The effort took all his concentration.

When the pain lessened, he first thought it meant he was dying. Cracking his eyes revealed he was still lying on the roof, but his sight had improved. Encouraged by the progress, he pulled harder on the energy stores, then gasped when he seemed to hit a wall. A gushing wave of exhaustion hit him. He pressed his eyes shut again and gasped to breathe. The pain felt more manageable, but his complete enervation made him panic.

*I need more energy. A lot more. Where can I—*

He craned his neck to find the greenhouse—a mere twenty feet away. Stretching his senses, he failed to connect with the abundant foliage inside. While the agony was momentarily better, it intensified with every second he took. A groan escaped his lips as he pulled his body with his elbows. His legs scraped across the roof. Sharp pains redoubled in his body, so intense he nearly vomited. He worked closer, inch by inch. His lungs felt like they would burst. His pulse grew impossibly fast. Every pull with his arms felt impossible.

Genoris had stopped walking. His head cocked, and he stared at Kaleth.

A hint of life prickled Kaleth's senses. He strained his focus and found energy. It was distant and weak, but it trickled into him. His lungs eased their strain. His pulse settled. *Need more!* He used the newly found strength to move faster. He brought up his knees and crawled. The closer he grew to the greenhouse, the more readily available the energy was.

It refilled him, giving life and strength. After passing through the door, vitality surrounded him. Although he no longer felt fatigued, the debilitating pain in his body persisted. He lay on his back, soaking up as much energy as he could. When he felt he could fit no more, he directed the nearly bursting power toward the poison.

His body shuddered as if being attacked from inside. Discomfort from the attempted healing warred against the pain of the poison. He willed his body to heal. He pressed a hand to his hip as if pressure on his father's glyph would work better. The stabbing sensation lessened until it was a dull ache. He continued. The shaking of his limbs eased. He pushed more. As if breaking past an invisible barrier, the pain was gone.

It took effort to blink his eyes open. When he did, a view of the greenhouse ceiling awaited. He sat up with a start, sucking in air through his nose. The movement caused him to groan. A dull throbbing of soreness covered him. He looked down at himself. No cuts. No wounds. No poison had eaten its way out of his stomach.

Getting to his feet took effort. After standing, the sight of the greenhouse took his breath away. Plants in the closest quarter of the space had turned completely brown. Their fronds and petals had withered and curled as if they had been deprived of water over months.

After absorbing fresh life, his aches and pains were gone. His limbs felt renewed. He stepped out of the greenhouse to find a gawking headmaster.

Genoris stood on the far side of the decorative stone with his eyes open wide. "I knew it." His words were breathy and weak.

Kaleth frowned. He kept his eyes up while bending to retrieve his lost knives. "Knew what?"

"Your strength. Your father. It was the only thing that made sense."

The hair on his neck prickled. "What about my father?"

"Why do you think I trapped you in your room back when you started?"

"That was you?"

"Why do you think I tried to have you killed so many times?"

Kaleth's head spun. "You knew my father?"

"The chance was too great. You were a greater threat than anyone."

Kaleth held up a hand. "Wait! What are you talking about? How am I a threat?"

Genoris' words were little more than a whisper. "Because you're a Forcebinder."

## CHAPTER FIFTY-FOUR

# PROTECTING THE ACADEMY

The unfamiliar word hit him like an anvil. The F on his hip. His secret ability that no one knew about. *It has a name!*

"What does that mean?" Kaleth stepped closer. "What is a Forcebinder? How did I get this?"

Genoris backed away. His eyes grew wider as his knives raised.

Kaleth paused. "You're afraid of me."

"No!" The headmaster straightened. With a metallic hum, his knives glowed again. His arms seemed to be lighter and move quicker. "I'm not afraid." His shaky voice betrayed him. Reaching into a pocket, he pulled out something small, then slid it onto a finger of his right hand. A blue ring reflected the lamplight.

Kaleth sucked in a breath.

While Genoris stepped from behind the large stone, multiple rocks lifted off the rooftop as if pulled by invisible strings. The stones spun while suspended in the air, holding as if waiting on a command. The headmaster waved his glowing knives among the floating stones, showing off both rings.

Kaleth dodged as a rock hurtled toward his face. Narrowly missing him, the projectile crashed through a glass pane of the greenhouse. A large metal watering can sat on the floor. Kaleth snatched it and held it up as a shield.

"Kaleth?"

He spun to the top of the steps where Rayd stood watching them.

"Rayd!" Kaleth shouted. "Go! Warn Aurik! Soulbinders are coming, and Genoris is one of them!"

A projectile crashed into Rayd's face. The initiate cried out and toppled. Kaleth rushed up the steps to his side. A bloody gash ran across his squad leader's cheek.

Rayd's wide eyes turned toward the headmaster. Floating stones hovered, ready to strike.

"Kaleth, this is your chance," Genoris called.

"What?"

"Rayd—your father's killer—no one would know."

Kaleth's sinuses cleared. He looked at the collapsed initiate below him. Injured and fallen, Rayd was vulnerable.

"He ruined your life. He put the rest of your family in danger. He forced you into this place."

Rayd's eyes opened wide.

"You've wanted revenge against him all year. This is your chance. Take it!"

Conflicting emotions raged through Kaleth. He had nearly given up his quest for vengeance, but his squad leader continued to vex him at every turn. The only thing that had held him was fear of jeopardizing his place in the academy.

"Killing him will move you up in the ranks. There will be no repercussions. Don't you want to become a Lightbinder and save your mother and your sister?"

He gripped his knives tighter. Helpless below him, Rayd stared back. Kaleth thought of the abuse he'd endured from the squad leader. His heart pounded.

*No repercussions.*

The temptation was great, but something else stayed his hand. Rayd wasn't *just* the one who destroyed his father's book. He was also someone who was trying to do his best—attempting to please his parents. He was a Kalshian.

"Kaleth," Rayd whispered, holding his hands in front of his face. "Please."

The tension in Kaleth's arms lessened. "I won't kill you, Rayd. You're not the enemy here." He extended a hand.

Rayd blew out a long breath. With Kaleth's help, he made it to his feet.

"We'll both go, but we need to hurry."

A rustling noise caught his attention. Kaleth spun.

An eerie laugh came from Genoris. "Too late, Kaleth-il-Valorr. The time for warning has passed."

The sound seemed to come from multiple directions. He peered into the night, but all he found was blackness. He stepped toward the edge of the balcony, squinting at a trick of light. A strange object grew closer. *Is it a bird?* His mind reeled, growing more confused as the flying mystery came more into focus.

"What is that?" Rayd breathed.

It was a wooden platform, eight feet squared with something covering it. It looked like gray boulders or piles of laundry. When it drew closer to the balcony, the platform lowered until it settled to a stop.

After what Kaleth had experienced from his father's ability and lightbinding, he didn't bat an eye at the impossibility of a flying object. His muscles were primed and ready to act. He stepped forward, trying to get a better understanding of what had just landed.

The gray objects moved, and nine bodies rose from crouched positions. They wore similar gray-and-yellow uniforms except with differing patches on their chests. Some patches had crossed swords while others displayed an elaborate "S".

*Soulbinders!*

Felyra tensed when she looked up. Unsure if she would even run into him or not, Kaleth was the first person she saw. He stood with Rayd—the rude one from Fairdre—and held a knife and a metal can out in defense. They backed up until a stone wall stopped them. An older man in a Lightbinder uniform seemed relaxed at their arrival.

The fighters on her ascender stepped out to the balcony as the other three shuttles arrived—one next to theirs and the other two near what looked like a greenhouse.

Celedar approached the Lightbinder. "Genoris, is everything ready?"

"They're still alive," the man named Genoris said.

"Who's alive?"

"Everyone. They're in the dining room."

Celedar's face turned hard.

"I thought you said you could kill them?!" Janduan stepped forward. "We were supposed to only face two Lightbinders!"

"How many are there?" Celedar asked.

"In Central Tower? Fully trained?" Genoris said. "Nine."

"Bind me!" Janduan threw up his arms and paced.

"And what about the others?" Celedar asked.

"Around, um . . ." The Lightbinder wouldn't look him in the face. ". . . thirty Blade guards and another ten initiates."

Janduan turned to Baloran. "I told you we couldn't trust him."

"We can still take them," Genoris said. "How many did you bring?"

"Eight Soulbinders, and twenty-eight infantry," Celedar confirmed.

"That's it?"

"They were all supposed to be dead!" Janduan shouted.

"Well, that makes nine Soulbinders including me," Genoris said. "We have the element of surprise, Celedar. Our numbers are about the same, but no one down there knows you're coming. They're gorging themselves on wine and meat right now."

Celedar, Janduan, and Baloran exchanged a tense look.

"If they're on alert, this will be futile," Celedar said.

"I'm positive. They have no idea."

He looked toward Kaleth. "And what about those two?"

"Initiates. They're no one. You can kill them now."

Felyra felt the blood drain from her face.

Celedar nodded toward her group. The others she had flown with snapped into action while she lingered toward the back of the crowd. She pulled Ruane to linger with her. "That's him," she whispered.

Ruane frowned. "What? Who?"

Felyra didn't speak, but tried to communicate through the intensity of her gaze.

Her friend's eyes opened wide. "Kaleth? What?! You never said he was—"

"Shh! Don't say anything." She pulled her hood farther forward.

Dropping his can and pulling out a second dagger, Kaleth moved faster than she expected. He dodged the Thravian swords, knocking them away, spinning and jabbing at successive attackers. Not only did he protect himself, but he assisted Rayd, who appeared sluggish in comparison. Kaleth alternated between striking down his own assailants and picking off Rayd's. Each time one of her fellow Thravians fell, she felt a mixture of dismay and relief.

After ten fighters had fallen, Janduan shouted, "Enough!" The Thravian infantry halted. He pointed at Genoris. "Have him do it."

The headmaster scowled. "You don't trust me, Janduan. After all I've done?"

"We don't know what you've done. Prove you're one of us."

He looked at Celedar, who nodded in approval.


KALETH GLANCED toward the door to the office, but Thravian soldiers had already blocked the escape. His heart pounded. They were surrounded. He didn't even try to fight the fear that surged through him. But he also didn't let it stop him.

Genoris took his time climbing the stairs. When his knives burst with light, the Thravian soldiers near him muttered to each other, shifting their hips. The headmaster seemed to notice their unease, and the glowing light dimmed as floating stones gathered before him.

"Sorry, Kaleth," Genoris said. "You had your chance."

Kaleth picked his metal can back up as if the small object could help him defeat the most powerful enemy in all of Kalshia. A rock hurtled at his face. Processing its movement with his rapid brain, he jabbed the bulbous can in its path. It hit the metal with a deep thunk, shaking his hand before the stone fell to the roof. The impact dented his shield.

Genoris' eyes narrowed as multiple stones leaped into action. Several came at Kaleth and a few toward Rayd.

Kaleth's mind whirred. His arms flew. His body and limbs jerked to dodge what he could. Metallic thunks peppered the air as he used the can as a shield to knock away rock after rock. The ones headed toward his squad leader took more effort, but jabbing the can took them out, one by one.

Rayd shrank under the onslaught, covering his head with his arms.

Careening stones fell into the crowd of onlookers.

After sending a barrage of projectiles, the headmaster bellowed a frustrated grunt. Kaleth inspected his can. It was mangled after the salvo of stones. Part of the metal had even torn open.

"Is this a game, Genoris?" the one named Janduan asked.

His knives glowed brighter, taking more of the surrounding light from the binder lamps. The reduction cast a shadow across the rooftop, but Genoris charged forward. Kaleth dropped the can and barely got his knives up in time. The headmaster moved as fast as a snake, jabbing with infused blades that seemed to move of their own will. Kaleth struggled to keep up, even with his extra energy. He dodged and blocked, spinning away from jabs and ducking under slashes.

While the headmaster was devastatingly fast, he wasn't powerful. With Kaleth's muscles as strong as iron, stopping each strike was like batting a frenetic fly with a stone paddle. A blade nicked his arm, drawing a wince.

Rayd stood ready with knives of his own, but the headmaster ignored him. The squad leader feinted in and out as if deciding whether to attack. When he attempted a thrust toward Genoris' body, the headmaster knocked it away with an arm block. Spinning, he jabbed a glowing blade into Rayd's upper arm.

The squad leader cried out and dropped one of his knives. He grabbed his arm with his other hand while stumbling backward.

With the headmaster facing Rayd, Kaleth jabbed at the man's side, where the leather jacket stopped. Genoris was quick but late. The tip of Kaleth's knife cut into flesh, not deep, but enough to open a gash and start a steady flow of blood down his leg.

"Enough of this!" Celedar called. "The longer we wait, the more at risk we are of them being alerted. You finish him; we'll ambush the group below."

Soulbinders and Thravian soldiers rushed through the doorway into Genoris' office. Wary eyes watched Kaleth, but they kept their distance.

"Gotta—warn them," Rayd said, wincing through pain.

Kaleth nodded. While the Soulbinders continued their stream into the office and Genoris held the wound on his hip from a distance, Kaleth stepped toward the edge of the balcony.

"What are you doing?" Genoris asked.

Kaleth leaned toward the edge and looked over. It was a long way down to the paved stones in the corridor outside Central Tower. "Hey, Soulbinders!" he called.

Celedar peeked out of the office doorway while the Thravian force slowed.

"And what are you going to do if you lose the element of surprise?"

The Soulbinder frowned. "If we . . . what do you mean?"

Kaleth looked to Genoris. Deep furrows cut into the headmaster's brow. "What are you going to do?"

Kaleth reached into his jacket and pulled out the fist-sized ball from Genoris' desk. It was hard, like metal, but it hummed with a simmering energy inside.

Genoris' eyes opened impossibly wide. He rushed forward, lunging toward the object with his hands outstretched. Before he arrived to snatch it away, Kaleth tossed it over the side of the balcony.

"No!" Genoris shouted.

Everyone on the balcony stood for several agonizing seconds.

When the binder orb exploded, a deep rumble shook the air, unlike anything Kaleth had heard before. The balcony trembled.

While Genoris stood frozen like a statue, Kaleth looked back over the edge. The first person outside was Aurik. With glowing knives at the ready, he glanced in each direction before finally looking up.

Kaleth waved an arm, then yelled down, "Soulbinders are here! We're under attack!"

A hush fell over the soldiers on the roof. Their original plan had been ruined. Their backup surprise attack was thwarted.

"Back to your shuttles!" Celedar called, waving the Thravians out of the office. "Full retreat."

"N-No!" Genoris spluttered. "We can do this. I—I—"

The Soulbinders paid him no more mind as they pushed their way out of the narrow office doorway and returned to their wooden platforms.

Genoris' chest heaved as he took in the sight of the Thravians running past them to leave. When his eyes turned toward Kaleth, they simmered with a renewed fury. "You ruined everything!" Ignoring the wound in his side and the blood dripping down his hand, he surged forward with raised knives.

Kaleth tried to keep out of range but kept bumping into Thravians. He alternated his attention between Genoris and the enemy infantry, even though they seemed focused on fleeing.

After backing into a hooded Thravian, Kaleth wrapped an arm around their neck and pulled their body in front of his. It was a woman, strong but lithe. She lifted her sword to fight back, but Kaleth kicked it out of her hand.

"Stay back!" he shouted at Genoris. He raised a knife to his captive's neck, pressing it against the gray hood. With him blocking the doorway to the office, most of the Thravian force paused inside the tower, trapped.

Janduan roared with laughter from where he had returned to a platform. "Good luck with that threat, Kalshian. She's trying to be a Soulbinder. If you put her out of her misery, we'll all thank you."

Kaleth ignored the man. He counted the seconds in his head,

hoping the delay would be enough time for the Lightbinders to get up the tower.

Genoris' narrowed eyes didn't flinch. "You think threatening one soldier will stop us? We will sacrifice hundreds, even thousands, to get what we need."

"You're already stopped, Genoris. The Kalshians below will live, and Thravia doesn't get whatever they're trying to steal."

The woman in his grasp jerked her head, trying to slam it into his. Through his tight grip, he avoided the danger. Her arms pulled against his, but he worked the dagger around the hood, pressing it into the soft flesh of her neck. The Thravian soldier sucked in a breath and stilled.

"We may not win today, but we will," Genoris growled.

"Not you, though," Kaleth argued. "You're done. You'll stand trial as a traitor and will be executed."

He shook his head. "No, I won't."

Genoris' confidence gave Kaleth pause.

"You won't tell Aurik or the others about my involvement. We were all ambushed up here: you, me"—his eyes flicked to Rayd—"and your unfortunate squad leader who died in the fight."

Rayd tensed as Genoris stepped closer.

"You need me alive, Kaleth."

"I don't need you!"

Genoris lowered his chin and lifted his eyebrows. "You have . . . questions, don't you? Questions that need answers."

In the fracas, he'd forgotten about it. *Forcebinder. Father's secret. The tattoo. Where did it come from? How did it work?* He had so many questions, and Genoris was the only one who might answer them.

"You want to know what I know."

"No!" He belted it in a deep voice. It turned the heads of the Thravians who were getting into position on their platforms. "I will not let my squad leader die, and I will not let you get away with this."

He adjusted his grip on his hostage, causing her hood to slip. He looked at her neck to ensure the tip of his knife was secure. "Kalshia needs to know what—"

Words failed him. He tried to speak, but the breath had been sucked from his lungs. He stared at the partially visible chin of his captive—a chin of olive skin. A chin with a white scar. A face he had spent hours cleaning and watching while its bearer slept. Curly black hair peeked out from the hood. His arm went numb. The iron grip he'd maintained crumbled. He pulled the dagger away and flipped her hood down. She angled her head away until Kaleth grabbed both shoulders and spun her toward him. His gasp shattered the silence.

Felyra's vivid green eyes looked anywhere but at him.

His legs wobbled. Trying to speak was impossible. His jaw only wavered. After the shock of seeing her faded, his reaction jumped from shame to anger. He had never told her who he was, but it seemed she already knew.

*Was she a spy all along?*

With his focus distracted, Thravians who had been trapped in the tower fled to their platforms.

Free of his grasp, Felyra backpedaled. "I'm sorry, Kaleth. I should have—" She never finished her sentence.

Lost in staring after her, Kaleth was gutted and oblivious to the rest of the world. He felt numb and lethargic. It was almost too late when the massive object registered in his peripheral. The decorative stone beside the greenhouse no longer rested inert. It didn't hum with lightning, but it did hurtle through the air toward him. Dropping onto the balcony, he flattened his body as well as he could. The bottom of the stone grazed his jacket but failed to crush him. Having missed, it knocked into a retreating Thravian, hurtling itself and the body off the side of the tower. Taken over by gravity, both objects arced toward the ground, ready to pulverize whatever lay below.

Genoris' rage-filled attack followed the flying stone. Kaleth jumped to his feet as the barreling headmaster crashed into him. He blocked an arm, preventing a glowing knife from skewering his side. The headmaster attempted to get behind him, but Kaleth pivoted.

The trickling Thravians steered clear of the fight. They hurried around the men and continued loading up their platforms. Rayd tottered, gripping his wound. His loss of blood had turned his face white. Fresh shouts echoed through Genoris' office, on the far side of the clogged doorway. The Lightbinders were coming.

Attempting a thrust of his own, Kaleth's attack was blocked by a quick move from Genoris. As if operating from muscle memory, he fell into the rehearsed Circle of Thrusts. He hooked his knife in a loop and cleared the headmaster's weaker arm. A rapid slash drew a red gash across the man's arm. Genoris cried out and jumped back, causing Kaleth's circle thrust to fall short. Rather than allow that to be it, he adjusted his measure, taking a short step forward. With both of his opponent's hands low, Kaleth executed the final move. The quick jab dug into the meat of the headmaster's neck. The wet, fleshy squelch turned his stomach.

Blood squirted onto the balcony. Genoris staggered backward and dropped his knives. One hand pressed against his neck, but the streaming red stain continued down his body. "Kaleth," he gurgled. One arm wobbled out for balance. "You're a good kid. Too bad—" The headmaster staggered, then blinked hard as if trying to clear the encroaching death. Blood dribbled down his chin. "Too bad you're on the wrong side."

Genoris didn't cry out when his legs hit the low railing or when his body continued over the side. The headmaster fell into the darkness.


"Let's go!" Celedar shouted.

Felyra stood next to her ascender but hadn't gotten into position yet. She stared after Kaleth, filled with a mixture of sorrow and guilt.

Something new caught her eye through the congested tower door. Glowing objects backlit the remaining Thravian fighters still pushing through the doorway. Shouts filled the air. Steel clanged. Someone tripped—no—was pushed. The Thravian stumbled forward, knocking into Headmaster Baloran. Both fell to the floor. The fighter's hood fell back. Felyra gasped. It was Ruane. Grax jumped over her prone body, running for the closest ascender.

Lightbinders surged onto the balcony. Some had dual knives, and some used a short sword in one hand. Ruane and Baloran struggled to rise.

"Take off!" Janduan yelled from his huddled position at the far end of his half-filled platform.

"No!" Felyra jumped off the ascender just as it lifted.

"Hold the shuttles!" Celedar shouted.

Felyra ran toward Ruane and the headmaster. She lifted her sword as a glowing blade lowered toward her friend's head. The blow almost ripped the weapon from her hand. She held on. Despite the ferocity with which the Kalshian attacked, she placed herself between him and the fallen Thravians. "Get up! Go!" she shouted over her shoulder.

The Lightbinder's short sword danced through the air. Its moves were too fast for her to process, so all she could do was guess in which direction it would flow. After a lucky series of correct guesses, the man paused to catch his breath.

Scrabbling feet sounded behind her. She risked a glance to see Baloran and Ruane back on their feet. Ruane limped. Supported by the headmaster, they both hurried toward the closest ascender. "Felyra, come on!" she yelled.

*They need more time!*

Two Lightbinders took the one's place. Their grim visages turned her blood cold. *I can't take them.* Despite the impossible odds, she lifted her sword and bared her teeth. The display seemed to give them a moment of pause because they hesitated in their attack.

"Felyra!" The shout came from Baloran. "Now!"

The firm command got through. Trusting the headmaster, she turned and ran. The ascenders hovered off the balcony. Footsteps echoed behind her as the Lightbinders closed. Her hip tweaked, sending a spark of pain shooting up the side of her body. She kept her feet under her, pumping her legs as fast as she could. The floating platform had moved past the safety of the balcony. If she missed her shot, she would be trapped with the Lightbinders. She would be dead. Pushing off the railing with one foot, she leaped into the air. Her hair trailed behind her. A glimpse of the drop below her turned her stomach. The ascender was too far.

*I won't make it!*

She slammed into the side and wrapped her arms around the railing. Her chin scraped. The collision against her stomach knocked her breath away. The impact jostled the delicate stability of the platform. It tipped. The jolted Thravians shouted and raised hands for balance.

Felyra held on tight as her legs dangled over the open air. She gritted her teeth and held on. When the equilibrium resettled, Ruane grasped her arm. Both of them pulled, straining and grunting. After a terrifying struggle, she rolled onto the ascender.

She panted and looked back at the tower balcony. She was safe. The charging Lightbinders stopped at the edge, just out of reach. But she didn't look at them. Past their shoulders, Kaleth's wounded blue eyes held hers. His shoulders slumped. She knew exactly what he should be feeling—betrayed and hurt. She was the enemy.

*But so is he.*

As her shuttle dropped into the night, his lips pulled up in an ironic smile—one that matched her own feelings.

## CHAPTER FIFTY-FIVE
# THE FINAL CUTS

Kaleth exited the crammed binder lift, spilling into the hallway with the guards he'd ridden with. He stumbled down the hallway in a stupor. The corridor spun, but he managed to walk a straight line.

*Felyra.*

He couldn't get her out of his mind. Why did she send a warning letter? Had it been planned from the beginning? Was saving him in the river a calculated plot? Did she sell herself into slavery as a trap to gain his confidence? He chuckled and shook his head.

*That's ridiculous.*

She was a girl. A girl he randomly ran into. A girl who happened to be in training to become his mortal enemy.

*What would Mother and Father think?*

The thought of his father brought the other blast of information to his mind.

*Forcebinder.*

The F glyph on his hip. His father's secret. It had a name, and others knew about it. The thought both terrified and encouraged him.

Everyone related to the academy already filled the dining hall as Kaleth descended the grand staircase. The fortress guards had left, but the instructors, trainers, and initiates remained. They all spoke in loud rumbling groups, flustered by the recent chaos. He spotted Rayd's father talking with other men, but neither Jairus nor Kaleth's family were anywhere to be seen.

He caught sight of Jovi. His friend jumped out of the gaggle of initiates and ran toward him. "Kaleth! You're all right! *Are* you all right?"

"I'm fin—"

"I choked on my food when that binder orb went off. What happened?"

Kaleth opened his mouth to speak, but Jovi cut him off.

"We heard Genoris is a traitor and an army of Soulbinders showed up. I expected something like this would happen. Did you really kill every one of them?"

"No, I didn't ki—"

"The Menders took Rayd to bandage him up. He was pretty out of it but said you saved everyone. You. Kaleth. You saved us. Is that true?" His friend stopped talking.

*Saved everyone.* "Jovi, I'm exhausted. I've been answering questions for the last hour."

Jovi raised his eyebrows higher, still waiting for the answer.

Kaleth huffed a laugh. "Um . . . yeah, I guess it's true. Kind of."

Jovi grinned. "What were they doing? Trying to kill everyone?"

"No. Well . . . Genoris tried to kill everyone with the poisoned wine. The Thravians were here to take something. He mentioned something about the return of Stones."

"Stones?"

Kaleth shrugged. "He didn't explain, but the Thravians were only expecting two Lightbinders." He leaned closer and lowered his voice. "Where can you think of that has two Lightbinders who *weren't* at the feast?"

Jovi's eyes grew wider.

"That's right. I think the Thravians were here to steal whatever is in that jungle room down all those steps."

"Did you tell Aurik?"

"He waved it off. I think he knew but didn't want to say anything."

Jovi nodded until his face snapped into a huge smile. "Oh, yeah! I've got some other good news for you."

His friend was cut off by Principal Aurik clapping his hands together. The buzzing crowd quieted. Aurik stood at the front of the room while everyone took seats.

A bandaged Rayd rounded the corner and caught Kaleth's eye. The squad leader nodded as if recognizing what Kaleth had done for him. Seeing the antagonistic squad leader acknowledge his actions caused the corner of his mouth to rise. He nodded back.

"It's been an eventful night," Aurik said.

Nervous laughs peppered the room.

"Not only did the last test not go as planned, but it seems our late headmaster was a spy, working with Thravia. Thankfully, his actions were thwarted by the presence of Rayd-il-Stonne and the quick thinking of Kaleth-il-Valorr."

Hoots and claps surrounded him. Kaleth's neck turned red as initiates slapped him on the back. While he relished the appreciation, none of it mattered unless he was able to move up to sixth in the rankings.

"While I'm sure you all are tired, we have one more topic to discuss. Your year is finished. The tests are complete. Rankings are finalized. It's time to reveal the final Lightbinder appointments." He opened a hinge on a wooden box. Inside, six rings with green gems gleamed.

Kaleth's gut twisted. He winced. It could have been a lingering effect of the activated poison, but more likely, it was nerves.

"Ranked sixth, we welcome Jovi Strapper to our ranks."

Kaleth's nerves evaporated as pride surged through him. He grabbed his friend's shoulders and shook. "Congratulations!" Claps and cheers filled the room.

Jovi's mouth hung limp. A beaming smile had taken over his face.

"I expected this would happen," a grinning Kaleth said over the applause.

Jovi stood and walked to the front, where the principal slid a green ring on his finger.

"Fifth is Rayd-il-Stonne."

The applause lessened like a sail deflating after losing the wind. Mutters rumbled around the room. Kaleth had figured the squad leader would end up higher, although his performance at the last test and up on the tower couldn't have helped.

"Congrats," Kaleth grudgingly whispered as his squad leader passed by him to receive his ring.

Rayd's father stared with crossed arms from the front of the room. His judgmental smirk indicated a mixture of feelings.

"Fourth is another from Dragon Squad: Roselle-el-Pelim."

After a fleeting moment of hope at recognizing his squad, Kaleth sighed. He offered compulsory applause, but his heart ached. With each name called, his hope of making it grew increasingly impossible. He was about to be cut. His mother and sister were about to die.

"From Iron Squad, third is Torrek-il-Valrec."

An obvious choice. Torrek had been near the top all year. The muscle-bound young man sauntered to the front of the room and thrust his splayed fingers before the principal.

"Bromar-il-Rone leads Claw and takes slot number two."

The name was expected. Everyone knew Bromar should make it. He was a beast and led every activity they'd performed. Kaleth prepared for the inevitable death sentence of his family to be proclaimed with the next name. Jairus wouldn't care that he had single-handedly saved everyone's life there. All he cared about was the money owed.

"And for single-handedly saving the life of everyone in this room . . ."

Kaleth's ears perked.

"For demonstrating bravery and skill beyond anything we've seen in the final test. For making such a dramatic improvement during the year, I'm proud to announce our number-one initiate and future Lightbinder: Kaleth-il-Valorr!"

Kaleth tried to breathe, but his lungs wouldn't work. He had heard the words, but his brain had trouble making sense. A ringing filled his ears. He was aware of applause, but it all sounded muddled. His head wobbled, flung by an enthusiastic shaking of his body from Lainn. He could no longer see the rest of the room because everyone stood. As the ringing and muffled effect faded, the roaring applause registered. He lifted a meek hand and mouthed "thank you." He stood and walked to the front of the room.

Aurik's proud grin helped him feel at ease. The principal held up the last ring and nodded toward Kaleth's hand. Cold and heavy, the ring slid on his middle digit. With numb steps, he walked to the far end of the line of inductees.

Roselle clapped him on the back. "Congrats."

An unsmiling Rayd nodded—as positive an interaction as Kaleth could hope for from the antagonistic leader.

Jovi jumped out of line and wrapped him in a hug. "You did it! I always knew you could."

His friend's tight embrace allowed the stress and fear that had dominated his life for the previous year to trickle away. He gripped back, savoring the safety and celebrating the victory.

Once the applause settled, Aurik continued, "You six make up our next Lightbinder class. After your hard-earned two-week break, we'll teach you how to use those rings."

When the ceremony ended, the new Lightbinders all turned to congratulate each other. Jovi had other plans, though. He grabbed Kaleth's arm and pulled. "Come on!"

"What? Where are we going?"

Jovi ran out the door of Central Tower and headed toward the Grand Courtyard. Memories of giant spiders sent a shiver up Kaleth's spine, but the wide grin on his friend's face eased any fear. Jovi jogged toward the doors that had led to their test.

"What are we doing?"

Jovi opened the door, letting Kaleth go first. "There's something you need to see."

When Kaleth entered the arena, the stench of death made him cover his nose. Four large spider carcasses dominated the scene. Despite their legs curled in death, he eyed the closest one with wary attention.

Jovi stepped around a monster and led him to an armless corpse of a man who lay on his chest with his head facing away. The body had been tossed from the wall—a short man with a bald head. His neck was a mangled mess, bloody and torn from what was likely a skewering spider leg. The site of the missing arm marked a large bloody patch on the grass. He spotted a black beard pressed into the ground.

Kaleth stepped closer, not daring to breathe. He grabbed a lifeless arm and tugged it to the other side, flipping the corpse. The scarred ear confirmed it. Jairus, the Night Saber, the man who had threatened to kill his family, was dead. A quick laugh escaped his mouth.

Jovi grinned. "It's him, isn't it?"

Kaleth nodded. His body felt numb. *Could this be true? What will it mean?*

Shuffling feet made him look up. Jairus' two goons entered the courtyard from a door on the opposite wall with a stretcher carried between them. They paused at the sight of him. The man who had held the crossbow said. "We were looking for you."

Kaleth stiffened and lifted his chin.

"I saw what you did. What you were capable of." The man's voice trembled. He glanced at his partner before turning back to Kaleth. "Your mother and sister will be released. Your debt is waived."

The cascade of good news was almost too much. The light feeling he'd had for the last few minutes escalated to a new level. *Lightbinder. Seventy-five gold bonus.* Now the man who started it all was dead and his family was free.

The man nodded his head behind him. "They're back in the corridor."

Kaleth ran. He tore across the grassy courtyard, then burst through the indicated door. A passage through the Kalistor fortress lay beyond. His sister jumped at the intrusion. Her hair was matted, and dirt marred her cheeks. His mother sat. Eager eyes showed a desire to stand, but she remained on the ground.

"Kaleth!" Sora cried. A smile covered her face.

He ran to them and crouched next to his mother. Sora kneeled and the three of them shared a vigorous hug. Their bony limbs pressed against him, shaking as they wrapped him up. His mother and sister both shed tears of relief. Kaleth joined them. The hard work, blood, and sweat he'd given over the previous year had all paid off. His family was safe.

"He says you're free," Kaleth said. "The debt is paid."

"We heard," Sora confirmed, wiping her eyes. "What took you so long? I'm sure Jovi would have freed us by the morning at the latest." Her playful wink proved she was feeling better.

"And now we're rich."

His mother's forehead creased. "What do you mean?"

A grin covered his face. "I made Lightbinder."

THEIR RACE to the Lagrash River was nothing short of exhausting. Felyra's legs and hip complained the entire way. They barely stopped to breathe, much less eat or sleep. Janduan barked at them whenever someone stumbled or slowed. The enemy knew where they were, and they would be in hot pursuit.

Splashing across the river was much less stealthy than the previous fording. A company of Soulbinders and infantry from Twainford greeted them on the far side. When their group finally stopped, Felyra collapsed, letting her body become one with the ground and her back with a dead tree trunk.

Baloran, Janduan, and Celedar stepped aside to speak with the fresh Soulbinders, leaving the initiates from Soulbinder Academy clumped together in a bedraggled group.

Felyra sucked in several breaths and dropped her head between her legs. A braced hand kept her from falling over. When her pulse settled, she looked up. The other initiates seemed in the same shape, but the number shocked her. They had been so busy running that she hadn't checked. Only five of the initial twelve initiates remained. A hard lump formed in her throat. Kaleth had killed the others.

*He was just defending his kingdom. That was his job—just like mine would be in the same situation.*

Ruane leaned forward to whisper in her ear. "Your boyfriend seems like a handful."

Felyra tensed, but her friend's curling smile set her at ease.

"Relax. I won't say anything. You should have told me, though."

"I was hoping he wouldn't be there."

"I take it from his reaction that he *didn't* know about you."

She shook her head.

"How do you think he's gonna take it?"

"I don't know. He might think I was using him."

Ruane nodded for a long moment. "Well, I'm glad I could confirm one thing."

"What?"

"He *is* cute."

Shuffling feet lifted her gaze as Headmaster Baloran approached. "Felyra, come with me a moment."

The command made her groan—not at talking with Baloran but for having to get off the ground. After she made it to her feet, they walked to the edge of the river.

"Nice job back in Kalistor."

Her neck grew hot. Sarcasm wasn't the headmaster's style. "I'm sorry, sir."

He frowned. "What do you mean?"

"I let that Kalshian hold me hostage. I should have been more careful."

He chuckled. "I wasn't talking about that. That could have happened to anyone. Plus, he was as quick as any fighter I've seen." He cocked his head as if an idea had just come to him. "Did he know you?"

She held her breath. It took a concerted effort to shake her head, then croak out, "No, he couldn't have. Must have thought I was someone else."

Baloran nodded, seeming content. "I was speaking of coming back for Ruane and me. You were the only one to help."

"Oh."

"And the way you held off that Lightbinder. That was impressive."

A smile fought its way onto her face.

"Anyway . . . I wanted to thank you before we headed back to Revalle."

A pit formed in her stomach. She had been dreading when she had to split from Ruane and everyone else. "So, from here . . . do I head to Twainford with the others?"

"We had twelve finalists. We were planning to choose *six* Soulbinders from the group. We do have six rings allotted."

His emphasis on *six* sent tingles through her body. She glanced back at the five remaining initiates of their class. *Don't let yourself hope. Don't get carried away.* It was too late. Her hopes were as high as the tower they'd just flown to.

"I think we made a mistake in sending you off. I'd like to reconsider and offer you a spot as one of our newest Soulbinders."

Her heart stopped. She looked at him with wide eyes and fought to not gape. After a brief pause, she nodded. "Yes." The word was little more than a rasp. She cleared her throat. "Yes, I accept."


KALETH SAT on the stairs with his arms draped over his knees and his hands clasped. His foot bounced incessantly. Three of their new Lightbinder group had already taken turns entering Carrick's office. They each were inside for around twenty minutes before they left. Each time, the ones still in line peppered them with questions, but the finished initiates said nothing. Not knowing what was coming created a tense mood that left even Jovi speechless.

When the door opened, Kaleth looked over. Rayd exited without making eye contact or speaking. The anticipation had grown, and now he was next. Aurik stood at the open doorway and motioned for Kaleth to enter. He nodded at Jovi beside him, then rose and stepped into the room.

Kaleth had been in the Chief Mender's office before, but everything felt darker and more ominous. Carrick sat in a chair with a table of bottles and needles next to him. Aurik took a stool and motioned for Kaleth to sit in the one next to the Mender.

"Let us see your hip," Aurik said with a blank face.

Kaleth's throat constricted. "My—my hip?" *How do they know about my secret?* His pulse raced. His throat felt dry.

"Yes, please pull your pants down, just on one side."

Realizing he may be safe, he lowered the hem of his pants on the side without the Forcebinder tattoo.

Carrick inspected the skin. "That will work." He unstoppered a bottle.

"Lightbinders have secrets, ones you must guard at all costs," Aurik said. "Do you promise to uphold this secrecy and keep safe the knowledge entrusted to you?"

Kaleth nodded. "I do."

Aurik nodded at the Mender.

"This will sting a bit," Carrick said. He picked up a needle and dipped it into the bottle.

*Ink. He's giving me a tattoo! Is it what I already have?*

The Mender got to work, pricking the skin to deliver ink just below the surface. He paused occasionally to wipe away blood.

Kaleth cringed from the low-level pain as the man worked, but it was much easier than doing it himself. Carrick started with a circle, then worked on intersecting curved lines. So far, it was identical to the glyph Kaleth had cast himself.

When the lines were finished, he held his breath. *Is he finishing with an F?* Carrick began a vertical line as if confirming his theory. He wasn't sure which he felt stronger: relief over the familiarity or disappointment at it not being something new.

When Carrick had finished the vertical line, Kaleth nearly gasped. The man didn't return to form the top line of the F. He continued along the bottom. *Is he making it in reverse? Or upside-down reverse?* Kaleth frowned as the man worked. It wasn't until the Mender wiped off the final bead of blood and leaned back in his chair that Kaleth realized what had happened.

It wasn't another F for Forcebinder. *Of course.* He felt stupid for not seeing it coming. It was identical to what he had—same circle and same lines—but the center contained an L.

*Lightbinder.*


FELYRA TOOK her time ascending the steps inside Soulbinder Academy. It felt good to be back. The familiarity comforted her. Their group had rested at Twainford for two days before the six Soulbinder initiates continued back to Revalle.

Her hips were tired. She longed to remove her pack and rest. No longer staying in the large bunk room, the remaining initiates had been assigned smaller single rooms.

When she tossed her pack on the clean bed, paper crumpled.

"What was that?" Ruane asked, peering around the door frame.

Felyra rolled her pack over and held her breath. An envelope with her name on it waited on the mattress.

"Is it him?"

Felyra picked up the envelope with a trembling hand. She stared at it for a long moment.

"Open it!"

She looked at her friend. "What will he say?"

"You'll find out when you *open* it."

"He's going to hate me."

Ruane paused. "You don't know that." The hesitation and soft words spoke volumes.

Felyra ripped open the envelope and pulled out the letter.

*Felyra,*

Not "Silvertail," but her actual name. *Not a good sign.*

*You lied to me—*

"He hates me. I just know it!"

Ruane pointed at the paper. "Just *read* it!"

*You lied to me. I lied to you, too, and for that, I'm sorry. I never intended to deceive you. I kept back some of who I was because I didn't want to scare you. I have no hatred for you or even Thravia. As I told you, I was here to pay off a debt, which is now complete.*

*My mind ran through so many scenarios around our meetings. The mountains. The river. The slave auction. Did you orchestrate it? Was I your target all along? I don't think so, otherwise, why would you warn me about the attack. The only explanation I can come up with is that every-thing between us—between just you and me—was real. The letters. The feelings. I meant them all, and I think you did too.*

*Is this impossible? We come from opposite worlds—each other's sworn enemies, set on impractical paths that could never end well. If we can't do this, tell me now, and I will leave it behind. I will give it up.*

*But maybe we can. Surely we can't be the first Lightbinder and Soul-binder to fall for each other.*

*Kaleth*

Felyra lowered the letter. Her mouth remained cracked as she stared without focus, out the window.

"What did he say?" Ruane asked. "Does he hate you? Was it all a trick? Was he using you to get information? What?"

A laugh escaped her mouth. "He said—" She turned to her friend and felt the smile taking over her face. "He said he's falling for me."

THE CLUNK from his boots echoed off the stone walls. Commander Brigador walked with purpose, masking the fear that he couldn't show. He spotted the instructors outside of Central Hall, talking as if they had no worries other than what the weather may bring.

"Aurik!" he bellowed.

The Lightbinder principal jerked to attention and looked his way. The hand of a hasty salute shook. "Commander, we didn't know you were coming." The instructor he had been speaking with shrank backward.

"Is the object safe?"

Aurik took a moment to find his words. "Y-Yes, sir. It was—"

Ignoring the principal, Brigador walked past and pushed open the door to the hall.

"We repelled the invaders." Aurik hurried after him. "With our initiates' help, actually. The Soulbinders didn't even come down the tower to fight.

Brigador crossed the dining hall to reach the back hallway. "I need to see it for myself."

The principal followed but didn't say anything more. The stairs into the belly of the fortress descended on and on. The air grew damp as the moss thickened.

When the commander stepped into the room at the end of the second stairwell, the two posted Lightbinder guards reached for their weapons. It took only a moment before the alarm in their eyes changed to fear.

"Step aside," Brigador ordered.

The guards did so without argument. The mahogany door creaked as it opened, fighting to fulfill its rarely used purpose.

A small room waited behind the door. Without moving, the commander pulled light from the lamp behind him and infused the dim lamp attached to the wall of the room. A wooden chest sat on a stone pedestal, but no rock was to be seen. Moss and weeds grew on every surface of the walls, floor, and ceiling. Even the chest itself looked more like a mound of vegetation than a man-made object of wood and metal.

"As promised, it was not disturbed," Aurik said.

Brigador released the front clasps. They groaned as he pulled down the latches. With two hands on either side of the lid, he held his breath. His pulse pounded in his head. He lifted the lid, his mind racing with what he could potentially find.

Light from the binder lamp poured into the chest. He froze as he stared.

The stone inside was a perfect sphere. Spotless and untouched by the rampant foliage outside the chest, it rested on a velvet pillow.

The commander released his breath in a loud sigh. The tension in his shoulders melted like butter in the sun. He lowered the lid, content to have allayed his fears.

"I told you, we took care of it," Aurik said. "Our guards are the best."

"Of which I have no doubt." Brigador's harsh tone had been replaced by an air of respect and appreciation. "You have always done well. Still, this is important enough for me to verify."

"I understand."

"If it had been lost—" His words faltered as a lump formed in his throat. He shut the latches on the box and worked the clasps. His hand shook as he fixed the last one. "If it had . . . we would all be dead."

———

THE LIGHTBINDER SERIES continues in 2026 with *Soulbinder*. Learn what happens next with Kaleth and Felyra!

"Dad, this book was so good that I think I want to be a Lightbinder when I grow up. Is this how they dress, or do I just look like a burrito? Either way...I'd like to leave a review online to tell everyone how great your book is, but these paws make typing hard. Could you help me out? What I want to say is, 'Five out of five dog bones! This book was not RUFF to read!'" - Charlie

PLEASE leave an honest review on Amazon or wherever you got the book from. Do it for Charlie.

Get a FREE prequel novella to the Shadow Knights series - Shadow Knights: Origine - by signing up for my mailing list at www.subscribepage.com/michaelwebbnovels or scan this QR code

# ALSO BY MICHAEL WEBB

———

**The Shadow Knights Series:**

Prequel Novella - Shadow Knights: Origine

**The Shadow Knights Trilogy**

#1 - The Last Shadow Knight

#2 - Rise of the Shadow

#3 - Shadow of Destiny

**Shadow Knights Generations**

#4 - Shadow of Betrayal

#5 - Shadow of Sacrifice

#6 - Shadow of Hope

———

**Treasure Hunters Alliance:**

#1 - Fortress of the Lost Amulet

#2 - Legend of the Golden City

———

**Lightbinder Series:**

#1 - Lightbinder

#2 - Soulbinder

# ACKNOWLEDGMENTS

Thank you fans, friends, and family for believing in me and enjoying my work! This book has taken longer than I originally planned, but I hope you'll agree it was worth the wait. Life has been full recently. Full of good things, but full nonetheless. And sometimes, good things take time.

Thank you SO much to my beta readers: Eli, Tara, Jeff, Junie, Manton, David, Andreas, Aden, Johnny, Don, Beckham, Kent, Andrew, John, and Dylan! I could not have done this without you. You all made so many good suggestions that helped tighten up the story. And Scott and Cherie, thank you for helping clean up my final product.

Starting a new series is both exciting and terrifying, but I'm proud of the final result. I have lots more exciting things planned for Kaleth and Felyra, so stay tuned for the rest of the series!